Dray was sta
into swung open.

She was at eye level with a broad chest and shoulders. The intoxicating scent of cologne teased her nostrils without overwhelming her. Yet, she couldn't help wanting to press her nose to his chest to get a big whiff of it.

Was there such a thing as love at first scent? Because if so, she was in serious danger of it.

"Dray?"

She took a step back, tipped her chin and gazed up at the man who'd uttered her nickname in a voice that sounded all too familiar. But it just couldn't be...

"Kahlil?" She studied the familiar face. His medium brown skin was a bit more weathered than it'd been when she'd last seen it twenty years ago, and he wore his hair cut much lower. But he was more handsome than ever...and the fluttering in her tummy indicated that her attraction to him hadn't subsided either. "What on earth are you doing here?"

An excerpt from *A Bet Between Friends* by Jules Bennett

The last thing Mason needed was to screw up the very best friendship he'd ever had.

Hell, Darcy was the *longest* relationship he'd ever had. Perhaps that's why this was the strongest bond he'd ever formed…and the very reason he couldn't risk pushing anything beyond friendship.

He sure as hell was in no place to enter a relationship, let alone an experimental one that could fail.

Darcy stretched her hands high above her head and stretched. "That felt amazing."

That slight band of skin between her tank and her jeans gave him a glimpse of an area he knew would feel silky beneath his fingertips. Thankfully for his sanity, her stretch didn't last long, but still long enough to add fuel to his fantasies.

"You want to start demolishing anything in here?" she asked with a sweet laugh.

"I'm good for the day."

Her eyes did a little traveling of their own over his bare torso and a flare of desire spread through him. He'd seen her in a bathing suit before and dolled up for proms. Why did a fitted tank and wayward hair with adorable tortoiseshell glasses get to him?

REESE RYAN

&

USA TODAY BESTSELLING AUTHOR

JULES BENNETT

WORKING WITH HER CRUSH
&
A BET BETWEEN FRIENDS

HARLEQUIN
DESIRE

Recycling programs for this product may not exist in your area.

ISBN-13: 978-1-335-45785-1

Working with Her Crush & A Bet Between Friends

Copyright © 2023 by Harlequin Enterprises ULC

Working with Her Crush
Copyright © 2023 by Roxanne Ravenel

A Bet Between Friends
Copyright © 2023 by Jules Bennett

For questions and comments about the quality of this book, please contact us at CustomerService@Harlequin.com.

Harlequin Enterprises ULC
22 Adelaide St. West, 41st Floor
Toronto, Ontario M5H 4E3, Canada
www.Harlequin.com

Printed in U.S.A.

CONTENTS

WORKING WITH HER CRUSH   9
Reese Ryan

A BET BETWEEN FRIENDS   235
Jules Bennett

Reese Ryan writes sexy, emotional stories featuring thirty-plus-somethings finding love while navigating career crises and family drama.

Reese is the author of the award-winning Bourbon Brothers series and an advocate for the romance genre and diversity in fiction.

Connect with Reese via Facebook, Twitter, Instagram, TikTok or at reeseryan.com. Join her VIP Readers Lounge at bit.ly/VIPReadersLounge. Check out her YouTube show, where she chats with fellow authors, at bit.ly/ReeseRyanChannel.

Books by Reese Ryan

Harlequin Desire

The Bourbon Brothers

Savannah's Secrets
The Billionaire's Legacy
Engaging the Enemy
A Reunion of Rivals
Waking Up Married
The Bad Boy Experiment

Dynasties: Willowvale

Working with Her Crush

Visit the Author Profile page
at Harlequin.com for more titles.

You can also find Reese Ryan on Facebook,
along with other Harlequin Desire authors,
at Facebook.com/HarlequinDesireAuthors!

Dear Reader,

When Jules Bennett approached me about collaborating on a writing project, I couldn't say *YES!!!* fast enough. Devising every element of this project and working with Jules—who is incredibly chill—was an absolute dream. I'm so proud of the series we put together, and I'm excited for readers to meet the characters and explore the world we created.

In this series, old Hank Carson—the man who owns and runs most of Willowvale Springs, Wyoming—dies without family and leaves his beloved ranches to four men who worked for him in their teens. The unexpected inheritance brings the prodigal sons home and forever changes their lives.

In *Working with Her Crush*, Andraya had an unrequited crush on her former childhood friend, Kahlil. The two own their past mistakes, heal old wounds and renew their friendship before exploring the possibility of something more. This is the first book of the Dynasties: Willowvale quartet. Be sure to return to Willowvale Springs to see what happens next.

For book news, giveaways and more, be sure to visit ReeseRyan.com/DesireReaders and join my newsletter list.

Until our next adventure!

Reese Ryan

WORKING WITH HER CRUSH

Reese Ryan

To Jules:
Thank you so much for inviting me to join you on this project and for being both incredibly creative and unbelievably accommodating. It was a joy to work with you.

To our readers:
Thank you for joining Jules and me for the ride!

To my family:
Thank you for your love, patience and support.

To K. Sterling & Leigh Carron:
Thank you for being there every day both cheering me on and telling me the unvarnished truth when I need to hear it. Love you both!

One

Tech entrepreneur Kahlil Anderson paced the floor of his pricey Seattle condo. His temples throbbed, a hole gnawed at his gut and he'd been popping antacid tablets for the past five days straight. He'd never felt such pure panic in his entire thirty-eight years of life.

A week ago, he'd discovered that his business partner, Armand Moreau, had vanished with *his* ex-wife. He'd been devastated by the news. Not because his former college roommate and long-time business partner had broken the unstated bro code by apparently dating his ex-wife in secret for the past year. He and Meridia were over, and he had no desire to revisit that particular mistake. Kahlil was far more upset that Armand had such little regard for their decades-long friendship.

And the real devastation had occurred two days later

when Kahlil's company accountant quietly informed him that Armand had emptied one of the company's accounts. Worse still, the check bore both his and Armand's signatures. Only Kahlil hadn't endorsed the check. The forgery was quite convincing. But he recognized the tiny deviation that indicated the true author of the signature: his ex-wife, Meridia.

Kahlil had spent the past five days trying to decide how to handle the situation. He'd hired a private detective who'd followed their trail to Venezuela—a country from which extraditions to the US were rare. The money trail had gone dry courtesy of untraceable accounts in the Cayman Islands.

How long had the two of them been planning this heist? The entire year since the divorce? Or had their clandestine relationship begun before his and Meridia's had ended?

Kahlil made himself a Tom Collins and moved to the little alcove where he enjoyed his unobscured view of Elliott Bay. Normally, the view calmed his nerves and put him at ease. But today, the sense of dread and the impending doom weighed on him far too heavily.

He held the sweating, icy glass to his temple as he slumped in his chair with his eyes closed. "I am completely fucked."

Over the years, Kahlil, Armand and Meridia had started and sold a variety of technology entities: mobile apps, SaaSs and industry software. But out of all of the projects they'd developed, this one—by far—was the most meaningful. It was medical software designed to help monitor patients with MS across the various specialists required to manage the illness. It was a project he'd become obsessed with after attending a charity event for families battling the disease.

Armand hadn't touched their operating account—a small kindness. So they had enough to keep functioning for three to six months. But if there were any sudden expenses or the development took any longer than six months, they'd run out of capital before they could get the software to market. And while a forensic scientist could surely tell the difference between his signature and his ex-wife's, there would still be a cloud over his head. So he hadn't told anyone the truth—other than the company accountant and his lawyer, both of whom were sworn to secrecy.

Kahlil took a generous sip of his drink and heaved a sigh. Even if he sold his condo and emptied out his personal accounts, it wouldn't come close to replacing the eight-figure amount Armand and Meridia had absconded with.

The front door buzzed, startling Kahlil who was busy imagining a hundred different scenarios to make the situation right. Maybe he hadn't been the one to make off with the investors' money. But Kahlil had initiated the project, and he'd clearly trusted the wrong people.

So how could this not be his fault?

Kahlil peeked through the peephole, holding out the tiniest hope that it was Armand having come to his senses and saying that he'd returned every last dime of their investors' money.

No such luck.

"Hey, Bernie," Kahlil greeted the building doorman. "What can I do for you?"

"This came for you a bit ago, sir." The genial older man smiled broadly as he held up an envelope. "Ada just signed for it, and we thought you'd want it right away."

"Thank you, Bernie." He reached into his pocket, peeled off a few bills and discreetly stuffed them into the older man's hand before bidding him a good evening and closing the door.

Still hoping Armand or Meridia had had a change of heart, Kahlil studied the envelope.

From the Estate of Hank Carson of Willowvale Springs.

Kahlil frowned, guilt tugging at his chest. He'd been to Willowvale Springs twice in the past twenty years. Both times it was to attend one of his younger sisters' weddings. And he'd left just as quickly as he'd arrived, not bothering to stay overnight.

Two weeks ago, his sister had informed him of old Hank Carson's death. He and Armand had visited a possible investor in Houston at the time of the funeral. So he hadn't gone back home for it. Hank Carson had been synonymous with the town of Willowvale Springs. In fact, he'd owned the majority of it. Three or four different types of ranches. The general store. Several rental homes. And lots of undeveloped land.

Kahlil had worked on the wealthy landowner's horse ranch for two summers transporting horses and as a general stableman. And he'd done some IT work for Hank, who'd just been coming around to the idea of using the internet for advertising and banking.

The old man could be moody and cantankerous. But he'd also been benevolent to the town and its residents. Despite his dire situation, Kahlil couldn't help chuckling as he recalled some of his interactions with the sometimes crotchety old man, whose bark had been far worse than his bite.

Still, he couldn't imagine why Hank's estate would want to contact him. The last time he'd spoken to the old man had been at his sister's wedding five years earlier.

Kahlil tore open the envelope and pulled out its contents. He scanned the lengthy document reading it once, then again.

"No fucking way." Kahlil pressed his free hand to his forehead. "I'm definitely not that lucky."

Not that it was lucky that the old man had died. But for Hank Carson to leave Kahlil his beloved thoroughbred horse ranch at a time when he was in dire need of the cash… There had to be some sort of catch. Or perhaps this had all just been some elaborate prank and Armand, Meridia and Hank would pop out to say *gotcha*.

No, Hank Carson hadn't been the prankster type. And while Armand was a constant jokester, one thing the man did not play about was his money.

Kahlil reached deeper into the envelope and pulled out a flash drive. He connected it to his computer and opened the sole file.

Hank's weathered face appeared. The man had always seemed like a giant to Kahlil. Even once he'd grown bigger and taller than him. But here he looked tired, frail and…*human*.

"I'll get to the point, son. You know Edith and I never

had kids of our own. It was the one thing I could never give her. The kids we watched grow up in Willowvale Springs were the closest we ever came to having family. Some more than others." The old man launched into an awful coughing fit, waving off someone who offered him a bottle of water before continuing. "You made an impression on me during your time on the horse ranch. And I've been following your career. I'm damn proud of you, son. And maybe he's too damn stubborn to say it, but I know that daddy of yours is proud of you, too."

Hank seemed choked up, and Kahlil's gut twisted in a knot, thinking about his father who'd barely spoken to him since Kahlil had walked away from the family ranch, opting to follow his own path.

"This horse ranch has always been my pride and joy. Edith and I had lots of happy memories here. I'm leaving the horse ranch and the neighboring rental properties to you. You can do with it as you please, son. But this place means so much to a lot of folks here in town. I'm trusting you'll consider that when you make your decision as to what to do."

Hank said a few more words, then he signed off.

Kahlil stared at the documents in his hand. The horse farm contained hundreds of acres of land. And it had been known far and wide as one of the best horse ranches around.

The thought of selling Hank's old place made his heart feel heavy. But there was no way fate had handed him a gift like this—at just the right time—if he wasn't supposed to use it. The entire town of Willowvale Springs was Hank Carson's legacy. It wasn't as if the old man would be forgotten if Kahlil sold the horse ranch. And the project he was developing had the potential to save thousands of lives.

Wouldn't Hank have wanted him to move forward with it?

Kahlil pulled his phone from his back pocket and dialed his accountant. "Hey, Matt. I think I've found the solution to our problem. But first, I'll need to make a trip home to Willowvale Springs."

Andraya Walker rode her sorrel-colored American quarter horse, Gingerbread, as he walked along the river that spanned the back edge of Willowvale Springs Horse Ranch. The serene, beautiful area had been one of her favorite places on the ranch from the very first day she'd come to work there as a horse groom at the age of sixteen. That'd been twenty long years ago, and since then, she'd come to love this place even more. According to her mother and sisters, this ranch was her life.

They probably weren't wrong.

Except for the years she'd spent away at college, Dray had spent most of her life on either her family's farm or this horse ranch. She'd been the ranch manager for the past five years and was often the first to arrive and the last to leave. In the beginning, she'd worked seven days a week. Not because she had to, but because she felt most at peace on the ranch. She'd dialed it back to five days a week because her boss had told her she was too young to end up like him—with no life outside the split-rail fence surrounding the place. He'd insisted that she at least take weekends off.

This ranch, along with most of Willowvale Springs, had belonged to Hank Carson. But three weeks ago Hank had succumbed to a long, protracted illness and died.

Hank Carson could be cantankerous and picky. Particularly in his later years. But he'd been a kind and generous man who'd taken good care of the people who'd worked for him. He'd taught her everything she knew about running the ranch. Made her as excited about this place as he'd once been. Hank had been like a second father to her.

Dray sighed heavily, her eyes stinging with tears when she thought of how Hank's prolonged illness had ravaged his body over the past seven years. An illness he hadn't wanted most people to know about, though it had become evident to anyone who knew him that something was wrong.

She sniffled and wiped at her damp cheeks with the back of her wrists, hoping not to upset Gingerbread. He was a docile, empathetic creature who was far more attuned to her emotions than any human she'd ever known. That included her family, who simply couldn't understand why she hadn't found someone and settled down, and the trifling exes they'd expected her to settle for. The only person who'd come close to understanding why she loved this place so much was her best friend, Alejandra Price.

But even Allie didn't quite understand how devastated Dray was that Hank hadn't left her the ranch.

Hank and Edith Carson had never had children of their own, but they'd both loved and tended to the town of Willowvale as if it was their offspring. In the years since his wife had died, Hank had lost his zest for life and had become a cranky semi-hermit. But he'd still been kind enough to mentor her. And he'd seemed pleased by how much she loved the old place.

Dray loved the old man. She missed their weekly lunches together. The mornings when she'd surprise him with doughnuts or some home-baked goodies. The rare occasions when she'd gotten him to ride out here, take in the incredible scenery and have a small picnic. It had been a softer side of the old man. A side he hadn't shown often.

Andraya hadn't taken this position or fussed over old Hank because she'd wanted or expected anything from him. But knowing how much he'd once loved these old ranches, she'd thought for sure that he would've wanted them to go to people he could be sure would love and care for them, too.

It'd been three weeks since Hank's death. But with the exception of the general store, which he'd left to Mabel Miller, who'd been running the place since she'd been knee-high to a grasshopper, no one in town had any idea to whom Hank had left his vast properties.

Hank did, however, leave her Gingerbread as well as; a black Straight Egyptian Arabian horse he'd named Diablo; the little two-bedroom, two-bath Craftsman bungalow she resided in as the manager of the ranch; and a considerable amount of cash. She was incredibly grateful for Hank's final generosity. But she'd trade all of it for the horse ranch that meant so much to her. And that was exactly what she hoped to do.

If the rancher's new owners were willing to strike up

a deal, she'd sell everything she owned besides Gingerbread and leverage as much cash as possible to acquire the ranch. But until she knew who the new owners were, she was in a holding pattern where she could do nothing more than hope and wait.

Suddenly, a voice crackled from the two-way radio on her hip. Gingerbread stopped, his head raised and his ears pricked as if wary, despite being familiar with the voice on the other end.

"Everything is fine, boy," she whispered, patting the horse's warm neck. She'd been feeling guilty that her own anxiety seemed to transfer onto Gingerbread in the weeks since Hank's death. But she could even hear the tension in her stable boy's voice. "We all just need to relax."

She answered the two-way radio when Antonio called her again, his voice sounding more frantic than it had the first time. "What's wrong, Tonio?"

"There's a man here who says he's the new owner," the boy informed her, fretfully in a loud whisper. "Should I let him in?"

Andraya drew in a deep breath and tightened her grip on Gingerbread's reins. She forced a smile, hoping it would translate in her tone and ease some of the boy's anxiety.

They'd all been in mourning for the old man. But in the days since Hank's funeral, there had been a notable sense of dread among them. They were waiting for the inevitable other shoe to drop regarding whether or not they still had jobs.

"It's okay, Tonio," Dray said in the same tone she'd used with Gingerbread. "If he's the new owner, he should have keys to the place anyway. Go ahead and let him in. I'm out by the river. I'll get back to the stables as quickly as I can."

Andraya heaved a quiet sigh before turning Gingerbread around and racing back toward the stables. Her body hummed with the same wariness expressed by her trusty steed.

Before she'd arrived at the stables, Antonio had hailed her on the two-way radio again to inform her that the man was headed over to the log cabin on the adjacent property. It was the largest of the rental properties and not far from the house Hank had left to her.

When Antonio asked if he should inform the other workers of the new owner's arrival, she asked him not to. After all, there was no need to send panic rippling through their staff before she had a chance to assess the situation.

Andraya changed directions and headed toward the house rather than the stables. When she arrived at the beautiful log cabin—the newest of the properties—she tied Gingerbread's lead to the hitching post and made her way up the stairs. Her heart raced, and her palms were damp thanks to this especially warm day at the end of summer.

Dray rang the doorbell and caught sight of herself in the reflection of the glass of the gorgeous double door that she'd always admired. Given the physical and often dirty nature of her job, she rarely gave much thought to her appearance. She wasn't trying to impress her fellow ranch workers, and the horses certainly didn't care if she looked rumpled or wasn't wearing makeup. But as she studied her reflection now, she couldn't help cataloging all the things about her that looked...*wrong*.

She was hot, sweaty and dirty. She probably smelled like a horse—not that she noticed anymore. Her old Stetson—a gift from Hank when she'd won her first riding competition—was dented and in need of a good steaming and a scrub. And how could she not have realized that there was a tear in her favorite plaid shirt?

Dray—busy scrubbing smudges of dirt from her face—was startled when the door she'd been staring into swung open. She was at eye level with a man's broad chest and shoulders. Intoxicating cologne teased her nostrils without overwhelming her. She couldn't help wanting to press her nose to his chest to get a big whiff of it.

Was there such a thing as love at first scent? Because if so, she was in serious danger.

"Dray?"

She took a step back, tipped her chin and gazed up at the man who'd uttered her nickname in a voice that sounded all too familiar. But it just couldn't be...

"Kahlil?" She studied the familiar face. His medium brown skin was a bit more weathered than it'd been when she'd last seen it twenty years ago, and he wore his hair cut much lower. But he was more handsome than ever. And the fluttering in her tummy indicated that her attraction to him hadn't subsided, either. "What on earth are you doing here?"

Andraya had gone to great pains to avoid Kahlil over the past two decades. She'd ensured that she hadn't been in town for either of his sister's weddings. Something she still felt guilty about. And he clearly hadn't been eager to return to Willowvale Springs, either. So what was he doing there now?

"Are you staying at the cabin while you're in town?" she prodded when he didn't respond.

"Yes." He shoved his hands into his pockets.

Obviously still not much of a talker. No worries. She wasn't here to see him anyway.

"I must've misunderstood Antonio. I came to meet the new owner of the horse ranch. He must be staying in the smaller log cabin." Dray drifted backward, her face hot and her pulse racing. "Well, I'm sure you're busy with…you know…your life. So I won't keep you. Goodbye." Dray hurried toward the stairs, desperate to escape the incredibly awkward meeting.

"I *am* the new owner," Kahlil said.

Andraya froze, then turned slowly on the worn heels of her favorite cowboy boots. She stared at the boy who'd once been her best friend. The boy who'd boarded a bus to Denver for college, promising to see her at Christmas, and never returned. The man who clearly hadn't wanted anything to do with her or the little town of Willowvale Springs anymore.

This had to be someone's idea of a cruel joke. There was no way in the world Hank Carson would've left his beloved horse ranch to a deserter like Kahlil Anderson.

Would he?

Dray stared at her old friend in disbelief, her heart dropping to her stomach and her throat suddenly dry. She shook her head, taking another step back. "No... I don't believe it."

Two

Kahlil studied the face that had once been so familiar to him. The large, expressive brown eyes, pouty lips, and deep brown skin. The tattered plaid shirt and worn jeans streaked with dust indicated that her sense of style hadn't evolved much. But everything else about the girl next door who'd once been his best friend had been completely transformed.

Dray's once-boyish figure—typically drowned in oversized clothing—was soft and curvy. Rather than hiding her body, the shirt and the tank she wore beneath it highlighted full breasts he definitely didn't remember her having at sixteen. The jeans she wore clung to her tantalizing curves. And the vision of that perfect ass when she'd turned around to leave… Kahlil wasn't sure it would ever leave his brain.

It'd been twenty long years since he'd seen Andraya Walker. But in some ways, it felt like he was seeing her for the first time. Had she always been this beautiful? Or had he just not noticed because Dray had always been one of the guys?

Kahlil forced his gaze to meet hers as he leaned against the door frame. "Well, if I can't convince my old friend I'm the new owner, I'm not off to a very good start today, am I?"

Dray stared at him, blinking. He watched her elegant throat work as she swallowed hard and tried to formulate her next words.

"Why?" Dray said, finally.

"Why am I here, or why did Hank leave me the horse ranch?"

"*Both.*" She practically spat the word at him. There was pain, anger and unshed tears in her dark brown eyes.

He'd barely been in town two hours and already his presence was the equivalent of a wrecking ball.

"Honestly, Dray? I'm as shocked as you are that the old man left the place to me," Kahlil admitted. He stood to his full height of just under six feet and folded his arms. "But Hank Carson did, in fact, leave me this place. I executed the documents with his lawyer this morning."

"His lawyer? You mean *my brother*." She slapped a hand to her chest, and his wandering gaze couldn't help but follow.

There was practically smoke coming from Dray's ears. Kahlil was pretty sure he could fry up a steak on

Dray's head right now. He wasn't sure whom she was angrier with—him for inheriting Hank's ranch or her brother, Phil, for not disclosing that information to her. Their next family get-together would undoubtedly be awkward, to say the least.

Kahlil cleared his throat, meeting her eyes again. "I've watched the video Hank left me a dozen times, and I still can't quite figure out why he'd leave the place to me. But you're welcome to see it if—"

"Yes, I'd like to see it, *please*." She glared at him with her arms folded and her chin tipped when he didn't respond. As if defying him to deny her request.

Kahlil sighed, then pushed open the gorgeous wood and glass front door, permitting Andraya to enter.

As she squeezed past him into the great room, he was reminded of all the familiar scents of working on a ranch. Sunshine, sweat, the great outdoors, bales of hay, horses and a soft, warm scent that was uniquely her own.

Dray removed the worn, old, beige Stetson from her head and dragged her sleeve across her glistening forehead. Taking off the hat revealed more of her lovely face and her straight, black hair, which had been flattened by the hat. She wore her hair in a single braid that ended somewhere between her shoulder blades.

She placed her hat back atop her head and stared at him a moment before speaking again. "So…the video?"

"Right." He dropped his gaze from hers momentarily. "First, can I get you something? Maybe water or an ice-cold beer? You look really hot… I mean…

warm," he faltered. "Because it's pretty damn hot out there today."

Andraya raised an eyebrow, her nostrils flaring. "Just the video will be fine, thanks."

Kahlil led her to the sitting area where he'd been working in the octagonal solarium—an outstanding architectural feature he'd been pleasantly surprised by. The warm space had lots of windows and overlooked the crystal clear creek that ran behind the cabin. He sank onto the sofa in front of his laptop and unlocked it.

He pulled the flash drive from its original envelope, lying on the table. When he plugged it into his computer, the sofa sank beside him, and Dray's thigh-clad thigh brushed against his. His skin blazed beneath his jeans, and a rush of heat filled his body.

Kahlil cleared his throat and tried to ignore it. He pulled up the video, set it to full screen and played it. "Satisfied?"

They'd watched the video together, and Dray had been rendered speechless again. She stared at the screen, her expression a mixture of bewilderment and disappointment.

"Again," she said, then turned to him, her eyes hazy. "Please, Kahlil. I need to see it again."

"You can watch it as many times as you'd like, Dray. It won't change the fact that Hank left the thoroughbred ranch to me." Kahlil felt like shit for causing her pain again.

"I know. I just really need to… I need to understand why Hank would do this. Why he would choose you when you clearly haven't given a damn about the ranch, this town or anyone you left behind here." She glared at him momentarily, her eyes glossy and filled with tears. Dray wiped at them angrily. "And as much as I could really use that beer right now, I'd gratefully accept that bottle of water you offered earlier."

"You've got it."

Andraya clearly needed some space as she tried to process the fact that he was the new owner of the ranch. He didn't need to prove anything to his old friend. But it was a small concession given the pain in her eyes.

Kahlil stood and gestured toward the computer. "I'll be back with your bottle of water. You're welcome to watch the video as much as you need to."

He went to the kitchen, taking his time as he grabbed a bottle of water for her and a beer for himself. Then he returned to the solarium and settled beside her on the sofa, handing Andraya her water.

She accepted the bottle and sniffled, her eyes watery and red. Then she removed the top and downed nearly half the bottle before capping it and setting it on the coffee table.

"You obviously don't plan to relocate here." She turned to him, her steely gaze not meeting his. "So what do you plan to do with the place?"

"You could barely stand Hank Carson that one summer you worked on the ranch before I left." Kahlil drank a little more of his beer, then set the bottle on the opposite side of his laptop. "So why do you care so much about my plans for it?"

He studied her face, and it seemed to make her uncomfortable. She popped up from the sofa and paced the floor in front of him.

"You might not believe this, Kahl, but an awful lot can change in *twenty* years." The derision in her tone and expression made his gut knot with guilt.

Don't make such a big deal out of me leaving. We'll see each other again in a few months at Christmas.

The words he'd spoken that warm summer day when Andraya had driven him to the bus station in Cheyenne still haunted him. He'd honestly meant them. But by the time the holidays had rolled around, Kahlil had been too slammed with schoolwork and the demands of an exhausting job to return to Willowvale Springs.

"Okay, tell me what's changed." Kahlil's gaze followed her as she paced the floor.

"So now you care about my life?" Dray laughed bitterly. She stopped pacing and folded her arms. "That's rich coming from you, Kahl."

Her words felt like a stake being driven into his heart.

"I'm sorry if it seemed like I was ghosting you after I went away to college, Dray. But I was genuinely overwhelmed with my classes and my part-time job. I tried to explain that I—"

"Save the insincere apology, Kahl." Andraya held up a hand. "Let's just focus on what's happening right now."

He heaved a sigh, his chest heavy. "If that's what you want, Dray."

"I do." Her expression was unreadable.

Was she grateful that he'd agreed so easily or disappointed that he hadn't put up more of a fight? Either way, it was clear there would be no future friendship for them.

Fine. That made things easier on him.

"Working at the horse ranch was an obligation to you, Kahl. It was your way of getting out of here. But for me...it was the opposite. I found passion and purpose here. And I fell in love with every part of the process. For the first time in my life, I didn't feel like that awkward girl who didn't fit in anywhere. I felt like I belonged. And I found the thing I was really good at." Her voice trembled. "Except for the time I spent away at college, I've worked here on the ranch ever since."

"You've been working for Hank all this time?"

"I've done just about every job there is on this ranch. And for the past five years, I've been the ranch manager," she said proudly, standing taller. "I have a considerable stake in who owns this place and their plans for it. So I'm asking you again...why are you here, Kahlil? And what exactly are your plans?"

"I'm selling the place." He folded his arms, prepared for a fight.

"Great." Her response stunned him. She sank onto the sofa, leaving considerable space between them this time. She turned her body toward his. "Because I'd like to buy it."

"You can afford to buy this place?" Kahlil carefully regarded the gorgeous woman seated less than two feet away.

"Not outright, no," she admitted. "But I've got a substantial down payment, and if I take a second mortgage on my house and move around a few assets, I can make it happen, if the price is reasonable," she added. "I was thinking something like this…"

Andraya picked up a pen and scribbled a figure onto a nearby pad, then slid it over to him.

Kahlil glanced down at the figure and snorted. He slid the pad back to her. "I'm a businessman, not a charity, Dray. You know damn well that's nowhere near what the place is worth."

"What it *was* worth," Dray noted with a shrug. "As I said, a lot can change in twenty years."

"So did you intentionally run the place into the ground so you could buy it dirt cheap, or do you just suck as the ranch manager?" Kahlil spoke calmly, even though he knew his words would make her furious. "Old McGhee would never have allowed the place to deteriorate the way it has."

"I have done everything I could within my power to keep this place going." Dray scowled and her body tensed, but her words were measured. "But after Ms. Edith died… Hank just wasn't the same. He could barely bring himself to care about…*anything*. It was all I could do sometimes just to get him to sign off on the basics. Hank put an end to the equestrian events, and we stopped breeding prizewinning racehorses."

"That explains why the place is barely in the black."

He'd been shocked when he'd arrived at the horse ranch and discovered that it wasn't the showplace he remembered anymore. He'd hoped to sell the place as is. But in its current state, there was no way he'd get anything close to the figure he had in mind. He'd been preparing himself mentally for option two—liquidating the place. He could parcel out the land and sell all of the equipment. There was a good chance he could get much more for the property that way. But as he stared into Dray's wide eyes now, he felt guilty for even considering it.

"We were in the red for years before I became the ranch manager and talked Hank into expanding the stables so we could board horses and give riding lessons," Andraya said. "Look, Kahlil, I know this place...this town doesn't mean anything to you. But it means *everything* to me. If I had millions of dollars to pay you for the place, I'd gladly hand them over. But I don't. So maybe we can come to some arrangement. Just give me a few months and—"

"A few months?" Kahl stood and paced the floor. "Sorry, Andraya, but I don't have that kind of time. I need to move on the sale as quickly as possible."

"There's no way you'll get top dollar for the property in its current condition," Dray said, her game face firmly in place. "I can't give you what you want for the ranch, but I'm sure we could work out a more equitable figure. I'd just need to arrange to finance the deal."

"No, Andraya." He shook his head. "I'm sorry."

They were miles away from each other on the sales price of the ranch. And the probability that Dray could get financing for an eight-figure deal when she was barely offering seven figures was highly unlikely.

Andraya winced, momentarily crestfallen. But then she pulled her shoulders back and lifted her chin prepared for a fight.

That was the reaction he'd been expecting.

"Then your only other option is to renovate the place—something I've been begging Hank to do for more than a decade. With state-of-the-art facilities, you can name your price," she said calmly.

"With respect, that isn't my only other option," Kahlil said. "The other option is that I could liquidate the place. Divide the property into several parcels rather than just one. Surely some builder would be happy to create a planned neighborhood in such a perfect location right along the edge of the river."

Dray looked horrified. She shot to her feet. "You wouldn't!"

"The place belongs to me now, Andraya. And I have every right to do whatever I want with it." He stared into the dark eyes that were practically shooting flames. "I don't need your permission or the town's. I've already clarified that with Phil."

"I'm gonna kick my brother's ass," she muttered under her breath. "I'm not challenging your right to liquidate the ranch, Kahlil. I'm simply stating that it would be an incredibly shitty thing to do to the people who rely on this place to board their horses. Not to mention for those of us who count on this place for our livelihoods."

"The place is barely making money."

"But it will if we renovate the old buildings, start breeding prizewinning stallions again and reinstitute the equestrian events," she said matter-of-factly.

"*We*, huh?" Kahlil folded his arms and hiked an eyebrow. "Is that the royal *we*, or do you plan on putting up any money to achieve these grandiose ideas of yours?"

"Let me buy in partial ownership, and I'll gladly supply an infusion of cash for the renovations," Dray said.

Kahlil was trying to unload this money pit of a ranch in the dead-end town he'd fled as a teen, not become a rancher. And he certainly had no desire to take on an opinionated, pain-in-the-ass business partner. He'd already had one of those, and it hadn't ended well.

"Pass," he said.

"But you can't just—"

"I can do anything with this place I damn well please." Kahlil's tone was much firmer this time. "This entire exercise was a courtesy to you because we were once friends, Andraya. The final decision on what happens to the ranch is solely up to me."

"You *asshole*," she whispered, tears streaking down her cheeks. He was pretty sure he'd only ever seen Andraya cry one other time. The day he'd boarded that bus for Denver. "You've never cared about anyone but yourself, have you?" She dropped her gaze momentarily. Then she stood taller and glared at him. "Well, I won't help you run this place into the ground and ruin the lives of everyone who depends on the ranch. So consider this my formal resignation. Effective immediately."

She turned on her heels and headed for the front door.

"Why are you behaving like a petulant child?" He strode ahead of her with his long legs, standing between her and the front door. "You're a bright, sensible person. You had to realize that the ranch would be sold after Hank passed."

"I did. But I never imagined he'd leave his beloved

horse ranch to someone with a personal vendetta against the place." She folded her arms and cocked a hip.

"I do *not* have a personal vendetta against you or this town. None of this is personal, Dray. It's business. And let's face it, the ranch isn't a profitable business anymore. I'm making the same logical decision any other investor would make. Maybe that's why Hank left the ranch to me. Because he knew I'd approach this decision logically rather than allowing sentiment and emotion to cloud my judgment."

Her eyes widened. Perhaps because she was insulted by his implication that she was being emotional rather than logical about this. Or maybe because she recognized that his assessment of Hank's decision was probably right. He'd bet it was a little of both.

Hank had been unable to part with the ranch because of its connection to his wife and all the memories they'd shared there. Had he left it to Andraya, she would've held on to the place tooth and nail, even if the accounts were in the red and bleeding her dry.

"Being logical, detached and devoid of any human emotions has always been your gift, hasn't it, Kahl?" she said coolly.

The derision in Dray's tone and dark eyes cut him deep, but saying so would do nothing to resolve this impasse. Just like twenty years ago, they were in opposite camps about what he should do, but it was *his* life, *his* choice. He'd make the decision that was best for him—even if that meant hurting her.

"Maybe you're right. Maybe that is why Hank left

the place to you rather than to me or any of the rest of us who actually care about it. But I still believe in this ranch and the people behind it. I'll *never* stop fighting for them."

"Your way of fighting for this place is by having a tantrum and quitting, huh? Brilliant, Dray." Kahlil matched her glare with one of his own, then stepped aside, gesturing toward the door as he swung it open. "Well, don't let me stop you."

Andraya cut her eyes at him as if she wanted to tear him apart with her bare hands. She bumped him hard with her hip on her way out of the door.

Kahlil closed the door behind Andraya, watched her mount her horse and head back toward the ranch, riding as if her hair was on fire.

He squeezed his eyes shut and dragged a hand across his forehead, his temples throbbing.

He'd often thought of what he'd say to Andraya Walker if he saw her again. How to explain his previous state of mind and how to best apologize for being such a shitty friend. But their encounter today had taken him completely by surprise. And he'd only made things worse between them.

This unexpected windfall was supposed to solve his problem. Instead, it only seemed to be compounding it.

Kahlil pulled his phone from his back pocket, scrolled through his contacts and pulled up a number he hadn't used in years. He needed the help of a real estate professional. So he called his old friend: local kid turned real estate mogul Paxton Hart. If anyone could help him see his way out of the tangled mess Hank had left him, Pax could.

But as for Andraya, any chance he'd had of making amends had just flown out the window.

Three

Dray stood back and admired the freshly painted walls of her bedroom. The color, Maison Blanche, was a soft, calming khaki color recommended by her mother. Given the amount of pinned-up rage she'd been experiencing since Kahlil Anderson had blown into town and ruined her plans, she needed a calm space.

Her phone rang, and her older sister Alana's smiling face filled the screen. Dray wiped the perspiration that had formed over her brow and dropped the paintbrush into the tray. Then she picked up her phone, propped on the edge of her drop cloth-covered dresser.

She answered the video call. "Hey, Lana, what's up?"

"A better question is what are *you* up to? You look a hot mess," her sister peered into the screen. "I thought you quit your job at the ranch."

"I did."

"Then why do you look like you've been mucking out stalls or something?" Alana asked, sunshine filling the screen. Her sister, who was a registered nurse, was evidently outside the hospital on her lunch break.

"Love you, too, boo." Dray frowned at her sister. "And for your information, I'm repainting my bedroom."

"What for? No one but you ever sees it." Alana had propped her phone up somehow and was now nibbling on her sandwich.

Dray flipped her sister off, which only made Lana dissolve into laughter.

"How about you worry less about how much action I'm getting and check out my impressive paint job." Dray flipped the camera on her phone so she could show her sister the freshly painted walls. She slowly scanned the space. When she turned to face the door, Lana screamed and she did, too, nearly dropping her phone.

"What the hell are you doing in my house?" Dray demanded, her heart racing and her face flaming with anger or maybe embarrassment. She wasn't sure which.

Kahlil Anderson might've owned every other piece of land around her, but the bungalow and the land adjacent to it belonged to her, thanks to Hank.

"Who the hell is that?" Alana was saying. "Wait… is that Kahlil?"

His expression softened, and he smiled, offering a small wave for the camera. "Alana, right? Good to hear your voice again."

"Wow, Dray, you neglected to tell me how hot your old bestie is now. Way to bury the lede."

"The man is selling off the ranch I've worked at my entire adult life, and you really think the fact that he's more handsome now is the lede?" Dray frowned at the screen. Then she raised her eyes to study the man standing in her doorway looking finer than ever. "And I asked a question—what the hell are you doing in my house?"

"I knocked. You didn't answer. The door was open and the music was blaring so—"

"Are you here to lodge a formal complaint?" Dray propped her free hand on her hip. "Because if so, you'll need to call 1-800-You Can Go Fu—"

"Andraya Walker!" Alana screeched her name in the same chastising voice her mother and older siblings had used her entire life. "Those are lovely flowers, Kahlil? Did you bring them for Dray?" Alana quickly pivoted the conversation in a more amiable direction.

Andraya scowled. How had she not noticed that the man was carrying a gorgeous bouquet of flowers? Not that they were for her. That much she was sure of.

"Yes, they are," Kahlil confirmed sheepishly. "As for why I'm here… We got off on the wrong foot yesterday. I was hoping we could start over."

"Aww…that is so sweet," Alana said. "Handsome *and* thoughtful. You should totally bring him to Mom and Dad's forty-fifth-anniversary party. Otherwise, you know Mom is dead set on finding you a date."

Dray glared at her older sister, who promptly broke into laughter. Was it any wonder Dray had buried all her sister's Barbies in random crops on their family farm when they were kids? "We'll talk about the anniversary party and Mom's badgering later. *Goodbye*, Lana."

"Okay, little sis." Lana flashed a mischievous grin, then stabbed her salad with a fork. "Love you."

"Love you, too," Dray said begrudgingly.

"Bye, Kahlil! Hope to see you at—"

Dray ended the call before her sister could finish. She slid her phone into her back pocket and folded her arms, one hip still cocked.

"So if you're here bearing gifts, I have to assume that selling the ranch wasn't as easy as you hoped." Dray smirked when Kahlil's eyes widened. "Does that mean you're ready to entertain my offer to buy the place?"

Kahlil cleared his throat and stood taller. "No."

"Then we have nothing to talk about." Dray brushed past him as she stepped into the hallway and jogged down the stairs.

"At least give me a chance to make my proposal before you toss me out." Kahlil was on her heels as she descended the stairs and headed into the kitchen.

Dray lifted onto her toes and opened one of the high cabinets over the refrigerator. "I'm trying to get a vase for the flowers. So instead of watching me struggle to reach that glass vase, maybe you could grab it for me." Dray had lifted onto her toes as high as she could, but at five foot six in her bare feet, she couldn't reach the vase on the far side of the cabinet over the refrigerator without her step ladder, which was upstairs in the bedroom.

"Of course." Kahlil set the flowers on the counter and stepped behind her. The front of his body grazed the back of hers. And his warm, spicy scent with hints of leather and cedarwood tickled her nose. Her skin heated, her nipples suddenly felt tight and the space between her thighs pulsed.

Andraya held her breath and sank her teeth into her lower lip. She reminded herself that her body's reaction was a lot less about who was standing behind her and more to do with the fact that—as her sister had so rudely indicated—it'd been a while since she'd entertained company in her bedroom.

Not that she needed anyone else. Her collection of brightly colored vibrators scratched the itch far better than the few guys she'd been with.

Kahlil pulled the vase down and handed it to Dray. She stared at him for a moment, and he stared back. Then his gaze dropped to her nipples protruding through the tank top she was wearing with no bra.

Shit. She'd forgotten about that. Then again, she hadn't been expecting company this afternoon, had she?

Andraya clutched the vase, her arms strategically shielding her chest as she moved to the sink and turned on the water. "I get that I didn't answer the door when you knocked. But that doesn't give you permission to just walk into my house."

"And for that, I apologize." Kahlil held up his open palms in surrender, and she wanted to punch him for looking so damned sweet and adorable. Just like the nerdy, oblivious boy she'd once been head over heels for.

Dray's heart ached a little just thinking of how much she'd once adored Kahlil. And how he hadn't cared a single whit about her. It had broken her heart, but it also taught her never to be gullible and overly trusting again.

"Unlike Lana, I'm not buying the 'I was really hoping we could start over again' routine," Dray mimicked the tone and cadence of his voice as she arranged the beautiful, fragrant stems in the glass vase now filled with cool, clear water. "There's obviously something you wanted to talk to me about. So spit it out."

Kahl's expression crumpled, as if he was genuinely hurt by her assessment of the true motive for his uninvited visit. But he didn't deny it. Instead, he shoved a hand into the pocket of the distressed, dark wash jeans that hugged his fine ass. They probably cost more than her entire collection of jeans acquired from her favorite clothing store—the *Tarjay* over in Casper. But from where she was standing, those jeans were worth every penny.

"Still as straightforward as ever, I see." Kahlil rubbed his bearded chin.

She folded her arms over her chest and nodded. To her, being called straightforward was the highest of compliments. As in she wasn't the type of person to bullshit people by making promises she had no intention of keeping or showing up at their doors unannounced bearing gifts because they needed something.

"So I'll get to the point. You said you still believe in this ranch and the people behind it. That you'd never stop fighting for it and for them," Kahlil said.

"And I meant it." Dray stood taller and tipped her chin.

"Well, here's your chance to prove it." Kahlil studied her, as he had so often studied people in the past.

Back then, she'd thought it was an indication that he

liked her, too. But now she realized it was just his curious nature. He observed people the same way scientists in a lab studied mice.

"And how do you propose I do that, since selling me the ranch is off the table?" Dray hated that she was intrigued by his proposal.

"I want you to come back to work for the ranch."

"Because you're tired of getting calls from the ranch hands about the day-to-day running of the place—which you know nothing about, by the way." She pointed an accusatory finger, then quickly drew it back and folded her arms when his gaze suddenly dropped to her right breast.

"Yes, Andraya, you are clearly the glue that holds that place together," he admitted, folding his arms, too. "Is that what you want to hear?"

"What I'd like to hear is that you'll sell me the horse ranch for a reasonable price. But I'd settle for hearing that you plan to stay and actually run the ranch. That you give a damn about the place that Hank left you and the town that made you." Dray balled her hands, buried beneath her armpits, into fists. Her voice was surprisingly calm.

"I *do* care." Kahlil had that pained look on his face again. "After your impassioned plea about how much the ranch means to you and to everyone in this town… I've asked the listing agent to ensure that the place remains a working horse ranch."

"You aren't going to sell the land to a developer?" Andraya was genuinely stunned. When Kahlil had declared that the ranch was his to do with as he pleased, she was sure she'd seen the last of the beloved place that held so many memories for her. "But...why?"

"You'd rather I parcel the ranch out to land developers?" Kahlil frowned, one of his thick, neat eyebrows lifting.

"No, of course not. I just wondered what made you change your mind." She shifted her gaze to just over his shoulder.

Kahlil didn't answer right away. "People around here already seem to think I'm a heartless ingrate who doesn't give a shit about the town or my family." He looked at her pointedly, then shrugged. "The last thing I want to do is prove them right."

"Oh." Dray tried not to sound as disappointed as she was. But what had she expected him to say?

You, Dray. I did it for you.

Seriously, she needed to stop dreaming.

"So you still plan to sell the place—you just want to ensure that whomever buys it maintains it as a horse ranch. How will you manage that? Once someone buys it, they can do whatever they want with the place. And what would be most lucrative for them is to either develop the land themselves or sell it to someone else who would."

"Given the current condition of the ranch, the only way we can both get what we want is to follow your suggestions—renovating the old buildings, reviving the breeding of prizewinning stallions and reinstituting the equestrian events." He ticked each item off on his fingers.

"All of that comes with a hefty price tag. You're

willing to do all of that to save the place?" she asked incredulously, still expecting someone to jump out and tell her that this was all one big cruel joke.

"It appears I am." Kahlil heaved a long sigh, then ran a hand over his close-cropped waves.

She couldn't help smiling, thinking of the wave brush that had been Kahl's near-constant companion when they'd been growing up. That, at least, hadn't changed.

It was good to know he'd been able to maintain at least one relationship. Too bad it was with an inanimate object.

Then again, her longest relationship had been with a vibrator she called Pete, so who was she to judge?

"How do I know—"

Dray was cut off by the personal ringtone she'd set for her best friend, Allie. She held up a finger. "I need to take this call."

Kahlil shrugged as if he didn't much care either way.

"Hey, Allie, I'm in the middle of something. What's up?"

"I thought you said Kahlil was going to liquidate the ranch?"

"I know. I was sure that was the case." She glanced at Kahlil, who studied her. She lowered her voice as she turned away from him. "But now I'm not so sure. Why? What have you heard?"

"He just paid a big fat deposit and engaged my family's company to renovate four of the old buildings on the property. Sounds like he's ready to upgrade the place to a state-of-the-art, world-class facility. Make it better than it ever was when old Hank was alive," Allie said in a loud whisper. "So what do you think his real plan is?"

"He's standing in my kitchen right now." Dray glanced back at Kahlil, who wore a nearly imperceptible smirk. "So I guess I'm about to find out."

"He's at your house right now? You might've led with that, you know. Does he look as good as he did the other day?"

Dray looked him up and down surreptitiously and lowered her voice. "Affirmative. But I've gotta go. We'll talk about that later."

She ended the call, sticking the phone back into her back pocket and raising her gaze to his.

"Manny said you and his little sister, Allie, were best friends. I assume that was her confirming what I just told you?"

Did he have to sound so damned self-satisfied?

"Yes." Dray heaved a quiet sigh of relief. She studied his handsome face and the dark eyes that regarded her curiously. "Thank you, Kahl. What you're doing... it means a lot."

But before he could respond, she hugged him, and it took both of them by surprise.

Kahlil rocked back on his heels when Dray unexpectedly tackle hugged him. She'd done the same thing when she'd dropped him off at the bus station in Cheyenne. It had surprised him just as much then.

Dray hadn't exactly been the warm-and-fuzzy type. She'd been a tomboy through and through. Andraya Walker was far more likely to punch you in the gut and tell you to get your shit together than to say she loved or missed you.

This hug felt even weirder than their last one.

Dray smelled like citrus and sunshine. Her soft, warm body was cradled against his, and he was hyper-aware of her firm nipples pressed into his chest through the thin fabric of her white tank top. He hugged her back, his hands low on her waist, perched just above the full, round bottom that had been teasing him as he'd followed her down the stairs in those tight, cut-off jean shorts.

"I…uh… You're welcome" was all Kahlil could manage to say as he extracted himself from her arms, glad that spontaneous human combustion wasn't a real thing. Still, he was pretty sure his cheeks and forehead were on fire.

And the sensation rising below his belt in response to having his old friend—voluptuous, sexy and more gorgeous than ever—wrapped around him braless and in the tiniest of shorts—that feeling was *definitely* real.

"So does that mean you'll come back to work at the ranch?" He hoped to God his face didn't appear as flushed as it felt.

"I don't know." Dray folded her arms, seemingly amused by his discomfort. She cocked her head and made a face as if she was weighing the prospect. "That depends."

"It depends?" he echoed. "You've got to be kidding me. You're the one who was so insistent that we save the ranch. Now I'm asking you to come back and be a part of it and your response is… I don't know, that depends?" He huffed. "I swear to God, I will never understand women," he muttered under his breath.

"I'm not *women*," she said indignantly. "I'm a woman who's dealt with you before. You didn't honor your commitment before. Why should I trust that you'll do it now?"

"First of all, I was eighteen." Kahlil dragged a hand over his head. It was a gesture he'd often be repeating if he and Dray were going to be working together for the next two months. "Second, I never promised anything, Dray. Yes, I'd planned to come home. But things changed. I tried to talk to you about how I was feeling, but you didn't want to hear anything else. You just kept insisting—"

"Hey, let's try to stay focused, all right?" She held up a hand. "This isn't about what happened between us then. I'm asking you if you're willing to make a commitment to the ranch and to this town *now*."

Kahlil counted backward in his head and held back all the things he wanted to say. Like reminding Dray that *she* was the one who'd stopped accepting his calls.

"I just gave your friend's family a hell of a lot of money to get these renovations started. I'd think that would indicate my commitment to this project."

"Okay, that's great. But exactly what kind of renovations are you doing? And how would you have any clue what we'll actually need?"

She gestured wildly as she spoke, her full breasts swaying with each motion.

"Are these gonna be a problem?" Dray asked finally, her thumbs pointed toward her incredibly perky and distracting breasts.

"What? No. Of course not. I just…"

"Haven't been able to take your eyes off of them," she said indignantly. "Yes, the breast fairy visited me after you left town. No, I don't typically walk around with them unleashed in mixed company. Also, you're an uninvited guest in my home, and I had no idea you were going to let yourself into my house. You're lucky I have on pants." Dray propped her fist on her generous hip.

Kahlil swallowed hard and diverted his eyes. "Okay, yes. They're very distracting," he admitted. "But it's fine. It's not like I haven't seen breasts before."

"Well, good for you, pal," she said. "But I need you to stay focused right now. So have a seat. I'll be back in a sec."

Dray headed up the stairs, and Kahlil tried his very best not to watch her incredibly enticing bottom as she hurried up the steps. He failed miserably. Then he wandered around her living room, looking at photos of Dray and her beloved horses along with a handful of photos of her family. Her older sister and brother were both married with children.

"My sister has had another kid since then." Dray returned wearing the same clothes, but she'd clearly put on a bra.

"Nice." Kahlil already missed those glorious headlights.

"So…if you want my help, I want to truly be involved in this project. If you're just going to consult me after the fact, this isn't going to work," Dray said.

"I came to you right away."

"*After* you'd selected the construction company and

made renovation plans," she noted. "Either we're in this together or you're on your own."

"You would never have made such a demand of Hank when he owned the place."

"Hank knew how to run the place. You don't."

"Fine. I'll consult with you before the fact. But as the owner, I make the final decision." He jabbed a thumb in his direction.

"Sure, pal. Whatever you say." She shrugged. "Now, we need to talk about the plans for the renovation. Should we order in pizza? Because I'm starving. And in case it wasn't obvious, you're paying, *boss*."

"Gladly." Kahlil chuckled.

"And speaking of payment…you won't let me buy in as a partner? Fine. But if I'm taking on more responsibilities, I should be paid for it. After all, you're planning on making a killing on this place, right?"

Kahlil sighed. "Fine. A three-percent raise."

"I was thinking twenty."

"Have you lost your ever-loving…" He drew in a deep breath and counted backward in his head again. "Five percent."

"Fifteen."

"Ten," he said, fully aware that the veins in his temples were likely bulging. "That's highway robbery and my absolute final offer." When she didn't respond, he added, "And I'll be your date for your parents' anniversary party."

She snorted, as if his offer held little appeal. But then she rubbed her chin, as if considering it. "And help me put the furniture in my bedroom back in place once the paint dries?"

Kahlil heaved a sigh and rubbed his forehead. "Yes. Fine."

"Then ten percent it is." She shrugged. The impish grin on her lovely face actually made her even hotter. "I'll call in the pizza. A supreme okay?"

"Fine. Just please tell me you have beer or wine or *something*. I'm gonna need it before this night is over."

Andraya burst into laughter. "You've got it. Make yourself comfortable, and I'll grab one for you."

He sank onto the sofa as she headed for the kitchen. But suddenly she stopped and turned back to him.

"By the way...thank you for the flowers, Kahl. They're beautiful." A soft smile lit her dark brown eyes, and she looked even more gorgeous.

Kahlil sighed quietly as Andraya made her way to the kitchen. Working with his former best friend was going to be the death of him.

Four

It was more than a week after his return to town when he'd finally visited his family's ranch. The old place looked achingly familiar yet surprisingly different. There was a fresh coat of paint in a new color—robin's-egg blue trimmed in white. A brand-new split-rail fence surrounded the ranch. A new swing and ceiling fan had been installed on the front porch. And they'd added a sunroom onto the house.

It was a gloriously sunny late afternoon, and the house and the property surrounding it seemed so idyllic.

Kahlil was eager to see his mother and sisters again. But the prospect of seeing his father tightened the knot that had been sitting in his gut since he'd returned to town.

His parents, sisters and their families had been on

a cruise to celebrate his parents' fortieth anniversary when he'd first arrived in town. A cruise he was supposed to be on. He'd canceled when he'd learned that Armand and Meridia had made off with the company's funds. Who knew he'd end up back in Willowvale Springs after all?

The visit was short and sweet. His mom and pregnant baby sister, Salena, were thrilled to see him. His sister Farah ribbed him for his extended absence in her typical smartass way. His father did his best to ignore him. The old man grunted in greeting, perturbed that Kahlil's visit had interrupted the viewing of his favorite old Western shows. Then he disappeared the moment Kahl turned his back.

It seemed that rekindling a relationship with his dad wasn't in the cards, either.

Kahlil stayed for maybe an hour but politely declined an invitation to stay for dinner, which his mother and sisters were busy cooking. He said his goodbyes, then his mother insisted on walking him back to his rented SUV. She practically glowed as she related how thankful she was that his sister Farah, her husband and children lived next door in the house that had once belonged to Andraya and her family, and that Salena and her husband lived a stone's throw away.

When they got to the Tahoe, she glanced around, then leaned closer and lowered her voice. "You need to speak with your father."

"I just tried talking to Dad," Kahlil reminded her. "He grunted and left the room. So I'm pretty sure he doesn't want to talk to me."

"You've both dug your heels in, and neither of you seems to know how to let go of all of that pent-up hurt and anger. If you ask me, that's why you and Dray are stuck in the past, too. Though I'm glad that the two of you seem to have found some middle ground." She squeezed his forearm and flashed a sad smile. "So maybe there's hope."

"For whom? Me and Dad, or me and Dray?"

"*Both*." The way she'd uttered that single word…it came off as more of a directive than a plea.

Kahlil rubbed his stubbled chin. "Yeah, I hope so, too, Mom."

"Unlike me, you're not relegated to the sidelines *hoping* that things will turn around. You're at the center of this thing, and you can fix things with both your dad and Dray. You have to because…because…" His mother's voice wavered, and her eyes filled with tears. She produced a napkin from the pocket of her apron and dabbed at the corners of her eyes.

Kahlil's mouth went dry, and there was a sudden burning in his chest. This was unlike his mother. Something was genuinely wrong.

He placed a hand on her upper arm and leaned in. "What's going on, Mom? And I know this is about more than the tension between me and Dad. Is it the ranch? Is everything all right?"

There had been some lean years on the ranch when either his mother or Farah—who was now running the place—had come to him for help. He'd gladly gifted them the money, grateful that he was in a position to assist. Not that his father had ever seemed impressed by his eagerness to help save their family homestead.

"No, things are fine here, honey, in no small part thanks to you." She sniffled, wiping at her eyes. "This is much bigger than the ranch. It's about your father."

Kahlil leaned against the SUV, his shoulders tensing. "What about Dad?"

"He's sick," she said.

"How sick?"

"*Very.* He has chronic kidney disease caused by hypertension. His doctor wants him to begin kidney dialysis as soon as possible, but your father refuses to consider it." The tears fell faster than his mother could wipe them away. Still, she tried her best.

"Why?"

"Says he doesn't see the point in it. That he'd simply be delaying the inevitable and leaving his family with unnecessary hospital bills. But I know it's mostly the cost, the inconvenience and his not wanting to feel vulnerable."

"Stubborn old goat," Kahl muttered, then heaved a sigh. "He'd rather go out on his own terms than to feel like he's at the mercy of anyone or anything else."

"*Exactly.*" His mother's expression was pained as she dabbed at her tears. "He might be a stubborn old goat, but he's *my* stubborn old goat and I love him. Maybe I'm being selfish, but forty years together isn't enough. Your father finally retired and is letting the girls handle the ranch business. We just started traveling. I want us rocking on that porch swing together, surrounded by our grandchildren—including your kids." She poked him in the chest. "For years to come."

"Farah and Salena have you covered on the grandkids," he teased, glad to see a ghost of a smile on her lips. "I'll talk to Dad if that's what you want. But you see how he is with me. Wouldn't it make more sense for the plea to come from his beloved baby girl or his fiery-tongued doppelgänger of a daughter instead of the son he considers a traitor to the family and a general disappointment?"

"I know he isn't very good at showing it, but your father *is* proud of you, Kahlil." She placed a hand on his shoulder.

Sure. And pigs can fly and camels can swim.

"Besides, he made me promise to let him tell the girls himself when he's ready," she said.

"They don't know?" Kahlil blew out a long breath and rubbed his chin. His sisters would be devastated. They were both daddy's girls, but Salena especially.

His father had spoken barely twenty words to him in the twenty years since he'd left for college. He'd begrudgingly attended his undergrad and graduate commencement ceremonies and his wedding. If his father hadn't forgiven him in twenty years, what could Kahlil possibly say that would make the man listen to him?

But he would do anything for his mother and his sisters. So if there was even the slightest chance he could change his father's mind and ease his mother's despair, he had to try.

"I'll talk to Dad. But let's give him a chance to process the fact that I'm back home, first. Okay?"

"But you *will* speak with him?" The hopefulness in her voice broke his heart.

"I promise." He smiled.

"Good." She seemed relieved. "We have dinner plans this Sunday. But we were planning on having a family dinner the following Sunday. Maybe you could talk to him then?"

"That sounds perfect, Mom," he said.

Farah brought out a bag filled with what looked like enough food to feed a small army.

"It's good to have you home again, baby." His mother hugged him tight. Then she and Farah returned to the house, arm-in-arm.

Kahlil climbed into the SUV, settled against the headrest and groaned. Life was way too short to let petty differences destroy a relationship that had meant as much to him as his friendship with Andraya once had.

Too bad Dray didn't feel the same.

His phone rang. It was the lead software engineer on the project, Titus Gibson. Tye was a brilliant, focused engineer who only ever reached out if he ran into a problem.

"What's up, Tye?"

"I've been wracking my brain all week on some of the security concerns I have for the end-user if we stick to all of the deliverables the investors want." The man sounded exasperated.

"What've you tried?"

"Everything!" Tye said. "Nothing seems to be ticking all the boxes without posing a security risk."

"I doubt that you've tried *everything*." Kahl tried to keep his tone upbeat. "But I have some time available tomorrow. If you'd like, we can—"

"Actually, Tim needs the changes by tomorrow," Tye

said sheepishly. "One of the investors asked for a status update and inquired about this issue in particular. So I'd like to have some sort of viable answer for him before then."

"You might've tried leading with that, Tye." Kahlil rubbed his forehead and groaned.

"Sorry, boss. Tim said this is normally the kind of thing Armand would be able to schmooze his way out of. Any idea when he'll be returning?" Tye asked.

"No time soon." Kahlil's jaw clenched.

Eventually, he'd have to come clean with his team about their missing chief marketing officer. But not today. For now, he needed to keep up the facade. He couldn't take a chance on the investors or the team losing confidence in him or in the project. So he needed to dive in and help Tye get this problem figured out.

"Give me twenty minutes to get back to my computer, then the two of us will put our heads together and get this resolved."

That meant he'd have to reschedule his meeting with Dray. He only hoped she'd understand.

Andraya paced her bedroom, still pissed about Kahlil canceling on their working dinner. The man hadn't even had the courtesy to call her. He'd sent a text message which she'd just happened to see after spending an inordinate amount of time rummaging through her closet for something to wear.

Something important came up. Need to reschedule. Rain check?

Dray had screamed in exasperation. Kahl clearly hadn't even cared enough to make up a good lie. He'd gone with the generic *something came up*.

Was it a family emergency? A business meeting? A case of food poisoning? Had aliens invaded? Or perhaps a zombie apocalypse was looming.

Andraya squeezed her eyes shut and huffed, angry with herself for caring.

Did it matter *why* Kahlil had canceled their meeting? The point was that he had. More importantly, it was the third time they'd rescheduled.

This wasn't about her being disappointed personally. Though Kahlil blowing her off again did feel pretty damn personal. No, this was about his interest in the ranch. Or rather, his lack of interest.

Dray could hear Kahl in her head reminding her that he was the owner of the ranch. Therefore, he didn't owe her an explanation. Maybe that was true. But his flippant disregard for her time and lack of urgency where the ranch was concerned seemed to be a harbinger of things to come. If so, this entire exercise would be a waste of time.

Like it or not, Kahl was at the helm of the horse ranch now. So if he wasn't all in, the project was doomed.

Andraya sank onto the edge of her bed and stared out of the window that faced Kahl's cabin and scowled. In anticipation of their evening feast, Dray had worked through lunch and hadn't bothered to pick anything up for dinner. So yes, maybe she was a tad bit hangry. But she also had every right to be upset.

This wasn't Seattle. This was Willowvale Springs,

where you picked up the phone and had the courtesy to call your dinner companion when you were canceling on them.

Andraya glanced at the watch on her wrist—a gift given to her by Hank when he'd appointed her ranch manager. He'd hugged her and told her how proud she'd made him, that she was the daughter that he and Edith never had.

Her eyes stung with tears thinking of the old man. More so when she thought of the fact that he hadn't trusted her with keeping the legacy of the ranch alive. Well, Hank wasn't there, so she couldn't tell the old man just how she felt. But Kahlil was. He was probably sitting on the sofa over in his cabin watching some sci-fi marathon.

The more she thought about it, the more annoyed she became.

Andraya went down to the kitchen to look for something for dinner. Nothing quick and easy was on hand, and after a long day at the ranch, she wasn't in the mood to cook a meal from scratch. That meant she would need to go out and get something.

She grabbed her wristlet wallet and the keys to her pickup truck—a black GMC Canyon Hank had left her along with the house. But before she got into the truck, she glanced over at Kahlil's cabin. The lights were on, and his SUV was in the driveway.

She should just hop into the truck, drive into town and get a pizza. But she slammed the door, shoved her keys into the back pocket of her jean shorts and made her way to Kahlil's cabin.

If he wasn't taking this project seriously, she needed to know now so she wouldn't get her hopes up—or those of the ranch hands whose livelihoods depended on it.

Kahlil stood and stretched, his back aching and his fingers cramped after spending the past five hours hunched over his computer as he and Tye had gone over a variety of scenarios and proposed possible solutions. Twenty minutes ago, they'd finally had a promising breakthrough.

Tye had initiated a unit test to ensure the functionality of the code they were proposing before integrating the changes into the software. If all went well, they'd move forward with the process and take the next steps.

"How's it looking, Tye?" Kahlil asked.

"So far, so good, boss." Tye shoved a pencil through the messy bun atop his head he'd pulled his shoulder-length locs into. "We should know if this code is viable in a few more minutes."

"Let's hope this works. If so, maybe we'll both get to bed before midnight." Before Kahlil finished his sentence, the doorbell rang. He glanced at his watch. It was after 9:00 p.m.

"Sounds like you've got company." The usually serious younger man flashed a mischievous grin. "You probably had plans tonight. If you need to go—"

"I did have plans," Kahl admitted. "But I rescheduled them because this is important. No doubt you did the same."

Armand had floated in and out of the office and spent most of his time wooing investors. But Kahlil had been determined to demonstrate the same work ethic and level of commitment he expected of his team. That often meant long nights in the office.

The doorbell rang again, and maybe it was Kahl's imagination, but this time it almost sounded angry.

"Doesn't sound like they plan on going away anytime soon," Tye noted.

No, it didn't seem they did.

"Be right back." Kahl walked toward the front door. He'd forgotten to turn on the porch light, so he couldn't make out the figure standing at his door. When he switched on the light, it illuminated the gorgeous woman standing on his front porch, one hand propped on her generous hip. Fire blazed in those dark eyes, and she was clearly unhappy. But she looked damn good in a fitted white tank top worn beneath an open, long-sleeve plaid shirt. Her cutoff denim shorts highlighted thick but toned brown thighs and made her legs look a mile long.

Kahlil swallowed hard and willed himself to stop thinking inappropriate thoughts about his former best friend who was now his employee.

He opened the front door. "Hi, Dray. Did you not get my message?"

"Your *text* message?" she asked indignantly. "I did. But only after I skipped lunch and spent an hour getting ready."

"It took you an hour to come up with that?"

Shit.

Kahlil regretted the words the moment he heard them

coming from his mouth. Dray's look of outrage confirmed that he'd indeed made a boneheaded mistake.

"I mean…not that you don't look great. You absolutely do. Not that I'm… I mean…it's not like I'm looking. I'm just saying—"

"Stop. Talking." There was practically steam rising from Andraya's ears. Her full breasts rose and fell with each angry breath as she narrowed her gaze at him. "And stop staring at my boobs. God, grow up already!" She stormed past him into the house.

"Well, come right in, I guess," Kahl muttered under his breath as he closed the door behind her. He turned to Dray and forced a smile. "Like I said, I sent a message to cancel our meeting—"

"For the *third time*." Andraya shook three fingers angrily. "Look, I'm sure you've got better things to do…like watch sci-fi or porn or whatever the hell you're doing. But this meeting is important." She shoved a finger into his chest.

She seemed surprised at the resistance she encountered. Dray raised a brow, then poked his chest again, more tentatively this time.

"You done?" Kahl folded his arms.

She stepped back, eyes wide as if she'd momentarily forgotten he was there. He could only imagine how those cheeks of hers must've been stinging with heat beneath that gorgeous brown skin.

Andraya stood taller, her gaze somewhere in the distance over his left shoulder. She cleared her throat. "The point is…this isn't Seattle or New York or LA. Here, if we're going to cancel an important meeting for the *third time—*" she emphasized, in case he'd missed the earlier mention "—we have the common decency to pick up the telephone and call a person. We don't send them a cowardly text message."

Kahl rubbed his forehead and heaved a sigh. As annoyed as he was with Andraya right now, she made a good point. Shooting off a quick text message had been the most efficient way of informing her. But things worked differently in a small town. He was well aware of that and should've acted accordingly.

"You're right. And I'm sorry." He folded his arms over his chest. "It would've been better if I'd called."

Dray looked stunned by his apology. She eyed him suspiciously but quickly recovered. "It would've been *a lot better* if you hadn't canceled."

"That couldn't be helped," Kahl countered.

"Why? Because there's a *John Wick* marathon tonight? I love Keanu Reeves as much as the next person, but we need to discuss ranch business, Kahl."

There was a tick in his jaw, and his hands tightened into fists at his side. A lot of things had changed between them. But Andraya clearly still knew how to get underneath his skin.

Normally, he was able to stay pretty clearheaded and keep his emotions in check. Even through this entire mess with his former business partner and ex-wife, Kahlil had managed to keep it together. But tonight, he was exhausted, frustrated and concerned for his father's physical health and how his mother and sisters would handle it. Oh, and he was ravenously hungry, too. He'd been so busy working on the project that he'd completely forgotten about the food his mother had sent home with him.

"You claim to have been running the place, even when Hank was alive." He gritted the words out through clenched teeth. "I'm paying you more than the old man was. Because I have a business of my own to run back in Seattle, so why can't you just create a formal proposal with your key recommendations? I'll look it over and either approve or deny your requests."

Andraya's widened eyes quickly met his. The dark pools flared with anger, but she also seemed genuinely wounded by his words.

What was it about Andraya Walker that got him so off-kilter? He would've thought she'd be happy to produce a list of her wants for the ranch without having to debate him over every single one of them. No matter what he said or did, he could never seem to win with her.

"Inheriting this place has been a *huge* pain in the ass for you, Kahlil. I get it. But the ranch is important to me, to this town and to all of the people who depend on it. It's important to everyone involved *except you.*"

"It's not that I don't care. I'm just busy tonight. Like I said…something came up."

"*Right.*" Andraya rolled her eyes incredulously. She brushed past him and swept into the other room. "I swear to God, Kahl, if you canceled on our meeting again so you could spend all night playing *Grand Theft Auto* or *Overwatch*…" Suddenly she screamed. One hand was pressed to her mouth, and the other was pointing at the curved, thirty-four-inch, ultrawide computer monitor he'd set up. "Is he… Are you… I'm sorry. I didn't mean to interrupt your date…or whatever."

"I am *not* on a date," Kahl objected.

"Definitely not. I would've made him order me dinner," Tye piped. "Besides, Boss Man is cool and all but definitely not my type," he said the last part in a loud stage whisper behind his palm. "I'm already way too serious, and he's always hyper-focused. I honestly don't need that kind of stress in my personal life." Tye was clearly amused.

"Kahl can't help it." A slow grin spread across Andraya's gorgeous face. Her dark eyes twinkled. "He's been that way as long as I've known him, and we met when I was five."

"You two realize that I have the power to fire both of you, right?" Kahlil stepped into the view of the camera. He narrowed his gaze at Dray, then shifted it to Tye.

Dray and Tye exchanged glances through the screen, then they both burst into laughter. As if firing either of them was as improbable as the earth spinning backward.

They were right.

He needed them both desperately. But he wasn't about to admit that.

"How's that unit test coming, Tye?" Kahlil asked the question of the man on the screen, but he glared at Dray who gave him an adorable, apologetic shrug.

He remembered why he'd never been able to stay mad with her when they were best friends.

"Great, actually. I was just waiting for a break in your conversation with…"

"Andraya," she interjected, pressing a hand to her chest. "But please, call me Dray."

"Hi, Dray. I'm Titus Gibson. My friends call me Tye."

"Great, now, that we're all friends. About the unit test...you were saying?" Kahlil bit the words out through clenched teeth.

Before tonight, Kahl wasn't sure he'd ever heard Tye laugh. Two minutes with Dray and the man was joking and sporting a goofy grin.

Was he indignant because Tye had never seemed that comfortable with him? Or was it because the other man was staring at his former best friend like she was the last prime rib sandwich at the Wyoming State Fair?

Definitely the latter.

"The code checks out," Tye announced proudly. "Now I'll try integrating it into the software and running a smoke test. But we've been at this for hours. You and Dray clearly have business to discuss, and I don't need you for this part. I'll run the next few tests and shoot you a quick text after the software passes each checkpoint."

"I'm not going to just abandon you," Kahl said. "After all, we've been at it this long."

"Which is why you need a break." Tye smiled, but Kahlil was pretty sure it was directed at Dray not him. "I'll be fine."

"If you're still at work, you must be starving," Dray said to Tye as she studied the office cubicles in the background of the screen.

"I'm good. Had a KIND Bar in my desk." Tye held up the empty wrapper.

"Really, Kahl?" Dray whipped around to face him. "You could've at least ordered dinner for Tye if he's going to be working all night." She sounded genuinely disappointed in him.

"Now that you mention it… I could eat," Tye said sheepishly.

"I think he owes us both dinner." Dray's eyes sparkled.

The teasing lilt of her voice did things to him, and he honestly wasn't sure what was happening in his head.

Yes, she'd acquired her share of grown-woman curves and was more beautiful than he'd realized back then. But this was still *Dray*. She'd always just been his friend. One of the guys. He hadn't thought of her as anything more. Not even once. But since he'd rolled back into town, he hadn't been able to stop thinking about what an insanely gorgeous and remarkably enticing woman his best friend had become.

Or clearly, she always had been. He just hadn't bothered to notice. Either way, he was here to take care of business. Not to get involved with Dray or anyone else.

"Kahl?" Dray placed a gentle hand on his forearm. "Are you okay?"

Kahlil's neck warmed and his cheeks heated with embarrassment. Exactly how long had he spaced out just now?

"Fine. Text me what you want, and I'll have it delivered. And keep me up-to-date on those tests you're running. If you encounter a problem—"

"Got you on speed dial." Tye picked up his phone and tapped something out on it.

Kahlil's phone dinged in his back pocket.

"That would be my order." Tye set the phone down again. "Pleasure to meet you, Dray."

"You, too, Tye." She beamed.

Before he could pepper the younger man with a slew of additional questions, his image disappeared from the screen.

Khalil yanked his phone from his back pocket, read Tye's order, then opened a delivery app.

"You're costing me a fortune, you know that, Dray? First the renovations at the ranch. Now a ribeye steak for Tye. I'm surprised he didn't order the lobster. *Jeez*," Kahl muttered.

A smirk lit her eyes. "But I'll bet he'll be willing to work twice as hard for you the rest of the night. And he won't forget what you did for him. That'll matter one day when some other tech company comes along and tries to recruit him. So...you're welcome."

Damn. She wasn't wrong about that, either.

Kahl folded his arms and heaved a sigh as he studied her, trying his hardest to keep his focus on her gorgeous face without being distracted by the soft curves that had him mesmerized since she arrived on his porch the day he'd returned.

"I know it's late, but since you're here and presumably haven't eaten, either, maybe you'd like to help me polish off the meal my mother sent me home with this evening. I think there's probably enough food to feed five people." Kahl shoved his phone into his back pocket.

"Your mother cooked?" Her brows lifted with interest.

"Chicken-fried steak, baked macaroni and cheese, garlic mashed potatoes and stir-fried green beans."

"Dude…you know how much I love your mother's cooking. You had me at chicken-fried steak. I'm definitely in. And since I'm here, maybe we can go over some of these items we were supposed to discuss?" There was hopefulness in her expressive dark eyes.

Kahlil groaned quietly. He was tired, hungry and about ten minutes from falling asleep if he sat still too long. And yet…he seemed wholly incapable of saying no to Dray.

"Looks like our working dinner is back on after all."

Five

Andraya washed her hands and took the meal Kahlil's mother had cooked out of the refrigerator, preparing both of their plates. It was the least she could do since he was willing to share his mother's legendarily good chicken-fried steak and macaroni and cheese. Besides, Kahl had gotten a call from Tye and they needed to go over a few more things.

She brought out their plates, just as Kahl was ending their call.

"At the table or—"

"Would you mind if we eat here on the sofa?" He didn't bother lifting his head as he tapped quickly on his laptop set up on the coffee table.

"No, of course not." Dray set his plate on a piece of junk mail on the table to protect the wood. Then she settled onto the sofa beside him.

Dray didn't dig into her food, despite being hungry enough to eat a bear. It didn't seem right to begin eating his mother's food before he did. After a few minutes of silence, as he furiously tapped away on his laptop, she set her plate down, too.

"Look, about earlier… I didn't mean to interrupt your meeting with Tye. I thought you were blowing me off again."

Kahl stopped typing and glanced over at her. "It might seem to you like I don't care. But I have as much riding on the horse ranch as you do. Maybe more. It's just that *this*—" he indicated his laptop "—has to be my primary concern. It's difficult enough running my firm and managing a project of this magnitude remotely. So when there is a time-sensitive emergency like tonight, I have to drop everything and tend to this first. Understood?"

"Yes, of course." She fidgeted with the tattered edge of her cutoff jeans. Dray felt like a scolded child. But then again, she deserved it.

Tye would probably tell Kahlil's entire staff about overhearing their conversation earlier. It was honestly a wonder Kahl was willing to share his meal with her after that. He was clearly furious with her, but he'd done a fair job of hiding it. Still, despite spending two decades apart, she knew that look. The tension in his shoulders. The tightening of his jaw. How the already quiet man would mostly grunt out two-word answers.

"From now on, if you say you're busy, then I'll take you at your word. And you're obviously busy tonight." She gestured toward the laptop he was pecking on furiously again, then stood. "So why don't I just take my food to go and get you that formal proposal you asked for?"

Kahlil didn't answer. He continued typing as if she hadn't said a word. Finally, he sent the email he was working on and shut his laptop. He turned toward her on the couch.

"After you made a huge deal about how important and time-sensitive these topics are?" Kahl chuckled bitterly. "Not on your life. Now, sit down and eat your food before it gets cold." He gestured toward her plate.

She sank onto the sofa beside him without a word.

Kahl stuffed a forkful of his mother's macaroni and cheese into his mouth and murmured. "God, I miss home cooking."

"Then maybe you should come home more often," she noted, drawing a raised brow from her ridiculously handsome ex-bestie.

Dray hadn't intended to shoot another barb at Kahl, but the words had tumbled out of her mouth before she'd even had a chance to think about them, let alone reel them back in.

"I'm just saying…your mom and sisters really miss you." Dray picked up her own plate and took a bite of his mother's macaroni and cheese. "And I know your dad can be stubborn and ornery. The man is like a bulldog with a pork chop bone when it comes to holding a grudge…"

"Sounds familiar," Kahlil muttered, casting a side-eye in her direction as he cut up his chicken-fried steak and ate a piece.

He wasn't wrong, so it was best that she ignore the comment.

"But despite your dad pretending as if he doesn't care about you staying away all this time... I know that he does. He's just hurt." Dray scooped up some mashed potatoes. "He's lashing out like a wounded bull so that you can't get close enough to hurt him again. And maybe he thinks that if he acts as if what you did doesn't matter, it won't hurt anymore."

"And what makes you think you know my dad so well?" Kahl's voice was laced with irritation.

"Let's just say I can relate." She ate a piece of mouthwatering steak.

Kahlil grimaced and set down his plate as if he'd suddenly lost his appetite. He draped an arm over the back of the leather sofa and turned toward her. "About what happened back then..."

"This isn't about me and you, Kahl. I'm just saying that I understand how your dad feels. So despite what he says, don't give up on him." Dray's eyes burned with tears, and she wasn't even sure why.

"Like I gave up on you?" he asked quietly.

Andraya raked her teeth over her lower lip as she shoved the food around on her plate, but she didn't address his question.

"You should talk to your dad, Kahl. I know it won't be easy. He's as stubborn as they come. But our parents are getting older. If you don't talk to your dad, someday you'll regret it."

"I was just at the house earlier today. My mother asked me to talk to him, too." Kahl rubbed his whiskered chin, his brows furrowing. The pained look on his face made Dray's heart ache. "My dad's sick, and he won't accept treatment. Between work and dad…" Kahl heaved a sigh. "That's why I was so grumpy tonight."

"Kahlil, I'm so sorry." Dray set her plate on the table, too, then turned toward him. Her bare thigh brushed his jean-clad one. She gently gripped his forearm. "I swear I didn't know."

"I shouldn't have said anything." Kahl seemed angry with himself for telling her. "My sisters don't even know. So you can't tell anyone about this."

She squeezed his arm, prompting his gaze to meet hers. "I won't say a word. I promise. You can trust me." She offered him a weak smile when the tension in his shoulders seemed to ease. "Why is your dad refusing the treatment?"

"My mom thinks he doesn't want to feel like a burden to her and the girls." Kahlil dropped his gaze again. "She wants me to get him to change his mind."

Despite all of the hurt, anger and distance that had grown between them, she would've done anything to take away the pain and guilt her old friend seemed to be feeling.

"Then you should talk to him." Dray slid her hand into Kahlil's and squeezed it.

"If he won't listen to my mom, why on earth would he listen to me?" Kahlil rubbed the back of his neck with his free hand. "He can barely stand to be in a room with me for ten minutes."

"That's all bluster and ego," Dray assured him. "Your dad loves you, Kahlil. That's why it hurt so badly when you walked away from the legacy he built for you and your sisters."

"I get that. Especially after what happened to…" Kahlil drew in a deep breath, just short of uttering his brother's name. He swallowed hard. "I appreciate why my dad feels the way he does. But being a rancher just isn't the life I saw…*see*…for myself. He's my father, and I'm grateful for everything he's done for me. But he doesn't get to dictate what I do with the rest of my life, Dray." He settled his gaze on hers. "No one does."

His words landed like a direct torpedo hit to her chest.

Dray's throat was suddenly dry. She nodded. "You're right. No one else has the right to dictate our lives. That includes our parents and—"

"Our best friends?" His brows furrowed.

She tugged her hand away, but Kahlil held onto it firmly, his gaze meeting hers as if awaiting a response.

"Okay. I was wrong to be angry with you for not wanting a life in Willowvale Springs. You had your sights set on bigger and better things. Things that didn't include me." Dray's eyes stung. "Like your dad, I took that rejection really hard. I couldn't accept that you'd outgrown our friendship."

Kahlil frowned, releasing her hand. "I didn't reject you, Andraya, and I *never* claimed to have outgrown our friendship. I had a lot on my plate. Classes, clubs, a part-time job."

"You didn't have to *say* you'd outgrown our friendship, Kahl. Every conversation we had made it obvious. It was even more apparent in the conversations we *didn't* have. You were screening my calls most of the time, and when you did answer the phone, you were always too busy to talk."

"Maybe I was slow to respond, but I *never* stopped taking your calls, Andraya." There was a deep ache in Kahl's voice.

Dray felt every ounce of the anguish reflected in Kahl's sad, dark eyes. Her gut knotted and her chest ached with regret.

"I reacted poorly," she admitted with a shrug as she blinked back tears. "But I could see the end of our friendship looming, clear as day. Maybe it was immature of me, but I thought if I was the one who pulled the plug on it, losing you would hurt less."

"And did it?" Kahl watched her intently, his voice sincere.

Dray shook her head. The emotions invoked by the admission rendered her speechless.

Kahlil raised a hand and swiped a thumb over her cheek. Was she crying?

What the hell?

Dray rarely ever cried. She'd been thrown from horses, bitten by a dog and broken an ankle when she'd tripped and fallen down the stairs. She hadn't cried during a single instance despite the excruciating pain. But Kahlil Anderson had been back in town for a week and suddenly she found herself all weepy and emotional.

Her cheeks and forehead flamed with embarrassment. She squeezed her eyes shut, but that only wrung more tears from her eyes.

"I shouldn't have disturbed you. I should go." She stood suddenly.

"Andraya." Kahl stood, too. He caught her elbow, his grip gentle but firm enough to hold her in place. "Losing your friendship was devastating for me. I know it might've seemed like I didn't care or that I was too busy for you. But the realization that I'd lost my best friend… it hurt like hell. And it took a really long time for me to get over it. But when I came back here and saw you standing on the porch that day…"

Kahl drew in a deep breath, releasing her arm. "That's when I realized that I wasn't over it at all. That I'd just kind of stuffed all of my feelings down and tried to ignore them. Maybe you've done the same. Either way, I just want you to know how sorry I am if I ever made you feel like I didn't want you in my life anymore. That wasn't true. And I'd love it if we could be friends again."

Andraya stared at Kahlil, unsure of what to say. Her heart felt full in a way that felt unfamiliar and yet oddly comforting. Her pulse raced, and electricity seemed to crackle along her skin.

Kahlil wanted to renew their friendship, but the feelings she'd been battling since his return…they were more than just *friendly*. She hadn't admitted that to Kahl when they were teenagers, and she sure as hell wasn't going to admit it now.

"I'm sorry, too," she said finally. "About then and now. On top of the feelings of rejection over our friendship, I was hurt that Hank left you this place when it was clear how much I loved it. That there was no one who would take better care of it."

Kahlil shoved a hand into his pocket. "I don't doubt that's true, Dray. And in an ideal world, I'd love to sell the place to you, but… I can't settle for that low of a price. If circumstances were different, I'd let you buy it in a heartbeat."

"I understand." Dray folded her arms and nodded. She wiped at her damp cheeks with the back of her hand and cleared her throat. "And I'd like for us to be friends again. But if you plan on finishing your business with the ranch and then riding off into the sunset for another twenty years—" she hunched her shoulders "—I don't really see the point. Maybe it would be better if we agreed to wipe the slate clean and then just keep the relationship businesslike and cordial."

Andraya tipped her chin and stared at her old friend. Her words were firm, and she'd regained her composure. What she'd proposed was the best, most sensible path. She truly believed that. So why couldn't she stop hoping that Kahl would disagree?

Six

Kahlil dragged a hand across his mouth as he regarded the gorgeous woman standing just a few feet away from him. Her eyes still glistened, and her cheeks were damp, but the tears had stopped.

God, she was beautiful.

Her words echoed in his head.

If you plan on finishing your business with the ranch and then riding off into the sunset for another twenty years, I don't really see the point.

His best friend had always been direct. And while many things about her had changed, her trait of absolute honesty, which he'd always admired, certainly hadn't.

She'd made a fair point, and she deserved an honest response.

He took a step closer, and she jumped slightly. Her breathing seemed shallow and her eyes blinked rapidly.

"Our parents aren't the only ones getting older, Dray," Kahl said. "I don't know about you, but I've been through a lot in the past twenty years. Highs, lows, successes and disappointments, marriage and divorce. I've thought of you a lot in those moments. Regretted my part in ruining the friendship we had."

"But not enough to come home or to call," she noted.

"Maybe you weren't the only one afraid of being rejected." Kahlil rubbed the back of his neck. "I didn't try because I envisioned it going pretty much like it did… only worse. You haven't come at me with a double-barrel shotgun yet, so I'd say it's already a win."

Andraya shook her head and laughed. "I'm more of a pocket-derringer kind of girl, 'cause I keeps it classy." She blew on the barrel of an imaginary pistol, then holstered it.

They both laughed and it alleviated the tension between them.

"Seriously, Dray, I understand if you don't think repairing our friendship is worthwhile. But I'm at a point in my life where I've come to truly value family and genuine friendships. I promise to make regular visits— even after I sell the horse ranch."

"You promised to come back before." Her tone was serious but not angry. "One of my ranch hands thinks you can't be trusted. You let me down then, Kahlil. Why should I trust you this time?"

Another fair question.

"Only you can answer that," he said. "But my decision to save the horse ranch…why do you think I did that?"

"Because it was the right thing to do," she responded quickly. But something in her eyes indicated there was something she wasn't saying.

"True. But I came to that conclusion because of you, Dray. And because I didn't want to do anything that would hurt you again."

Dray wrapped her arms around herself, a soft smile curving one edge of her sensual lips. "You did this for me?" she practically whispered.

"Yes." He shoved both hands in his pockets again. "I just hope that it—"

Before he could finish his sentence, Dray launched herself into him and wrapped her arms around him, her cheek pressed to his chest.

"Thank you, Kahl. This means the world to me and to everyone at the ranch."

It felt *good* to be wrapped up in her hug, inhaling her delicious scent, with her soft curves pressed against him. So good he froze. By the time his brain screamed at him to hug her back, Dray had already pulled away.

An opportunity lost.

"Most of the ranch hands are really excited about the renovations and reviving the equestrian shows," Dray continued. "That's why I've been pushing so hard for us to get everything finalized. I want to reward their confidence before our resident pessimist can sow seeds of doubt and kill the morale."

"Then *stay*. We'll hash everything out tonight. Deal?"

Dray cocked her head, studying him for a minute.

A soft smile spread across her face, and her eyes lit up. "Okay."

"Great. Then why don't you reheat the food, and I'll make some coffee while you tell me exactly why you hate my plans for renovating the equestrian center." He flashed her a sly smile as they grabbed their plates and headed into the kitchen.

It felt good to be working with Dray. For them to be laughing and joking again. She hadn't answered his question about the possibility of repairing their friendship. But this felt like a hopeful start.

Kahlil and Andraya ironed out the remaining details of the necessary renovations and decided on the dates for the equestrian events while they shared a meal and reminisced about old times.

Revisiting fond childhood memories was something Kahlil hadn't done much. But seeing his sisters earlier had reminded him of how much fun his family had together before his younger brother's accident. There had even been a few good memories after his family had suffered that tragic loss.

As he and Dray recounted some of the mischief they'd gotten into as kids, he felt a little nostalgic, accompanied by growing feelings of regret.

Kahlil had been viewing his early years there in Willowvale Springs through a skewed lens. He'd conflated his memories of this town with all the opportunities he couldn't have, had he stayed. As if Willowvale Springs was some sort of prison. But the truth was that he owed a lot to the town and the people in it. People like Dray and Hank.

"The old man…was he sick a long time?" Kahlil handed Dray another beer and sat on the sofa beside her.

The broad smile on Dray's face disappeared. Her eyes filled with sadness.

"For much longer than any of us knew. He kept it to himself until he had no choice but to reach out for help. Then he told me and a handful of others. Still, he tried to hide how much pain he was in, and he didn't want most folks to know how sick he was." Dray's voice cracked, and she swiped a finger beneath her eyes. She sniffled. "But despite everything, he was generous to so many of us. Made sure we would be okay once he was gone. That's why…" Her words trailed off as she glanced up at him.

"That's why you were shocked that he'd left the ranch to me." Kahl took a swig of his beer. "Believe me, I was just as stunned." Kahlil's chest ached with guilt over not keeping in touch with the old man and not returning for his funeral. "In the video he left me…the things he said…he'd obviously followed my career. Said he was proud of me."

"He was," Dray confirmed with a soft smile. "He was beaming with pride over you, Mason, Vaughn and Paxton. Like he'd raised the four of you himself. I didn't appreciate it much at the time," she admitted. "I didn't want to hear about how well you were doing. Then I'd be forced to acknowledge that you were right to leave all of us behind." Dray took a long drag of her beer.

The air between them was suddenly thick, the silence awkward.

"Leaving town was something I needed to do, but I shouldn't have distanced myself from everyone here the way I did." He heaved a heavy sigh. "I kept in touch with my mom and sisters. And since both you and my dad had cut ties… I figured that was enough. But the truth is I was avoiding the hard conversations and pretending like losing you both didn't matter. I'm sorry Hank is gone," Kahlil said. "But I'm grateful that—"

"He left you the ranch." Dray snickered drily.

"I'm grateful that inheriting the ranch forced me to come home. And not just for a day or two…like when my sisters got married," he added. "Long enough to see that I've been wrong in how I saw this town and the friends and family I left behind."

Andraya tilted her head and assessed him carefully as she ran her fingers through her low ponytail.

"About you wanting us to be friends again… I'd like that, too," she said, a hint of wariness in her voice. "But you need to understand that my obligation, first and foremost, is to my ranch hands and the folks who board their animals with us. So I need you to be honest with me about something." Dray set her beer on the coffee table and turned her body toward him on the sofa.

"Of course. Ask me anything," he said.

He hadn't told Andraya or anyone why he desperately needed to sell the ranch for a premium price. He hoped like hell she didn't plan to ask him. Because he wouldn't lie to her. But he couldn't risk telling her the whole truth, either.

"If your real intention is to turn all of us out onto the street and liquidate the place, I need you to be honest with me about that right now. Don't go through the charade of pretending to care about this place or about me only to let us all down." Andraya shook her head. "I honestly couldn't take that, Kahl."

He felt like a heel for having hurt her the way he had and for not making amends sooner.

Kahl set his beer down and turned toward her, his knee resting against hers. He took her hand in his and met her concerned gaze. "I would never do that to you, Dray. Not now that I know how much this place means to you and to the town. I *am* going to sell this place. But I promise to do everything I can to ensure it remains a horse ranch and that it's better than ever."

"What if developers are the only buyers who'll give you anything close to your target price?" Dray dropped her gaze to their joined hands.

Pax had prepared him for that possibility. And he wouldn't lie to her about it.

"Then I'd tell you that." He lifted her chin, forcing her gaze to meet his. "I'm not going to bullshit you, Andraya. And I promise to keep you informed about the process. So if anything changes, you'll know as soon as I do. All right?"

"Okay." Dray nodded, seemingly relieved. "Then I trust you. And I'll do what I can to instill that same confidence in the rest of the team."

"Good." Kahl grabbed his beer and settled back on the sofa, creating a little space between them again. He gulped down the rest of his cold beer, hoping it would cool the heat rising in his chest. He cleared his throat. "I know some of the older guys probably have their doubts about me and about my motives. Any suggestions on how I can gain their trust?"

A wide smile spread across Andraya's face and her eyes twinkled. "Glad you asked, because I have the perfect idea. But you're gonna need some new clothes, cowboy. Because for the first time in twenty years, you're about to do some actual work. That's the best way to connect with the guys. It's how I earned their respect."

Shit. He had to ask, didn't he?

Working the ranch was the last thing he wanted to do, but there was no way he was backing down.

"You're on. Just…can we make it a day other than tomorrow? It's late, and I'd at least like to get a full night of sleep before you have me mucking out horse stalls."

"Fine." Dray grinned triumphantly. She glanced down at her watch. "Oh! I didn't realize how late it was. Maybe you don't have to go to the ranch first thing in the morning, but I do. My boss is a real pain in the ass, so I don't want to be late." She winked, then started gathering their empty beer bottles and remaining dishes.

"Don't worry about the dishes. I'll get them."

She raised an eyebrow. A look that indicated that his protestations were pointless.

He chuckled, following her to the kitchen.

"At least let me walk you home." Kahlil stood in the doorway as she rinsed the plates and silverware, loading them into the dishwasher.

"I'm just a couple of doors away. Besides, what if

Tye needs you?" She closed the dishwasher and dried her hands.

"He'd call first, and I've got my phone." Kahl patted his back pocket. "Now, come on so we can get you into bed." He cringed the moment the words came out of his mouth. "I mean…"

"I know what you meant." Dray punched his arm playfully. She picked up her wristlet, and they both headed for the door.

"It's a beautiful night," Kahl marveled, looking up at the dark sky punctuated by twinkling stars.

"It is. But the sky is like that here most nights."

They walked onto Dray's porch, and she punched in an entry code, then opened the front door. She turned to him and smiled, neither of them speaking. As if she was just as reluctant to end their night together as he was.

"Well, I'm glad we finally got that meeting out of the way. Great work tonight," Kahl said, his hands shoved into his pockets. "You should get some sleep. In fact, you should sleep in tomorrow. I have a feeling that pain in the ass boss of yours won't mind if you come in a little late."

"Well, that's awfully nice of him. Too bad the horses wouldn't be quite as forgiving." She grinned. "Good night, Kahl. And…thank you. I know this isn't what you had in mind when you inherited the ranch. I honestly can't thank you enough."

Andraya lifted onto her toes and pressed a soft kiss to his cheek, her open palms resting on his chest. She pulled away so slowly that it felt like it was happening in slow motion. Her dark eyes studied his as if she was waiting for him to react.

This was an opportunity he wouldn't miss.

Kahl slipped his arms around her waist, lowered his head and kissed the soft, full lips that had teased him all night.

Dray leaned into him as his mouth glided over hers.

He tucked her closer, reveling in the sensation of her soft, luscious curves pressed against him. One hand moved to cup her cheek as he angled her head, permitting better access to the sweet mouth he'd spent the better part of the past week fantasizing about kissing. The hand pressed to her back glided lower.

Suddenly, his phone rang, and they both froze.

"You should get that." She pulled back just enough to meet his gaze as he held her in his arms. "It's probably Tye."

He pulled out his phone and checked the screen.

Kahl groaned. "I have to take this."

"And I need to get to bed…to sleep," Dray clarified. She pulled out of his hold reluctantly, her gaze still meeting his. "Thank you for dinner and for making time for our meeting."

"Of course." Kahl nodded. "And thank you for being open to repairing our friendship."

Though kissing Dray probably hadn't been in the interest of friendship. It would only make the already tenuous situation between them even more precarious.

"Don't make me regret it, cowboy." Dray pointed a finger at him, then stepped inside her house.

"Don't worry," he said. "I won't."

Kahlil quickly answered Tye's call before it went to voice mail. Then he headed back to his cabin. Tye had run into another problem, and the two of them would probably be up the rest of the night trying to resolve it. Yet he felt like he was floating on air, eager to see Andraya again.

Seven

"You're in an awfully good mood this morning, Dray. Hot date last night?" Antonio stood in the doorway of Andraya's office.

He grinned as if he was privy to the scene that had been replaying in her head for the past two days: the moment Kahlil had finally taken the hint and leaned in to kiss her.

A shiver ran down her spine thinking of it now.

"Don't be silly." Dray's cheeks heated, despite her denial.

It wasn't a lie. First of all, she and Kahlil hadn't been on a date. It had been a working dinner. Second, they'd had dinner together *two* nights ago—not last night. But Antonio was right about one thing: she'd been in a particularly good mood ever since.

Andraya had been floating around her office humming "Butterflies," by Kacey Musgraves. And she'd gotten up a full hour early to make egg, bacon and croissant sandwiches for the ranch hands.

"Sure smells good in here." Antonio stepped inside, peeking over at the warming platter where she had the sandwiches stacked.

"Where does all that food go?" Dray shook her head and chuckled. Antonio was nineteen and hungry all the time. He could eat his weight in food, but he never seemed to gain an ounce. She lifted the little door and grabbed one of the sandwiches wrapped in plastic. She tossed it to the young ranch hand. "Here you go, Tonio. Coffee is on the counter outside, and there's orange juice and apple juice in the cooler underneath it."

"Thanks, boss." Tonio grinned, removing the plastic as quickly as his fingers could manage. He took a bite and murmured. "That's why you're my favorite."

Antonio had started working at the ranch when he was sixteen, just like she had. And he was, in fact, her favorite. He was smart, hardworking and eager to learn. But like a parent, it was better if she didn't admit to having a favorite kid.

"I'll bet you say that to all the ranch managers who make you homemade breakfast croissants." Dray smiled.

Antonio's grin widened and his dark brown eyes sparkled before he disappeared to grab a bottle of apple juice—his favorite.

"Do I smell some good eats?" Ben appeared in the doorway rubbing his hands together. "Because Alice has been feeding me oatmeal for breakfast every day, and I could use some *real* food."

"You'd better not get me in trouble with Alice." Dray pointed a finger at the older man, then handed him a sandwich. "Got coffee and juices just outside the door.

Ben thanked her and started opening the wrapper. "Been a while since you made us breakfast, Dray. What's the occasion? Is this where you tell us we no longer have jobs?"

"No, it isn't."

Dray and Ben both turned toward the unexpected voice.

Kahlil hovered in the doorway wearing a pair of Timberland boots, some lived-in blue jeans and a green, short-sleeve Henley shirt. He looked like a rugged model in a commercial.

She was pretty sure her mouth had fallen open. There may have been some drool involved.

"So *that's* why you fixed us breakfast. We got company." The old man was as terrible at whispering as he was at being optimistic.

"Stop bellyaching, and eat your free sandwich." Dray elbowed Ben in the side and spoke in a hushed tone. "And don't you dare go starting no trouble today, Ben. *I mean it*." She narrowed her gaze at the old man before turning to their guest who watched them with amusement.

"Good morning, Kahlil. You remember our award-winning horse trainer, Ben Baxter," Dray said.

"Of course." Kahl shook the older man's hand. "Good to see you again, sir."

"Just Ben is fine," the old man grumbled. He took a bite of his sandwich. "You come down here to size us all up? 'Cause I might have a little more snow on the roof and a couple of replacement knees, but up here—" he tapped the crown of his Stetson with his index finger "—I'm fit as a fiddle."

"I don't doubt it." Kahlil's pursed lips quirked into a lopsided smirk as he stepped aside so the older man could leave. All Dray could think of was how those lips had tasted two nights ago and how much she wanted to sample them again.

Kahlil shut the door behind Ben, startling her from her temporary daze. He sank onto the chair on the other side of her desk. "Let me guess… That's our resident pessimist?"

"That's right." Andraya grabbed one of the sandwiches and tossed it to Kahlil before sitting behind her desk and waking her laptop. She opened her email and scrolled through her messages. "Yesterday, I shared some of the details of the renovation and the date for our first equestrian event. That put a damper on Ben's negativity. But the man is nothing if not persistent. It's the reason he's been able to train even our most stubborn stallions."

"First, this sandwich is delicious," Kahl muttered through a mouthful of it.

"Thank you," she said without looking up from her screen.

"*You* made this?" Kahlil seemed genuinely shocked.

"It's eggs, bacon, cheese and a croissant, not beef Wellington." She glared at him over the screen, then resumed typing an email. "I know you've been gone for a while, but I've learned a few things while you were away."

"No, of course. I didn't mean to imply…" He sat up

straight in his chair and cleared his throat. "It's just that…
when we were teenagers you were diametrically opposed
to your mother's attempts to 'domesticate' you." He used
air quotes. "Said you were like a wild horse that wouldn't
be broken." He chuckled, then took another bite of his
sandwich. "I've eaten breakfast sandwiches from gour-
met shops that weren't half as good as this."

"Again…thank you." She nodded, glancing up at him.
"Back then, me not wanting to learn to cook…it was an
act of defiance. My mother was always on about Alana
and me needing to learn to cook so we could *catch* a
good man. Like we were hunting elk or something."
Dray shuddered. "Even now, the thought of it makes
me sick to my stomach."

She printed the document she was viewing, then
walked over to the printer as it warmed up.

"Why'd you change your mind?" Kahl watched her
thoughtfully as he nibbled on his sandwich. Something
about his gaze warmed her chest and sent zips of electricity down her spine.

"Again, it's not a four-course meal. It's a *sandwich*,"
she emphasized. "But yes, I happen to be a damn good
cook. At some point living on my own, I realized that
I deserved good food and I shouldn't have to run home
to mama to get it. I was talking to Hank's wife, Ms.
Edith, about it. She was eager to help me learn to cook
so I could surprise my parents. The time we spent in the
kitchen together was special. For both of us, I think."

Andraya forced a smile and fought back the tears that
stung her eyes. She missed both Ms. Edith and Hank.

They'd been like family to her and to so many of the folks in Willowvale Springs.

"Ms. Edith was an amazing woman. I can only imagine how tough it was for Hank once she passed. She was everything to him," Kahl said solemnly. "The two of them…they were lucky to have a love like that that lasted an entire lifetime."

"They were," she concurred.

An awkward silence settled over the room as Kahlil finished his sandwich and she reviewed her document. Dray sat down at her desk again. She made a few corrections to the document, attached it to the email, then sent it to one of their boarders.

"Coffee?" she asked, already on her feet to make a cup for herself.

"Please," Kahl said.

She grabbed two coffee pods from the drawer beneath her single-serve coffee maker, then two mugs. She started on his cup first, then turned to him.

"About the other night…" They said the words simultaneously, then broke into nervous laughter.

"You go first," Dray said.

"Okay. Umm… I just wanted to say that I haven't been avoiding you since our kiss. I slept in a bit yesterday, then I was handling calls with a couple of investors."

"I didn't think you were dodging me," she said. But now that he'd said it, the thought planted itself inside of her head and instantly grew roots.

Had he been avoiding her?

And though the kiss had been wonderful and exactly what she'd wanted, what did she expect would happen next?

Okay, so maybe there was a small space in the back of her head that daydreamed about the kiss changing things. That Kahlil would suddenly realize how much he missed her and his family and want to keep the ranch and make a life there in Willowvale Springs. But it was just as wild as imagining that she'd someday become Mrs. Michael B. Jordan. She had no delusions about that.

The reality was that when the renovations were done and Kahlil had secured a buyer for the horse ranch, he'd be on a plane back to Seattle faster than she could say goodbye. In fact, now that she thought about it, he probably wouldn't stay through the whole process. Why would he when he had her to oversee the project?

Kahl would probably be traveling back to Seattle soon because *that* was his home.

Andraya's protective instinct flared instantly. The one she'd honed to shield her heart and keep her from becoming more heavily invested in a potential relationship than the other party. The instinct had protected her from repeating the heartaches and disappointments of the past.

Never again would she be that heartbroken teenage girl waiting for her best friend to return so she could admit she loved him.

"Andraya…" Kahl was waving a hand, trying to get her attention. "Did you hear me?"

"No." She'd completely spaced out. *Embarrassing.* "I was thinking about an email I need to send." She immediately felt guilty about lying to Kahl.

She'd made him promise to be honest with her,. but that was about business. People's livelihoods. This was personal. A silly crush leftover from her teenage years. It certainly wasn't the same thing.

"What did you say?" Dray handed Kahl his cup of coffee, then set a small ceramic tray with packets of sugar and creamer pods in front of him.

"I said I realize that this isn't the time or place, but we should probably talk about that night." Kahlil tore open a few packs of sugar and poured them into his coffee.

Andraya swallowed hard, her heart thumping in her chest. She returned to the coffeemaker, removed his used pod and inserted a fresh one for herself.

"Let me save us both some awkwardness and anxiety, Kahl. There's nothing to discuss."

Kahl stopped pouring creamer into his mug and stared at her with a bewildered expression. "What?"

"It was late, we'd both had a few beers and we were reminiscing over the past." Dray grabbed her cup of coffee and sat down at her desk again. "I have no illusions that the kiss meant anything to you…to either of us."

"That's not exactly what I was going to say," Kahl muttered beneath his breath, then sipped his coffee.

"And what were you going to say? That you're only in town for a few weeks? That you're not looking for anything serious right now? That it's only been a year since the divorce and you're not ready to get involved again yet?" Dray tried not to sound facetious because she honestly wasn't trying to be.

"No, I wasn't… I mean…not all of it. And how did you know that it's been a year since my divorce?"

"One of your sisters might've mentioned it. In passing." Dray cleared her throat, her face and cheeks suddenly red hot.

"Why am I surprised? Farah sent me a gift package that included a *Ding-Dong! the Witch is Dead* mug after the divorce was finalized." Kahlil rubbed at his whiskered chin, and she could tell he was trying to hold back a laugh. "My sister has never been very subtle about her feelings for Meridia. Another reason I wasn't eager to come home while the two of us were married."

"Well, I might've been with Farah and Salena when they picked out that gift." Dray drank some of her coffee, also trying to hold back a grin. "By the way, how'd you like that new beginnings candle and the sage smudge home-cleansing set?"

"You and Salena were in on it, too, huh?" He chuckled, and she couldn't help laughing, too. Kahl heaved a quiet sigh, then gripped his mug tightly. "But if all that's true…why did you… I mean, you did want me to kiss you, right?"

Andraya bit her lower lip and sighed.

"I did," she admitted after another sip of her coffee.

"Why?" He studied her carefully.

Dray got up and grabbed a sandwich of her own, which she had no intention of eating at the moment. She just needed space and something to do. She'd hoped that Kahlil would take the hint and change the subject. Instead, he crossed one leg over the other and stared at her intently, awaiting a response.

"Look, it's no secret that I had a huge crush on you

when we were teenagers. So maybe some part of me still needed to know——"

"Wait. We're not gonna just pretend like you didn't say what you just said," Kahl held up one hand as he sat up bone straight in his chair. He set his mug on the table. "You had a crush on me?"

"Really? That's the game we're going to play right now?" Dray propped a hand on her cocked hip.

"I'm not playing a game, Dray." He stood, too. He looked as if she'd just told him something improbable like that the earth was flat or made of cotton candy. "I honestly had no idea that you were into me back then."

"Your sisters teased you about it all the time," she reminded him.

"And you pointedly denied it," Kahl noted. "Besides, you never did or said anything that remotely indicated that you wanted to be anything other than friends."

"You were the *only* person I ever let use my lucky baseball mitt," she said. "I literally wouldn't let anyone else touch it."

"I thought that was because you were my best friend, not because you *liked me* liked me." He dragged a hand over his head. "Besides, you were vocal about everything else you liked or didn't like. So why didn't you just *tell* me?"

"I tried." She sank onto her chair. Her voice sounded small and defeated.

"When?"

"When I was driving you to the bus station." She sighed. "I was getting all worked up and flustered, and you told me——"

"Don't make such a big deal out of me leaving. We'll see each other again in a few months at Christmas," Kahlil recited the words ruefully. He sat on the back edge of her desk, his extended leg brushing her thigh. His freshly showered skin, still dewy, emitted the warm, spicy scent of cedarwood and leather. "Probably the single most regrettable words I've ever uttered."

"Because you knew even then that you weren't coming back?"

"No, I honestly intended to return for the holidays. It's just that life got—"

"Busy." She sucked in a deep breath, willing herself not to get hurt or angry all over again. "Forget it, Kahl. It's all water under the bridge now." Dray forced a smile.

Andraya stood abruptly and made her way around Kahl's long legs as she made her way toward the door. She gripped the handle but didn't open it.

She turned back to him. "There's more coffee and juice just outside the door. I need to speak with one of my groomers before she gets started this morning. Then I'll introduce you to everyone and get you set up working with Antonio today. In the meantime, make yourself comfortable. I'll be back in a bit."

Andraya slipped out of the door before Kahl could respond.

Her pulse was racing and her heart ached. But Dray wasn't sure if it was because Kahl had honestly been clueless about her crush on him then or because, just as then, nothing would ever come of the crush she had on him now.

* * *

Kahlil collapsed onto the bench beneath a sheltered outdoor picnic area where the ranch hands frequently gathered during mealtimes. He slid the straw cowboy hat Andraya had loaned him off his forehead, wiping away the sweat with the back of his wrist.

It was a scorcher beneath the hot sun, despite it being mid-September and a few degrees warmer than it would be back home in Seattle. Not that the temperature outside mattered much. Kahlil spent most of his days in a climate-controlled office hunched over his computer. But he wasn't back in Seattle in the comfort of his office anymore.

He'd spent most of the morning working outdoors with the young ranch hand, Antonio. They'd mucked out stalls, fed the horses, mended fences, hauled hay and kept the troughs filled with water.

Several of the workers had thanked him for saving the ranch after Andraya had introduced him around that morning. They were polite, even grateful. Still, they regarded him cautiously. As if they expected him to pull the rug from underneath them at any moment. Kahlil couldn't blame them. He'd have felt the same, had he been in their position.

You don't care about anybody but yourself. Not this family or this town. That ain't how I raised you, son.

Kahlil could hear his father's words echoing in his head across the two decades since he'd uttered those words. He'd been trying to live his vision for his life while also proving his father's analysis of him wrong ever since. He could think of no more obvious way to prove his dad wrong than pulling off this resurrection of Hank's dilapidated old horse ranch.

But as admirable a goal as it was, he was going to pay for it over the next couple of days. Because the tasks he'd performed had called for him to use muscles he'd forgotten he owned. But if this was what he needed to do to prove to the workers and the town that he really did want what was in their best interest, it was a small price to pay.

Kahlil circled one shoulder while kneading the tightness on the opposite side of his neck.

"You're gonna want to pop a few ibuprofen and take a *long*, hot soak in a tub with some Epsom salt tonight, or you won't be able to move for a week." Dray smiled, her hand shielding the sun from her gorgeous face.

Andraya Walker was probably the only human being in the world who would look that damn good in a pair of worn, tattered jeans, a white tank top and a plaid shirt—her preferred "uniform." A worn Stetson was pushed down on her head, and her ever-present low ponytail hung from the back of it.

He still couldn't believe he hadn't known that she had a crush on him back then. And he couldn't get her advice about soaking in a hot tub out of his mind now. Or the vision of her soaking with him, with all of her glorious deep brown skin on display.

"I'll take that under advisement." Kahl shifted in his seat, his body reacting to how well those worn jeans hugged Dray's impressive ass.

It had felt weird noticing her body that first day he'd returned to town. Because despite her earlier revelation about having a crush on him, he'd always considered her just a friend. One of the guys. Truth be told, Andraya hit a baseball, rode a dirt bike and roped a steer better than he ever had. But in the days since then—and especially since their kiss—those tantalizingly glorious curves and soft brown skin were all he could think of. Oh, and Dray braless in a thin, white tank top. That vision was permanently etched in his brain.

"Would you mind getting Gingerbread and Rex ready for us, Tonio?" Andraya asked the young ranch hand who had retrieved two ice-cold bottles of water from a cooler.

"Sure thing, boss." Tonio tossed one of the bottles in Kahlil's direction. "I'll have 'em ready in five."

"Great. And when you're done, I saved a couple of those sandwiches from this morning for you. They're in the fridge in my office. Heat them up a little in the microwave."

A wide grin spread across the young man's face, and he pressed his hat down on his head. "Yes, ma'am. Back in a flash."

"I could go for one of those sandwiches, too." Kahl leaned back with his elbows perched on the table behind him.

"Don't worry, cowboy. I've got you covered." Dray patted a sable-brown rectangular backpack she'd set on the table. The pockets on either side of the bag held thermoses. She sat beside him on the bench and leaned her elbows on the table behind them, too. She glanced around as if ensuring that no one else was within hearing distance. "Seems you've made quite an impression on the crew today."

"I'll just bet I did. Tonio had to save my ass more than once." Kahl chuckled drily as he assessed the busted knuckles on his left hand. He guzzled the last of his water. "I forgot how grueling ranch life can be."

"You've gone soft, city boy." Andraya nudged him. "Growing up, a morning like this would've been nothing for you."

"I'm not a spry young kid anymore, Dray." He circled his shoulder again. "And today, my body made damn sure I remembered that."

"I know this morning might've been a bit rough, but the trust and camaraderie you built with the ranch hands were invaluable," Dray assured him.

"Let's hope," he said. "Now, where are we with getting the horse breeding program started again?"

"We only have one ranch-owned horse that would make a viable candidate, and that's Scout," she said. "So I've identified a handful of potential stallions available for acquisition. We can go over the details after lunch."

"After our ride?" Kahl's belly grumbled, protesting the idea of waiting for perhaps another hour or more before eating.

Andraya chuckled. "Do you need a Snickers or something to tide you over until then, Kahl?"

"I'll do my best to survive." He reined in a grin and slid the cowboy hat back down, shielding his eyes from the midday sun. After a few moments of companionable silence, he said, "Thanks for the hat, by the way. I wouldn't have survived out here today without it."

"It's one of Hank's." A soft smile curved Andraya's pretty mouth. But this time, the memory of Hank didn't seem to make her sad. "His collection of hats was one of the things he left me. I keep a few of them here for days when someone needs them. Usually a noob like you." She grinned. "Kept the pricier ones for myself."

"Is that one of them?" Kahl indicated the worn, beige Stetson atop her head.

"No. This was a gift from Hank. He bought it for me when I won my first riding competition. Said every cowgirl needed herself a good hat." Dray's dark brown eyes sparkled in the sunlight. "I hadn't worn it in a while. But since Hank died…" She shrugged. "I dug it out. Been wearing it pretty much ever since. It seems silly, I know."

"No, it doesn't seem silly at all. It's sweet. Hank and Ms. Edith weren't just lucky to have each other, Dray. They were really lucky to have *you*."

"Thanks." Now her dark eyes glistened with gratitude. She smiled, their eyes meeting. "I was really lucky to have them, too." Her gaze lingered on his.

The quiet moment between them stirred something in his chest. Was it friendship? Nostalgia? *Desire?*

Kahlil wanted desperately to lean in and taste her lips, frosted in a shimmering nude-brown gloss, beckoning him. But he understood what a mistake that would be.

They were in a common area. And as the owner and the ranch manager, they both had reputations to protect. As a woman holding the highest position of authority on the ranch, Kahlil could only imagine how Andraya must've had to fight for every ounce of respect she'd earned from the mostly male crew. He wouldn't do anything to jeopardize the position it'd taken Dray years to acquire when he'd be gone in just a few weeks. But he couldn't stop thinking about kissing her.

His less-than-pure thoughts were interrupted by the clomping of hooves and neighing. They both turned toward the sound. The expression on Dray's face reflected the guilt Kahlil felt as Ben sized the two of them up, as if he'd caught them making out.

"Ben, I thought you were working with the Horvaths' new filly today." Dray stood quickly and approached the older man, reaching for the reins of the sorrel-colored American quarter horse that she'd ridden away from his cabin on that first day he'd returned to town. She stroked the horse's neck.

"I was," Ben confirmed. "She done real good, too. So I've given her a little playtime."

Dray looked at the other horse—a beautiful black stallion—then frowned. "I asked Tonio to bring out Gingerbread and Rex," she said.

"I know. But one of old Rex's shoes looked a bit loose. I had him sent over to Dustin, our new farrier. He needed some help, so I sent Tonio over to help him and brought Diablo instead." Ben seemed exceedingly proud of himself.

Of course the horse's name was Diablo. Why couldn't he have had a nonthreatening moniker like Midnight, Smokey or even Ace?

Andraya's agitation with Ben was clear as she narrowed her gaze at the old man who walked past her with a smug grin and headed straight toward Kahlil.

"This here is Andraya's other horse," the old man said.

"A Straight Egyptian Arabian." Kahlil studied the gorgeous animal who also assessed him. Diablo didn't seem as easygoing in nature as Gingerbread.

"That's right," Ben chuckled. "I guess you do remember a little something about horses after all."

Kahlil had driven the trailer for Hank, delivering horses to buyers. After once delivering the wrong horse to a client, he made it his business to recognize the different breeds. He'd also recommended a few fail-safes to ensure that it wouldn't happen again.

"A little," Kahl climbed to his feet and approached the horse slowly, meeting its wary gaze. The horse snorted and groaned. He took a step backward, his ears pinned back.

Kahl froze.

He'd grown up handling horses on his own family's farm and then on Hank's for a few years, starting at the age of fifteen. But it had been a long time since he'd ridden or handled one. He hadn't thought much about it when he'd arrived. Because he'd had no intentions of riding a horse. But as he stood in front of the majestic, towering animal that clearly didn't have an affinity for him, it instantly took him back to that fateful day more than twenty years ago. The day he'd lost his younger brother, Amir.

Eight

Kahlil's youngest brother, Amir, had been smart and funny. Curious and adventurous. He'd been the spitting image of their father. Yet he'd had the broad smile, kindness and good-natured personality of their mother. His younger brother had loved animals—horses especially.

There had been a particularly stubborn stallion his father had been struggling to train. Their father had threatened to sell the horse if he didn't show improvement soon.

Amir had been adamant that he and Kahlil could train the horse themselves, so their father wouldn't sell him. Kahlil had had zero interest in training a stubborn horse. In fact, his interest in ranch life had been waning as his love for computers and technology had grown.

One Saturday his parents had driven to Riverton,

one hour away, to spend the day together. With his parents gone and his sisters at a sleepover, he'd just had Amir to watch. He'd set his brother up with a bunch of snacks and told him he could watch all of the cartoons he wanted. Then Kahlil had put on his headset, cranked up some music and worked on building a computer from scratch.

He'd been so absorbed in what he was doing that he hadn't realized his younger brother had snuck off to train the problem stallion. It wasn't until he'd gone to check on Amir two hours later that he'd discovered him out in the horse pen, his back and neck broken from a fall.

It was a scene he'd had vivid nightmares about for three years. A memory he'd worked damn hard to forget. Even if it meant leaving his family, his friends and ranch life there in Willowvale Springs behind.

He'd ridden a horse a few times since his brother's accident. But that had been more than twenty years ago. Now, as he stared at the majestic animal standing in front of him, his shiny black coat glistening and a fierce look in his narrowed, dark eyes, Kahlil's chest ached—like it was being compressed. Every single ounce of oxygen was being wrung from his lungs.

He couldn't move. Couldn't speak.

"We've got it from here," Andraya snarled, her tone and glare biting. She snatched Diablo's reins, taking the old man by surprise. "We *will* talk about this later," she growled in a low voice, making it clear to Ben that he'd been dismissed.

"Yes, ma'am." The old buzzard had the nerve to look

contrite, his gaze downward as he sauntered off with his tail between his legs.

Too bad Kahlil was too preoccupied with the overwhelming sense of grief and guilt he was suddenly drowning in to truly enjoy it.

Andraya was furious with Ben. Her face was hot, her heart thumped in her chest and it had taken everything in her not to curse the old buzzard out six ways to Sunday.

Ben likely didn't know that Diablo looked incredibly similar to the horse Kahlil's younger brother Amir had been attempting to ride bareback when he'd fallen to his death. But Ben *was* aware that Diablo didn't care for male riders he didn't already know well. The stallion had been owned by an abusive man prior to Hank buying him.

She'd deal with Ben later. Right now, her only concern was Kahl. The distress on her old friend's face made her gut twist and her heart ache.

Dray quickly tied the reins of both horses to a nearby post. Then she carefully approached Kahlil, who still hadn't moved. She placed a gentle hand on his forearm and squeezed it.

"Kahl, I'm so sorry. I would *never* have intentionally put you on a horse that looked so much like—"

"I know you wouldn't." He swallowed hard. His expression reflected all the turmoil he must've been experiencing.

His absolution only made Andraya feel more guilty.

Andraya wrapped him up in a tight hug, her eyes

closed as she leaned into him. After a moment, Kahlil hugged her back.

He heaved a quiet sigh, and the tension in his back eased the tiniest bit. "It's okay."

"No, it's not okay." She pulled out of Kahl's embrace and folded her arms. "Ben was trying to show you up by bringing out Diablo. He's an asshole, but he's not cruel enough to have done this purposefully."

"I figured as much. And I honestly thought I was over the trauma of…" Kahlil ran a hand over his head and sighed. "Clearly I'm not."

"Why don't you call it a day?" Andraya forced a smile. "You've certainly done enough around here today to prove that you're all in with trying to save the ranch. You don't need to ride Diablo or any other horse. And you have nothing to prove to Ben or anyone else who might've been behind this stunt."

"Maybe. But maybe I have something to prove to myself," he said. Kahlil stared at Diablo for a moment, his expression still pained. "You obviously prepared us a lunch." He indicated the backpack on the picnic table. "I don't want to ruin your plans."

"Who cares about my plans?" she said. "You can take the food. I don't care. I just need to know that you're okay. When I saw you like that…" Andraya shook her head, diverting her gaze from his. "I can't tell you how sorry I am."

"*I* care," Kahlil said. "What kind of horse rancher is afraid to ride a horse?"

"You're not actually a horse rancher," she teased, hoping to lighten Kahlil's mood. "You're just a guy who inherited a horse ranch and plans to sell it. There's a difference."

"Not to them. Not if I want them to trust the process and work with us toward our goal of revitalizing this place. That's why I *do* need to prove myself to these guys." He nodded toward the stables. "So I'd like to go for that ride."

"All right, Kahlil," she said. "But I'm not letting you ride Diablo."

"You don't need to coddle me, Dray. I know it's been a while since I rode a horse, but—"

"I'm not coddling you. Even Ben won't ride Diablo. Only Tonio and I do," she said. "Now, c'mon and let me introduce you to Gingerbread. He'll take good care of you. Promise."

Kahlil heaved a reluctant sigh and nodded.

She'd wanted to remind Kahlil of all of the great memories they'd had riding horses together through the pastures owned by their families when they'd been kids. Instead, she'd reminded him of all the reasons he'd left this place. And why he hadn't wanted to come back.

Certainly not the best way to convince him to stay.

Kahlil sat on a blanket, basking in the afternoon sunlight. He rested his folded arms atop his knees as he took in the surrounding terrain. Water trickled over the rocks as it followed a path down the crystal-clear creek just a few yards away. Acres of verdant pasture surrounded them.

"It's beautiful out here." Kahl leaned back on his elbows. "So peaceful and serene. No wonder you come out here to have lunch every day."

"I'm lucky that I get to do what I love and that I get to call this my office." Andraya removed her hat and glanced around as if seeing the splendid scenery for the first time. A soft smile curved those full, sensual lips of hers, and her dark eyes sparkled in the afternoon sunlight.

God, she's beautiful.

Kahlil kept repeating this refrain to himself like a broken record. But he'd been kicking himself for never noticing how gorgeous Andraya had been beneath that purple-billed Colorado Rockies baseball cap she'd worn pulled down over her face as a teen. And he was still stunned by her earlier confession about having had a crush on him.

When he'd been a teenager, obsessed with computers and gaming tech, his father had accused him of having a one-track mind. Maybe his dad had been right. Because as he'd been hauling bales of hay and refilling the horses' troughs earlier that morning, he'd had time to think. As he'd replayed their past interactions in his head, it had suddenly become obvious that his friend had a crush on him.

How can someone so damn smart in one area be so damn clueless about everything else?

He recalled Farah saying those words to him after he'd declared that Dray had asked him to "hang out with her" at the school dance.

It's a date, dumbass. Your best friend just asked you out on a date. Farah had stared at Kahlil that day as if he was the dopiest human being on the face of the earth and she was ashamed to be related to him.

He'd accused his sister of reading too many of their mother's romance novels. But Farah had been right. He'd been unable to see what was right in front of him.

Once he'd started down the path, he'd thought of at least a handful of other instances in which his friend had hinted at there being more between them. And it suddenly made sense why she'd been so upset that he'd gone to prom with his friend Manny's cousin, Ellen. Something he'd done purely as a favor to Manny, not because he'd actually liked Ellen.

When he'd asked Dray why she'd cared so much, she, too, had looked at him as if he was clueless. But she'd insisted it was strictly because Ellen Price was a high school mean girl and she was tired of them winning.

She'd considered Ellen getting to go to prom with him *winning*. Even that had gone over his head at the time. His father and sister were right. He'd been clueless about so many things in his life. From his best friend's crush on him to how well his former best friend and ex-wife had always gotten along. More importantly, he should have known that his little brother would try to train that horse that day.

All Amir had wanted was the chance to spend the day with his big brother. But Kahlil had been too preoccupied with his own desires to spend time with him. Since that fateful day, Kahlil had gone to bed every night wishing he could spend one more day with his younger brother. Wishing that Amir was the one still here instead.

"You just drifted away again." Andraya stared out at the plain in front of them. She rested her chin on her knees and wrapped her arms around her legs. "Thinking about Amir?"

"Yeah." Kahlil sucked in a quiet breath and nodded. "And you."

"About me?" Dray seemed stunned as she met his gaze. "Why?"

Kahlil sat up and heaved a sigh. "Because I was a terrible brother and a terrible friend, and you both deserved better."

"You weren't a terrible friend, Kahl." Dray shrugged, her gaze not quite meeting his. "You were my best friend, and you were always there for me. You never treated me like a reject like all the other kids did. You didn't think I was weird because I cared more about baseball and NASCAR and riding horses than fashion or makeup. You always accepted me for exactly who I was, when even my own family was set on 'fixing' me. And you weren't a bad brother, either. What happened to Amir was awful. But it was an *accident*, Kahl. And it could've happened when anyone was there with Amir. Even your parents."

"But it didn't." Kahl winced, the guilt he'd carried for the past two decades weighing heavily on his chest. "That's something I'll always have to live with."

Andraya sighed quietly, her brows furrowed. She slid closer to him, put an arm through his and rested her head on his shoulder. She'd done the same thing back then. It'd been one of the single most comforting moments he'd experienced in the days following his brother's death. And it had the same effect on him now.

They sat quietly, neither of them speaking for a few minutes. The sun warmed his face. The sound of trickling water and birds in the distance calmed him. And the touch and comfort of the woman seated beside him eased the tension in his chest and soothed his soul. Made him feel at home in a way he hadn't felt in so long.

Part of him wished they could sit there forever, enjoying the warmth, the breeze and the incomparable peace of that moment. That they could enjoy each other's company the way they always had.

"I've missed you, Dray," Kahl said finally. "And I'm *really* sorry about the way things worked out between us. About all the lost time. I realize nothing I could ever do would make up for everything we both lost. But I'd really like to try."

"Me, too." Dray lifted her head and studied his face. A soft smile lit her dark eyes and warmed his chest. "But I'm afraid the role of best friend has already been taken. I know Allie seems like an adorable little sprite, but don't underestimate that woman. I think she could probably take you in hand-to-hand combat."

They both laughed, and it was the lightest he'd felt since the day he'd discovered Armand had cleaned out their company account.

"I'll keep that in mind." Kahlil studied his friend's face, his gaze drawn to her full lips. Despite the voice in his head screaming for him to stop, he slowly leaned in and captured her soft lips in a kiss.

Dray leaned into him, her hand cupping his face as

his lips glided over hers. She tipped her head, her lips parting as she sighed softly.

Kahlil's tongue glided along the seam of her parted lips. He heaved a quiet sigh, his tongue gliding along hers as he held her face in his hands, his thumbs brushing her cheeks.

Her mouth was sweet and tangy with the taste of the lemon meringue pie she'd brought for their lunch. The more he kissed her, the more he desired her. He desperately wanted to take her back to his cabin and kiss every inch of the skin that smelled like sunshine, hay and something sweet and floral. Her own unique scent simmered beneath it all and reminded him of home.

There was a part of him that wished their lives were as simple as they'd once been. And that he'd known about Dray's feelings for him back then. How would their lives have been different?

Would she have been willing to leave Willowvale Springs with him? Would he have been willing to return to town after school and make a life here? Or maybe their teenage romance would've flamed out before he'd ever climbed onto that bus for Denver.

How could they possibly know?

Kahlil squeezed his eyes shut and forced all of those maddening thoughts from his brain. He focused on what was happening between them here and now instead.

He pulled Dray into his arms and deepened their kiss. A kiss that was growing hungrier and more intense. Her beaded nipples pressed into his chest as he swallowed her soft, breathy murmurs. His body hardened, and his skin grew hot and tight. And all he could think of was taking Dray back to his cabin, showering together and spending the evening getting to know each other in ways they hadn't before.

Kahlil's erotic fantasies were interrupted by static and the crackle of the radio, followed by Tonio's voice.

"Hey there, Dray. I hate to interrupt your lunch, but Manny Price and his guys are here to get started on the renovations and he needs to see Kahlil."

They shared a collective sigh, their eyes meeting.

Dray unclipped the radio from her belt and responded. "Got it. Please direct Manny and his crew to the equestrian center. Kahlil will meet him there as soon as he can."

Kahl climbed to his feet, then tugged her up. He held on to her, reluctant to let her go. He dipped his head and kissed her, but as the kiss began to escalate, Dray pulled out of his arms.

Andraya picked up her hat, then shoved it down on her head. "Manny's waiting for you over at the equestrian center, Kahl. We have to go."

He groaned as he stooped to help her gather their things and pack them into the cooler backpack.

"I know you said we don't need to talk about this—"

"And we don't," Dray said quickly. She glanced at him momentarily, then zipped the bag and lifted it onto her shoulder.

Kahlil took the backpack from her and strapped it onto his back instead. He watched as she folded the blanket they'd been seated on.

They walked toward the post where Gingerbread and Diablo were tied.

"Okay, if you say we don't need to discuss whatever is happening here…then fine. But I won't risk hurting you again, Dray." Kahl caught her elbow, halting her escape. He met her gaze when she turned back to face him. "So I do need to know what you expect of this. Because what you said this morning is true. In a few weeks, I'll be returning to Seattle for good and—"

"Then you already know that I'm not looking for anything serious and that I don't expect anything of you."

She said it as if she was completely fine. As if it didn't matter to her at all that he'd be leaving again soon. But as angry as she'd been with him all these years… How could that possibly be true?

"Don't do that." Dray tipped her chin in his direction. "I can practically hear the conversation you're having in your head about whether I actually mean what I'm saying. I do."

Dray broke into laughter when his eyes widened with shock.

They'd been apart for a long time. Yet Andraya still knew him well.

Dray stepped a foot into her stirrup, then mounted Diablo. She glided a gentle hand up and down the horse's neck. Diablo shot a warning glare at Kahlil.

Noted.

"Okay." Kahl shrugged. "If you say everything's fine, then everything is fine." He mounted Gingerbread, then adjusted in his seat.

"Good." Dray offered a wooden smile that bordered on a frown.

Andraya Walker could be as stubborn as a mule, and she clearly had no intention of changing her position on this. Pushing her on it would only irritate her. So he changed the subject instead.

"About me coming to your parents' anniversary party—"

"You're not backing out on your end of the deal, are you?" There was a hint of alarm in her voice. "I mean…it's not like I asked you to be my date. *You* offered. And I wouldn't even care, but I already told my mother and sister…so they could add your name to the guest list…and if I have to go back and tell them you aren't coming—"

"I'm not canceling on you, Dray," Kahlil said. "In fact, I wanted to ask you a favor."

"Okay." She held a hand up to protect her eyes from the sun. Both Dray and Diablo seemed a bit restless. "What is it?"

"My mother wants me to come to dinner Sunday after next. I promised to talk to my dad then."

"Okay?" There was a puzzled look on her gorgeous face. "And…"

"I was wondering if you'd come to dinner with me."

"Are you sure they'll want me there?" Dray tightened the restless horse's reins as he tried to walk away.

Clearly, Diablo was already over this conversation and ready to return to the stables.

"My family adores you," he assured her. "It'll be like the old days when you were always at the house."

Dray seemed to digest his request and mull it over for a moment. Definitely not the enthusiasm he was hoping for. But she hadn't declined his invitation yet, so there was that.

"You're about to have a really sensitive conversation with your father, Kahlil. Are you sure you want me to be there at such a tough time for your family?"

"This isn't going to be a family conversation. I'll be talking to my dad alone. In fact, I was hoping you could help run interference. Keep my nosy sisters preoccupied while I talk to my dad," he said. "Besides, Dad has always liked you. He'll be on his best behavior if you're there."

"I do love your mother's cooking." Dray stroked Diablo's neck thoughtfully. After a few moments of silence, she nodded. "All right, Kahl. I'd love to join your family for dinner. But I do have a request."

"Okay. Let's hear it." Kahlil repositioned himself on Gingerbread's saddle.

"I'm excited about reviving our friendship. I've missed us, too. But as for…whatever else this is we're doing… I don't think we should tell anyone else about that. Like you said, you'll be leaving soon. And while *I* don't have any expectations…you can just imagine how knowing about us might complicate things with our families. Right?" Dray offered a smile that seemed almost apologetic.

"I could definitely see how that might be an issue. But we are grown-ass adults pushing forty."

"*You're* pushing forty, friend." She pointed a finger at him. "I am thirty-six. *Period.*" Dray laughed, the sound light and sweet.

He couldn't help laughing, too. "Fine. *I'm* pushing forty. Either way, we're a little old to be sneaking around."

"I don't know." Dray shrugged, a mischievous smile on her face. "Sneaking around sounds like fun. Besides, I know it's no big deal to you, but I'm the one who'll be left behind with our families and friends." Andraya frowned. "I can't deal with people asking me about you all the time again. That was one of the worst things about before. The constant questions and the looks of pity." Her eyes lowered, and her voice trailed off.

Kahl hated that he'd hurt her. Hated that even now that pain still seemed fresh.

"I didn't think about that," Kahl admitted. "So we're going to my parents' for dinner and to your parents' anniversary party as friends. Not on a date."

"Right." Dray cued Diablo to start moving forward.

"And this isn't like when you asked me to 'hang out' at the dance that time, right?" Kahlil cued Gingerbread to follow.

Dray laughed and glanced back at him, her ponytail swinging in time with the horse's movement. A mischievous grin lit her dark eyes. "Actually, it kind of is. Only this time, it's our families who'll be clueless instead of just you."

Before he could answer, Dray and Diablo transitioned from a walk into a canter, and he and Gingerbread were in pursuit.

Maybe Andraya was right not to make a big deal about their attraction and to just go with it. As teens, despite their close friendship, they'd been very different people with completely opposite aspirations for their lives.

That hadn't changed.

Kahlil heaved a sigh, leaning into his two-point stance. His weight was balanced between the stirrups as he stood, his bottom no longer touching the saddle, as they strode toward the equestrian center, also near the back of the vast property.

Her life was there in Willowvale Springs. His was in Seattle. There was no point in acting as if this could be anything more than a fling at best.

Getting involved with Dray—even temporarily—could be disastrous to the friendship they were trying to rebuild. Yet as he watched Dray riding in front of him, he already knew that he wanted to kiss her again.

Nine

Andraya felt slightly self-conscious about her attempt to go a tad bit more dramatic with her makeup than usual as she stared at her reflection in Kahlil's mostly glass cabin door. A cool evening breeze rustled her hair hanging loose from her ponytail and blowing a few strands across her face as she held on tight to a covered ceramic dish with both hands.

"Hey." Kahlil opened the door, his full mouth spread into a slow, sexy grin as he regarded her with a heated stare that warmed her from the inside out and made her skin…and other parts…tingle. "Thanks for coming."

When she stepped inside, Kahl leaned down and dropped a kiss onto her cheek, his stubbled chin grazing her skin. Dray inhaled the subtle scent of cedarwood and leather emanating from Kahlil's freshly showered skin.

Her shoulders tensed, her face and neck suddenly felt too hot. Electricity crackled along her skin and shot down her spine.

"Thanks for the invitation," Dray stammered.

"What you got there?" He stood back, arms folded. Kahl inhaled deeply, then his dark eyes danced with recognition. "Don't tell me you brought banana-walnut bread?"

"Homemade and fresh from the oven with that sugar crunch topping you love so much." Dray held out the still-warm dish, and Kahl accepted it eagerly.

"Just like my mother's recipe?" The affection in his eyes made her tummy flutter and her heart feel full.

"Actually, it *is* your mother's recipe with a few tweaks of my own." She peeked through the tiny space between her forefinger and thumb.

"But how—"

"Willowvale Springs has a quarterly town magazine now." Dray grinned, inexplicably thrilled about how elated he was by such a small gift. "Your mom shared her recipe in the town newsletter a couple years back. I've been making it ever since. It reminds me of those Saturday afternoons when I hung out at your family's place trying to avoid my mother teaching me to cook to impress a man someday. Ironic, right?"

Kahlil broke into a deep belly laugh. Dray did, too.

Something about laughing together about a moment rooted in their past…in their history, their friendship… made her heart dance.

It felt good to laugh with Kahl again. Despite the

oddness of their open attraction for each other and the fact that they'd kissed twice now.

He took the dish to the kitchen and set it on the counter.

"Seems nothing about this visit is going quite as either of us would've anticipated." He shoved his hands into the pockets of his jeans and smiled.

Not true.

As a fifteen-year-old girl, she'd often daydreamed about the two of them dating, getting married and living happily ever after. But it seemed best not to mention that.

Dray resisted the urge to fidget with the ruffled hem of her thigh-length denim minidress. Instead, she lifted the charm worn around her neck, fiddling with it as she glanced around the room. Anywhere but at Kahl. The man looked incredibly delicious in a size *smedium* black T-shirt that showed off his impressive musculature and a pair of frayed, broken-in jeans that highlighted his perfect hind parts.

"You cooked dinner." She shrugged. "I figured the least I could do was bring dessert."

"I wouldn't go straight to *cooked*." He chuckled. "It'd be more accurate to say that I ordered our meals and I'm heating them up. I subscribe to one of those precooked-meal delivery services," he said. "But the food is delicious. I promise," he added, countering her doubtful expression.

"Is there anything I can do?"

"Nope. I just popped the bruschetta in the oven, which I am making myself." Kahl grinned proudly. "In the meantime, can I get you a beer or maybe a glass of wine?"

"White wine, if you've got it."

"You've got it. Make yourself comfortable and have a seat." Kahl gestured toward the solarium, then ducked into the kitchen.

Kahl was barefoot, so Dray slipped off her sandals, too. She made her way toward the space where they had hashed out arrangements for their upcoming equestrian event. Dray sank onto the sofa and folded one leg beneath her.

Kahlil brought their drinks and sat beside her. His jean-clad leg brushed her bare thigh, and warmth spread over her skin.

What was it about Kahlil Anderson that made her instantly revert to a giddy, smitten teen?

She was a confident, self-sufficient woman at peace with being single. So why did she feel like she was right back in high school scribbling hearts inside her notebook and imagining how her name would look with his last name appended to hers?

"So…you've been working on the ranch since you returned from college." Kahlil handed Dray her glass of wine, then took a sip of his beer. "There are horse ranches all over the country. You never considered venturing outside of the state? Or even outside of town?"

"Never." Dray sipped her wine. It was crisp and fruity with just a hint of sweetness. "My family and friends are here. The ranch is here. Besides, I always saw Willowvale Springs as a land filled with adventures. Most of which I had with you." Dray bumped

Kahl's shoulder. Her cheeks tightened with an involuntary smile. "But to you, Willowvale was a wall holding you back from everything you ever wanted."

Andraya took another sip of her wine and tried to dismiss the sadness that descended over her.

"I was obsessed with computers and eager to learn everything I could about them. I wanted to explore new technologies and use that knowledge to make a difference in the world. I couldn't do that here." Kahlil swigged his beer, the mood suddenly thick and heavy, the room echoing with silence.

"Well, you realized your ambitions." Dray ran a finger around the base of her wine glass and forced a smile. "You're the CEO of your own company, and you're out there slaying all kinds of tech dragons." Dray forced a smile. "Despite whatever feelings I might've had about being left behind, I'm so damn proud of you for doing exactly what you set out to, Kahl."

"Thanks, Dray. That really means a lot. Other than my mom and Hank in that final video, no one else from home has ever really said that." Kahlil seemed to be moved by her words, and she felt guilty for not having had this conversation with him sooner.

"You never really talk about your life in Seattle *outside of work*, though," Andraya noted. "Since you kissed me, I'm assuming that you aren't involved with anyone right now."

A bitter snort erupted from Kahlil, as if him being involved was a ridiculous probability.

"Definitely not. I've been on maybe two dates since the divorce. I hated the idea of being thrust onto the dating scene again. To be honest, maybe I was never really cut out for it. You know better than most how oblivious I can be when it comes to relationships."

"That I do." Dray sipped her wine. "But you evidently figured it out enough to get married. How long were you and…"

"Meridia," he supplied.

"Meridia," Dray repeated her name. "How long were the two of you together?"

While she hadn't remembered the woman's name, she had remembered her face. Farah and Salena had shown her pictures from the wedding. Mrs. Kahlil Anderson had been beautiful with honey-brown skin, hazel-colored eyes and a figure like a classic Coke bottle.

Meridia was sleek, elegant and fashionable. Her makeup, her dyed, beachy, blonde waves and Vogue magazine cover-worthy wardrobe looked perfect in every single photo or video she'd seen of the woman. She moved as gracefully as a gazelle, and her speech at the wedding had been clever and moving. She was the anti-Andraya, if ever she'd seen one.

It had almost made Dray feel better to think that she was so far removed from the kind of woman Kahlil was attracted to that she'd never even stood a chance. At least that way she could convince herself that it wasn't her *specifically* he hadn't been attracted to. Kahlil was just far too oblivious to fall for anyone who didn't look like the blonde edition of Black Barbie.

"Dated two years, married for five and separated for a year before the divorce," Kahlil said bitterly, shifting in his seat. "Before that we were friends. Meridia went to school with me and Armand. He was my best friend and business partner," he clarified in response to her questioning look.

"*Was?*" She sipped more of her wine. "Don't tell me you disappeared on him, too."

Dray winced as soon as the words left her mouth. She'd been half teasing. But they were in the early stages of repairing their friendship. Too soon to make such a deep jab. Unfortunately, the words had escaped her mouth before her brain could corral them.

"Actually, Armand disappeared on me." Kahl chuckled bitterly, then drained the last of his beer. He set the bottle down on the table with a thud.

"If Armand is your business partner, how could he just…vanish?" Dray studied Kahlil's furrowed brows.

There was more to this than her friend was saying.

"Been asking myself the same question the past few weeks." Kahlil stood as soon as Alexa proclaimed that the bruschetta was done. He seemed grateful for the interruption.

Stop prodding and let it go.

The topic was evidently a touchy one. But her mother had often accused her of being like a dog with a bone once she got on the scent of something. And maybe Mama was right. Because Dray needed to know if Kahlil had a history of driving off his best friends.

"You're not concerned that something might've happened to him?" Dray settled onto the bar stool as he took the pan of toasted bread from the oven.

Kahl froze, his shoulders suddenly stiff. He reached

into the fridge, pulled out their meals and microwaved the first.

"That was my first thought—that something had happened to him," Kahl said finally. "But when I checked his place, he'd packed everything that meant something to him and canceled his lease. I even hired a private investigator. He confirmed that Armand had intentionally taken off."

"Without giving you any kind of a heads-up?" Dray was angry on Kahl's behalf when he confirmed it to be true. "Deciding you no longer want to be friends is one thing. It's every human being's right. But bailing on a friend you own a business with? That's horrible. Is that why you seem so stressed about work?"

"It's a big part of it," he admitted. "We're at a tricky juncture in this project. Close enough to see the finish line, yet still just far enough away for everything to fall apart. So if our investors and the rest of our team—many of whom Armand recruited—knew that he'd just up and left…" Kahlil heaved a sigh and rubbed his forehead.

"It'd be disastrous." Dray squeezed his forearm, understanding what a tenuous position her friend found himself in. "I'm sorry this happened, Kahl. I can't imagine how stressful that must be."

"Thanks." Kahlil's handsome features pinched as he moved to retrieve the first meal from the microwave. He transferred it onto a plate along with a few slices of the bruschetta, making a lovely presentation. Kahl set the dish in front of her, then he microwaved the second meal.

He changed the subject, asking about her parents

and siblings as he made and plated his meal. Then he topped off her wine glass and sat down beside her, picking up his utensils.

Dray cut into the tender chicken breast and took a bite of the succulent, flavorful meat. She involuntarily murmured in response to the explosion of flavor on her tongue.

Kahlil watched her with satisfaction, his gaze hooded, and his dark eyes filled with heat. He cleared his throat and dug into his meal before pivoting back to their earlier topic. "I'm sure you understand why I can't afford for Armand's disappearing act to become public knowledge."

"I do, and I won't say a word," she assured him. "But surely your team has questions about your business partner's whereabouts."

"I'm the one who was in the office every day. Armand would pop in a few times a month. He spent most of his time courting the investors and discovering new talent. So it isn't odd for him not to be in the office for several weeks at a time. But the story is that he was long overdue for a vacation. So he's spending a couple months in South America." He took another bite.

"Which is true…just not the entire story." Dray took another bite of her food.

"Precisely. The people who need to know the truth do." Kahlil shrugged. "Now, enough about my exes. What about you? Your family sold their farm to my parents. My sister and her husband are raising their kids in the house where you grew up. That must be tough for you."

"Not really," Dray said, almost meaning it. "By the time my parents decided to sell the place, the farm had been declining for years. Besides, they'd been encouraging us to get out of agriculture since we were in grade school. That's why Phil eventually became a lawyer and Lana became a registered nurse. They wanted me to become a teacher, a dentist, a veterinarian or an accountant. *Anything* but a ranch worker."

She forced a smile and pretended she didn't care how much it hurt that her parents were disappointed by the career she'd chosen.

"It's like we were born into the wrong families." Kahlil chuckled bitterly as he grabbed another beer from the freezer. "My dad wanted me to stay and run the family ranch, while yours wanted you to become a career professional."

"Here's to being equally huge disappointments to our families." Dray held up her glass, and he clinked it before taking a sip of his icy beer.

"Look, maybe you didn't choose the path your parents wanted for you. But your parents aren't hard-asses like my dad." Kahl set his bottle down and resumed eating. "There's no way your parents are disappointed. You've done well for yourself, Dray. And you're a terrific ranch manager."

"You'd be surprised just how disappointed they are that I'm not married, haven't given them children, and chose a career that requires manual labor," Dray mimicked her mother's voice.

"There's nothing wrong with the choices you've made, Andraya." Kahl stabbed the green beans on his plate. "Besides, being married to the wrong person is far worse than not being married at all."

"Try convincing my grandchild-obsessed mother of that," Dray muttered, then shoved a forkful of creamy, delicious mashed potatoes into her mouth.

"It's tough straddling that line between being an adult and still being your parents' child," he acknowledged. "I still don't know what the hell to say to my dad about his medical situation." Kahlil put down his fork and folded his arms, as if he'd suddenly lost his appetite.

She put her utensils down, too, and turned toward him on the stool. "Your dad is a straight shooter, Kahlil. So be direct and don't bullshit him. Be honest about your feelings. Tell him that you'd desperately like to fix things between the two of you. So you're begging him to do whatever he can to ensure that you'll have time to repair your relationship."

"Thought you said don't bullshit him." He snorted.

"If you don't see that fixing this thing with your dad *is* what you want, then the only person you're bullshitting is yourself." Andraya poked a gentle finger into his chest.

His dark eyes flickered with annoyance, or maybe realization.

At his soft, gooey center, Kahlil Anderson was still that wide-eyed little boy who wanted to make his father proud. When he'd decided to forge his own path and that no longer seemed possible, Kahl had tried to convince himself that he didn't care what his father thought. But they both knew that wasn't true.

* * *

Kahlil sank onto the sofa beside Dray after dinner. He handed her the remote, and she scrolled through the streaming services looking for something to watch. He rested his leg against hers as she sat with one leg folded beneath her. The smooth, creamy brown skin of her thighs teased him.

He couldn't help watching Dray as she focused on the large TV screen on the wall above the fireplace. Kahl found it equally comforting and disconcerting that after all this time, his childhood best friend still knew him so well. It was even more confounding that he couldn't look at her without appreciating what a gorgeous woman she was.

Andraya had such stunning features. Big, expressive, doe eyes. Luscious, full lips. Smooth, creamy, dark brown skin. She was toned yet deliciously curvy in all the right places. Dray wasn't much for the pricey designer fashions that had been staples in his marriage to Meridia. But the woman could rock the hell out of denim.

A pair of lived-in, ass-hugging jeans, which seemed to be her go-to for working at the stables. The tiny denim shorts she wore when she was hanging out at home. The flirty light-wash thigh-length denim dress with the ruffled hem she was wearing tonight.

Andraya toyed with the charm hanging around her neck again, and his eyes were drawn to the hint of cleavage exposed by the unfastened buttons at the top of her dress.

Kahlil forced his gaze back to her face and inhaled

quietly. Tried to pretend that his brain wasn't spinning and his blood wasn't overheating every moment he found himself in close proximity with her. He hadn't been affected this way by anyone in a very long time. Maybe never.

Sure, he'd been into other women. Had even lusted after a few. But there was something magical about the combination of his history with Dray, their friendship and this jumble of feelings he had for her.

Familiar friendship. Deep affection. Inexplicable protectiveness. A burning desire. *So much desire.* Enough to keep him awake at night, staring at the ceiling and imagining all of the ways he wanted to pleasure that gorgeous body of hers. Fuzzy, warm feelings which hinted at the beginnings of something so much deeper. Feelings he had no right to hope Dray reciprocated.

Maybe Dray had stopped taking his calls, but it was his unwillingness to prioritize their friendship that had triggered its unraveling. And now he was having all of these unexpected romantic feelings toward his old friend. Whenever they were alone, he couldn't stop obsessing about pulling her into his arms and kissing her again.

"Earth to Kahlil." Dray waved a hand in front of his face, startling him. "You seem tired and distracted tonight. I should go."

He'd completely spaced out fantasizing about her again.

"No, I'm fine." Kahlil forced a smile. "I mean, yes. I'm a little tired. But no, I'm not ready to end the night.

My thoughts just drifted for a moment. What did you say?"

"I asked if you've seen *The Harder They Fall*," she repeated.

"I haven't," he admitted.

He'd been intending to watch the cowboy movie featuring a Black cast and headlined by heavy hitters like Idris Elba, Regina King, Jonathan Majors and LaKeith Stanfield. It'd been on his watch list since before the movie had been released. But with his crazy life and schedule, he just hadn't gotten around to it.

"It's been a wild couple of years," he explained in response to her look of utter outrage.

"Well, until you see it, your Black cowboy card is *definitely* revoked." Dray shook a finger at him only half teasing. "We're watching it tonight. You're not squeamish or anything, are you? Because this one has a high body count."

"*The Departed* is one of my favorite movies." Kahl chuckled, draping an arm over the back of the couch. "I think I'll be fine."

"Good." Dray adjusted her position so that she was practically snuggled beneath his raised arm. She lifted the remote, then started the movie.

They were thirty minutes into the film when Dray's phone rang. She glanced at the screen, and her sister Lana's face was smiling back at them.

"I'll call her after the movie." Dray put her phone facedown on the coffee table, but it immediately rang again. It was Lana. "It might be important. Do you mind?"

"Of course not." Kahlil paused the movie and pulled

out his own phone to check his email. He'd been expecting a project status update from Tye.

"Hey, sis. What's up?" Dray made her voice sound
tired and drowsy.

"Where are you right now?" Lana's voice came
through the phone.

"At home. Why?" Andraya looked incredibly guilty.

Kahlil resisted the urge to laugh.

"Is that right?" Lana responded. "Well, that's funny
because I'm standing in your kitchen, and I don't see
you here anywhere. You're over at Kahlil's cabin, aren't
you?"

Kahl burst into laughter, and Dray elbowed him in
the ribs, which only made him laugh more loudly. Not
that it mattered—their clandestine night together was
totally blown. He wouldn't be surprised if the entire
town knew about it by the end of the night.

*Did you hear the latest news? Andraya Walker was
over at Kahlil Anderson's place alone the other night.*
After dark.

Kahlil shook his head. They might even make the
town's next quarterly newsletter.

"Okay, fine. Yes, I'm at Kahlil's place. But it's no big
deal. We had dinner, and now we're watching a movie."
Andraya sounded like the pouty little sister, and it was
fucking adorable.

"If there's nothing going on, why are you being so
weird about it?" Lana demanded.

"Because I knew that you and Mom would make a
big deal out of it, that's why."

"Put me on speakerphone," Lana said.

"What? Why?"

"Put. Me. On. Speakerphone." Lana said each word as if it was its own sentence.

"Fine. You're talking so damn loud he heard our entire conversation anyway," Dray muttered, tapping the phone to put it on speaker.

"Hi, Kahlil," Lana said in a sweet singsong tone. "Since you two are officially hanging out…or whatever…it's my ninth wedding anniversary, and we're just doing a small family dinner at my parents' house tomorrow evening. I'd love it if you joined us."

Dray's eyes widened. She looked at him, then back at the phone but didn't respond.

"It's really kind of you to invite me to such a special family event. But I wouldn't want to make your sister uncomfortable. And she looks *really* disturbed by the idea of me coming to dinner." Kahl tried to hide a smirk.

Dray shoved his arm. "Kahl!"

"Well, you do look uncomfortable right now. So either you don't want me to go or we're looking at a possible case of food poisoning," Kahl said.

Lana broke into laughter. "That's my sister's 'the thought of change chaps my hide' expression, all right. But that doesn't mean she doesn't want you to come. It just means that she's struggling with processing shifts in her world. She'll be fine. Right, Dray?"

Kahlil studied his friend's embarrassed frown. Was that steam rising from her ears?

It's fine. He mouthed the words. *I'll just say no.*

"Yes. It's fine. I just figured he'd be busy with work stuff, that's all," Andraya said hurriedly.

"Then I guess we'll see you tomorrow night. Thank you for the invitation, Lana," Kahl said.

Were they going on a first date? Or had tonight been their first date and they just hadn't realized it?

"Wait a minute." Dray stood suddenly, one hand planted on her waist. "You said you're in my kitchen. Why are you at my house, Lana Bouvier?"

"Because you didn't answer the door. *Duh.*" Her sister chuckled. "I was worried that you were lying on the kitchen floor bleeding out or something. Plus, I need that cake pan of mine and, like, five other things that you borrowed and didn't return. I have the cake stand, but I can't find a few of the other items. So if you just tell me where they are, I'll let you two get back to your *friendly* little evening."

Dray rolled her eyes, then listened as Lana rolled off a list of items. The face she made indicated that she didn't remember borrowing the items and certainly had no idea where they were.

Kahlil covered his mouth to dampen the sound of his laughter.

"Just stay there. I'll be home in five minutes. Bye."

"Sorry. I didn't mean to ruin your date—"

Andraya hung up the phone before her sister could say anything else. She set the phone down on the table and sank onto the sofa beside him and huffed. "I'm sorry to end our night early, Kahlil, but I have a feeling this might take a while. Can I get a rain check on the movie?"

"Of course. Go ahead and take care of your sister. And about tomorrow. If you'd really prefer that I don't go—"

"No. I want you there." Dray's tone and expression

softened. "Besides, other than my nieces and nephews, I'll be the only single person in the room. It'd be nice to have an ally."

"Then I'm your man," he said, then cleared his throat. "Not literally… I just meant…" More throat clearing. "Tell me what time to pick you up tomorrow night, and I'm there."

"Would five thirty be too early?"

"No. That's perfect." He picked up the remote.

"Great. But do not watch the rest of the movie without me," she said.

"I won't. Promise." He clicked off the television. "C'mon, let me walk you over before your sister thinks you're naked and needed time to get dressed." He winked, then walked her to the door.

"You can watch me to my door from here." Dray slipped on her sandals. "I'll see you tomorrow at five thirty. Thanks for dinner, and good night."

Dray lifted onto her toes and pressed a kiss to his stubbled cheek. Then she hurried across the little cul-de-sac to her place where her sister greeted her at the door and waved to Kahlil.

He waved back, then closed his door and went to his computer.

He'd had a lovely evening with Dray, and he was eager to see her the following night. But he had work to do and emails to return. So maybe it had been a good thing that their night had ended early. Because his plans had been to kiss Andraya Walker senseless and carry her to his bed.

That would surely complicate the beautiful friendship between them that was beginning to bloom again, like a lotus flower emerging from the mud and muck. And that was something he just couldn't risk. Because having Dray in his life again felt amazing. And this time, he wouldn't be the reason that their relationship came to an end.

Ten

Andraya dug a tub of ice cream out of her freezer and grabbed a spoon from the drawer. Less than half of the pint was left.

"I just had a little of your ice cream while I was waiting," Dray mimicked her sister's voice and shook her head. "'A little' my ass. I hadn't even opened this."

Dray bumped the utensil drawer closed with her hip, then dug into the carton and spooned some into her mouth. She sighed with delight.

It was getting late and she should get ready for bed, but Dray was still too wound up after a fun night with Kahl. And still too disappointed about the premature end of their evening. She padded through the kitchen, sank onto her sofa and resumed rewatching the first season of *Living Single*. She pushed play on "A Kiss Before Lying," the episode where Max asked her mortal frenemy, Kyle, to pretend to be her boyfriend in order to impress her engaged ex-boyfriend. Max and Kyle's antagonistic, love-hate relationship always made her laugh.

When the doorbell rang, she moved to the door and peeked through the window. She opened it.

"Hey, Kahl. What's up?"

"You left your phone on the coffee table." He produced it from his pocket and handed it to her. "I thought you might need…" He gazed over her shoulder at the television on the wall. "Is that the episode where Kyle pretends to be Max's boyfriend?"

"It is," Dray said excitedly. "I'm rewatching all five seasons. Did you want to watch it with me?"

"I haven't seen *Living Single* in years." Kahlil grinned, stepping inside.

They settled onto the sofa together and watched the episode, laughing till they cried. Then they watched another and another.

It felt good to be with Kahl again. To talk about their lives and their families. To cheer each other on and have someone to share things with.

She had Allie and Lana, of course. And she adored both of them. But Kahl would always be her OG best friend. Laughing with him like this and just *being* with him…it soothed her soul.

Dray believed Kahl when he said that he'd work hard to maintain their friendship, even after his return to Seattle. But it still pained her whenever she thought of him leaving. And all of the other feelings she had for him… it only made all of this more complicated.

Kahlil finally saw her as more than a friend. But in a few weeks, he'd be gone. So what was the point of getting involved romantically? Still, she couldn't stop wanting him.

"Hey, is everything good?" Kahl's brows were knitted with concern. "I didn't realize it had gotten so late. You've got an early start tomorrow. So——"

Andraya's heart was in her throat, and she couldn't speak. But she'd regret it if she didn't kiss Kahl right now.

Dray pressed her lips to his, her tongue sliding between his full lips and gliding along the tongue that tasted of her homemade banana bread.

Kahl didn't hesitate or seem surprised. Instead, he cupped her face in his large hands and tilted her head, taking control of the kiss. His kiss was hungry yet deliberate. Like he was savoring the taste of her mouth and the feel of her skin as he stroked her cheek with his thumb.

Dray's body was filled with heat and electricity. Her beaded nipples ached. And the space between her thighs felt damp and heavy with need.

Maybe it was unwise to get involved with Kahl when what she wanted most was to restore their friendship. Then there was the fact that he still held her fate and the fate of her fellow ranch workers in his hands. But she couldn't pull away, and she didn't want to fight her feelings for Kahl anymore. After fantasizing about this moment more times than she could count, she wanted to be with him.

Even if they later deemed it to be a mistake…at least

it wouldn't be an unanswered question lingering between them. And she honestly needed to know what it
would be like to finally be with Kahlil.

Andraya pulled out of their kiss. Her head was spinning, and her breathing was shallow and unsteady. As
much from their kiss as from her nervousness and fear
of rejection. And if he said yes, the anxiety over wondering what would happen next.

She stood, turned off the television and slipped her
hand into his, leading him toward the staircase. Dray's
knees felt like Jell-O as they climbed the steps and entered her bedroom. She turned on the bedside lamp,
then rejoined Kahlil a few feet from her bed.

Dray's hands trembled as she grasped the hem of
his black T-shirt and helped him lift it over his head
and drop it onto the floor. Her gaze lingered on the
contours of the chest she'd admired through the fabric
of Kahlil's shirts since that day he'd first returned to
town. Mapped out the path of the trail of hair that disappeared below his belt and drew her attention to the
ridge beneath his zipper.

Andraya's throat was suddenly dry. When she looked
up, Kahl's hungry gaze met hers.

Kahl reached for the ruffled edge of her dress. His
eyes never leaving hers, as if seeking permission. It
was a refreshing change from past experiences. She'd
been pawed at on first dates. As if buying her a medio-
cre chicken dinner automatically entitled them to sex.
But Kahlil seemed determined to let her set the pace.
To ensure her ease and comfort.

Andraya lifted her arms, and a sexy little smirk

curved one edge of Kahl's mouth. He slowly raised the hem of her dress. First to her waist. Then over her head and onto the floor atop their growing pile of clothing.

Kahl stood back and rubbed his stubbled chin. He slowly scanned Dray as she stood before him in her bare feet, wearing nothing but a pair of black, lacy boy shorts and the matching black bra.

His reverent gaze warmed her bare skin and made her feel exposed yet cherished in equal measures. Her breathing became heavier. She clasped her hands, hoping Kahl wouldn't notice how much they were shaking.

"Wow," he whispered, his gaze still roving over her skin. "You are beyond *fine*, Dray." He reached for her hand, and she offered it to him. Kahl tugged her closer. "You, sweetheart, are a fucking masterpiece. You know that?"

Andraya sank her teeth into her lower lip and swallowed hard. Should she say thank you? Tell him that he, too, was a stunning specimen?

None of it seemed quite right. And her throat was too dry, and her tongue felt like it was glued to the roof of her mouth. So she stared at him dumbly and nodded.

"I'll just bet you do." Kahl chuckled softly.

His hooded gaze was filled with a hunger that made her nipples so hard and tight they ached. The space between her thighs pulsed though he hadn't even touched her there. And she was sure that the thin fabric shielding her sex was already soaked through.

Dray swallowed hard, then shifted her gaze to his waist. She fumbled with his leather belt, loosening it and then slowly tugging it through each belt loop. She tossed it onto the floor, then unfastened the button at his waist before slowly unzipping his jeans.

Kahl watched her with keen interest, his eyes filled with a heat that practically seared her skin. When she'd unzipped his pants, he shoved them to the ground and stepped out of them, kicking them aside.

Dray's chest rose and fell more quickly with every shallow breath as she studied his tented boxer briefs and the outline of his erection beneath the fabric.

Kahlil Anderson was well endowed, to say the least.

Dray drew in a quiet breath, her hands trembling more noticeably as she reached for the waistband of his underwear. But Kahl swept her up into his arms instead and carried her the few steps to her bed. He deposited her there, then climbed onto the bed.

Kahl resumed their kiss, and some of the tension in her body eased as she got lost in their increasingly hungry kiss. Her body was filled with a raw, ferocious energy that made her feel as if she was going to slither out of her own skin like a snake.

Kahlil gently nudged a knee between her legs, his hands slipping behind her and unfastening her bra. He slid the garment from her shoulders and tossed it onto the floor. His hungry eyes widened, and he licked his lower lip before lowering his head and kissing her neck, then her shoulders and chest.

When he sucked one of her rock-hard nipples into his warm mouth, her spine stiffened and she found it harder to breathe.

Was it the unexpected mixture of pain and pleasure?

The weight of his body on hers? The sheer disbelief that this was finally happening?

Andraya squeezed her eyes shut. Her breathing was ragged. As if there suddenly wasn't enough air in the room. The trembling in her hands and legs increased notably. Her heart thundered in her chest just as Diablo's hooves had as he raced across the pasture.

"Sweetheart, are you okay?"

Dray's eyes fluttered opened to find Kahlil's thick, neat eyebrows furrowed as he studied her with concern.

She froze. Flames licked at her ears and neck—hot with embarrassment. She tucked her arms at her side, fighting the urge to cover her bare breasts, which she was painfully self-conscious about.

"I'm fine, why?" Her neck and cheeks tingled.

"You're trembling, your muscles are tied in a knot and there was a moment when I'm pretty sure you stopped breathing." He offered a soft smile. "I'd understand if you've changed your mind or you're just not ready."

"I haven't changed my mind, and I *am* ready," Dray insisted a little too fervently.

Kahlil cocked his head, one brow hiked. A looked that called bullshit.

Andraya sucked in a slow breath and shut her eyes momentarily before meeting his gaze. Just how much of her personal history did she really need to share?

"It's okay, Dray." Kahl gingerly stroked her cheek. "It's late. We've both got an early morning planned. I should go." He moved to climb off the bed.

"No, Kahl, wait." Dray lifted onto her elbows and squeezed him between her thighs, halting his escape.

This might be their only shot at this. And if she let Kahl leave now without leveling with him, there was a good chance this was *never* going to happen.

"You're right. I am nervous," she admitted. "But not because I'm unsure about this. I know *exactly* what I want, Kahl. *You*. Right now," she stammered, then swallowed hard. "I guess I just want tonight to be perfect."

"You're overthinking it, Dray. It's just me."

"I realize that the thought of us being together like this is a new concept for you. But it's something I've wanted for a *really* long time and—"

"You're worried whether the reality of us will live up to your fantasies of us." Each word seemed to be turning over in his head as he spoke.

"Yes," she admitted. "But not because of you. It's more me. I just…" She drew in a deep breath.

Just say it.

"I don't have a ton of experience, okay. And the experiences I've had weren't very good. Which is why it's been…a while for me. That's why I'm a little nervous, I guess."

There. She'd said it.

"Ahh… I understand." Kahl's voice was warm and soothing without the slightest hint of derision. When he lifted her palm to his mouth and pressed a gentle kiss there she breathed easier. "First, I'm sorry that's been your experience. Second, thank you for trusting me enough to share that with me. Lastly, if we're going to do this now, I need you to relax. I know that's easier said than done, but do you trust me?"

A smile quirked those sensual lips of his, and the

racing of her heart slowed the tiniest bit. She didn't need to think about the answer to his question. After all, hadn't he changed his plans to liquidate the horse ranch because she'd pleaded with him not to?

"Yes, Kahl. I trust you." She stroked his stubbled cheek and returned his widened smile.

"Good. Then lie back, close your eyes and relax. Because I've got you," Kahl whispered, following the reassuring promise up with a kiss to the shell of her ear.

She did as he requested, lying back on the bed, her eyes closed as she took slow, measured breaths and tried not to think about the fact that she was half-naked with the man who'd been her childhood crush.

Andraya continued breathing slowly…in through her nose, out through her mouth…as Kahlil kissed his way down her chest. He licked, sucked and teased her nipples until they were hard as diamonds again. Kahlil planted kisses down the valley between her breasts and down her belly—still taut with unease.

Kahlil planted soft kisses to the band of skin just above her panties. Then he slowly tugged the fabric down her hips and off of her legs.

"It's just me, Dray," Kahl said again. "And you're doing fine. Just keep breathing and relax. If you don't like something that I'm doing, just tell me, and I'll stop. If you want more of something, you can tell me that, too. All right?"

Before she could open her mouth to respond, he'd parted her with his thumbs, and she felt the first lash of his tongue against her slick flesh.

"Oh my God." Andraya gripped the sheets beneath

her, her chest heaving as Kahl continued his deliciously slow, teasing licks of her flesh. Her heart rate sped up, and her pulse raced. "More, more, *more*," she demanded, like a child that had yet to learn niceties like *please* and *thank you*.

Dray could practically feel Kahl's lips pressed into a smile as he feasted on her. She squirmed with pleasure, her grip on the sheets tightening and her back arching as Kahlil took her higher and higher. Until she was teetering on the edge, her heels digging into the mattress.

When he shifted his focus, grazing her clit with his tongue, her hips lifted off the mattress as if of their own accord.

"More. *Please*." The breathy plea hardly sounded like it had come from her.

Kahl obliged, licking and sucking the hypersensitive bundle of nerves. Then he inserted what felt like two fingers inside of her until he was stroking a spot deep inside that she'd feared she might go to her grave with no man able to find.

"Yes. Yes. Please." The varied sensations felt so good, heightening her pleasure and bringing Dray so close to the brink that she could practically taste it.

But when Kahl reached his free hand up and tweaked one of her painfully erect nipples, the added sensation sent her spiraling into a stratosphere of unbridled pleasure she'd honestly never known.

She cursed and cried out his name, her hips lifting off the bed and her heels digging into it as she rested her hands atop his head. Her heart beat wildly, and her body stiffened. A sense of euphoria washed over her, seemed to sate every single cell in her body. Her head felt light as her core pulsed, clenching the two fingers still inside of her.

"You can open your eyes now," he said in a gruff, sexy voice.

When she did, he pulled his fingers from her and sucked them. A wide grin spread across his face in response to her widened eyes. Then he pressed gentle kisses to her still-quivering sex as she slowly came down from the incredible high.

"Now you look relaxed." He winked, pressing a kiss to her belly, then another to her neck.

It would be more accurate to say she was floating on a cloud of pure pleasure—and ready for more.

Kahlil gathered Dray in his arms and kissed the top of her head. Her skin was warm, and her body felt like heaven cradled against his. Andraya Walker was an incredibly beautiful woman under any circumstances. But sated and naked with a flush that spread beneath her brown skin…she was a fucking goddess. He would never get the vision of her falling apart as he gazed up at her from between her thighs out of his head. And he didn't want to.

Kahl ran a gentle hand up and down Dray's bare back as she held on to him, her cheek pressed to his chest. Her breathing slowed, and the thump of her heart against his chest eased. If they lay like this the rest of the night, he wouldn't regret a thing. Because seeing Dray reach such heights of pleasure and knowing that he'd been the one to take her there had given him immense satisfaction.

It'd also given him an immense hard-on. But he could worry about that later. Because if this was all she was ready for, he'd be okay with that.

Dray lifted her head and flashed a shy grin that made his heart flip and his stomach do summersaults.

"*That* was pretty damn perfect," she said dreamily before lying down again.

"It was just *pretty* perfect, huh?" Kahl chuckled. "As in not quite. Okay. I'm gonna earn that perfect badge. Bet."

"And that's why you always leave a little room for improvement on a performance review." Dray dissolved into laughter.

The joyous sound vibrated in his chest and made his heart expand.

He'd spend the rest of his life kicking himself for not realizing that his best friend had been into him all those years ago. This time around he knew. But the end results would be the same.

He'd return to his life in Seattle, while Dray would continue her life there in Willowvale Springs. There would be no happy ending for a romantic relationship between them. That cold, hard reality reached into his chest, gripped his heart and squeezed. But he wouldn't permit his worries about the future to ruin what had been an amazing night. Regardless of how it ended.

"No pressure…but how are you feeling about things now?" Kahlil lay on his back while Dray lay on her side. He twirled a few strands of her hair, which had come loose from her ponytail, around his finger as his chin rested atop her head.

Andraya raised her head again. Her seductive eyes met his, and those pouty lips curved in a mischievous grin. She pressed her lips to his.

Their kiss grew hungrier, more intense. His dick hardened painfully, his desire for Dray building like a head of steam.

Kahlil glided his hand down her back, then lower. He squeezed the full, sexy bottom that he'd come to adore. He swallowed her small gasp in response, hoping he wouldn't leave a bruise on her brown skin.

He flipped them over so that Dray lay flat on her back and hovered over her as he kissed her with fervor and an unexpected longing. He settled between her open thighs, his belly damp as she moved against him, as if desperate for her next fix.

Kahlil pulled himself away just long enough to retrieve the strip of three condoms he'd inserted into his wallet after that first time he and Dray had kissed. Maybe it had been a bit presumptuous of him, but he'd much rather be presumptuous than ill-prepared.

Kahl stripped off his final piece of clothing, then sheathed himself before returning to the bed. As he lay over Dray, he could feel the tension in her shoulders again. He pressed a soft kiss to her lips. She wrapped her arms around him, her hands drifting down to his ass and pulling him forward, making it clear that she wanted him. *Now.*

He gripped his painfully hard shaft at its base, pressing himself to her slick entrance. He continued their kiss, inching inside her until he was fully seated.

"Fuck, you feel so damn amazing, Dray." He whispered the words into her ear, pressing another kiss there.

Kahl rocked his hips slowly at first. Rotating them so his pelvis made contact with her clit.

Dray's titillating, breathy murmurs of pleasure seemed to grow more vocal with every stroke. The sounds—a reward for hitting just the right spot—made him want to bring her more pleasure and brought him closer to finding his own.

Kahl swallowed hard and tried to gather himself. He lifted one leg over his shoulder and adjusted his angle, focusing on each movement until he found the position that got an instant reaction.

"Yes. Right there. Do that again," she pleaded, her eyes wild.

He obliged. Hitting that spot deep inside her again and again while grinding against the stiff bundle of nerves. Until she finally cried out his name, the corners of her eyes damp.

Kahl repositioned himself, his hips moving harder and faster until he came hard, his back stiffening and his arms trembling as he hovered above her.

He fell to the mattress beside her, both of them gasping to catch their breath.

"Did I earn that perfect score yet?" Kahl teased.

Dray laughed, then rolled over and pressed a long, hard kiss to the mouth that still tasted of her. Her expression was more serious now.

"Tonight was beyond perfect, Kahl. Thank you for being patient. That matters. *A lot*," she said.

Growing up, Dray had sometimes been guarded and insecure. She worked hard not to put herself in a position to be hurt. So she often acted as if she didn't care about being teased or that she wasn't invited to the "cool kids'" parties. Should it really be surprising to him that she hadn't felt comfortable enough to tell him how she really felt about him?

But tonight, she'd been open and vulnerable. Had laid her body and her heart naked. Kahl was moved by Dray's willingness to let him inside after all they'd been through. But if he said as much, it would only make this arrangement feel that much weirder. So he'd keep it simple.

"*You* matter a lot to me, Dray," he said. "You always have."

She smiled, but there was sadness and unshed tears in her eyes as she pressed her cheek to his chest and wrapped her arm around him, like she never wanted to let him go.

He understood exactly how she felt.

Eleven

The following afternoon, Dray settled into the passenger seat of Kahlil's luxury rental SUV and leaned against the headrest. He closed the door behind her and walked around to the driver's side.

Last night had been nothing short of amazing. She'd felt like she had been floating on a cloud of satisfaction and had been giddy the entire day, but she'd tried her best to hide it. She'd had minimal success.

She found herself daydreaming about their night together during a few conversations with her ranch hands. And more than one old timer had asked who it was who had her grinning to herself like that.

Ben, of course, had to ruin it.

That friend of yours might be smiling in your face and making you all happy now. But the minute it works

*out in his favor, don't be surprised if he stabs you—and
all the rest of us—in the back.*

Dray gritted her teeth and sighed, trying to get the
old man's words out of her head.

"Everything okay?" Kahlil put a gentle hand on her
knee, startling her from her thoughts about crotchety
old Ben Baxter.

"I'm fine." Dray tucked her hair behind her ear. It
still felt weird to be wearing her hair loose rather than
in her usual low ponytail. She set the gift bag for her
sister and brother-in-law on the floorboard beside her
feet. "Maybe a little nervous about just how much my
family is going to show their ass about me bringing a…
someone to dinner."

Kahlil chuckled. He hadn't missed her nearly referring to him as her date. "You're the one who doesn't
want it to be known that we're…seeing each other," he
continued.

"And I explained why," she said gently, her shoulders tight. "I'm staying.; You aren't. I don't want to be
the topic of gossip from here to eternity about how you
came back to town, used me to maximize the sale of
the ranch, then ditched me…*again*."

"Is that what you think? That this is me using you?"
Kahlil turned to her and gestured between them.

Andraya had tried to state the scenario matter-of-
factly. But maybe there was a part of her that had worried about as much, too. And perhaps that had come
through in her words to Kahl.

"I'm not saying that's how *I* feel." Dray slapped a
hand to her chest. "But it is what some people in town

will be thinking and saying. I'd like to avoid that, if at all possible."

Kahl sighed quietly and gripped the steering wheel tightly as he backed out of her driveway. He pulled up to the stop sign at the end of their cul-de-sac, then proceeded onto the road in the direction of the new development her parents lived in on the outer edge of town.

"I wasn't sure we were still on for tonight," Kahlil said. "Until an hour ago, you hadn't answered your phone or responded to any of my messages. I thought maybe you regretted last night." He glanced over at her.

"I don't regret last night even the tiniest bit." She turned toward him. "In fact, I've been walking around the stables smiling and humming all day just from memories of last night and reading your text message. I thought it best not to risk someone overhearing our actual conversation," she said.

"I haven't been able to get last night out of my head, either." He reached for her hand on the console between them and threaded their fingers. "Thanks for leaving me breakfast, by the way." He lifted her hand to his mouth and kissed the back of it. "But I would've much rather had you for breakfast." He winked.

Andraya's eyes widened. Her nipples suddenly felt tight, and she felt a heaviness between her thighs.

"You're bad." She pointed a finger of her free hand at him. "Also, that sounds amazing. Let's put a pin in that for a day when I don't have to be at the stables at six."

"Yes, ma'am." Kahl chuckled, his laughter filling the cabin of the vehicle.

Dray laughed, too. She was counting the minutes

until she and Kahlil could return to her place and recreate the magic of last night. Only this time, she wouldn't be the least bit anxious.

Andraya had dug out the old gag gift Allie had gifted her one year on her birthday. It was a T-shirt that said *Save a Horse. Ride a Cowboy.* She planned to wear that T-shirt and a pair of sheer lace panties. And she would do just that.

"Kahlil, how wonderful to see you." Andraya's mother hugged Kahl, then turned to her.

Gloria Walker surveyed Andraya with her best shocked face. As if Dray had donned a floor-length ball gown and a pair of two-thousand-dollar stilettos.

She hadn't. She was simply wearing a thigh-length, sunflower-gold floral sundress with a ruffled hem. Her fashion sense was clearly limited.

"Andraya, sweetie! You look adorable. This is the nicest I've seen you look since Hank's funeral."

Quite honestly, the sundress—which Allie had talked her into buying—and her standard funeral dress were among the few pieces of clothing she owned that were neither denim nor a T-shirt. Still, she didn't appreciate her mother making such a big deal about her having put a little more effort into her look tonight.

"You're being melodramatic, Mom," Dray said in a hushed voice, hoping her mother would take the hint.

"No, she's not." Alana studied Andraya with her arms crossed and her eyes wide. "And if I had legs like that… I'd *never* wear pants outside of the hospital again. Thanks for coming, sis." Lana kissed Dray on the cheek before she could raise a stink about her comment. "Good to see you again, Kahl." Lana hugged him. "Come on in. We'll eat as soon as Phil gets here."

"Lana, show Kahlil to the den so he can say hello to the boys," her mother said.

"Come on, Kahl. You can say hello to Dad and meet my husband, Robbie. He's not from Willowvale Springs, so you two have never met." Alana grabbed Kahl by the hand and dragged him toward the den where their father, brother, and Dray's brother-in-law always posted up before and after dinner for fear they might be asked to help out with cooking or cleanup.

Kahlil glanced back at Dray, and she could swear that his eyes were pleading, *Help me!*

Andraya laughed. If they were dating, Kahl being a bit nervous about getting reacquainted with the men in her family might be cute and comical.

Okay, it still was.

"Someone certainly has eyes for their *friend*." Her mother, who'd been watching her, used air quotes. A wide grin lit up her face.

Dray hadn't seen her mother this happy since the last time Lana had told their parents she was making them grandparents again.

"Mom, please *do not* start." Dray followed her mother into the kitchen and spoke in a hushed tone. "I told you, Kahl and I are just trying to revive our friendship. And even if I did like him as anything more than a friend—which I'm not saying that I do—he's going back to Seattle when this is all done."

"Then you'll have to find a way to change his mind.

Just like your sister changed Robbie's mind. We Walker women have a special talent for making our men move heaven and earth to be with us." She winked, then lifted the top from one of the steaming pots on the stove.

"*Eww*, Mom!" Dray's response was on delay when her mother's meaning finally hit her. "We are not having this conversation."

"I'm not just talking about *s-e-x*, honey…"

"I'm pretty sure that every adult in this house and the kids can spell that word," Dray muttered, dragging a hand down her face.

"I'm just saying that we are strong, determined women who know who and what we want. For you, that person has always been Kahlil Anderson." Her mom replaced the top on the pot and grabbed Dray's hand. Her smile was warm and compassionate. She stepped closer and lowered her voice. "I might be an old woman, Dray, but I'm not clueless. And there's nothing wrong with your heart wanting what it wants. You've never been afraid to go after anything else. Why change now?"

Her mother's smile widened. She dropped a kiss onto Andraya's cheek. "Now, call your brother and see what's taking him so long."

"We're here, Mom." Phil stood in the doorway with his arms folded looking grumpier than usual. "The twins are studying for a big test tomorrow, so we didn't bring them. And Michelle will be in as soon as she finishes her confidential client call," he said of his wife who was also his law partner since they'd left their respective firms to start Walker & Walker. He shifted his gaze to Dray. "You look…*nice*."

"My God. What is wrong with you people?" Andraya shoved her brother's shoulder and whisked past him out of the kitchen. "It's informal, but it is Lana and Robbie's ninth anniversary party. Is it really that strange that I'm wearing a dress?"

"*Yes*." Her brother, mother and sister—who'd returned to the dining room—all responded in unison, then laughed.

Kahlil, who stood a few steps beyond Lana, frowned. He didn't seem amused by her family's teasing.

"Then again, when you can pull off casual and denim the way Dray does…all the other embellishments aren't really necessary, are they?" Kahl shrugged. "It's just a matter of taste and preference. And Dray knows what she likes. I appreciate that about her."

When Kahl met her gaze and smiled, Dray's heart felt like it leaped in her chest. It reminded her of all the times Kahlil had defended her in school to mean girls who had teased her about her lack of fashion sense and not-so-sleek edges. Her heart swelled in her chest, and she wanted to run over to him and kiss him on the lips, right there in front of her entire family.

But she managed to stay rooted in place and give him a subtle nod before turning back to her mother, brother and sister, who stood there speechless.

"I suppose you're right." Her mother offered an apologetic smile, then turned to Phil. "Would you mind calling your niece and nephew in for dinner? They're playing out back."

"Yes, ma'am," Phil said without hesitation. He glared at Kahlil momentarily on his way out of the door.

Phil had never been keen on the fact that Dray's best friend was the boy next door. He hadn't trusted Kahl back then, and it seemed that he still didn't trust him now.

"I'll go tell Dad and Robbie it's time for dinner and see if the baby needs changing." Alana turned on her heels and headed back toward the den.

"And I'll start bringing everything to the table. Dray and Kahlil, would you mind giving me a hand?" her mother said.

"No ma'am. We'll be right there," Kahl said, following her toward the kitchen.

Andraya grabbed his elbow, thankful that it was just the two of them left in the room for now. She tugged on his shirt, pulling him down into a quick kiss. "Thank you, Kahl."

He nodded, his eyes as dreamy as hers had been earlier when she couldn't stop smiling about the night they'd shared.

"Of course. You're my girl." He tapped his chest and smiled. "I've got you."

Her mother's words echoed in her head.

Then you'll have to find a way to change his mind. We Walker women have a special talent for making our men move heaven and earth to be with us.

She wished that was true. Because every moment they spent together made it clear that friendship with Kahl would never be enough.

Kahlil finished off his second serving of pot roast, homemade mac and cheese, and green beans almondine, wishing he was at home alone and could lick the plate clean.

His mother was an amazing cook, but Dray's mother was no slouch, either.

"You want more of my pot roast, don't you?" Mrs. Walker grinned. "Don't worry. Got plenty. I'll send you both home with leftovers. But right now, you need to leave at least a little room for dessert."

"Thank you, Mrs. Walker." Kahl grinned.

Aside from how she sometimes pushed Dray to be the ultrafeminine girlie girl she'd hoped for, Kahlil really liked Andraya's mother. In fact, he liked the entire Walker family. It was Phil who had never been his biggest fan.

Phil had been cordial and businesslike when he'd met with him to dispense Hank's estate. But the Phillip Walker staring at him now was the big brother who'd never trusted Kahl's relationship with his little sister. Given what had happened between him and Dray the previous night, maybe Phil had been right all along.

"Dray, Michelle, help me clear the table and bring out the desserts." Mrs. Walker stood, wiping her hands on the white half apron tied around her waist.

"Yes, ma'am." Dray and her sister-in-law, Michelle, both stood and began gathering dishes. "Oh, I forgot to bring in the gift bag. Kahl, would you mind bringing it in? I left it on the floor in your SUV."

"Sure thing." Kahl headed out to the SUV. He retrieved the black gift bag with a festive gold bow attached to the handle and was headed back to the house when Phil appeared outside. He leaned against the house with his arms folded.

Kahlil stopped a few feet in front of the man, meeting his icy gaze. "You obviously have something to say, Phil. So why don't you just save us both some time and tell me what that is?"

"What the hell do you think you're doing?" Phil's voice simmered with anger like a pot of Wyoming stew.

"Okay." Kahl folded his arms, too, the gift bag dangling from one wrist. "I'm going to need you to be more specific."

"Don't get cute, Anderson." Phil seethed. "I mean what the fuck are you doing with my sister? You're running around town 'dating but not dating' her. Taking afternoon picnics with her by the creek. Got her lying about being at home when she's over at your place doing God knows what."

The more "offenses" he listed, the angrier Phil got. At this point, the man was practically frothing at the mouth.

"My sister was devastated when your friendship ended. And for twenty years, you couldn't be bothered to make so much as a phone call to Andraya. Now that you need her—"

"Whoa. That is *not* what this is about." Kahlil held up a hand in objection.

"Now that you need her," Phil repeated with a snarl, "you're treating her like some sort of princess. Making her think you're really into her. But what happens when the deal is done and you've got your money? You're going to ride off into the sunset, and she won't see or hear from your ass for another twenty years. She'll be devastated all over again."

"Inheriting the ranch provided an opportunity for us to reconnect. But it isn't the reason I'm spending time with her." Kahl's face was hot. He dropped his hands, balled into fists, at his sides as he glared at Phil.

There were so many things he wanted to say but couldn't because he'd promised Dray he wouldn't.

"I care about your sister, Phil. Dray was my best friend, and I hope we can get to that place again. I'm sorry that you believe there's some sinister plan at work here. But there isn't, so that's your problem to work out. I don't need to prove myself to you or to anyone else except Dray."

"Great speech, tech boy." Phil slow clapped sarcastically. "But inheriting a ranch doesn't make you a cowboy and pretending to be my sister's friend doesn't mean that you are. So while my sister might be in la-la land about her former bestie, just know that not all of us are fooled. So I've got my eyes on you." Phil gestured with two fingers that he'd be watching him, then turned and hurried back to the house.

Kahl rubbed the back of his neck and sighed. Maybe Phil was wrong about his intentions toward Dray. He wasn't wrong about the fact that Dray would be hurt by him leaving again. But Dray wasn't the only person who'd be devastated when it was time for Kahl to leave. He didn't just care for Dray. He loved her. Only this time, the love he felt for her was different than before. And his chest ached at the thought of leaving her behind again.

Twelve

"You aren't nervous about going to my parents' house tonight, are you?" Kahl's question dragged Andraya out of her daze as she stood at his kitchen stove making bacon, eggs and hash browns for breakfast. "My family actually likes you."

Andraya laughed. She was wearing one of Kahl's college T-shirts that barely covered her butt cheeks and a pair of panties. Kahl slid behind her in a pair of jeans and no shirt. He wrapped his long arms around her waist and nuzzled her ear while she tried her best to flip the rest of the bacon.

"You're not being fair." She put the tongs down and turned around in his arms. "My family likes you, too."

Kahl raised an eyebrow, and Dray dissolved into laughter. She lifted onto her toes and gave him a quick kiss before going to the fridge to get a can of frozen orange juice.

"Okay, Phil distrusts you more than he dislikes you. That's just a big-brother thing to do." She rummaged through the cabinets for a pitcher.

She'd helped purchase the utensils for the rental units, so she knew there was a pitcher around there somewhere.

Kahlil opened an upper cabinet, retrieved the pitcher and handed it to her. He folded his arms and leaned against the counter while he watched her. "Either way, I wouldn't turn my back on the guy."

"That's probably a good idea." She giggled, only teasing. Phil would never hurt Kahlil. Because if he did, she'd kick his ass.

"I'm actually looking forward to dinner with your family this evening. You know how much I adore your mom and your sisters. I guess I was just thinking about your conversation with your dad. Have you decided what you're going to say to him?"

The jovial expression on Kahlil's handsome face moments ago had disappeared. It was replaced by what looked like regret and pain. He massaged the back of his neck and sighed heavily.

"I've been thinking a lot about what you said, actually. In some ways, I guess you still know me better than I know myself." He shrugged. "Because you're right. I do want to fix this thing with my dad. As much as I want to fix things between us."

Andraya stopped stirring the frozen orange juice and shifted her gaze to her friend. The man she found herself a little more enamored with every single day. Her heart swelled, and emotion seemed to clog her throat.

She grasped his bearded chin, the wiry hairs tickling her palm, as she leaned in and gave him a slow, sweet kiss again. Andraya pulled away and caressed his cheek.

"You will fix things with your dad, and so will we." She smiled. "So don't worry. Just tell him what's on your heart—" she tapped one finger to his chest "—and everything will be fine. Maybe not today or this week. But he will come around. Promise."

It was a bold promise to make. But that was how sure she was that Jed Anderson had been waiting for this opportunity to make amends with his son.

"I hope you're right, beautiful." He kissed her cheek, then glanced at his watch which had just beeped with a message. "Do I have a few minutes to make this call before breakfast?"

"Five minutes, Kahlil Anderson." Dray pointed a finger at him. "Do not let my food get cold."

"I won't. Promise." He kissed her again then went up to the spare bedroom he'd begun using as an office.

Since their first night together, Kahlil had either spent the night at her bungalow or she'd spent the night at his cabin. They had an unspoken pact to spend every available moment together between now and the time that Kahl would leave for Seattle again.

Whatever they had brewing between them had been lovely but also slightly strange. But being intimate with Kahl had only been part of the dream.

She hadn't been a sentimental kind of girl growing up, but she had imagined the two of them being together *forever*. Dray thought of her mom's favorite Rolling Stones song.

Maybe you couldn't always get what you wanted, but sometimes if you tried, you could get what you needed. Mick Jagger would have to excuse the paraphrase. But the fact was even if she couldn't get the thing she really, really wanted—Kahl in her life and in her bed forever—then they could at least have this for now. And being with him right now was exactly what she needed.

"Tim, you have *got* to buy us some time. It's going to take a little more time to liquidate the assets than I thought. Matt said we're good for at least another month or two."

Kahlil spoke in a hushed tone as he paced the floor of his office. He'd been forced to level with Tim about what had really happened with Armand—bringing the total number of people who now knew the whole ugly truth to three.

"Matt's the accountant, Kahl. He's simply telling you how long we can afford to keep the lights on. I'm telling you that our biggest investor, Hollis Randle, is getting antsy. Armand was the one who brought him onto this project, and now he's just *disappeared*." The man lowered his voice when he said that final word. "Armand took Hollis out every few weeks to update him on the project. Now Armand is gone, and it's been radio silence. I know that schmoozing was his thing and you've always been the one doing the real work behind the scenes. But you've got to give Hollis *something* or he's gonna be asking a lot more questions. And if he jumps ship, he's going to take the rest of our investors with him." The panic was evident in the other man's voice.

Kahlil was panicking, too. But for the sake of his project manager, he did his best to stay calm. "Okay. I'll handle it."

"How?" Tim asked.

"You said Hollis wants an update. So I'll give him a call tomorrow."

"What are you going to tell him?" Tim asked.

"Let me worry about that later." Kahl ran a hand over his head. "But thanks for the heads-up."

"Oh, one more thing…" Tim said. "Hollis sent tickets over for that big charity ball of his coming up in a couple weeks. He expects someone from our company to be there. It's for Armand and a plus-one."

"That's it." Kahlil snapped his fingers. "Have Vivian reach out to Hollis's office. Ask him to change the name on the guest list. I'll attend the charity ball, and I'll update him on the project then. We can kill two birds with one stone."

"Aside from the fact that I've never actually seen anyone kill two birds with one stone, seems like a pretty solid idea," Tim said. "Buys us some more time, plus you'll be in a more friendly environment where he'll want to keep up appearances and probably won't have you killed."

Kahlil chuckled bitterly. "Hollis Randle is a legitimate businessman, Tim. Not a gangster."

"Aren't all billionaires really gangsters on one level or another?" he asked. "I mean, I adore Oprah and RiRi, but I wouldn't put it past either of them to disappear someone if they started fucking with their money. Rihanna literally has a song called 'Bitch Better Have My Money.'" Tim let out a nervous laugh.

"You watch too many damn gangster movies." Kahlil chuckled. "I think the man would be more likely to put me in jail if he thought I was the one who stole his money."

"Who are you taking to this thing?" Tim asked.

"Taking? As in a date?" Kahl hadn't considered taking a date. This was a business obligation, after all. He just wanted to get in and get out as quickly as possible.

"Yes. There's a ticket for a plus-one, and if you attend the event with a date, that'll help keep things friendly," Tim said. "And before you ask, it's the night of my daughter's ballet recital. If I miss one more event, she and my wife would disappear me without a second thought. So who else you got in mind?"

"Breakfast is ready!" Andraya called from downstairs.

Kahl rubbed his chin. "I think I just might have someone in mind."

Kahlil pulled up to his parents' ranch and turned off the SUV. Before he could reach for the handle, Andraya grabbed his hand.

"Kahl, is everything okay? You haven't quite been yourself since you took that call earlier today," she said.

He frowned. A part of him wanted to tell Dray everything. About Armand running off with Meridia. About Hollis Randle breathing down his neck. About the apprehension of his employees. His concerns that if he couldn't pull this off and the truth about the missing money came out, he'd never be able to clear his name.

But all of the words were stuck in the back of his throat. Despite the deep regard and affection he had for Andraya, he'd already told her too much. What if she slipped and mentioned some of this to Allie, Lana or even Phil and it got out? It would ruin his firm's reputation and the name he'd built for himself in the industry.

Armand had stolen enough from him. He wouldn't allow him to take his company and reputation, too.

"It's just work stuff, babe. Sorry if I wasn't as attentive as I should've been."

"You don't need to apologize." Her dark eyes glinted in the sunlight. "I just wanted to make sure you're okay."

"Right now, being here with you... I couldn't be better." He forced a smile and leaned in to kiss her cheek. "Thanks again for agreeing to be my wing woman on this operation."

"What are best friends for?" She smiled, then pointed a finger. "Do *not* tell Allie I said that."

"No worries. I won't." Kahl laughed as he climbed out of the SUV, then opened her door. "But there is one other thing I wanted to ask you."

"Okay?" Dray stepped down out of the truck. "What is it?"

"There's this big investor...our chief investor, actually. His annual charity ball is coming up in a couple weeks, and he expects a member of our management team to be there."

"But Armand is gone, so you'll have to do it." Dray

frowned, her brows furrowing. "Which means you're returning to Seattle."

"I don't have a choice." Kahl closed the door.

"You aren't coming back, are you?" The pain in Andraya's eyes knotted his gut.

"Of course I'm coming back," he assured her.

"Then why are you being so weird about it?"

"Because I'm trying to ask you if you'd like to be my date. I'm just doing a shitty job of it." Kahl flashed a nervous smile.

"You want me to be your date at some fancy charity event *in Seattle*. The woman whose entire wardrobe consists of denim and a funeral dress." Dray cocked her head and raised a brow, as if she was awaiting the punchline to a joke.

"*This*—" he indicated the short, flirty dress whose hemline had teased him with flashes of the smooth, thick thighs he now knew so well "—is definitely *not* a funeral dress." He grinned. "And to answer your question, yes, I want you to be my date."

"So to be clear…you're asking me to go away with you for the weekend?"

"Also yes." Kahlil tried to hold back a grin. "So if you need some time to think about it, I completely—"

"Yes." Dray grinned. "I'll be your date for the charity ball."

"Just like that?"

"Would you rather I say no?"

"Point taken." Kahlil chuckled and extended an elbow. "We can talk about arrangements on the drive home."

Kahl felt a huge sense of relief that Dray had accepted his invitation. It would primarily be a business trip, but still, they'd get to spend some quality time together.

As they approached the front porch, his mother's Chihuahua, Sergeant, started barking his head off from the other side of the screen door.

"Relax, Sarge. I know you probably don't recognize the man because he's hardly ever around, but this is my son." Jedediah picked up the still-yapping Chihuahua in one arm and opened the door with the other.

Shots fired.

And they weren't even on the front porch yet.

Before he could respond, Dray slipped her much smaller hand into his and squeezed. She whispered, "Hurt people hurt people. Don't let it get to you. It's going to be okay."

Kahl drew in a deep breath and squeezed her hand back before she slipped it free as they walked onto the porch.

"Hello, Mr. Anderson." Dray smiled broadly.

"Andraya Walker." His father grinned. "Well, it sure is good to see you, darlin'. Thought they were pullin' my leg when they said you were coming to dinner with Kahl." His father, still clutching the growling dog, gave Andraya a one-armed hug.

Andraya, he was definitely glad to see. Him, not so much.

"Hey, Dad." Kahlil shook his father's hand. "Good to see you, sir."

His father nodded but didn't respond in kind. He

simply stood back and gave Kahl and Dray room to step inside.

Dray was greeted by his sisters, who hugged her as if she lived in a far-off galaxy rather than in town and just up the road.

Kahlil hugged each of his sisters, greeted his brothers-in-law and Farah's two children: his adorable niece and nephew. Then he went into the kitchen to find his mother.

"Hey, Ma, what's for dinner?" Kahl lifted the top to one of the pots simmering on the stove.

"Is that the way I raised you to greet your mother?" She placed a fist on her cocked hip. "'Cause if so, we need to go back to the drawing board."

"Sorry, Ma." He kissed her cheek. "How are you today?"

"Just fine, baby. Especially now that you're here."

"Great. Now, what's for dinner?" Kahl rubbed his hands together.

She elbowed him in the midsection, and he doubled over in laughter. "Smart aleck."

"Fine. Then surprise me," he said.

"I will," she retorted. Then she looked past him and lowered her voice. "I hope you plan to finally talk to him today."

"I am," he said. "But I can't promise you that it'll make a difference. I wasn't even in the house good and Dad's already firing cheap shots."

"You know your father." She sighed.

"One other thing, Ma… I'll talk to Dad, like I promised, and let him know how we feel. But what he does with that information…that's *his* decision. We need to respect whatever choice he makes about his medical care. Once all of the cards are on the table, if Dad still insists on not seeking treatment…will you be able to do that?"

Eva Mae Anderson sighed quietly. "I guess I won't have much choice."

He hugged his mother, both of them hoping he could find the right words to make his father change his mind.

Thirteen

Kahlil drank a beer as he watched his sisters and their husbands; their mother and father, who were doting grandparents; and the woman who was once his best friend and had since become so much more. He couldn't be happier that Hank's unexpected gift inheritance had finally brought him back home to spend time with the people he loved.

They'd had an outstanding dinner: bison steaks and bison burgers grilled to juicy, tender perfection; loaded fries with smoked applewood bacon and aged cheddar; and roasted Brussels sprouts. But it was getting late and Farah's kids were getting restless. His sister Salena—who was six months pregnant—looked exhausted, and her husband was patiently rubbing her back.

"You should get Salena home. She looks completely

wiped out," Farah said to their brother-in-law. She turned to her own husband. "I'll help Mom straighten up, then we can get the kids home to bed." She shielded her mouth as she yawned.

"Actually, you should hit it, too. Dray and I have got it," Kahl said.

"You've got a lot of nerve volunteering Andraya," Farah propped a hand on her hip. "She has to be at the stables early. Besides, she's *a guest*, Kahl. She shouldn't have to—"

"I volunteered," Dray said. "It's my way of bribing your mother. I'm hoping to get a few more of her recipes."

"Besides, Dray and I have lots of catching up to do. You two go on home and get the kids to bed. Salena, take a quick soak in a warm tub for your back." Their mother hugged each of them.

His father said his good-nights, then said he was going to the den. He extended no invitation for Kahlil to join him—implied or otherwise.

Kahl drew in a breath, his eyes closing for a moment. When he opened them, his mother gestured with her head for him to follow his father. As if that wasn't already the plan.

As soon as she disappeared into the kitchen, Andraya turned to him and took his hands as she met his gaze. "This will probably be one of the most difficult conversations you've ever had. Be honest with your dad about how you feel, Kahl. No matter how he responds, you will have said your piece. And that's going to feel like one hell of a relief."

He nodded, grateful Dray had agreed to come to dinner with him. He gave her a quick kiss. "Yep. I've got this."

When he appeared in the doorway of the den, his father looked disappointed. The old man grunted and paused the episode of *Gunsmoke* he was watching.

"You plan on just hovering in the doorway, or you got something you wanna say?"

Kahl counted to five in his head.

"Actually, there is something I'd like to talk to you about, Dad." Kahlil cleared his throat and sat on the sofa. "Mom wanted me to talk to you about you not wanting to go to dialysis."

"Dammit, I asked her not to say anything to you all about this." His father slapped his knee in frustration.

"No…you asked Mom not to talk to *the girls*. Clearly, you think I'm the kind of asshole who doesn't care enough about his father to want to know that he's gravely ill and refusing treatment."

"Watch your mouth, son." His father pointed a finger.

Kahl raised his hands in surrender. A silent *Tell me I'm wrong.*

His father heaved a sigh and leaned back in the recliner. The old man huffed. "Maybe that's because I probably wouldn't care much what happened to my old man, either, if he'd been an asshole to me the past twenty years."

Kahl was taken aback. He replayed his father's words in his head again and again. Jedediah Anderson wasn't much for apologies, and he never admitted he was wrong. Though, as husbands went, he could grovel with the best of them whenever he'd pissed off their mother. But what he'd just said…it came dangerously close to admitting…

Kahlil shifted in his seat. "Wait…did you just say—"

"*Yes*. All right? I'm saying this thing with me and you—I could've handled it a hell of a lot better." His father sighed. Regret and maybe grief deepened the furrows in his forehead and the lines around his mouth. His dad ran a hand over his thinning gray hair as he glanced around the room. "I built this place with my own two hands. Scrimped and scraped and did whatever I needed to do to make sure that I'd have something to leave to you kids. So maybe I took it kinda hard when you didn't want to be a part of the legacy I created for you."

"I know, and I'm sorry, Dad. You wanted me to be like you and—"

"Is it so bad for a father to want his sons to take up his mantle? Walk in his shoes?" The old man seemed agitated.

"No, Dad, it's not. Lots of parents have hopes and dreams for their kids that don't align with what their children want for themselves once they have a choice. But most parents don't hold a lifetime grudge against their kids because of it," Kahlil said.

His father's expression twisted, and he looked contrite again. "I know. Like I said… I didn't handle it so good. I figured I had myself two boys—one of you surely would want to run this place. But then…" His father rubbed a hand over his mouth, unable to finish the sentence.

"But then we lost Amir, and it was just me. And I let you down," Kahlil said.

"*We* didn't lose Amir," his father said, his eyes filled with anger and pain. "*You* lost Amir." He shoved a finger in his direction, his voice elevating.

Kahlil grimaced, his heart feeling like it had turned to stone and then split into two. "You're right, Dad. It's my fault that we lost Amir. I… I should've done a better job of watching him. I shouldn't have been so focused on myself. And I would do anything, and I do mean *anything*, to switch places with Amir. He should be sitting here right now instead of me. And I think about that every single day of my life. I not only lost my brother, but I lost you, too. Because things have never been the same between us since then."

"I never told you before today that I blamed you." His father still seemed stunned by his own admission.

"You didn't need to. You've barely said two sentences to me in twenty years. Even before I chose a career that would take me away from the ranch…you'd clearly already written me off. I blamed myself enough for Amir's death. I couldn't deal with your silent condemnation, too. So I left. And with you and Dray hating me…didn't feel like I had much reason to come back."

His father regarded him momentarily, then sighed. "Guess we ain't give you much to want to come back home to."

"The important thing is that I'm here now. For you. For Dray. For Mama and the girls, who by the way have been holding down the ranch and doing a damn good job at it." Kahlil tapped the arm of the sofa for emphasis. "You were so determined that the ranch should be left to one of your sons that you completely ignored the two incredibly capable daughters you have who've been running this place better than I ever could."

"Farah and Salena are two pretty amazing women," his father acknowledged, rubbing his chin. "I almost feel sorry for some of the vendors who run up against Farah, thinking she's gon' be a pushover 'cause she's a woman." He cackled. "It's a mistake those jackasses don't make twice, I'll tell you that."

"I can just imagine." Kahlil laughed, too. "Serves 'em right."

"That it does," his father agreed. "Guess it serves me right, too. You leaving this place and not coming back." His father's voice cracked. "I know it ain't rational to blame you for what happened to your brother. Amir loved horses. He snuck out and rode 'em plenty of times when I was watching him, too. Just never told y'all that." His father glanced out of the window that looked out onto the yard, where there was once a horse corral. "Thought I was doing a good job of hiding any resentment I mighta felt toward you after we lost your brother. Guess I didn't do such a good job."

The room was cloaked in an awkward silence as the two of them tried to absorb the long overdue conversation they were finally having.

"Let's just say that we both screwed up," Kahl said finally. "I will always regret the time I've lost with you and with Dray. But I'm here now, Dad. And I'd like to make things right between us. I can't do that if you're not here." Kahlil reached over to where his father was seated in his favorite chair and squeezed the old man's arm. "I'd like another shot at this. The only thing Amir loved more than horses was his family. It'd break his heart if he knew what his death has done to us. So please, *please*, Dad, give us the chance to finally get this right."

The old man's eyes filled with tears, and Kahlil's did, too. He fought like hell to keep them from falling.

"Please, Dad. Even if you don't care about us making amends, don't you want to be here to see your grandkids grow up? See what the girls do with the ranch?"

"Of course I want to make amends." His father placed his hand over Kahlil's, still perched on his arm. "Wouldn't mind seeing a couple grandkids from you, either." He wiped his eyes with his free hand, and they both chuckled.

"Don't know about that, Dad," he said. "In fact, it's a good thing Meridia and I didn't have kids. Things are complicated enough as it is."

"Not talking about you having kids with that woman." There was an unspoken indication that he'd dodged the bullet there. "I'm talking about that pretty little filly in the other room." His father grinned. "Been waiting twenty years for you to wise up and figure out that there is the woman for you."

"Andraya? C'mon, Dad. She and I have always just been friends."

"Oh yeah?" His father climbed to his feet slowly and with effort. He drew a circle around his mouth and nodded toward Kahlil. "So is that your lip gloss you're wearing? 'Cause the two of you wear the same color."

His father chuckled. "We're onto something here, son. Don't ruin it by lying about something me and your mama figured out the moment you called and asked if you could bring Andraya to dinner."

"Yes, sir." Kahlil stood. "But the two of us are still trying to figure out what this is. So if we could maybe not mention this to anyone else?"

His father clapped a hand on his back. "All right, then, son. But take my advice…a woman like that who knows you inside and out and still wants your finicky ass…" They both laughed. "That woman is a gem. Don't let her get away."

"It isn't that easy, Dad. Dray is here, and I'm…"

"You the boss, right, son? Seems to me you could be anywhere you wanna be." His dad shrugged. "Now, c'mon and let's see if there's any more pie left. Gonna need a snack while I'm watching *Gunsmoke*."

"Yes, sir," Kahlil said. "And about the treatments…"

"Tell your mama I'll begin treatments next month. I just need a little time to wrap my head around this. You can permit an old man that much, can't you?"

Kahlil nodded. "Yes, sir. We absolutely can."

"Good. Oh, and Kahlil…"

"Yes, sir?"

His father stared at him for a moment, then sighed. "Look, this little talk we had today… I realize it's not an instant fix for more than twenty years of boneheaded mistakes. But…" His dad's voice faded again. "I'm glad you're here, son. Next time, maybe don't stay away so long, huh?"

"I won't, Dad." Kahlil hugged his father. The man

who'd once seemed so much larger than life felt thinner...almost frail. Kahl held his father closer. "I'll be here as much as I can to see you through this. Promise."

His dad sniffled and patted his back, then stepped away. He dragged a hand across his face and cleared his throat. "Now...about that pie."

Kahl chuckled. "All right, Dad. I'll make sure you get your pie."

As they approached the kitchen, laughter rang out. Andraya and his mother were giggling together and having an animated conversation.

"Looks like your two best girls get along pretty damn well, son." His father elbowed him.

They did indeed.

And something about the joy on their lovely faces as they stood together smiling back at him made him happier than he'd been in the longest time.

Fourteen

Andraya tried her best to slow her breathing as she glanced around the gorgeous ballroom at an upscale hotel in Seattle that was decorated to look like a fairy forest. Fairy lights were strung everywhere, and greenery abounded. The servers were dressed in the most adorable fairy costumes. The guests were dressed to theme in expensive designer clothing and red-bottomed heels.

She was, too, thanks to Kahlil, who'd handed her his credit card and paired her up with a college friend who was a stylist.

Andraya was a cowgirl who preferred the company of her horses to most people. Wide open pastures and glorious mountains to the confines of the city. A lived-in pair of jeans and a comfy T-shirt to spending two hours being primped, pampered and stuffed into foundation wear akin to a medieval torture device. But she had to admit that the end result was amazing. In her pale pink off-shoulder floor-length gown with a thigh-high split, she barely recognized herself.

And despite her expensive clothing, perfectly applied makeup and fancy updo, she definitely didn't fit in here among the rich, famous and elite guests of billionaire investor Hollis Randle. People whose names adorned streets, libraries and hospital wings. Everything about being there made her uncomfortable. Like she was a little girl playing dress-up and pretending to be someone else. But she was here to support her friend who needed her.

Andraya gripped Kahl's arm tightly as they moved through the space. He'd stopped to greet a few of their fellow attendees, politely introducing her to people whose names she recognized from the news or products on her kitchen or bathroom shelves.

Kahlil looked incredibly handsome with a fresh haircut, a trimmed beard, a crisp, white shirt and a black Tom Ford tuxedo with thin, shiny lapels. He smiled and laughed, looked the part and was saying all the right words. But Dray could feel the nervous energy vibrating from her introverted friend who'd always been far more comfortable with his face buried in a book than he was at social events.

"You okay, sweetheart?" Kahlil whispered out of the side of his mouth as he nodded in greeting to a couple across the room. "I *have* to be here, but you don't. If it gets to be too much, just say the word. I'll have a driver take you back to my place."

"After you spent a small fortune on my hair and makeup and this dress?" Dray pulled Kahlil aside so they didn't interrupt the flow of traffic and met his gaze.

"Is it a little weird to be rubbing elbows with folks whose jewelry costs more than my house? A little," she admitted. "But you need to do this, and because I know this isn't easy for you, I *want* to be here to support you. Just like when you had to talk to your dad last week. Don't worry about me. Just focus on what you're going to say to Hollis Randle."

A soft, warm smile lit Kahlil's eyes and quirked the corner of those full, sexy lips she could never quite get enough of. Her heart fluttered, and electricity trailed down her spine. Her nipples—shielded by a damn good push-up bra—beaded. The space between her thighs warmed.

"Thank you, Dray. It means a lot to have you here." He leaned down and pressed a gentle kiss to her cheek.

"It means a lot that you want me here." Andraya's tummy fluttered and her heart felt full. "Now, let's do some schmoozing." She ugged him by the arm back into the flow of the crowd.

Kahl introduced Dray to their fellow guests as a childhood friend he'd been lucky enough to reconnect with. Each time, she was reminded that her feelings for Kahlil went far beyond friendship or even being lovers.

It was an ill-advised move, given that there could be no future for them. Yet she was definitely falling for her longtime crush.

* * *

Kahlil felt a sense of warmth and ease with Andraya at his side. Despite his own discomfort with social situations of this magnitude, he'd been more focused on making sure Dray felt at ease.

He remembered the cruel girls who'd made her feel like she didn't belong because she didn't dress or behave as they did. The boys who'd teased her either because their egos were bruised by her rejection or because they were pissed she could pitch a ball harder and hit if farther than they could. Kahl had always been there to defend his best friend and set anyone straight who spoke harshly of her. And despite his worries about his own fate, he'd been determined to make sure that she felt as if she belonged tonight.

Kahlil had charged Allison—a fashion-major friend with whom he'd attended undergrad school—with the task of making Dray look and feel like a fairytale princess. His old friend had done an amazing job.

They'd selected the perfect sleek body-con dress in a shade of pink that popped against Dray's dark brown skin. Her hair, tugged over the shoulder bared by her dress, fell in soft, silky waves he was itching to sift through his fingers. Her subtle makeup highlighted the lovely features he'd grown accustomed to waking up to each morning.

She was easily one of the most beautiful women in the room. And Dray could hold her own with just about anyone. Still, she'd clutched his arm like he was her lifeline. And she'd frozen momentarily as they'd approached the entrance. Her breathing seemed labored and uneven as she was introduced to people whose fortunes rivaled those of families like the Rockefellers and Vanderbilts.

Her hesitancy and increased anxiety were understandable.

He had no choice but to endure the charity event. But he had no intention of putting her through a stressful evening if it made her feel uncomfortable. Still, he was grateful Dray had come tonight, and he was moved by her insistence upon staying and supporting him.

Andraya Walker was everything he remembered and so much more.

Kahl loved drifting off at night holding Dray in his arms. Sometimes, he lay awake lamenting the time they'd lost. But with every passing day he was thinking about more than just their past. He imagined what it would be like for Andraya to be part of his future.

It felt like a foolish, impossible dream. Because while their worlds were colliding for a couple months, the truth was that their lives were worlds apart.

What would happen once the renovations were done and the ranch had been sold?

He was committed to maintaining their friendship from now on. But he wouldn't string her along or set himself up for disappointment by committing to a long-term romantic relationship.

Yet he was clearly falling for his childhood friend.

Dray squeezed his arm, her hushed whisper stirred him from his thoughts. "Look, Kahl, coming this way. Isn't that—"

"Kahlil, how good of you to join us." Hollis Randle's

voice boomed from a few feet away. "Armand always said you'd rather chew off your own foot than don a tux and attend a charity ball."

The old man's boisterous laughter drew hangers-on who stood around, clamoring for his attention.

Andraya tensed at his side, apparently aggrieved by the joke at his expense. He rested a calming hand over hers and flashed a quick smile before freeing his arm and reaching out to shake Hollis's hand.

"I wouldn't go quite that far to escape a social event. But my gift is making magic behind the scenes. I usually leave the fun stuff to Armand." Kahl smiled broadly and slipped an arm around Dray's waist, tugging her closer.

"That's exactly what my team has always assured me," Hollis said. "So while I was shocked to learn that you'd be joining us for the charity ball this year, it was also a pleasant surprise. I like to get to know the folks I'm investing in." The older Black man, who wore his salt-and-pepper gray hair in a low-cut afro, turned his attention to Andraya. His dark eyes lit up. "And who is your lovely guest?"

"Hollis Randle, this is Andraya Walker. We were best friends growing up, but we recently reconnected."

"Lovely to meet you, Ms. Walker." Hollis kissed the back of her hand, taking Andraya by surprise.

She handled it with grace. "Call me, Dray, please. It's an honor to meet you, Mr. Randle. Thank you for permitting me to attend this fabulous event. Kahl has told me so much about you and all of the important philanthropic causes you support. I look forward to bidding on a few items during the auction."

"Call me Hollis. And you are more than welcome at this event anytime. Good luck with your bidding." He winked at Dray, then turned to Kahl. "How was it that you two reconnected?"

"I've had some business to deal with that's taken me home. But I've been running the project from Wyoming with no issues," he added, staving off the concern in the man's eyes. "Everything is right on schedule."

"Well, that's certainly good to hear. Got a bit worried when I hadn't heard anything from Armand. He usually takes me to lunch and keeps me posted every few weeks instead of just sending an email." Hollis's words were a clear reprimand setting his expectations for the future, delivered with a smile and the geniality of a Southern gentleman. "Where is Armand anyway? He's gone from being that annoying little gnat always buzzing in my ear to practically disappearing off the face of the planet."

The older man's furry white eyebrows lifted, and Kahl wondered how much he already knew. After all, a man as powerful and connected as Hollis Randle had eyes and ears everywhere. He could only imagine the number of secrets Hollis and his team had uncovered about the people he did business with.

Dray's gentle squeeze of his arm grounded Kahlil and reminded him of the words he'd rehearsed.

Tell the truth while leaving out the ugly parts.

"We've both been working pretty much nonstop the

past few years. Armand needed to get away for a bit,"
Kahl said. "He's taking a much-needed break."

"Where'd he go?" Hollis inquired.

"South America. The lucky bastard is lying on a
beach somewhere while I lead the team across the finish line." Kahlil forced a smile.

"Which country?" Hollis pressed.

Kahlil swallowed hard, hoping his voice didn't quiver.
"Venezuela."

"Interesting choice, but a lovely country," Hollis said.
He glanced over at a gorgeous blonde toting a clipboard
who was trying to get his attention. "Well, looks like
I'm needed. If we don't get a chance to speak again, I'll
go over the details in the recent status report you sent.
Just wanted to look you in the eye and get your reas-
surance that everything is okay. You two enjoy your
evening. We'll talk soon, Kahlil."

"Absolutely, sir." Kahl nodded—message received.
He exhaled slowly as the man walked away.

"Just breathe." Andraya turned into his embrace and
smiled softly. "You handled the conversation well."

Dray hailed a waiter dressed in a crown of leaves, a
green fairy costume, a matching cape and what Kahlil
was pretty sure were elf shoes. They both accepted a
glass of champagne and took a sip.

"Okay, the good stuff is *definitely* better." Dray held
up the glass filled with bubbly gold liquid and exam-
ined it carefully.

"Yes, it is." He chuckled. "And while I can't promise you champagne of this caliber, I do have a bottle or
two of some pretty damn good prosecco in my fridge at

home. Where I wish we were right now so that I could take my time getting you out of that dress."

"You don't like it?" Andraya frowned.

"Are you kidding me?" he asked incredulously. "I love it. Why do you think I've spent the past few hours fantasizing about stripping it off of you?" Kahl's shoulders finally relaxed rather than being hunched up around his ears.

"I've been thinking about how much I'd like to get you out of that tux, too." She grinned. "But you look so good in it. Maybe we should hang around for a bit. At least through dinner and the auction," she said. "You don't want to worry Hollis. I'm not sure he's buying your story about Armand. Have you considered just leveling with him about your partner ghosting you?" She glanced over in the direction of their host.

Hollis was watching them, too. He raised his glass and smiled before shifting his attention to another guest.

A chill ran down Kahl's spine.

If it were only a matter of Armand's disappearance, Kahl would be more inclined to level with the older man. But with the money being gone too, it would be a lot harder to convince the billionaire investor he hadn't been a part of his business partner's scheme.

"You're right." Kahlil nodded. "We'll stay through the auction. But the moment I get you home, I have every intention of devouring you."

Dray flashed a naughty smile, her dark eyes twinkling. "I'm counting on it."

She slipped her hand into his, and they went back to mingling with the other guests.

Kahl tried not to think about the meaning behind Hollis Randle's stare. Instead, he looked forward to ending the night back at his place and making good on his promise to Dray.

Fifteen

They were barely inside the door of Kahlil's condo before he'd pinned her back to the door and kissed her. The kiss was slow and sexy. A tease of what was to come. But then he locked the door, led her to his bedroom and resumed their kiss. This time it was filled with heat and longing. The frustration of wanting each other like this all night but having to settle for a hidden kiss here or a subtle touch there. All the while, their desires being revved up by the anticipation of the moment that they'd return to his bed.

Somewhere along the way, she'd kicked off her shoes and dropped the glittery rhinestone clutch she'd been carrying all evening. Kahlil toed off his shoes and stripped off his tuxedo jacket. Dray fumbled with the buttons of his shirt, still not accustomed to the full set of nails Allison had convinced her to try. Then she helped him shrug out of it and dropped it onto the carpeted floor as they continued their hungry kiss.

She reached for his belt, but he stopped their kiss, his eyes meeting hers, his chest heaving. There was something unspoken in his gaze. Like there was something he needed to say but he couldn't quite find the words.

Kahl swallowed hard, the muscles of his throat working, but still no words came out of his mouth.

"What is it, baby?" Andraya pressed a hand to his cheek.

"Dray... I know that we're just supposed to be friends with benefits. That this isn't supposed to be anything serious, but I..."

She smiled. Her heart overflowed with all of the feelings she had for Kahlil. Feelings that had persisted beneath decades of resentment. Like a hardy plant able to survive in the harshest of conditions. They'd renewed themselves and multiplied until her chest felt like it might burst, hardly able to contain them all.

"Me, too," she said. "But there are much better ways to spend our night than recounting all the things we can't have."

She forced a smile, her heart breaking with the realization that their feelings for each other were a double-edged sword. Wonderful and terrible all at once.

Dray slipped the stretchy, body-hugging material of her dress off her shoulders and then down over her hips as Kahlil watched her in silence, completely mesmerized. She kicked away the fabric and stood in front of him in the strapless black bra slip that had been compressing her curves to within an inch of their lives all night.

"Kiss me, Kahl," she pleaded. "We'll worry about everything else later."

He cupped her face as he leaned his forehead against hers and sighed softly. Kahl kissed her, slipping his arms around her waist, pulling their bodies closer as heat built between them.

Kahl traced the seam of her lips with his tongue, then parted them, claiming her mouth in a devouring kiss that sent heat rippling through her body. Her nipples tightened and the hot, wet space between her thighs ached with her growing need for the man who had returned to her life and turned it upside down. Made her feel things she'd begun to wonder if she'd simply been incapable of.

In the time they'd spent together, he'd shown her how amazing intimacy with the *right* person could be. He'd worshipped her body and made her feel as if there was nothing in this world he wanted more.

But he hadn't just awakened her body. He'd given a jolt to the heart that had seemed incapable of such deep love and affection. But he'd come back into her life, like the rain in spring, renewing everything that had once seemed lifeless.

Her heart had been awakened, and she wanted and needed Kahlil in her bed and in her life. But if there would be no happily-ever-after for them, at least they could have this.

Regardless of what happened next, she'd always have sweet memories of being with him. Of the nights they'd brought each other such intense pleasure that even the recollection of the moments they'd shared put her in an instant state of arousal.

He unfastened the strapless bra and pushed the sleek shapewear, with its built-in panty, down over her hips, leaving her completely naked. She stepped out of the garment, and he devoured her mouth in a kiss that felt hotter than all of the ones that had come before it. It filled her body with heat and deep longing. Made her desperate for the delicious sensation of having him inside her.

She reached for his belt. He unbuckled it, shedding his remaining clothing and sheathing himself before climbing into bed with her.

Kahl greedily sucked the pebbled tips of her breasts, then kissed his way down to the warm, slick space between her thighs, licking and sucking her sensitive flesh until she'd come completely undone.

She'd barely been able to catch her breath before he'd pressed himself inside her. She relished the delicious sensation of her body stretching to accommodate his. The way it felt as he moved inside her—slowly and deliberately, then more quickly.

Each brush of his pelvis against her extended, needy clit—still sensitive from his mouth and tongue—took her higher and higher. Until she'd reached a crescendo of ecstasy and bliss, calling his name without regard for the time or who might hear.

Kahl continued to move inside her. He cursed and groaned, the sounds getting louder as he got closer to the edge. Finally, his body went stiff and he cursed, arching his back as he pressed deeper inside her, emptying himself completely.

Kahl hovered over her for a moment, his eyes studying hers with a mix of sadness and affection. He kissed her, then stroked her cheek with his thumb. "Be right back."

Andraya watched his muscular ass and strong back as he made his way to the en suite bathroom. Her mouth curved in a soft smile at the sight. And for a little while, at least, it was enough to stave off the pain of knowing that one day soon, she would no longer be afforded the luxury of falling asleep in Kahl's arms.

They'd committed to ensuring their friendship first and foremost. As long as they kept their renewed friendship intact, she couldn't regret any of this. No matter how much it would hurt to watch him walk away from their shared bed for the last time.

Andraya awakened Sunday morning in Kahl's bed to a ringing sound. He'd arisen before the sun, kissed her on the forehead and told her something had come up and he needed to go into the office. He'd promised to be back in time for dinner, but he'd left takeout menus and money on the table so she could order something.

The ringing continued.

Kahl had apparently left his iPad in the bed amid the covers. She dug it out and set it on top of the duvet, too lazy to roll to the other side of the king-size bed and set it on the nightstand.

The missed call had been from Paxton Hart. He, too, had worked for Hank as a teen. Pax was the realtor Kahl was working with to sell the horse ranch once the renovations were done.

Now that she was up, her dreams of sleeping the entire day away like a lady of leisure were shattered. She got up and went to the bathroom to get ready for a day of exploring until Kahl returned.

Dray was eager to visit the famous Pike Place Market below Kahl's two-story condo. The condo was stunning and spacious. Several rooms offered a breathtaking view of Elliott Bay and the Olympic Mountains. It was no wonder Kahlil had fallen in love with Seattle and had made it his home.

She couldn't visit Seattle without visiting the famous fish market. It would be nice to score some fresh fish for dinner. She also hoped to get some flowers to go in the lovely vase on the dining room table. And she hoped to find a café or a little coffee shop to grab something to eat.

Andraya was getting dressed for the day when the iPad signaled a text message. She'd forgotten to set it on Kahl's nightstand, so she picked it up in time to see the message:

STOP ALL RENOVATIONS. Brandon located a land developer willing to give you close to your price w/o them. So you can stop wining and dining Andraya.

Dray dropped the device onto the bed as if it was on fire. Her hands shook, and her eyes stung with fat tears that blurred her vision and rolled down her cheeks. She covered her mouth and shook her head in total disbelief. "No. He wouldn't. He promised he wouldn't."

Her head suddenly felt light, and the room was spinning. Her heart raced, and her gut twisted in a knot.

How could he do this to her and to everyone who was counting on him to come through like he'd promised? Dray sank onto the bed, her shoulders shaking. She cried so hard that her head hurt and her throat felt raw.

Kahlil had promised to do everything he could to keep the place a working horse ranch. To save the place that she loved and the livelihoods of the people who worked there.

How was she going to explain this to Tonio and all of the ranch hands she'd convinced to trust her old friend? Ben had been right all along. Kahl had broken his promise the moment someone had waved a big enough check in his face.

As painful as the loss of the ranch would be, what hurt most was that she'd truly believed that they'd renewed their friendship. They were sleeping together, and just last night he'd claimed that he cared for her.

Had it all been an act?

Why would Paxton say that Kahl didn't need to "wine and dine" her anymore if Kahlil hadn't indicated that was exactly what he was doing?

She'd believed that Kahlil had good intentions and that he would keep his word—despite her brother's and Ben's warnings. And Kahl had played her for a fool.

How could she have been so naive? What had seemed so real to her had been nothing but a ploy to get what he wanted.

She picked up the phone and dialed Kahl's number, but her call went directly to voice mail. She tried calling again and again and got the same.

He couldn't even be bothered to answer her calls. What could he possibly say in his defense? Paxton's text message had been clear enough.

Dray willed herself to pull it together, then went to the closet to get her luggage.

Kahlil had convinced her to stay a few extra days so he could work in the office and take her to some of his favorite spots. Their original flight back was leaving in four hours. If there was a single seat left on that plane, she'd do whatever it took to secure it.

She just wanted to get back home and forget that she'd ever been gullible enough to believe that the past few weeks had been as real to him as they'd been to her.

Sixteen

Kahlil hurried back to his condo after a grueling but exciting day. It'd been pouring rain when he'd left in the early morning hours, juggling his bag, coffee for himself and the small crew of team members who had agreed to come in on Sunday morning to work on an idea he had to improve the software and his phone. Unfortunately, it was his phone that hadn't survived the trip. It'd fallen into a puddle and cracked. It hadn't shown an ounce of life since then, and given the success of his team's brainstorming session, he hadn't had time to get it replaced.

Without his phone, he hadn't had Andraya's number. Once he'd known he wouldn't be back in time for dinner, either, he'd called the front lobby of his building and asked the doorman to slip a note for Dray beneath the door. He'd been so involved with the breakthrough they'd had with the software, he hadn't realized that Dray had never called the office to confirm what she wanted for dinner, as he'd asked in the note the door-man had slipped beneath the door.

He opened the door as he balanced his bag in one hand and a pizza with bacon, caramelized onions and gorgonzola cheese from his favorite pizza spot, the Alibi Room, in the other. He set the pizza on the table and his bag in the chair, instantly noticing how dark the space was.

"Andraya, babe, you here?" he called out as he flipped on the lights.

He lived alone, so he was accustomed to coming home to a quiet place. But there was something eerie and foreboding about the darkness and silence when what he'd expected was to be greeted by the gorgeous face and soothing voice he'd missed all day.

Maybe she'd decided to take a late nap.

"Dray?" Kahlil walked into the bedroom. The bed was unmade, and there was no sign of Dray anywhere. He walked into the bathroom off his bedroom. The sink was completely dry, and there was no sign that anyone had been there for hours.

He walked toward the door to the hallway to check the guest room, but the ajar closet door caught his eye. Kahlil frowned.

She wouldn't have left without telling him, would she?

Kahlil pushed open the closet door and glanced toward the spot where Dray's luggage had been.

It was gone.

He went back to the bathroom and scanned the counter and the shower.

Her toiletries were gone.

Shit.

She'd packed her things and left without so much as a word?

Kahlil stood in the center of his bedroom and ran a hand over his head.

What the hell had happened?

Right now, he regretted his decision to eliminate his landline. And even if he did have access to a phone, all of the numbers he needed were in his cell phone—not committed to memory. In the age of technology and cell phone contacts, memorizing phone numbers didn't seem necessary. The only number he remembered by rote was his parents' landline number. It hadn't changed since he'd been a child.

First thing in the morning, he'd get his phone replaced. By then, maybe his cracked and flooded phone would be dried out enough to save. Besides, he'd backed up all of his info to the cloud. So he should be fine. But none of that explained why Dray had up and left, especially when he'd had a note shoved under the door for her.

Kahl went to the entrance way to look for any sign of the note. Had the new doorman forgotten to bring the note up?

He glimpsed a tiny piece of white paper peeking from beneath the doormat. Kahlil stooped and pulled it out.

It was the note informing Dray of what had happened and that he'd be home later than expected.

That explained why she'd never called.

Kahlil froze, listening for the sound of a phone ringing. He followed it to his bedroom. It was a call coming through on his iPad. Maybe it was Dray.

He looked on the nightstand, but his iPad wasn't there. He followed the sound to the side of the bed where he'd left Dray asleep this morning. He picked up the device. He'd missed a call from Pax and several from Dray.

A text message popped up on the device:

Do you ever check your voice messages? There's a reason I'm up at the ass crack of dawn, Kahl. This buyer is eager to acquire the property. Check my earlier messages and get back to me as soon as possible. Brandon is on vacation this week.

A buyer? They'd agreed not to officially list the place until the renovations were complete. Besides, hadn't he made it clear that he didn't want the ranch buildings to be razed to make room for a new development of homes? He'd promised Andraya that they would revive the horse ranch and that he'd do his best to sell it to someone who'd keep it that way.

Andraya.

Kahl quickly scrolled back through those earlier text messages from Pax to see what they'd said and when they'd been sent. He checked a message sent at 9:00 a.m. local time.

STOP ALL RENOVATIONS. Brandon located a land developer willing to give you close to your price w/o them. So you can stop wining and dining Andraya.

"Fuck!"

He was going to strangle Pax when he saw him again.

If Dray had seen that message sent earlier that morning, no wonder she'd packed her things and bounced. He knew his friend had only been joking, but Dray wouldn't have. So if she'd seen this text message, it would've been devastating.

The text message made it look as if he'd turned his back on his promise to her and to the workers at the ranch. She must've thought all of her earlier instincts about him had been true.

He quickly typed out a text message to Pax:

I'm with Dray because she's amazing and I adore her, Pax. Full stop. As for the deal... The ranch is no longer for sale. Dray and I have big plans for it. Sorry to have wasted your time. Look forward to seeing you soon. Enjoy Spain.

While three dots indicated that his friend was probably busy typing an angry message in response, he pulled up one of Andraya's missed calls and tried to call her.

His phone call went straight to voice mail three times in a row. Which could either mean she was on a plane home, had blocked his number or both.

Shit.

This was an absolute clusterfuck. He'd come home

looking forward to seeing Dray and sharing his exciting news. First: the breakthrough in the project that they'd been working on most of the day could shave several months off of getting the software to market. Second: He'd leveled with Hollis Randle about Armand and Meridia taking off with the money and being able to prove that it wasn't him who'd signed the check. The older man had surprised him, telling him he already knew. He'd known for at least two weeks about Armand jetting off to Venezuela with Kahl's ex. He just hadn't been sure whether or not Kahlil had been involved, too.

Randle had been understanding. Along the path to being the self-made billionaire he was now, he'd been betrayed by more than one business partner. He warned Kahl to let it be a reminder that he should be careful who to trust. And when he found someone he could put complete faith in, he should do whatever he could to hold on to them.

The old man had been ecstatic to learn that they were well ahead of where they were projected to be and could possibly take the software to market three to six months earlier than expected. Then he made a deal with Kahl: he was willing to invest more cash into the project, but he wanted a larger cut of the profits. And he told Kahl not to worry about Armand and Meridia. His team was working on that.

First, Kahl had clarified that it meant he was going to find a way to bring them to justice, *not* that they'd be swimming with the fishes. The man had nearly fallen out of his chair laughing. Then he'd assured Kahl that this wasn't an episode of *Power* and that everything would be fine. Kahl had accepted the deal.

Hollis Randle was drawing up the modified deal right now.

But Kahlil hadn't had a chance to tell Andraya any of that.

He took out his luggage and started to pack. Tonight, he'd eat his now-cold pizza. In the morning, he'd get a new phone and go visit his lawyer. Because he needed him to draw up a new contract and fast.

Seventeen

Andraya moved through the stable, turning on lights and greeting each of the horses by name.

Gingerbread stood at the door of his stall, whinnying as she approached.

"Hey there, boy. I missed you, too." Dray reached out to the stallion, and Gingerbread nuzzled her hand. Then he seemed to search her face as if asking what was wrong before gently leaning his forehead against hers.

Did Gingerbread recognize the gut-wrenching anguish she'd suffered in the forty-eight hours since she'd read that text message? Dray sniffled, her eyes stinging as tears wet her cheek.

How quickly things had changed.

Two days ago, she'd been having the time of her life with a man who made her happy, wondering if a future was possible for them. She was a smart, confident, capable woman. How could she have been stupid enough to believe that Kahlil really cared for her?

She'd had such a desperate crush on the handsome boy next door who'd been awkward and funny. She'd been head over heels in love with him, but he hadn't seen her that way then. And despite all of the intimate moments they'd shared these past few weeks, he clearly didn't see her as someone he could love. She'd simply been a means to an end, Kahlil's way of ensuring things carried on there on the ranch and that the workers stayed in line.

How could she be so gullible?

After arriving home late Sunday night, she'd taken off Monday, as planned. Allowed herself the time to lick her wounds and cry until she was pretty sure her body was devoid of tears. Apparently, there were still a few left.

Andraya squeezed her eyes shut and permitted herself the luxury of this animal's genuine love and concern. Gingerbread blew his warm breath into her face, and she smiled softly, despite the tears and heartache. It was one of the ways a horse showed affection, and it felt like a much-needed hug. Warm tears slid down Dray's cheeks.

She'd get herself together before the groomer and other stable workers arrived. Because she couldn't bear to be the object of their pity. Or worse, Ben shaking his head and saying, *I told you so.*

"Love you, too, boy." Dray kissed the white blaze

down Gingerbread's muzzle and forced a smile through her tears.

"Well, now I'm *really* jealous of Gingerbread."

The familiar voice startled Dray. Her panicked response agitated the horse. Gingerbread's nostrils flared, and he turned his wary gaze toward Kahlil, who stood a few yards away.

Kahlil appeared blurry through her tears. She sniffled, rubbing angrily at her face. The cracked leather of her fingerless gloves scratched the skin on her cheeks already rubbed raw from crying. The only thing worse than shedding tears for someone who didn't deserve them was letting him see just how devastated she was by his betrayal.

"It's okay, boy. I'm fine," Dray whispered, stroking the horse's neck. "We're fine."

"I hope that's true…or that it will be." Kahl's pained expression seemed to age him. He shoved his hands into the pockets of his worn jeans and moved a few steps closer.

"I saw Pax's text message." Dray folded her arms and bit out the words, her gaze landing somewhere over Kahlil's shoulder. "So please don't deny you're intending to sell this place."

Kahlil swallowed hard, moving a few steps closer. "I won't deny I came here with every intention of selling the horse ranch. I told you my business partner took off. I was too embarrassed to admit that Armand took off with my ex, Meridia, after the two of them drained the company's largest account. I needed the money from the sale of the horse ranch to keep the project afloat and ensure that critical software that could impact millions of lives makes it to the healthcare market. And to ensure my workers would continue to get paid."

Andraya had suspected that embezzlement had been behind the sudden disappearance of Kahl's business partner. But she'd been waiting for him to trust her enough to admit as much.

"I realize that the work you do is important. Life-saving, even. But what about the men and women who work here? Or the horse owners who rely on us to take care of their animals? What about…*me*?" Dray's voice broke, and she mentally chided herself for letting him see how broken she was by his treachery. This had just been business for him. She needed to keep that same energy. "I thought we were friends, Kahl. That you cared about me at least a little. But I realize now just how wrong I was about that and about you." Her eyes finally met his.

Kahlil winced as if her sharp words had pierced his flesh. He erased the space between them, cradling her wet cheek. "I fucked up by not being completely honest with you about my situation." There was a sheen over his dark eyes. "But don't *ever* think I don't care for you, Andraya." He stroked her cheek with his thumb.

Dray's eyes stung. The early morning chill in the stables nipped at her fingers and nose. But it was the pain and hurt she felt that chilled her to the bone. She slipped out of his reach, determined not to let him see another tear fall.

Kahlil Anderson wasn't worth her tears.

"My office," she said calmly. "*Now*."

The only sound in the barn was the swish of Andraya's jean-clad thighs as she stalked toward her office and his quiet footfalls as he followed her.

Dray had never allowed her personal life to take center stage at work. So they wouldn't be having this conversation where arriving workers could hear them. Or where Gingerbread, Scout, Rex, Diablo and some of the other horses might be agitated. She fumbled with her keys, barely able to unlock the door with Kahlil standing behind her and his delicious scent tickling her nostrils.

She ushered him into the office, clicked on the light, and immediately turned on the space heater. Dray sat at her desk and gestured for him to have a seat on the other side of it.

Kahlil sat on the edge of her desk instead, his body looming over her.

Dray pushed to her feet, pacing behind the desk. "How dare you claim to care for me when you lied to me, used me—"

"You're right. I was prepared to liquidate the ranch when I first arrived." Kahlil held a hand up, halting her as she counted his transgressions out on her fingers. "But after we talked, I chose to renovate the place. Would I do that if I only planned to raze the property?"

Dray stopped her pacing and glared at him, her brain spinning.

Why would he throw money away on renovating the place if he only planned to tear it down?

It didn't make sense, and Kahlil was nothing if not logical in his approach to business.

"I don't know." She folded her arms and tipped her chin, her eyes meeting his. "But I know what I saw in that text message from Pax. He said he found you a buyer who wants to tear everything down. And that…" Dray's voice broke, and her heart thumped in her chest. "That you were wining and dining me because—"

"I know what that text said, sweetheart." Kahlil rubbed his forehead and at least had the decency to look ashamed about the message from Pax. "Pax was making a joke. A joke in poor taste, but a joke nevertheless. I didn't even see his message until I got home at eight o'clock that night and discovered you were gone."

"You really expect me to believe that you hadn't checked your phone all day? That you didn't see any of my phone calls or voice mails?"

Dray was insulted by Kahlil's excuse. He wasn't even making an effort to dream up a believable story. No wonder Armand had been the one charged with dazzling the clients with the company vision.

"I dropped my phone into a puddle and broke it on my way into the office," he said. "Didn't get a replacement until yesterday morning when the store opened. So I hadn't checked my phone all day. When I got home, I saw the iPad on the bed, read the message and figured out what happened. I've been trying to call you ever since, but it seems I've been blocked."

Andraya furrowed her brows, and her cheeks and forehead were suddenly hot despite the chill in the air at this time of morning. After repeatedly being sent to voice mail, she'd figured he was screening her calls. So she'd blocked him.

"And while you might've seen Pax's message," Kahlil continued, "you didn't see my response to it."

He pulled his new phone—clearly several generations ahead of the old one—from inside his jacket. Kahl scrolled to his message thread with Pax and showed it to her.

"I don't need to see—"

"*Yes.* You do." He stood, his voice gentle and pleading. "If you still want to hate me after reading it, so be it. But at least give me a chance to explain. Please, sweetheart."

His soft plea tugged at something in her chest and made her stomach flutter.

What if she'd been wrong?

Dray accepted the phone. She reread the message that had broken her heart and sent her into a tailspin two days ago. Then she read Kahlil's response, which had come later that night, just as he'd said.

I'm with Dray because she's amazing and I adore her, Pax. Full stop. As for the deal... The ranch is no longer for sale. Dray and I have big plans for it. Sorry to have wasted your time. Look forward to seeing you soon. Enjoy Spain.

"You killed the deal? Why?"

Dray should just be grateful. Not look a gift horse in the mouth and all that. But she couldn't help herself. She needed to know why Kahlil had changed his mind.

Kahlil stuffed his hands into his pockets and offered her a sad smile. "Isn't it obvious why, Dray?"

"No, it isn't." She shook her head and stood taller, fighting back tears. "No more wishing and hoping or assumptions. I need to hear it directly from you."

Kahlil stepped forward, taking her face between his cold hands and pressing a tentative kiss to her lips.

Dray's back tensed, and her pulse raced. She should step out of his embrace. Not let him off so easily. But her body molded to his, eager for his warmth and touch. And her heart wanted him desperately. Wanted all of this to be real. Hoped that Kahlil wanted it, too. But she couldn't operate anymore on hope.

Andraya pulled away, just enough to break their kiss but not enough to step out of Kahlil's embrace.

"You didn't kill a deal of this magnitude just for me," she said softly, despite wishing it were true.

"You've spent the past couple months teaching me just how much this ranch means to the workers and to the community of Willowvale Springs. I can't take that away. Nor can I be a part of destroying something that meant so much to Hank." Kahlil stroked her cheek and smiled softly. His gaze locked with hers. "But the primary reason is I just couldn't break your heart again. I know how much this place means to you. And you... sweetheart, you mean the world to me. I love you, Dray. And I'd like to start a life with you right here in the place that means so much to both of us."

Dray studied his face, tears running down her cheeks. "You love me?" She'd barely been able to get the words out.

"More than I can say." His smile deepened, and so did its tug on her heart.

Andraya wanted to believe him. But they were just words. Anyone could say *I love you*. But how could she know that he actually meant it?

"I need to show you something." Kahlil pulled an envelope with her name on it from inside his jacket. He handed it to her.

"What's this?"

"Open it." He gestured toward the envelope and sat on the edge of the desk again.

She did, hands trembling, eyes teary. She could barely make heads nor tails of the blurry writing on what appeared to be a contract. Andraya wiped her eyes, reading the words faster and more intently. Then she started over and read them again.

"You're *gifting* me half of the horse ranch?" She looked up at him, stunned and not bothering to dry the tears that ran freely down her face.

He nodded. "No one cares for this place more than you, Dray. So you should have a stake in it."

"You're just *giving* me an equal stake?" she asked again, still feeling like this must all be some crazy dream. "A fifty-fifty split. Without any financial investment on my part?"

"The way I see it, the place should've always gone to you. And maybe Hank was counting on the fact that I'd want to run this place with you as an equal partner." Kahlil looped his arms around Dray's waist and dragged her closer, so she was standing between his open legs. "And I do want you as my partner, Dray. Not only here at the ranch, but in my life. But if that's not what you want… I'll understand, and we can still run the ranch togeth—"

Andraya covered Kahlil's mouth with hers, her tongue brushing his as tears flowed down her cheeks.

"Should I take that as a yes?" Kahlil asked when the two of them finally came up for air.

She nodded, leaning her forehead against his. Then she bolted upright, thinking about Kahl's financial dilemma. "What about the money you need for your business?"

"I leveled with Hollis Randle about Armand. You were right. He already knew about Armand running off, he just didn't know if he could trust me. Now that he knows I'm not involved, he wants to help because he not only believes in the project, his daughter is one of the people who'd be helped by it. Randle provided additional funding—for a larger share of the profits, obviously. But he's made it his mission to track down my partner and ex and recover as much of the money as he can."

"That's amazing news." Dray hugged him, sighing with relief. "I'm really happy for you."

"Thanks." He stroked her cheek. "I would've come yesterday, but I was waiting for my lawyer to draw up the new contract. Hollis let me use one of his planes, and I got here as soon as I could. I couldn't wait to see you again, Dray. And I needed to tell you what I was afraid to the other night—I love you."

Andraya laughed, feeling giddy and lightheaded. Her heart overflowed with love as tears of joy streamed down her face.

"I love you, too, Kahlil. I always have, and I always will." She kissed him again, her heart filled with a happiness she honestly hadn't known before. "I hope you'll still be my date for my parents' anniversary party."

"I wouldn't miss it for the world." He grinned.

Andraya had her best friend back. And he wanted to be both her business and life partner. She couldn't imagine anything that could possibly make her happier.

Epilogue

Kahlil paced in front of the entrance to the expanded and completely renovated equestrian center. The place was absolutely stunning, as were all of the recent renovations they'd made to the property. He could only imagine how proud old Hank would have been to see the place looking even more glorious now than it had the day he'd first opened it. Next, they'd begin work on a building that would be christened the Hank Carson Technology Center.

The technology space would house a local division of his company and accommodate future tech startups. They'd also offer technology classes to folks in the surrounding communities.

He couldn't believe the path that had brought him back home to Willowvale Springs and to the woman he loved more than anything. And as angry as he'd been with Armand and Meridia for what they'd done, it had saddened him when Hollis had informed him six months ago that Venezuelan police suspected that Meridia had murdered Armand not long after he'd put the checking account in both of their names. They'd found his body at the foot of a cliff. But she'd never reported him missing. She was currently in a Venezuelan jail cell, and Randle and his team were still working on recovering the money. But none of that mattered anymore.

Kahlil's life was completely different now.

Suddenly, the car wheels crunched on the gravel road leading up to the center.

His pulse raced, and he was sure his heart was trying its best to jump into his throat. Kahl closed his eyes for a moment and sucked in a deep breath as the car parked and footsteps approached.

"Okay, babe. I came straight here—like I promised. I assume this is about the signs." Andraya indicated the covered sign overhead on the front of the building as well as the sign in the parking lot. "I thought they weren't being installed until tomorrow."

She kissed him, then slipped her hand into his as they both faced the building. Dray was practically bouncing with excitement, and he couldn't be prouder of her.

Their first event in the newly renovated equestrian center—a dressage competition—would happen in just two weeks. Dray and her team had worked damn hard to plan and promote the event happening at their outdoor stadium, which was sold out. The indoor stadium would house a local bazaar featuring lots of local vendors—especially those with equestrian-related products and services.

"You should have the honor of revealing the sign," he said. "But I thought it would be nice if our friends and family were here, too." He gestured toward the front door for all of their friends and family to come out of the building where they'd been waiting to surprise her.

"I can't believe you invited everyone here just to watch me reveal a sign." Dray elbowed him before waving at their family and friends who'd gathered outside the building.

Tonio handed Andraya the rope attached to the cloth covering the sign on the main building. His handsome face was nearly split by his wide grin.

"Okay." Dray sucked in a deep breath, her bright smile making his heart dance. "You ready for this?"

"I am. But there's one thing you need to know first… I made an executive decision about the name. I wasn't quite feeling the Willowvale Springs Equestrian Center," Kahlil said quietly, so only she could hear him.

"What?" Dray's head spun in his direction, even as she maintained a smile for the benefit of their friends and family. "You changed the name without telling me? Why would you do that, babe? We always make decisions like this together."

"I know." He squeezed her hand. "So if you don't like the name, I promise to change it back and foot the cost myself." Kahlil pressed his free hand to his chest. "But I really hope you're going to love it. All right?" He dropped a quick kiss on her lips.

"Okay." She nodded, then stepped forward, gripping the rope with both hands and tugging it.

The black tarp shielding the sign fell away to reveal the name of the building, emblazoned in bold black lettering: The Andraya Walker-Anderson Equestrian Center.

Dray covered her mouth with both hands as their family and friends clapped and hooted. Her heart swelled in her chest, and her pulse raced. She turned to Kahlil, who was a blurry haze through her tears.

"You named the center after us?" Dray honestly couldn't believe that their names were emblazoned on this building that she hoped would once again be a crucial part of the local Willowvale Springs economy for decades to come.

"No, it's named after *you*," Kahlil corrected. "You're the reason we revived this ranch and this building in particular. You've been the heartbeat of this place for the past twenty years, Dray. And that's not just my very biased opinion," he added, his dark eyes twinkling. "It's a direct quote from Hank's will, and everyone here agrees." He gestured to the workers, who were clapping and smiling, then to their family and friends. "I can't think of anyone who deserves this more."

"Wait…you said it's named after me." Andraya turned back toward the sign, studying it carefully. "But it has both our names on the…" She sucked in a deep breath, covering her mouth. When she turned back to Kahlil with wide eyes, he was down on one knee, an open ring box in his hand.

"Oh my God." She pressed her hands to her mouth, tears streaming down her face.

"I love you more than anything in the world, Andraya Walker. This past year you've shown me everything that was missing in my life. How happy I could be if I took the risk of opening my heart again. You reminded me of the importance of family and community. And being with you has made me happier than I have ever, *ever* been." Kahlil sucked in a deep breath, and his voice faltered, filled with emotion. "I can't imagine my life without you in it, Dray. So I'm asking you to marry me and be my partner for life."

"Yes!" She nodded wildly, her pulse racing and her heart so full it felt as if it would explode. "I love you so much, Kahl. And I can't wait to be your wife."

Kahlil's hands trembled as he fumbled to remove the ring from the black velvet box and slip it onto her outstretched finger. He stood, wrapping his arms around her and kissing her as their family and friends clapped and cheered.

For a moment, everyone else seemed to fade into the background and it was just the two of them. Dray couldn't help thinking that this was exactly what Hank had wanted for them all along. And she would always be grateful to Hank Carson for giving her everything she'd ever dreamed of and more.

* * * * *

USA TODAY bestselling author **Jules Bennett** has published over sixty books and never tires of writing happy endings. Writing strong heroines and alpha heroes is Jules's favorite way to spend her workdays. Jules hosts weekly contests on her Facebook fan page and loves chatting with readers on Twitter, Facebook and via email through her website. Stay up-to-date by signing up for her newsletter at julesbennett.com.

Books by Jules Bennett

Harlequin Desire

The Rancher's Heirs

Twin Secrets
Claimed by the Rancher
Taming the Texan
A Texan for Christmas

Angel's Share

When the Lights Go Out...
Second Chance Vows
Snowed In Secrets

Business and Babies

Friends...with Consequences
One Stormy Night

Dynasties: Willowvale

A Bet Between Friends

Visit the Author Profile page
at Harlequin.com for more titles.

You can also find Jules Bennett on Facebook,
along with other Harlequin Desire authors,
at Facebook.com/HarlequinDesireAuthors!

Dear Reader,

Did you absolutely love *Working with Her Crush*? Reese and I are so excited to bring this fun series your way. We wanted to put a little spin on the whole inheritance trope, so why not four successful men who all had roots tied to one man with multiple farms, ranches and businesses?

In this second book, you'll meet Mason and Darcy, who have been best friends since childhood. She's a kick-ass pilot and he's a former professional baseball player who is now recovering from an injury back home in Willowvale Springs. I love a good friends-to-lovers trope and even more so when I can make the hero vulnerable. It's not always the shero that needs saving at the end of the day. :-)

I hope you love *A Bet Between Friends* as much as I loved writing it. There's nothing more fun than silly, sexy banter with a few harmless bets thrown into the mix. So cozy up with your favorite drink and a comfy spot to devour Mason and Darcy's happily-ever-after.

Happy reading,

Jules

A BET BETWEEN FRIENDS

Jules Bennett

A huge thank you to Reese Ryan for a quick *yes* when I asked her to do a fun, sexy series with no more plot than that. I love this little world we created and I loved our brainstorming sessions.

Prologue

Mason Clark stared out the floor-to-ceiling windows of his penthouse at the bustling city below. Lives were going on, people were milling about as cars rushed through the streets, and folks seemed to be speed-walking along the sidewalks, no doubt getting their start on holiday shopping. Everyone's world was rolling right along while he still remained a prisoner in his damn head, trying like hell to overcome the injury that had ended his career.

Not just his career, but his life. Or, at least, the only life he'd ever known.

What should he do now? What the hell else did he know how to do? He'd been part of the Major Leagues as a starting pitcher for nearly twenty years. Before that, there were the Minors and college. He'd played baseball since he was four years old. There had never been an option other than living his life out on the diamond.

Some said he should have retired long before his injury, but retire and go where? Baseball was his sole identity, not to mention all he loved.

His teammates were the only family he had. The traveling, the comradery, the joy of the wins and the disappointment of the losses—nearly every moment of his life had been about his career and those guys.

Until that one split second on his home-field mound when his entire world had changed.

Mason blinked and realized he'd been staring in the same spot at the little café on the corner. He needed something to do with his life other than watch the world go by and not participate. He'd been pouting in his Los Angeles penthouse apartment for the past few months, since his release from the hospital, even having his groceries delivered and his therapist come to his place.

Having a head injury was no joke, but day by day, he made progress and had nearly crawled back to his old self. He refused to believe or allow anything else.

The doctors had called him "lucky," but that implied something good had happened. Nothing good came from losing absolutely everything. His friends texted and came by at first, but they'd had lives to get back to, and their visits had waned. He didn't want to bother them with his pity party or look like he was begging for attention.

The only teammate he'd kept in contact with was his catcher and close friend, Dalton Allen. But he sometimes found himself avoiding Dalton's calls, too.

The buzzer from the lobby pulled his attention from the world outside the glass windows. He glanced over his shoulder and seriously considered ignoring the unexpected visitor.

He turned back toward the window, doing just that. He wasn't in the mood for company today, or anytime, really. After a bit, the buzzing stopped. If someone wanted him, they'd call. He wouldn't answer, but they could still call.

The cell in his pocket vibrated. On a sigh, he pulled out the device and glanced at the screen before answering. "Reginald, is there a visitor?"

"A letter that needs to be signed for, sir," the doorman replied. "Should I send the courier up, or would you like to come down?"

"Send them up. Thank you."

He disconnected the call and crossed his sunken living room, then headed down the hall toward the wide marble entryway leading to the elevator. What letter was so important that he had to sign for it? He'd completed the documents terminating his alliance with his team. Did he miss something? That had been months ago. Surely his former agent would've given him a heads-up if there was something else headed his way.

His life had already been ruined, so nothing could be worse than what he'd experienced. Maybe the letter was from some unknown deceased relative telling him he'd inherited the throne to a small country. At this point, he'd take any positive direction for his future, because he was at an absolute loss as to where to go next.

The moment the elevator doors slid open, the courier looked up and blinked. Mason got that quite a bit. People recognized him. That was nothing new, but it was that second glance, the one of pity, that grated on his every nerve.

"Mr. Clark, I just need you to sign here."

Mason signed, thankful that there would be no small talk and they could get to the point. The young courier handed over the letter and stepped back into the elevator. The doors slid closed, and Mason was alone once again. Just like he preferred.

He stared at the large envelope and stilled at the return address.

Willowvale Springs.

He hadn't been back to that place for years. Not since he'd hightailed it out of there when he went to the Minor Leagues. It hadn't taken long for the top dogs to notice him, and he hadn't looked back since. All of that bickering with his father over the sport had finally paid off. Funny that that success was fast becoming a distant memory. His injury had instantly severed that tie.

He still kept in contact with his best high school friend, Darcy, but she wouldn't send him something so secretive…especially since he'd pushed her aside since his accident.

But who else could there be? His father had passed, and he had never known his mother, so there were really no ties to that place. What the hell was this all about?

Mason headed back into his living area, crossing right to the spot he'd been moments ago. He loved this view and his city life. The fast-paced world suited him; it was as if he could almost get lost in the crowd and hide up here where nobody would know he was broken. He was just a shell of the man he used to be, the man he'd always known...

He tore open the envelope and pulled out a document. He didn't recognize the attorney letterhead as he quickly scanned the paper, wanting to take all the details in at once. The moment his eyes landed on "owner of Carson Farm and Estate," he had to go back to the top and start over.

What the hell? How did he just inherit a farm?

Not just any farm, but the one that he'd worked on as a teen for years. The one owned by Willowvale Springs's own Henry "Hank" Carson. The man had been a stable foundation in Mason's life from ages thirteen to eighteen. That farm had provided an outlet when he'd needed it most, not to mention cash to save for more baseball lessons, camps, new gloves. That farm had given him the work ethic that had carried over into his career.

Providing a solid foundation was one thing, but why had Hank left his estate to Mason?

A niggle of remorse crept up and pushed ahead of the shock of the paperwork. Hank had clearly passed, and Mason had had no idea.

His focus shifted back out the window as gray clouds rolled in over the city he'd called home for the past several years—eight, to be exact. Another blow to his life, one he didn't know he wanted to accept, but he was now the proud owner of a farm in Wyoming.

Looked like he'd found that direction he'd been seeking after all.

One

One Week Later...

"I've been waiting on you to show up."

Mason took his attention from the dilapidated home he'd been staring at for the past thirty minutes. He'd just stepped from his SUV into the snowy weather, ready to head inside and see the old farmhouse, when the familiar voice called from behind him. He'd been so transfixed on his past, he hadn't even heard anyone pull up.

"I've been driving by a few times a day thinking I'd see some flashy car here, knowing you wouldn't have anything else."

Darcy Stephens stood next to her old pickup truck with her hands in the pockets of her long puffy coat as the snowy Wyoming air blew around her. With a white knit cap pulled over her head and her adorable tortoise-shell glasses, she seemed even younger than her thirty-two years, and maybe even a little innocent.

And sexy. That term popped into his head, and he hated that after all this time, she still had that effect on him. He'd thought time and distance would have obliterated those underlying emotions for his best friend. Obviously not, which was completely ridiculous. They'd never shared anything intimate or gone beyond that line of friendship. The risk was too great for him to ever chance anything. In his unstable teen years, and then into his busy career, he'd needed her just where she was…as his friend.

Having her close and in person now, though, Mason couldn't keep his distance. He crossed the snowy yard and opened his arms. Darcy came at him and gave him a tackle hug that took him back years ago, when he'd been leaving for the Minors and she'd told him she wasn't letting him go.

A rush of memories hit him, and that flood of happy times warmed his coldest parts deep inside. Maybe coming back here wasn't the worst idea, even if Hank's will had forced his hand. Once upon a time, he couldn't wait to get out of town, to pursue his dreams and soar beyond his father's negativity and mockery. Willowvale had always been like a black dot in his mind, and the only bright spot had been Darcy.

She still embodied every single thing that had been good from this place. She'd always been that light in his life, the solid foundation anytime he'd needed it. And he'd turned her away over these past few difficult, hellish months. She didn't deserve that, not after the way she'd supported him and his dream for as far back as he could remember. She stood by him when nobody else did.

"Darcy, I'm sorry."

Her arms tightened around him. "Not now. I'm just glad you're here."

The heavy weight of guilt he'd been carrying eased a bit. Of course Darcy would still want to comfort and love him unconditionally. She wouldn't care about an apology, but *he* cared. She deserved nothing but the best from anyone in her life.

But they could get to all of that later. Right now, he had to figure out what the hell to do with the old farm that just landed in his lap. Not just any farm, but one that used to thrive and now seemed like something from a horror movie.

"This place is a dump," he muttered. "And it's too damn cold."

Darcy's chuckle vibrated against his chest. "It's gone downhill, and yes, it's winter in Wyoming. Welcome back home."

When she eased away, she rested her hands on his shoulders and peered up with those wide eyes framed by dark glasses. "How long have you been staring at the house and contemplating leaving?"

"Since I pulled in." Mason released her and let out a sigh as he turned back to the run-down two-story farmhouse. "What the hell happened here? Hank hasn't been gone that long, has he?"

"A few months." Darcy came to stand beside him

and take in the depressing view. "After Edith passed, he just gave up caring about everything. They were so in love, and her illness took a toll on every aspect of his life. His other properties were the same. He had nothing to live for without her."

Mason couldn't believe the gruff yet gentle giant who ran the proverbial tight ship had let anything slip like this. But Mason didn't understand that whole love concept either. His father and mother had certainly had nothing strong between them, which was why she'd taken off before Mason started school. His father had only loved himself, so clearly there had been no room for even his own son. So, no, Mason wouldn't know what a true loss like that could do to a man. He couldn't grasp the whole concept that a piece of you could die with your significant other. He'd never loved anyone so much that he thought he couldn't live without them. Nothing had ever fulfilled him the way baseball had. Which was why he fully understood feeling like there was nothing to live for or keep him going day after day. That dark, lonely headspace could be a scary place.

"So, what are your plans?" she asked after a minute.

"Do you mean for the day or long-term?"

"Both."

Mason adjusted his sunglasses against bright glare from the midday sun beaming off the pristine white snow. He typically contemplated all of his plans but at this point, he had nothing solid. He honestly hadn't thought beyond getting here. Never in his life did he think he'd return to this farm and see the shell of what it used to be. The run-down, depressing state of the once-thriving farm struck a nerve he wanted to ignore because this scenario hit much too close to home.

The parallel between his life and this place was not lost on him. But he couldn't breathe life back into a dilapidated farm, not when he could barely keep himself going day-to-day.

"I guess I could use lunch first. Preferably somewhere warm," he finally replied. "I was on the road early this morning."

Darcy jerked her attention to him. "You didn't fly in?"

Mason shook his head. "I left three days ago and drove the entire way."

Darcy blinked and snorted. "You are aware I'm in that line of work. I could have picked you up and had you here in a few hours."

Yeah, Mason was well aware of the kick-ass woman his Darcy had become. She'd gotten her pilot's license at the age of seventeen and had slowly grown so much in her field. She now flew a private charter, and he couldn't be more proud of the businesswoman she'd turned into. He always remembered her talking about getting her pilot's license, much to her parent's dismay. They were too much like his own father. Thinking her "little hobby" was a waste of money and time, Darcy's parents hadn't been supportive, and she'd been dead set on proving them wrong. How could he not admire her perseverance?

He'd known full well that one text to her and she would've been in LA to get him and fly him back home. But he hadn't wanted that, and he didn't want her to feel like she had to keep a watchful eye on him now.

"I needed the time to think and process," he explained, leaning back against his SUV. "I don't plan on staying here, but what the hell do I do with this place?"

Darcy shrugged. "I can't help you there, but I can take you to this new pub in town. They have the best beer and wings."

At any other time in his life, that deal would have sounded amazing, just another perk of starting a whole new chapter. But it wasn't that simple; he was still lost in so many ways.

"I can't have alcohol with my medication." He tapped his head. "I'm still broken."

In a flash, Darcy reached for his hand and held tight. "Don't you dare talk about my best friend that way. Wings and sodas will do just fine for both of us."

He stared back at her, waiting to see pity or something akin to that unwanted emotion. But there was nothing. Nothing but kindness and that friend he'd always confided in and adored. Damn it. He didn't want to feel warm about coming back to this town, but how could he feel anything else when he was with Darcy?

"I'll drive," he said.

Darcy's brows drew in. "You don't even know where the place is."

"Bet I can find it within ten minutes," he countered. "The town isn't that big."

"Ten minutes? Deal. What do I get when you lose?"

Mason pushed off the car and wrapped his arm around her shoulders as he led her to the passenger door. "I won't lose, but this needs to be fair. What do you want?"

"Can I keep my win in reserve and use it when necessary?"

Mason stilled as he reached for the handle. "That could be dangerous, but I trust you. Deal."

As soon as he helped her inside, Mason couldn't help but smile as he circled the hood. Just like old times. Their silly little meaningless bets. Maybe falling back into an old pattern with Darcy was just what he needed to transition into the next chapter of his life...whatever that might be.

Darcy couldn't believe he'd come back. In all honesty, she thought for sure he'd send an assistant or call a real estate agent to handle the farm and the old house. Mason Clark hadn't been back to Willowvale Springs in so long, not since he'd been called up by the Minor Leagues and realized his dream was turning into a reality. Oh, she'd visited him and gone to several games over the years. Even though they'd both advanced in their careers, as far as their personal lives went, they were all each other had. She'd been dating a local man, Tanner, but she'd recently told him that things weren't going to work out between them. Not that Tanner had gotten the memo; he was still holding out hope that she'd come around. The truth was, friends and relationships came and went, and acquaintances weren't there for the long haul. She liked knowing Mason was back, even if temporarily, and even if under duress.

She'd been lost after he'd gone off to fulfill his dream of one day playing in the Majors. At the time, she wanted to be angry with him for leaving her, but how could she be? He'd finally gotten the chance of a lifetime, and she'd been so damn proud that she'd walked around beaming for weeks.

Mason wasn't the same man he'd been when he'd left. There was a confidence, almost a cockiness, about him that made her smile. He already seemed too big for this town, as she'd always known him to be.

Something about him looked out of place here...or that could just be his flashy SUV rolling through the small-town streets and his dominating presence.

After spotting the pub's sign, Mason quickly pulled into a nearby parking space. They exited the vehicle and walked the short distance to the pub. Mason held the door open and gestured her inside. Darcy patted his bearded cheek as she passed by.

"Thirteen minutes."

He grumbled something about the pub being hidden down an alleyway and not being allowed to use his GPS, but Darcy laughed as she headed farther inside. It's true, The Getaway was off the beaten path. Granted, there was only one beaten path in the middle of downtown, but Mason had tried finding the pub without using technology. He had failed and had ultimately given in to the fancy system in his car that probably cost more than she made in an entire year.

Darcy would relish her win for now, and then again, when she cashed in her raincheck prize. She loved how they could fall so easily back into their old habits like no time had passed. Unfortunately, too much time and too many life instances had transpired for things to have really stayed the same.

As much as she wanted to pry and dig inside of his thoughts, she had to pace herself. He'd distanced himself even from their texts after his accident. The stubborn man likely thought if he avoided everything and everyone that his problems would disappear. No doubt he wanted to crawl inside a hole and ignore the world. But if he'd thought she was going to let him dodge her forever, he'd been sorely mistaken. If he hadn't come back to claim his inheritance, she would have gone to his fancy penthouse in LA and demanded to see him. No way would she let him go through any of this alone...despite his wishes that he do just that.

She wouldn't let him be alone now, just like she hadn't let him be alone when his first girlfriend dumped him for the starting quarterback on their high school football team. Regardless of the highs or the lows, they were always there for each other. He would insist on doing the same for her. They were a team, no matter what. A small team, but still a dynamic one. No matter where his headspace was right now, and she didn't mean the actual injury, she had to prove to him that nothing had changed. She still had his back no matter what.

Darcy still remembered watching that gut-wrenching game live on television, when that crack of the bat had sent the ball straight to the pitcher's mound—and Mason's head. He'd gone down immediately. She'd held her breath through the commercial break and knew things were bad when the break lasted longer than usual and the camera stayed off the mound. That had been the scariest moment of her entire life...more than trumping her landing the Cessna on her own for the first time.

"Where do you want to sit?" he asked.

Darcy glanced around the busy pub, and before she could reply, people started turning their heads, clearly recognizing who had just walked in. Some older folks knew Mason from his younger years, but the teens in here were looking at a hero and icon they'd never met.

"Maybe we should go somewhere else," he murmured into her ear.

"No." She glanced back and noted the fear in his eyes. She almost caved, but decided tough love was in order. He would have done the same for her.

"We'll stay. You can't hide forever."

The Mason she'd always known, the Mason portrayed on TV and during games, would never run from anything in his life. He always stood his ground in that confident, almost cocky manner. His head injury had clearly messed with more than she'd thought. But she would address all of that later. Right now, they were grabbing lunch and getting caught up on basic life topics.

"Mr. Clark."

Darcy glanced around to find a young man standing next to Mason. She instantly recognized him as the pub owner's son, Carter. Carter had grown up here at his dad's business by helping during summers and after school. Darcy guessed him to be about ten, but he was always eager to take an order or bring a round of waters.

"Hey, buddy," Mason said, immediately smiling as he greeted the boy. "Call me Mason."

Carter's eyes widened. "I can't believe you're really here. My dad said you went to school together, but I didn't believe him."

Mason laughed and glanced around. "Who's your dad?"

"Gabe Winn," Darcy stated, pointing behind the bar. "Remember him?"

Mason turned his attention to the back of the pub, where Gabe lifted a hand to wave before grabbing a pint glass and filling it with a pilsner from the tap.

"You mean you really do know my dad?" Carter asked.

"We played baseball together when we were about your age, until your dad joined the football team," Mason explained. "He was the best quarterback this town has ever seen."

Darcy watched as Carter led Mason to a booth toward the back, near the bar. She knew he'd get slammed with his popularity, but she'd gotten so used to his elevated status that she'd temporarily forgotten how it affected others. She'd been so damn excited he'd actually come home. She wanted to know how he was doing, because he'd always been vague or brushed off her questions in texts or calls. He either didn't want her to worry or he was in denial about his injury and end of his career…or, very likely, both.

Mason folded his long, lean frame into the booth, and Carter stood at the head of the table. Darcy patted his shoulder to get his attention.

"If your dad doesn't care, you can join us," she offered.

"Oh, man. Seriously?" He jerked his attention over his shoulder, to his dad. "Can I sit with Mr. Clark and Darcy, Dad?"

Gabe laughed and nodded. "After you write down their order and take it to the kitchen."

Carter turned back. "You guys need menus. Hold on."

"No need," Mason stated. "I hear you have the very best wings. Bring us a couple baskets of those, and I'll have a regular cola."

"I'll do a sweet tea," Darcy told him.

Carter scurried away, no doubt anxious to get back to their table. Seeing Mason interact with an impressionable child only added to his appeal. How could she not adore the man? In her eyes, he had no flaws. Or maybe because he was back and she could actually spend a considerable amount of time with him, she ignored anything that could potentially be a negative.

Mason was completely at ease chatting with a young boy, and just like she'd always known, he'd never let his celebrity life get to his head. He was still the guy who had just done his job for the love of the sport and not the padded bank account or recognition.

"I hope that was okay." Darcy crossed her ankles beneath the table and rested her elbows on the top. "I should have asked if you cared if he joined us, but I'm pretty sure he's starstruck."

They both removed their coats and shoved them to the seats beside them. Mason pushed the sleeves of his sweater up, exposing the tattoos she'd seen before—and some she hadn't. She felt a warm tingle spread low in her belly at the sight. *Where did that come from?* They were just two friends catching up. That was all.

"This is the best part of the job. The kids, you know?"

Mason cursed beneath his breath. "Was. This *was* the best part of the job. I love meeting fans, especially kids."

"You might not be playing the sport, but you're still a Major League player. Nothing can ever take that away."

"Everything was taken away," he grumbled. "But I'm not getting into that."

An emotion she'd never seen before flashed across his face. She couldn't imagine all the feelings he must be dealing with or the future he no doubt worried over. She had all the confidence that he'd bounce back and find a purpose in life as fulfilling as baseball was, but he didn't want a motivational speech right now, so she'd keep that in reserve.

"What's up with you?" he asked. "The guy you were seeing—was it Timmy, or Tommy—and the new business venture. Let's discuss that."

Darcy inwardly cringed. "Tanner. And let's not." Because both were colossal disasters.

"Going that good, huh?" He chuckled, stretching his arm along the back of the booth. "Last we talked, your guy had just left your house. What was that, just a couple days ago?"

"He left because I called things off, which should have happened months ago, but I kept waiting for that spark."

Mason raised one dark brow. "Nothing?"

Darcy shook her head. "I felt like I was kissing my brother."

"You don't have a brother."

"Exactly." She laughed. "It was even bad for a fake brother."

Mason had started to speak when Carter came back to the table.

"I want to know what's going on later," he murmured, moving over to make room for the young boy.

Darcy pursed her lips. "We'll start with you first. Deal?"

"We're not going to talk about me," he countered.

"Want to bet?" she asked. "You already lost one today. Already eager to go for another?"

Carter laughed. "Do you guys argue all the time like this?"

"Oh, we're not arguing," Darcy corrected him. "We like to bet. It's just our thing we've done since kindergarten, when he bet I couldn't go the whole distance on the monkey bars without falling off."

Carter's eyes went back and forth. "Who won?"

"Me, of course." Darcy pointed to herself. "I always get what I want, and I hate to lose."

"Don't let her lie to you," Mason chimed in. "She's lost plenty."

Carter and Mason picked back up chatting and talking baseball.

Darcy decided to take this opportunity to check her emails for more client referrals. She had a personal quota she wanted to meet each week, and so far, she was falling short. How could she reach the next level and grow her business beyond this tiny town, into something bigger?

Her love of flying stemmed from her days as a teen, when she'd wanted to find a way to escape reality. Being up in the sky overlooking the world below seemed to make any worry or care disappear. From her very first flight, Darcy knew being a pilot was the only path for her. Not only did she want to fly, but she wanted to own her own business. But this industry wasn't cheap, and she had to be patient. She just wished she'd known how frustrating this process could be.

For now, she shared her plane with another pilot. It wasn't ideal, but it was the only way she could afford to save up for a down payment on her own. Once she had that, she could start her own company anywhere she wanted.

Part of her had a sliver of jealousy that Mason had made a life outside of Willowvale Springs. He'd chased that dream and actually caught it. Here she was, thirty-two years old and still chasing hers. Would she ever catch it? Her mental spreadsheet of the timeline for her life hadn't been checked off in the manner she'd expected.

She thought for sure she'd have her own company by now with her own employees and her own fleet for charters. But her finances simply weren't at the level she needed quite yet.

Because of her career and her tanking love life, Mason's return couldn't have come at a better time. She wanted nothing more than to get lost in the memories she shared with her best friend, and to help him focus on his own healing. Fixing up the old Carson estate was just the distraction she needed.

Two

*H*ero.

Carter had called Mason his hero more than once. Mason was nobody's hero. He'd become a failure and a has-been. The only reason his name continued to circulate was because people were still talking about his injury…not because of how hard he'd worked to get where he was or his stats. Nobody cared about his strikeouts or wins, or his Cy Young Award.

Hell, there were days he couldn't recall those numbers and honors, either, and they'd been ingrained into his own mind. Why were pieces of his memory coming and going? He knew the injury had messed with a whole host of wires inside his brain, but—

"You missed your turn."

Darcy's soft voice penetrated his thoughts, and he

slammed on the brakes on the snow-covered backcountry road. When he started to fishtail, he eased off and carefully steered the opposite direction of the sliding to get the vehicle back under control.

His heart thumped hard in his chest at the rookie mistake of braking on snow. He should've been paying better attention to the drive and the conditions.

That sultry tone of hers had always warmed something deep inside him, but now a familiar humiliation was settling in. He didn't want her to worry and by getting lost in his own mind, she'd be doing just that.

"Need help getting back to the farm?" she asked.

"No," he barked. "I'm not an invalid."

Damn it.

He gripped the wheel tighter and ground his teeth. Darcy wasn't his target. This stupid injury was and she just happened to be in the crossfire. Shame consumed him both at his struggle and having Darcy witness every ugly part.

What he wouldn't give to go back in time and be whole again. To not feel like something was wrong with him and have the entire world see him crumble…to not have Darcy's concern and pity.

But her heart was in the right place, and he couldn't be angry at her for caring.

"Sorry," he grumbled.

Her hand came to rest on his thigh and he cringed, still staring straight ahead at the narrow country road.

"I don't want pity," he said.

"Good thing for you that's not what I was offering," she fired back. "I'll give you this free pass of being snarky and grouchy, because I don't know the full extent of what I'm dealing with."

Mason jerked his attention to her. "You're dealing with nothing. It's me. I'm the one dealing with everything."

Darcy's eyes narrowed as she slid her hand away. "First, I'm not offering pity. I know you better than that. Second, if you think I'll let you go through any of this alone, then you don't know me very well. I've given you space, I've let you ignore me, but that all stops now."

Mason returned his focus to the flurries blowing around outside the windshield, trying to figure out what the hell to say or do. He didn't want to take out his anger and frustrations on Darcy. From the hurt lacing her tone, she hadn't been trying to offer pity. But, to be honest, he didn't welcome her concern, either.

His teammate and friend Dalton had tried reaching out while he'd been on his road trip to Willowvale, but he was dodging him, too. He missed hanging with his friends, the people he'd come to think of as family. He knew they genuinely cared, but they had resumed their normal lives, while his was still…hell, he didn't even know what chapter he was in now.

The blare of a horn as a car eased around them pulled him from his thoughts.

Mason turned back to the wheel and put the car in Reverse as he glanced in the rearview mirror.

"I'm not ready to talk," he admitted.

He never wanted to be seen as a failure…especially to Darcy. They'd been so strong together through so many aspects of life. Now, more than ever, he had to appear as though he had his life together and his world hadn't completely crumbled, leaving him in a heap of despair.

Silence filled the confined space as he turned the car around and attempted to concentrate on his turn. He knew where to find the road. He'd lived here his entire life before his baseball career had taken off, and he'd worked for Hank for years. Why the hell did he have to think so damn hard?

"This next left."

Darcy's sweet tone washed over him, and as much as he hated her seeing his vulnerability, he also knew he had to accept her help this time.

"I didn't mean to snap earlier," he stated after making the correct turn. "It's just… There's a lot going on in my head, and now this ridiculous inheritance. I still don't understand."

There. Maybe he could deflect the conversation and mood away from his brokenness.

"Hank surprised several people with his will, to be honest. Kahlil inherited the Willowvale Springs Horse Ranch, and now he's engaged to Dray Walker. You remember her? She also used to work for Hank, and when Kahlil came back, they ended up on a rocky path but fell in love. That's a long story for another time, though."

Kahlil was back, too?

"What about Hank's other properties?" Mason asked, making another turn.

A sliver of relief slid through him that he remembered this one. He refused to continually look like a fool. No matter how much grace Darcy gave him, he expected—no, *demanded*—better of himself. His therapist would want to know about his brain blip, but Mason didn't think that would be necessary. He'd share the major occurrences, but he was going to chalk this moment up to the fact that he hadn't been back to Willowvale Springs in over a decade.

"The General Store was willed to Mabel since she's been the manager for decades. The dude ranch and the ranching resort were supposedly gifted as well, but the new owners haven't come to town yet. Maybe they're getting their affairs in order, or perhaps they're just going to send a real estate agent to resell."

"That thought definitely crossed my mind and is still a contender," he admitted. "I honestly don't know what I'm going to do now that I'm here."

"Are you staying at the house?" she asked.

Mason turned down the tree-lined drive leading to Hank's estate. He blew out a sigh, weighing his options, not that there were many.

"I guess. It's not like Willowvale is full of hotels. I hope the inside is in a little better shape than the outside."

Darcy laughed. "I haven't been inside in years, but I'm sure the place is fine. Hank has only been gone a few months."

Mason still couldn't wrap his mind around the fact that such a robust man, so full of life and stamina, could just be gone. But wasn't that just another reminder of how nothing stayed the same and life could take a drastic turn in the proverbial blink of an eye? He knew that better than anyone.

"Where did all of the animals go?" he asked.

"There were plans to take care of them until the new owners came to town," Darcy explained. "But a farmer Hank had dealings with in Cheyenne took them until they can be cared for here."

Mason pulled up in front of the house, the sight of its sad state still startling him. No window boxes full of evergreen branches covered with snow or lights around the doorways, no porch swing, and the gutter on one end was dangling precariously.

Edith had always prided herself on decorating for the holidays early. Well before Thanksgiving, she would have some of Hank's trusted employees out hanging garlands and lights. She claimed it was to get everything done before the weather took a turn, but everyone knew that woman loved Christmas. So her October decor didn't consist of skeletons or cobwebs but, rather, Santa and cinnamon candles.

He killed the engine and ran a hand over his jaw, trying to fully embrace this new normal. Much like his life now, everything about Hank's estate had changed.

"Want me to go in first and report back?" She laughed.

He'd missed that sweet laughter. That sound wasn't something that could be conveyed through a text. Seeing her in person had already caused a calming in him he hadn't even thought possible.

"We'll go in together." He turned to face her and blew out a frustrated sigh. "I'm really glad you're here. Can we forget that I was an asshole a minute ago?"

"A minute ago?" She snorted. "You've been an asshole since kindergarten. That's why I find you entertaining. But I know you also have a heart of gold, so I keep you around."

Mason reached for her hand and squeezed. "I don't let just anyone call me an asshole."

"I'm special, I know."

Yeah, she was. More than he ever realized until he saw her standing in the drive earlier. Since the start of his career, his agent and team owners had seen him as a money ticket. They had stressed more and more success because the more strikeouts he had, the more he would get paid, and the more higher-ranking teams would push for trades to get him on their team. The Cy Young Award had catapulted him to stardom, and then all of the teams had wanted him. He had known his value, his worth in the industry. Now he'd be lucky if all of his sponsors didn't drop him. So far, they hadn't. But that wouldn't last forever, either. Another, younger, better player would come up through the ranks, and Mason would be nothing more than a passing conversation between old guys at a bar.

"Hey." Darcy gave his hand a tug, pulling him from his thoughts. "Don't get lost in that head of yours. No pity parties. Got it? You're good, you're recovering, and now you're a new property owner. Let's keep it as simple as that."

Why did she have to be so damn logical? He wanted to be pissed and have the pity party he deserved.

"Ready to talk about that guy you just dumped?" he asked.

Darcy released his hand and groaned. "Not at all," she replied, giving the door handle a tug. "Let's get inside and see what we're dealing with. Then I'll get you some groceries so you can stock up on things you might need."

Stock up. That phrase sounded so permanent, as though he might be staying long-term. He had no intention of settling back down here. Granted, he didn't exactly know his next move, but being a small-town farmer sure as hell wasn't an option.

But maybe being at the Carson farm would give him the time he needed to figure out exactly where to go next…and heal privately. Because being around Darcy was starting to rattle him, and he wasn't about to stick around to find out why.

Darcy set her cell on the kitchen counter and glanced to where Mason ascended from the basement steps.

"Groceries are ordered," she told him. "I went ahead and chose delivery, so they'll be here in about an hour. I also ordered pizzas, and they'll be delivered, too."

Mason's dark brows rose toward his hairline. "There's a delivery pizza place in town now?"

"No, but my friend owns the place, and I asked for a discreet favor, so she's going to drop them off on her way home."

"You didn't have to go to any trouble."

Darcy shrugged. She respected his boundaries. If he wasn't ready to be out all the time, she understood. But that didn't mean she'd let him get too complacent with his yearning to hide away.

"I didn't do anything but make some phone calls. So, how's the basement look?"

"Water heater is shot, so until that gets replaced, I'm only using cold."

"You can shower at my place," she offered. "Hell, just stay at my place."

Mason shook his head. "I need the time alone to think."

"You've been alone with your thoughts long enough, right?" She crossed her arms and leaned back against the counter. "Can't you think at my house? I mean, it's probably not the posh living conditions you're used to, but I do have enough space for two people."

"I'm not the best company lately, and I don't want to take my issues out on you again."

"Fair enough. Though you'll be begging for my hot water before you know it."

Darcy adjusted her glasses and pushed off the counter. Mason's tormented look had her closing the distance between them and resting her hands on his broad shoulders. She still had to tip her head back to hold his gaze even though she almost topped six feet. She'd always been the tall friend and sometimes towered over her dates. But not with Mason.

"I'm here for you no matter what the need is," she explained. "Don't hide your issues to protect me or because you're too stubborn to admit you're human."

His eyes darted down, and she gripped his face between her hands, forcing him to focus on her.

"Stop avoiding this," she demanded. "Avoiding *me*."

"I'm not avoiding you. I'm here, aren't I?"

The denial stung as she dropped her hands and took a step back.

"What about all of my messages that you didn't answer, or calls that went to voice mail?" she fired back. "You're only here because you have nothing else to do but figure out what the hell to do with this farm."

The muscles in his jaw clenched, his lips thinned, and Darcy waited for more excuses or denials. She couldn't tiptoe around him because she was afraid to hurt his feelings. Yes, he might be recovering from an injury, but he still had to be held accountable for his actions.

Mason turned away and rubbed his hand over the back of his neck. As much as she had her own hurt from dealing with the way he'd treated her over the past several months, she had to push aside her selfishness and see that he struggled with the new reality he'd been given. Her heart ached for him, for the life he'd been forced into after the dream he'd been living.

"I'm not the same man I used to be." His murmured words sliced right through the pain that seemed to enshroud him. "I'll never be Mason Clark, the best pitcher in Major League Baseball."

Darcy pulled in a shaky breath and took a step around him. He needed to focus on his future, on what he had now, and she fully intended to make him see that the end of a career wasn't the end of a life. There could be new opportunities and other adventures.

"Nobody is taking your title away," she told him. "You are still one of the greatest pitchers the game has ever seen. Your name will be tossed around until the end of time. But stop and think of why you started. Was it for the fame and recognition?"

When silence greeted her, she knew he was in no mood for a pep talk or motivational speech. Likely he'd heard everything from his therapist. He needed a friend. He need a distraction.

"Bundle up," she ordered. "And follow me."

Darcy headed toward the old screen door leading to the backyard, assuming he would follow. She wasn't sure what she was facing with her best friend and his wounded soul, but she wasn't about to let him walk this path alone.

Three

Mason stared at the dilapidated chicken coop and then turned his attention to Darcy. His eyes landed on her as she stalked back from the barn that had certainly seen better days. His rich laughter pierced the air and she figured he was amused at the sledgehammer she had over one shoulder as she trudged through the snow.

"I hope you're not using that on me," he called.

"I'm not using it at all." She made her way through the yard and set the tool on the ground. "You are. Knock that coop down. Take out your frustrations and demolish this eyesore all in one. It's a win-win."

Mason eyed the sledgehammer and shrugged. Without a word, he picked up the heavy tool and seemed to survey the area to find the best place to start his attack.

He pulled the sledgehammer over his shoulder and

moved closer to the side of the crumbling structure. With one fast, strong swing, Mason cracked the tool right through the wood and wire. He pulled the hammer back and did it again. Over and over, until there was no way to tell what had been standing moments ago. The splintered pieces lay spread around the crisp white blanket of snow.

"Well done," she said with an approving nod. "Ready for something else to destroy now that we're warmed up?"

"I'll need a little more than this to hit that barn with," he joked.

"Oh, there's an old shed that we could both lay into. I could use an outlet myself."

Mason swiped his arm across his forehead. A sheen of sweat covered his dark skin, and the sun seemed to make him glisten like the freshly fallen snow…which were things she definitely shouldn't be noticing. Not from her bestie, not from her rock, who'd always been there.

"Want to discuss the issue with the ex?" he asked.

Darcy snorted. "Not particularly. But I'll just say, you'll meet him. Tanner doesn't stay away for long, and he's pretty persistent."

Mason's brows drew in. "Is he a problem?"

"Oh, no. He's harmless. He's just convinced we're destined for happily-ever-after together." Darcy slid her hands into the pockets of her coat. "I'm not even sure such a thing exists, let alone enough to try to attempt it with a guy that makes me feel like I'm kissing my nonexistent brother."

"So he thinks he's in love with you?"

Darcy shrugged. "He's never said the word, thankfully. But he does talk about our future together. I've tried as nicely as possible to act like I'm setting him free for someone better, but he swears there's nobody like me."

"He's not wrong."

Despite the heat from the physical exertion, those three words sent a shiver through her. His deep brown eyes locked on her and Darcy wondered why she couldn't feel this spark and connection with Tanner. Why did she have an inkling of attraction for Mason? Was it because she hadn't spent time with him in so long? Did she just miss him? Or maybe there was more to her sudden emotions. No matter the reason, she needed to check herself and keep control over these thoughts.

"Grab the sledgehammer," she told him. "Follow me."

As she headed toward the shed on the other side of the frozen pond, she had to keep repeating to herself that they were just friends. Nothing more. There could *be* nothing more.

Years ago, when they were in their late teens, she'd wondered if they should explore something beyond their friendship. But they'd never even kissed, and he'd never once indicated that he was interested in anything more than the relationship they'd already developed. He'd been so tied up with working for Hank and with baseball that there had not been room for dating or girls… though many ladies in Willowvale had tried to capture his attention.

Dodging any attraction she'd had for him had been the only option years ago. She'd wanted him to pursue his dreams, not allowing anything or anyone to hold him back…including herself.

And now? Well, she wasn't sure anything had changed. His career might have hit a major wall, but he'd come back stronger than ever. He had more pressing matters to attend to than her feelings. Not to mention, she was working toward her own goals. Mason wasn't in town to start anything other than his journey on the road to recovery.

If she focused on her own issues as well as helping her friend heal, maybe all of that would overshadow the unwanted need she had for the best person she'd ever known.

Mason reached behind his back and grabbed a handful of his T-shirt. He pulled the damp material up and over his head, discarding it on the kitchen table. Darcy hung her jacket on the one peg by the back door. They'd nearly demolished the shed, and despite the cold air, they'd both worked up quite a sweat. Darcy had made good use of her hard swings. She might have had more frustration built up than he did if her whacks had been any indication.

Who was this guy that was so hung up on her? Not that Mason could blame the dude. If someone was looking for a gorgeous, strong, independent woman to settle down with, who also happened to be a kick-ass pilot, there was no better option than Darcy. But clearly she didn't believe in fairy tales, not that he was surprised.

Her parents had divorced when she'd been young, and all of that bouncing back and forth had taken a toll on her.

Darcy pulled her sweatshirt over her head and folded it before placing it on the counter. She adjusted her glasses and turned to face him with a wide smile. That familiar grin sent a punch of lust straight to his gut, and not for the first time that day.

This bout of unwanted feelings and thoughts had to stop. He hadn't even been back in town a full day, and he'd already reverted back to the guy he'd always been around Darcy. He'd successfully dodged this magnetic pull of desire for years by staying busy with baseball and work. He couldn't cut her out of his life, not when she'd been his closest friend and confidant. But he also couldn't take the chance of stepping into intimate territory with her and ruining the best relationship he'd ever had.

Why did he let those tantalizing thoughts creep in? Why did he allow anything other than a platonic feeling enter their relationship? Even though she knew nothing of his years of wonder and infatuation with her, he had to find a way to make this stop. He'd lost so much already…losing his best friend would utterly destroy him. She was the last good, solid aspect of his life.

"Pizza should be here anytime, and so should the grocery delivery," she told him as she readjusted her ponytail. A few stray strands of hair clung to creamy skin on her neck, and that tank top seemed to hug every curve.

He forced himself to look away. The last thing he

needed was to put more muddled thoughts in his mind or screw up the very best relationship he'd ever had. Hell, Darcy was the longest relationship he'd ever had. Perhaps that's why this was the strongest bond he'd ever formed…and the very reason he couldn't risk pushing anything beyond the friend zone.

He sure as hell wasn't in any place to enter a relationship, let alone an experimental one that could fail and push Darcy away forever.

Darcy stretched her hands high above her head and stretched. "That felt amazing."

The small gap between her tank and her jeans gave him a glimpse of bare skin he knew would feel silky beneath his fingertips. Thankfully for his sanity, her stretch didn't last long, but it had been long enough to add fuel to his fantasies.

"You want to start demolishing anything in here?" she asked with a sweet laugh.

"I'm good for the day."

Her eyes did a little traveling of their own over his bare torso, and a flare of desire spread through him. He'd seen her in a bathing suit before, and dolled up for proms. Why did a fitted tank paired with wayward hair and adorable tortoiseshell glasses get him?

This was Darcy, and this was the safest he'd felt in months. Right now, that's what he needed, whether he wanted to admit such a thing or not.

He just hadn't been with a woman in so long. He'd focused on his game, then on his recovery. He'd pushed aside anything physical or intimate for the better part of a year, and the lengthy gap in his once-active social life was taking a toll on his common sense.

"You know you don't have to babysit me," he told her. "I don't forget everything, and I'm sure you have other things to do."

Darcy shrugged as she reached for her cell, which she'd left on the counter. She tapped a few things, her brows drawing together as she read something. Then she set the cell back down and focused on him.

"I already told you, I have no flights today, and if you are trying to get rid of me, just ask."

"If I wanted to get rid of you, I'd definitely ask. I just don't want you to feel like you have to babysit."

"Are we going through this again? I want to see my best friend. I certainly don't want to babysit a grown man. If I did, I'd still be dating Tanner."

Mason couldn't help but laugh. "Can't wait to meet the guy. What drew you to him in the first place?"

"I flew him and a couple of his buddies to and from a golfing trip in Oregon. He was adorable at first, and he had some pretty good flirty lines. I fell for it."

"So things changed when he kissed you?"

Darcy shook her head. "I don't really know. I mean, the dates were fun at first, and there were no expectations. Just, you know, a picnic or a movie. Really laid-back and nice. I never felt a spark, but thought maybe that would develop. Then a few kisses proved that wasn't happening. Unfortunately, *he* thought something magical happened, because he kept asking me to spend the night at his place."

Mason inwardly cringed. The instant image of Darcy

in some faceless man's bed really grated on his nerves. Which was positively ridiculous. She wasn't an innocent, and neither was he. Yet the idea of someone else knowing her on a deeper level didn't seem fair. He knew every single thing about her...except how to turn her on.

How was she in bed? Did she demand control, or would she relinquish it to her lover? Did she cuddle afterward or need her space? Did she have that one certain spot that would drive her wild? Like a kiss behind the ear or on the sensitive part where the shoulder curved up to the neck?

Mason muttered a curse beneath his breath and raked a hand down his bare chest.

Darcy took a step forward. "You all right?"

The concern lacing her voice and prevalent in her wide eyes had him cursing once again. No, he was not all right. He had unwanted thoughts flooding his mind, and she thought he had an issue because of his injury.

"I could use some sweet tea." He turned toward the cabinets and started searching for a pitcher or some leftover tea bags, though he doubted he'd find anything. "Think there's anything in here to make that?"

He turned back to face her and she crossed to him with those worry lines deepening between her brows.

"We'll come up with something, but you had a weird look on your face, and now you're dodging me." She tipped her head and shot him that look of worry he'd seen way too much lately. "You sure everything is okay?"

Not even a little.

"Perfectly fine," he lied. Thankfully, a knock on the

door gave him the out he needed. "You see what you can find for the tea—I'll get the door. I assume you're sticking around after pizza?"

She shot him a wink as she patted the side of his face. "You can't get rid of me."

Yeah, that's exactly what he both loved and feared.

Four

"I bet you can't go a week without someone asking for an autograph."

Mason curled his fingers around his can of soda as they sat on the floor in the dusty old living room. Darcy had found some old sheets in the storage closet and created a quick carpet picnic for their fancy pizza dinner. The groceries had been delivered and put away while she'd set up their dining experience.

"A week?" He scoffed. "Not a problem. I don't plan on leaving the house."

Darcy leaned back against the couch and extended her legs to cross her ankles.

"You're leaving the house," she retorted. "You can't hide here. What on earth would you possibly do?"

Mason shrugged, and she waited on him to give her

a valid excuse. She held his gaze and quirked her brow, offering a sweet smile and knowing she had him.

"See? No reason to stay holed up here," she added. "We need to talk about what you're going to do with the place, though."

Her cell vibrated by her leg before he could answer, and she glanced at the screen. She dropped her head back to the sofa cushion, unable to suppress a groan.

"Tanner?" Mason chuckled.

Darcy started to reach for the cell, but in a flash, Mason had beat her to it. He picked up the phone and tapped the screen.

"Hello?"

Darcy stared as Mason shot her a wink and a grin. That simple act sent a curl of desire through her. Why was he looking so darn hot right now? This wasn't the superstar Mason Clark so many people idolized on TV. There he sat, barefoot, with jeans and a tee that fit his excellent muscle tone all too well. His beard seemed a little more scraggly than usual, but he seemed content, and after all he'd been through, she'd take it. But still at that damn friend level.

Maybe she could help him find that road to happiness, that purpose for his life now that his career had been taken away. She couldn't imagine how he felt. If someone told her she couldn't fly anymore, she didn't know what she'd do.

"She's busy right now," Mason replied. "I'm happy to give her a message."

He waited a bit, still keeping his attention on her.

"This is Mason. You know about me, I'm sure."

Oh, there went that arrogance some might find annoying, but she found it…well, attractive. And honestly, at this point, she didn't mind him intervening in her calls from Tanner. The guy was nice enough, but he really needed to move on.

"I'll tell her you called." Mason tapped the screen once again and handed the cell back over. "He said it's urgent."

"I'm sure it is." Darcy took her phone and laid it back beside her hip. "Anyway, what were we talking about?"

"You were harassing me about not leaving the house," he reminded her. "Which won't be a problem. I'll need to be here to check on what needs to be fixed or updated. Meet with a real estate agent to see the value and worth of the property. I have a great many things to keep me busy without stepping foot off the estate."

"You're coming to my house tomorrow for dinner," she informed him.

"I am?"

Darcy nodded. "I have a couple of flights tomorrow, but I'm planning on making you dinner. I have a new recipe I've been wanting to try."

"Why am I the guinea pig?" He snorted. "Try it out on Tanner as you send him off on his final goodbye."

Darcy reached for the pizza box and closed the lid. She pulled her legs up and crossed them as she narrowed her gaze.

"I've already told him goodbye," she repeated. "And if I made him dinner, he'd drag me to the altar right then. No way can I chance that."

Mason came to his feet and stared down at her. "What time should I be there?"

Darcy checked her phone for her flights, because even though she knew the plan, she liked to have everything nice and neat in her world. Plans were her second-best friend.

"I'll be home around six, and it should take me an hour to make everything." She glanced from her flight plans to Mason. "Come on over anytime. I'll text you the code to get in now." She entered the digits, then pressed Send.

Darcy shoved her phone inside her pocket and started to stand, but Mason reached his arms out in a silent offer to help her.

She slid her fingers over his palms and let him tug her. The moment she came to her full height, she started to ease her hands away, but Mason held tight.

"I know you want to figure out what's going on with me, and I know every part of you wants to fix me." His eyes searched hers as he pulled in a deep breath, as if trying to find his words. "You have to understand that I might not be fixable."

Her heart ached for him, not only for everything he'd been through, but mostly because he believed he couldn't get better or have a fulfilling life now.

She held his hands tight between their chests. "And you have to understand your life isn't over and maybe something better is right around the corner."

He opened his mouth to say something, but she wanted to leave him with that thought, so she dropped her hands and stepped back. Mindful of the pizza box on the floor, she stepped around it.

"I have an early flight tomorrow, but like I said, come over anytime if you get sick of being here. You have my code."

She grabbed her coat and keys before heading out the door. Every part of her wanted to stay, to dig into his mind, but he'd dealt with enough on his first day back.

Did she want him to stay for good? Of course she'd love to have her best friend back. Part of her also wanted to explore her feelings, but there was too much fear in taking that risk.

Her worry over him had clearly clouded her judgment. Taking a chance on more could ruin absolutely everything. Was she ready to take that step? Was she ready to express the emotions that had lived deep inside her for so long?

If she only knew exactly how Mason felt, that would help with her decision. But there was no way to find out unless she just made a move…which left her right back where she'd started, with no clear answer.

The two-story cottage with a wraparound porch screamed *Darcy*. The place not only looked like her style inside, it *smelled* like her. Maybe coming onto her turf wasn't the smartest move right now. Perhaps staying at the musty, run-down farmhouse was the better option. He'd found a suitable bedroom there, a guest room on the second floor. Once he had hot water, he'd be golden.

Mason stood in the middle of her living room, which

seemed much more home and hearth than his penthouse suite in the city. With her plush white sectional dotted with colorful throw pillows, and the fat ottoman with a fluffy throw draped across it, she definitely had a thing for softness and comfort.

But it was all the photos on the walls and built-in shelving that really had him mesmerized. So many variances of Darcy either in the cockpit smiling from ear to ear or standing on the runway by a plane giving the photographer two thumbs-up. That radiant grin of hers had always been contagious. It was impossible to be in a bad mood around Darcy. She loved life and insisted those around her do the same. She wanted her neat and tidy little world to be all butterflies and rainbows.

Unfortunately, sometimes storms came along and knocked you down.

Mason started to take a seat on the sofa and scroll aimlessly through social media, but an unrecognizable chime cut through the cottage. He glanced around and out the front window, then realized her alarm system had alerted to someone in the drive.

He might not know too many people since leaving town, but he didn't have to think too hard to identify this stranger stepping from his SUV. The tall, lanky man had to be Tanner. Head down, he pulled his coat tighter around his neck as he strode with purpose toward the front door.

Mason was not at all surprised when the beeps keyed into the door slid the lock open. Tanner, or who he assumed to be Tanner, stepped right in as if he'd done so many times before...and likely, he had. Talking with

Darcy about not giving her code to people would be the first order of business when she got back.

Tanner's eyes widened as he stepped over the threshold.

"Tanner, I presume?" Mason asked, crossing his arms over his chest.

The unwanted guest nodded as he came in from the cold and closed the door behind him.

"Mason," Tanner said.

Of course the guy recognized him. Mason wasn't arrogant, but he was aware of his celebrity status.

"Darcy isn't here," Mason informed the guy.

Tanner slid his hands into his pockets and nodded. "I know. I called over to the airport, and they said her flight had just come in. She'll do her postflight check and be here anytime."

Mason gritted his teeth and resisted the urge to push this guy back out the door. But this wasn't his house, and Darcy would have to be the one to tell Tanner to go. Mason didn't have a leg to stand on, really. How could he be upset when he'd pushed her away these past few months? Clearly, Tanner had slid right in and made himself comfortable.

Still, the idea of this guy knowing so many aspects of Darcy's life and integrating himself in areas Mason should be involved in really irritated the hell out of him. For years, Mason had been gone, living his own life. Darcy had come to some of his games, and they had kept in touch through phone calls and texts, but after the accident, he'd closed in on himself and shut her out. All the while, this undeserving man had inched his way into Darcy's world. She didn't want him here—she'd told him as much—yet here he stood, in her living room, after using her private code.

Yes, she should be the one to tell Tanner to go, but that didn't mean Mason couldn't help things along and drive the point home.

"So, you're in town for good now?" Tanner asked after a long, awkward stretch of silence.

Well, Mason didn't feel too awkward, but the way Tanner shifted from one foot to another and couldn't decide to have his hands in or out of his pockets was a pretty good indicator that he wasn't comfortable with the turn of events.

"For now," Mason said.

No need to supply any more information than necessary. Even if Mason knew his plans, no way would he be sharing them with the guy who should be exiting Darcy's life.

Mason honestly had no clue what Darcy had ever seen in this guy. She'd mentioned some flirty lines and charm, all Mason saw was an unsure guy who looked like he wanted to turn and run.

The back door opened and closed, pulling Mason's attention from Tanner. Darcy stepped from the kitchen and into the living room and stilled. She was still wearing her puffy coat with her hair up and glasses in place. Her eyes darted from Tanner to Mason.

"Having a party without me?" she asked.

Mason knew that look, with her wide eyes and forced grin. She wanted out of this situation.

Without thinking, he closed the distance between

them and wrapped an arm around her. A gasp escaped her a second before he covered her mouth with his.

Finally.

After all this time, that's all Mason could think: finally. He'd wondered about this moment for years. Not that he wanted an audience, but damn. He couldn't pull himself away.

An overwhelming need consumed him. He hadn't known how much he had needed her until right this second. How could he have known how great his desire was before now? This one taste, this intimate touch... He wanted more.

Darcy sank against him and parted her lips, shocking the hell out of him. She was fully embracing the moment, and he wasn't sure how to unpack that important kernel of information. What would they do now that he'd pushed them both over that point of no return?

Mason eased back and forced himself to stay in this character he'd created.

"Glad you're home," he murmured, knowing Tanner stood only feet away, taking everything in. "Need help with dinner?"

Good grief. Where did this familial verbiage come from? He sounded like the husband who'd been waiting on his wife to come home from work. Even crazier, this whole scenario actually felt pretty natural.

"Mason."

His name came through her lips on a whisper, tightening that ball of lust in his gut.

He didn't know what to say to her, but he did know what to say to Tanner.

Keeping his arm around Darcy, Mason turned to face his new adversary.

"We're about to have dinner. Did you need something?"

Tanner's eyes darted back and forth, as if he didn't believe what he was seeing.

"Darcy, are you serious?" Tanner asked. "We have something between us."

"I've tried to tell you, Tanner."

Darcy's tone seemed both sorrowful and conflicted. Mason had to assume the conflict came from the impromptu kiss…the one that still had him shaken.

The man had the audacity to look wounded. "You didn't tell me you were cheating on me."

Mason unwrapped himself and took a step to stand between them.

"There's no cheating," Mason demanded. "She broke things off with you and has obviously moved on. It's time for you to do the same."

Tanner looked as if he wanted to say something, but apparently, common sense kicked in. He turned toward the door and let himself out without saying another word.

Mason watched through the window until Tanner got back into his car, turned it around, and pulled out of the drive. Only then did he let out a breath and face Darcy.

"What the hell was that?" she demanded.

"Tanner left."

Darcy jerked the zipper of her coat. She kept giving it a yank, muttering something about not believing what he had just done.

Mason moved across the living room and eased her hands away, noticing that they trembled. He slid the zipper down with ease and pushed the coat off her shoulders. He took the garment and tossed it over the side of the sofa before directing his focus solely on Darcy.

He placed his hands on her shoulders and stared down into her eyes.

"I can't believe you did that," she repeated.

"Did you want Tanner out of your life?" he asked. "Whatever you were doing or saying wasn't getting through to him. The guy used your code to let himself in. You can't keep giving that code out to people you're dating. You need to change that now."

Darcy snorted and rolled her eyes. "Are you kidding me? We're going to talk about my locks and not the obvious topic that needs addressed?"

Mason dropped his hands but didn't take a step back. How could he? That electric charge between them gave him no choice but to remain close. And he knew she'd felt it too, or she wouldn't have fallen into him, into the kiss.

The fire in her eyes matched the heat he'd experienced in her kiss. He'd seen her angry before over the years, but he'd never experienced that passion. Now that he had, he wanted to see more of this side of her.

"Someone needed to take charge," he explained. "It worked, didn't it?"

"Maybe so, but that kiss…"

She shook her head, as if she wanted to say something more. Because that kiss *was* something more.

"You felt it."

Her eyes widened and her mouth dropped at his bold statement.

"Is that what you want to talk about?" he asked. "The fact that you weren't just playing a part for Tanner? That you actually liked that I kissed you."

Mason didn't see her hand coming until she smacked his chest.

"You have no idea if I liked that or not." She snarled, her eyes narrowed and locked onto him.

"No?"

Mason leaned in, towering over her until she had to tip her head back to keep her focus on him.

"I bet I can get you to lean into me again," he murmured.

Part of him wanted her to make this stop. To stop him before he completely lost his mind and pulled them even further away from friendship and into something completely unfamiliar.

The other part of him, the primal, aching part, wanted her to shut up and let him put that mouth to better use.

"I bet you can't." She tipped her chin in defiance. "I bet this experiment is going to tank, and you'll see that I never—"

He crushed his mouth to hers, wrapping his arms around her waist. Flattening his palms against her back, he took everything she offered because she also was not holding back.

She melted against him just like moments ago…only now there was no audience and no reason to stop. But he had to stop. All he had wanted to do was to prove a point, and he'd done just that if the way she clung to his shoulders was any indication.

Mason released her mouth and his hold on her. When she stumbled and quickly caught herself, he merely smiled.

"Looks like I won that bet."

Shaky fingertips came to her lips for the briefest of moments before she squared her shoulders.

"So, you can kiss? So what?" she asked. "I haven't been kissed like that in a long time, so thanks."

Thanks? *Thanks?*

The ball of desire still hadn't uncurled from his gut and all she could say was *thanks*?

Fine. He didn't care to pretend if that's how she wanted to go about this.

"Do you need help with dinner?" he asked.

Darcy blinked, clearly surprised that he didn't press the kiss issue. He didn't have to. The way her hands had shaken, the way she had held on to him, the way she had returned his passion were all telltale signs that she'd enjoyed their encounter just as much as he had.

He just had no idea what the hell to do with that fact. He wanted her, that much was clear, and something he certainly couldn't deny anymore. On the other hand, he couldn't leave the friend zone behind. He had to keep her as his rock, his sounding board. She'd been the only constant in his life other than baseball, and now that was gone. He needed her more than he wanted to admit, and he'd just have to put his wants on hold until he could heal and think properly.

But that didn't mean he couldn't fantasize about that kiss.

Five

Darcy punched in her calculations once again and stared at the numbers. She hadn't even started her Christmas shopping, and she still wasn't at her goal. She'd set a specific number for each month so she could continue to save for her own plane, with the ultimate goal of hiring employees and buying a second plane. The ideal endgame for her would be to have her own fleet and her own company. She didn't want to just fly. She wanted to make a name for herself in the air charter business.

Sharing the Cessna wasn't convenient, but it did offer her a way to save money.

She sat back in the creaky old leather chair in the office she used at the airport. The place smelled like coffee and leather. She was the only female pilot, so they'd taken pity on her and given her a space of her own.

She'd brought in air fresheners, but the entire building still smelled like an old man.

Darcy stared at the glaring number and groaned. She had to figure out how to pick up more flights. At this rate, she'd never grow her business and have her own fleet. Growing up, she hadn't been too encouraged to chase her dreams. Her parents had thought her love of flying was just a hobby or something she would outgrow. They'd encouraged college and stuffy jobs, but she'd gotten her pilot's license and never looked back.

She wanted to be free, to have the ability to set her own schedule, but still enjoy her career. Making a living didn't have to be done inside four walls, and there was no reason not to go into a field she loved.

Unfortunately, her parents had never gotten on board with her flying career. They ended up divorcing, yet moving across the country to sunny Florida not long after Darcy graduated. They couldn't live together and they couldn't live apart. They had the oddest "marriage" she'd ever heard of.

She talked on the phone occasionally with her mom and even less with her dad, but she had a feeling they were still disappointed in her decision. Not to mention the fact that she still remained in Willowvale Springs, unmarried and far from the CEO of her own Fortune 500 company.

Honestly, she'd stopped caring if her parents were disappointed. She couldn't keep living her life for them and be all the things they wanted: perfect in her career and thriving in a big city with a husband and kids.

Having a husband wasn't necessarily in her cards or

something she'd put on her to-do list. She was just fine on her own, building her charter empire. Well, she'd start building it as soon as her bank account got a bit more padded.

But concentrating on how to generate more business was becoming a struggle since her thoughts kept drifting to her bestie. How could she remain focused on work when her still-tingling lips were stuck on last night. Mason had taken their relationship to a whole new level. Oh, he might have pretended he was playing some game with Tanner, but that kiss had been as real as it got.

Her cell dinged, and she glanced at the screen, sure she'd see either Tanner or Mason. Odd, she never thought she'd find herself in some love triangle. Not that she was in love with either man, or even in a romantic relationship with one, for that matter. Yet here she was, caught in some bizarro world of Mason's making, and she had no idea what move to make next. She still couldn't comprehend the kiss that had curled her toes or why her very best friend in the entire world had such a strong effect on her.

She couldn't deny her attraction to Mason, but why now? Why was he jealous and making a move now? Had he always looked at her this way? She had so many questions, and one just led to the next as she scrolled through her cell.

But her screen only showed a text from one of her pilot buddies, Mitch.

You and the ball player an item now? Heard he was back in town.

Darcy stared at the words on her phone and blinked, sure she'd read them wrong. But no. Somehow Mitch had already heard something about last night, and she had no clue how. Mason certainly wasn't talking to anyone about the kiss or Tanner. At least, she trusted him not to and she honestly didn't know who he'd go gossiping to. She sure as hell hadn't told anyone.

So that left Tanner. Who was he talking to? More importantly, why?

Goodness. What had he said?

Mitch had lived in Willowvale Springs for his entire seventy-plus years. He knew who Mason was, and "the ball player" really downplayed Mason's superstar status. But Mitch had never been impressed with celebrity status or fame. Oh, he thought it was cool that someone from their tiny town had made it big, but Darcy found his message somewhat amusing. Well, amusing once she processed the shock of his knowledge of events.

Darcy debated not answering, but staying silent would likely only make Mitch call or swing by her office.

She quickly typed a vague reply.

Mason is back but not to stay. I'm helping him figure out what to do with Hank's homestead.

There. Not one lie in her message. Mason had no intention of staying, though she loved having him back. They'd never spent a dull moment together in all their years of friendship. From kindergarten through their teenage years, and then off and on when they'd seen each other as adults.

But last night…they had entered a whole new level of adventure she wasn't sure she was ready for.

On the other hand, she couldn't ignore either of those kisses. Nothing even remotely as tantalizing or arousing had happened to her with Tanner. Hell, nothing as pleasurable had ever happened to her. She wasn't sure if that was pathetic or an eye-opener. Both, probably.

Darcy relaxed back in her seat and closed her eyes. She needed to focus on her career, on her goal of building her own company, and possibly moving from Willowvale Springs to do so. What started out as her proving to her parents that flying wasn't just a hobby, but a passion, had turned into her proving to herself that she could do even more. She could pilot the plane, yes, but she could have her very own fleet someday and make an impact in the male-dominated world of flying.

At this point in her life, her parents were the least of her concerns. She was setting out to change the world for herself by putting her dreams first.

Yet her mind simply wasn't having any of that today.

Mason had been back in town a whole day and was already muddling her plans.

Her cell vibrated on the desk once again, and she leaned forward, fully expecting to see Mitch's name, but she didn't recognize the number that popped up.

Her heart kicked up when she read the message and realized this was a new client asking about dates and services. Darcy had her regulars who wanted to get places quickly and with ease, but anytime she could get a new customer, she wanted to make sure they knew she would go above and beyond to meet their needs.

She checked her calendar and sent an immediate reply, securing two more flights for next week. This time of year could be tricky with Wyoming's finicky weather, but the picturesque area always brought in more tourism because of its beauty. And with Christmas right around the corner, everyone wanted to come here and experience the small-town magic, with its wintery white snow-lined streets and mountains.

This flight actually would be the family of some locals coming in for an early holiday visit from South Dakota. She almost had enough saved up to buy her own plane—used, but still her very own. From there, she had every intention of starting to look to add pilots under her. This business venture would be daunting and time-consuming and beyond costly, but she had an impeccable record and a stellar reputation. She loved everything about flying and wanted to dominate the private industry.

One day...

Darcy had just pulled up the schedule on her computer to input the flights and mark that the plane was in use when her cell vibrated again. Her hand hovered over the keys as she shifted her attention to her phone once again. This time the text was from Mason.

Meet me at the farm at six.

Wasn't that just like him to make demands? He'd always been that way, and at first it used to irritate the hell out of her, but then she realized she was his go-to.

He felt safest with her; he felt secure and always knew she'd be there for him.

Which is why when he'd been injured and he'd pushed her away, those months had stung. And that topic still needed to be discussed at length, whether he wanted to or not.

She finished logging all of her flight information before responding that she'd be there closer to six thirty. He might make demands, but that didn't mean she had to jump at them.

Although she very nearly jumped his entire body last night after that second kiss. The second kiss that proved the first one wasn't a fluke magical moment.

Darcy wasn't sure if she wanted him to keep his lips to himself or if she wanted him to take charge and kiss her again. Regardless of what she did or didn't want, people around the town thought they were an item. Now she had to figure out how to put out that fire before she went up in flames.

Mason kicked the loose piece of trim away from the wall. He'd gone from room to room earlier today, looking at the photos on the walls, trying to figure out what to do with the contents and wondering if he should renovate or sell as-is.

The old home had been built well over fifty years ago and had undergone the necessary updating and decor changes. But the trim was the same. The wide-plank floors were the same. Even the old banister leading from the entryway up to the second floor was the same. There were several components he'd want to preserve. Hank and Edith hadn't had children of their own, but they'd employed so many teens from Willowvale Springs and the surrounding areas. They'd taken in anyone who'd needed a job and could work hard. Now that they were gone, Mason had a sense of duty to honor both of them.

He'd had a new water heater installed because, a couple of cold showers later, he'd been convinced that quick investment was a matter of survival. But where did it end? He had the time to renovate, and he definitely had the financial means, but did he want to devote all of that time and money? Did he want to take all of this on alone and be stuck here for who knew how long?

Being back in town so close to Darcy, especially after their intimate moments last night, had really taken its toll on his mind. He hadn't slept well, which had only made him cranky. But even more so, he wanted to kiss her again. He wanted to do a hell of a lot more, but only a jerk would take advantage of the one constant and good thing left in his life. They were both in a vulnerable position, and he still didn't want her pity. Maybe she wasn't offering it, but he had to make sure it stayed that way.

There were so many moving parts in his life right now, he had no clue how the hell to keep everything straight.

Sexual frustration, coupled with confusion on what to do with this run-down farm, in conjunction with his head injury... Mason was ready to leave town and head to some tropical island alone where his only worry would be what time to have his meals delivered to his beach cabana.

He pulled his cell from the pocket of his jeans and checked the time once again. After six thirty and still no Darcy. No text, either.

His California lifestyle had him hating all this snow and cold. The weather wasn't great, but she'd never lived anywhere else. He hoped she hadn't gotten into an accident and was off the road somewhere. Worry had him going to the foyer and glancing out the old oak-and-glass door. No headlights yet.

He shot off a quick text asking if she was on her way. Like some anxious teen, he stared at the screen waiting for her reply. Nothing.

After ten minutes, he really tried not to let panic set in, but the flurries continued to fly. All he could think was that she'd been hurt and couldn't text or get help. Muttering a curse and developing a level of fear he hadn't experienced in a long time, Mason grabbed his coat by the front door and checked for the keys in the pocket. He'd just stepped onto the front porch when lights cut through the night and slowly made their way up the drive.

A wave of relief swept through him as Darcy pulled to a stop behind his SUV. He didn't even mind the chill that wrapped around him; he was just glad she'd made it.

Darcy stomped through the snow toward the porch, and he made a mental note to shovel the path in the morning. Thankfully, he'd only had a virtual walk-through with his old friend and real estate agent, Paxton Hart. Mason and Pax had worked many summers for Hank, but Pax had always seemed to land at the dude ranch, while Mason had kept his time at the farmstead.

"You're late," he stated as Darcy stomped up the steps.

She yanked her knit cap from her head, sending her dark brown hair falling down around her shoulders. But the look she gave him...something or someone had ticked her off.

"Bad day?"

Mason reached for the door and held it open for her, gesturing for her to get inside. She yanked off her coat and hung it on the hook, then shoved her cap into the side pocket. Mason shut out the cold and waited on her to answer, but she just marched on through the foyer and into the kitchen.

"Did you make dinner?" she asked, opening the fridge.

"Um...no. I can if you're hungry."

She whipped around. "What I am is annoyed. And I'm late because I had an office full of nosy men who are all aware of our relationship status, thanks to your little stunt last night."

Mason realized he still had his coat on, so he removed it and draped it over one of the old kitchen chairs around the table. He propped his hands on his hips and stared back at Darcy, who clearly had not had a good day and felt the need to direct her anger toward him.

Because of a kiss? He shouldn't find that amusing, yet he did.

"So, we're dating?" he asked, unable to hide his smile. "This might be my first relationship not broadcast all over the media."

Darcy's chocolate eyes narrowed. "We're not dating, Mason, and there's no need for the media to get involved. I like my simple life, and I despise lies."

He took a step forward, ignoring her dagger-worthy glare. "Nobody lied. If Tanner thinks we're dating, that's on him."

"You kissed me," she all but shouted. "What else did you want him to think?"

"I thought you wanted him to leave you alone and take the hint that he needed to move on."

"Well, I did, but now he thinks we're dating." She raked her hands through her hair, cursing when her fingers obviously hit a tangle. "I'm not sure who he told, but everyone at the airport knows, and I've been fielding texts and office visitors most of the afternoon and evening."

Mason shrugged. "Then Tanner is likely moving on. Do you want him back now?"

The thought of Darcy finding that sheepish guy attractive really irritated the hell out of Mason. She deserved someone strong, secure, someone who would do anything for her, and someone who would support her in everything she ever wanted. Tanner hadn't looked like he could support an ant farm.

Was it so silly that Mason and Darcy would date? Why? They clearly got along…and that was before the kiss.

"No, I don't want him back. I just have to keep my reputation intact and can't be going around just kissing icons." She scoffed. "Tanner is nice and all, but he's not my type."

"So I'm an icon and he's not your type. Sounds perfect to me."

Darcy rolled her eyes, and he realized that his thought had slipped out and hadn't stayed inside his own head. He would have liked to chalk that up to his injury, but he'd never been one to keep a filter on his thoughts to begin with.

"So, how long do we need to date?" he asked with a wink.

"We're not dating."

"Okay, honey. Now, what do you want to eat?"

"Don't 'honey' me," she grumbled. "I'm not in a fake relationship with my bestie. That's...well, it's wrong."

He didn't see the harm in a little PDA if they had to go into town for anything. Anyone who had lived here any amount of time knew full well that Mason and Darcy had always been inseparable as teens. People wouldn't think anything of it.

"Duly noted," he replied. "Now. Dinner. What did you have for lunch?"

"I ate a sleeve of crackers." She crossed her arms over her chest and sighed. "I'm hangry and cranky."

Mason wrapped his arm around her and pulled her in tighter. "I can see that. Let's get you fed."

"Why were you on the porch when I got here?" she asked.

"I was coming to look for you because you didn't answer my text and the weather is bad."

She snorted. "California made you soft. This isn't bad by any means. I just scheduled more flights. It's only bad if I can't work."

He slid his other arm around her, wanting her even closer. Maybe the city had gotten to him, or perhaps just worry in general had taken its gnarly talons and gotten a grip on him he couldn't shake loose. But the mere thought of her hurt or injured had shaken him in a way he couldn't describe.

"What did you need me here for?" she murmured against his chest.

More kisses.

"We can discuss that after you eat, but I'm torn on the house and need your help."

She nodded and took a step back. "I assume you're selling?"

Okay, maybe they were discussing now.

Mason couldn't bring himself to say those words just yet. Hank had loved this place. He and his wife had made this old farmhouse a home and touched the lives of so many local kids and families.

"I remember Hank always telling me that this was the first property he bought, and he never wanted to leave. I know he had several other properties and businesses in town, but he loved this house. He and his wife made this their home for decades."

Darcy flattened her hand against his chest as she offered one of her sweet smiles. "Are you getting sentimental on me?"

Damn it.

Mason shrugged. "Maybe a little," he admitted. "You're not allowed to tell anyone that."

"Oh, I wouldn't dare," she whispered.

"I spent all day here looking at the pictures on the

walls, seeing the quilts Edith made draped over the beds in the spare rooms, and it's difficult to believe the place I always thought would remain constant had changed drastically."

"That's the bad part about loving someone. They always leave in one way or another. But you have to lean on the memories and the time you spent here. Hank might have been a gruff old guy, but he loved the teens that he employed, and he helped shape an entire generation of hard workers in Willowvale."

Many of the guys from Hank's farms and ranches went on to achieve great successes. Mason knew for a fact that he wouldn't have had his strong work ethic and drive without Hank's guidance. Those weren't exactly lessons he could have learned from his own father, who had found baseball to be a hobby and a waste of time. At least Hank had supported Mason's decision and instilled in him a sense of respect.

"So if you're not selling, does that mean you're staying?" she asked after a bit.

"I can't stay here," he admitted. "You know I'm restless, and I've gotten used to a certain lifestyle. I love the city and all that goes along with it. The fast-paced world, social life, my penthouse. This country world isn't me anymore. Besides, I'm not walking away from baseball. I'm just trying to figure out where I fit now."

Her hand slid away. "So…what? You're going to keep the property and rent it or use it as a second home?"

Mason raked a hand over the back of his neck. "That's what I want your opinion on, but first, let's figure out dinner."

"I'll help." She turned back to the fridge and opened the door once again. "Let's see what we've got."

Yeah, he needed to focus on something other than his selfish wants. And the kisses with Darcy he couldn't repeat.

Six

"He also said that if we replace this whole en suite, that would up the value."

Darcy stifled a yawn as she followed Mason from room to room, going over what Pax had told him during their video walk-through. Darcy had only met Pax a few times, but she'd heard his of reputation of being an elite agent to celebrities. If anyone knew their real estate stuff, it would be him.

"You'd be dumping a good chunk of money into this place."

She leaned against the doorframe and eyed his broad shoulders and tall build inside this tiny room. Why did she have to find him desirable now? Why was she taking in those taut muscles beneath his T-shirt and the way his jeans hugged his narrow hips?

It was those damn kisses. How could those moments be altering her entire thought process? Now she couldn't look at him without feeling those lips on hers or his strong arms around her. He'd kissed her like he'd been starving for her affection for years.

What if he had? What if he'd wanted to kiss her? What if all this time he'd wanted more? Had he given her signals?

Darcy did a mental shake and realized that that line of thinking was ridiculous. Mason was living the high life, no doubt, with sexy women throwing themselves at him constantly. She was far from sexy or someone who turned heads. She wasn't sorry for her looks and definitely wasn't trying to be someone she wasn't. Never would she change for a guy to like her...not even her best friend who had curled her toes with his talented mouth.

All of this stemmed from Tanner and the fake kisses and dating. Maybe Mason was confusing his friend feelings and jealousy game for something more.

"Darcy?" Mason took a step forward. "You with me?"

She blinked, pulling herself back to the moment. "I'm here. Sorry. Zoned out for a minute."

His lips twitched. "I think that's my problem. Is everything okay?"

"Honestly, no." She straightened and moved farther into the room, which brought her toe-to-toe with him. "You've confused me, and I don't like it."

Mason jerked at his own confusion. "With the house?"

"No, not the house." She waved her hand in the air,

dismissing that thought. "I can't stop thinking about the kisses."

His lips twitched again, but now into a naughty grin. "Is that right?"

Darcy barely resisted the urge to roll her eyes. "I'm not complimenting you," she said. "And stop looking at me like that."

"Like what? Like I want to kiss you again?" He leaned over her, giving her no choice but to tip her head back. "Because I do."

Darcy's breath caught in her throat. She couldn't believe his bold words, and she certainly couldn't believe the effect they had on her.

"You don't," she stated without feeling any conviction behind her words. "You...you can't."

His lips barely feathered across hers, but it was enough to have her entire body heating up. She held her breath, afraid that even that bit of movement would break the intense moment. Conflict tore at her. She wanted to erase that sliver of space between them and take what he so blatantly offered. On the other hand, part of her felt she should step back and stop this madness before things truly got to the point of no return.

Then the devil on her shoulder told her she'd already gotten there. They'd kissed twice. What would be the harm of one more?

"Are we betting on this kiss?" she murmured.

"I'm betting that you can't say no."

His warm breath slid over her heated skin, and she decided this was one bet she didn't care if she lost. Why couldn't she take what she wanted...what they both wanted? They were adults. This didn't have to mean anything more, and they didn't have to change their friendship status just because they'd shared kisses. Right?

But at the same time, and at the expense of her sexual frustration, she knew Mason always got what he wanted…or, rather, *who* he wanted.

Darcy took a step back. "I'll take that win."

She patted his face as his eyes widened in shock. Yeah, she'd surprised herself on that one, too. But if he wanted her as a friend, then that's where she needed to be. If he wanted her as something more, then he'd have to come out and tell her—or show her. Their friendship was too fragile for anything to be done half-assed. He'd have to open up about his feelings one way or another.

And that's definitely something she'd have to think about if they reached that point.

"I need to head out," she told him. "I have an early flight. But I like the ideas of renovating, and you clearly have the money. You need to contact Allie Price. Remember her from school? She and her family have a top-notch construction company, not to mention she's a kick-ass designer. I'll text you her information."

Without another word, and because her heart was beating way too fast, Darcy stepped from the room and made her way down the stairs. She had to leave, not because of the early flight, but because she so desperately wanted to change her mind and see if those kisses meant something more than just some red-hot chemistry.

Was it worth exploring and risking years of friendship for something that might lead to absolutely nothing but heartache?

* * *

"So you guys are seriously a couple?"

Darcy propped her feet on the old coffee table Allie had found in an old abandoned home. The repurposed gift was absolutely perfect in the middle of her cozy living room.

"I mean, that's what everyone is saying, but you were so vague with your text the other day," Allie went on as she clutched her glass of chardonnay. "So I thought this might be something you wanted to discuss in person and over a nice bottle of wine."

"There's not much to discuss." Darcy crossed her ankles and took a sip. "You know I've been trying to break things off with Tanner."

Allie sighed. "Oh, Tanner. Such a sweet guy, but totally clueless."

"And you know I don't want to purposely hurt anyone's feelings, but he saw Mason kiss me."

Allie's mouth dropped. "He kissed you? Why didn't you lead with that? More importantly, why didn't you tell me when it happened?"

Because I was too busy kissing him again.

"It's not a big deal," Darcy stated. "We're friends. You know that."

"No big deal? That man is gorgeous. I'd be telling everyone if he kissed me."

Darcy couldn't help but laugh. The kisses were definitely worthy of praise and bragging, but she couldn't exactly tell anyone—not even Allie—how much she'd enjoyed Mason's lips on hers. Darcy still couldn't figure this whole new concept out herself. He confused her and made her want way too many things that she'd never thought of wanting before. He'd opened a new space in her mind, and a variety of thoughts and questions had come spilling out. By testing the boundaries of their friendship, they were overriding common sense. Even worse, she had regrets about walking out last night.

"So, do you have Christmas plans?" Darcy asked, hoping to turn the topic to anything else. "I'm sure you'll be with your family, but maybe we can do something fun one night."

"Fun like we fly somewhere for a nice dinner?" Allie asked with a wide smile.

Darcy nodded. "I'm in. You pick the place and we'll get all dressed up and make a night of it."

"Great. I have just the dress. Speaking of fancy nights out, are you still planning on going to the gala?"

The gala was an annual black-tie event held to raise funds for Willowvale's parks and recreation budget. It was also the perfect opportunity for Darcy to network and score more clients.

Darcy let out a sigh. "I had planned on going with Tanner, but that's obviously not happening. I honestly don't know."

Allie took the last sip of her wine and set her glass on the table before curling back up. "So, what about going with Mason, the local sports hero? I really think we need to talk about the two of you. Because I feel there's more, and the longer that rolls around in my head, I'm kind of liking the idea of you guys together."

Darcy gripped her glass and debated opening up about her feelings to her friend, but at the same time,

Darcy wasn't sure what she would even say. There was no way to explain what had happened or how she felt.

"Given the fact that he's practically a hermit these days, I don't think he'll be chomping at the bit to go to any fundraiser. Besides, we're not together, so don't get too hung up on that notion."

Allie snickered. "I'm not getting hung up on it, but I don't think I'll dismiss it, either. But we can table that topic for now. I don't want to push and scare you, because this might just be a good thing for you, so don't rush."

Yeah. Don't rush. She and Mason had been friends for years. They really couldn't take things slower than they had been, but still, since that first kiss... Darcy felt as if she was speeding downhill on skis with no poles.

"I actually might have another job for you guys if you have any quick openings for a friend," Darcy stated, turning the conversation around. "Mason is thinking of renovating Hank's old farmhouse to sell it. The place is pretty run-down."

Allie tipped her head back. "I haven't been to that farm in years. The house sits so far back from the road, I don't even know the shape it's in."

"It definitely needs love, both inside and out."

"Did you give Mason our information?"

Darcy nodded. Allie and her family had the most reputable construction company in the area, but Allie had taken things a step further and started designing as well. The family could work with any customer, from drab start to fabulous finish.

"I did. I'm sure you'll be hearing from him soon."

"Sounds good. So, that kiss?"

Darcy dropped her head against the back of the sofa and blew out a breath. *Yeah, that kiss...*

Seven

Darcy scrolled through the online images of the new-to-her Cessna she'd been eyeing for some time. Nothing wrong with revisiting the listings every now and then. She had to keep her eye on the goal, right? She'd worked hard to make a name for herself and saved every extra dollar. She wasn't much of a shopper and had no family to spoil. But bills and life just seemed to throw curveballs and she wasn't dumping nearly enough into her savings like she wanted to.

"You have a minute?"

Darcy glanced up at Tanner, who stood right next to her table at Rise 'n Grind, her favorite local coffee shop. She adjusted her glasses and nodded. His eyes landed on her laptop.

"Getting a new planc?" he asked, pointing to her screen.

"It's on my to-do list."

She hadn't opened up to Tanner since she'd known pretty early on that they wouldn't be together long-term. He never seemed to take her milestones or goals seriously anyway. That should be just another red flag as to why he wasn't the one for her. Plus he didn't kiss like Mason.

"Can I have a seat?" he asked.

Darcy hesitated. She didn't want to be rude, but at the same, she didn't want to give him the wrong impression.

"Tanner, I—"

"Hey, babe." *Speak of the devil.*

Mason stepped up on the other side of the table and leaned down to brush a quick kiss across her lips. When he drew back, he started unbuttoning his wool coat and glanced across to Tanner.

"Were you just leaving?"

Darcy inwardly cringed at his bold, impolite question.

Tanner's eyes darted back and forth between Mason and Darcy. She held her breath, hating any type of conflict. Yet here she found herself, smack dab in the middle of some weird fake love triangle—though there was nothing fake about the way her heart raced now when Mason was around—and she had no clue how to get her life back to normal.

"Take care of her," Tanner stated. "She's a good one."

When he walked away, Darcy felt sorry for him. But he'd find the right woman and eventually be happy he wasn't in her life.

Mason draped his coat on the back of the chair across

from her before taking a seat. Darcy eased her laptop aside and leaned closer.

"Why didn't you just come in and pee on me to mark your territory?" she whispered through gritted teeth.

Mason chuckled and rested his forearms on the table. "It's too cold, and I just came in from outside. Shrinkage, you know."

Darcy groaned and closed her eyes. "You're impossible."

"You'd be bored without me," he countered.

Yes, she absolutely would. He'd always been one to crack jokes and keep her smiling. She couldn't imagine her life without him, and now that he was back, she knew watching him leave again would be devastating. Especially now that those friendship lines had been blurred. Once she made sense of her new feelings, she'd have to live it up while he was in town and store all of those memories with her others.

"What are you doing here anyway?" she asked, focusing back on him. "I didn't think you were leaving the farm."

Mason shrugged. "I decided to get out and explore the town a bit to see what all had changed, but then I saw your car out front and pulled in."

He glanced at her laptop and then turned the computer to face him fully. The man knew no boundaries. She reached for her iced peppermint mocha and took a long drink, welcoming the sugary goodness.

"That's a nice plane," he murmured, tapping on the keys. "Seats twelve. Is that larger than what you're doing now?"

He glanced at her above the screen, waiting for her answer.

"I can do eight right now," she told him. "It's just a goal of mine. Something to keep me pushing forward."

"Why don't you just buy it?" he asked, turning the laptop back to her.

Darcy snorted as she closed the screen. "That's the mentality of someone with a padded bank account. I can't just buy a plane, Mason. That's not how the real world works."

She had no doubt, between his years of being the superstar pitcher for the best team in the nation, combined with all of his sponsorship ads and commercials, that he would have no problem "just buying" a plane.

"How much is it?" he asked.

Darcy started to answer when one of the baristas came up with a cup of coffee and a plate. She offered a smile, but the young woman only had eyes for Mason. Darcy couldn't blame her. He was quite the sight to behold, with his dark, flawless skin, nice square jawline, broad shoulders, and muscle tone that should be illegal... Yeah, people should be staring.

"Mr. Clark?" The barista's grin stretched across her face as she set the coffee and pastry down. "I'm sorry to interrupt, but I just wanted to bring this over and thank you. My dad passed away about six months ago, and I sat in his hospice room right before he died. We watched all of your games. But the one against the Rays where you had a shutout? That was our last game together, and one of your best."

Her smile faltered slightly before she pulled in a breath.

"Anyway, it's a memory I'll always have," she went on. "You were my dad's favorite player, and we would always watch."

Darcy's heart broke for the young woman who couldn't have been more than twenty. Darcy had been young when her parents up and moved across the country. Although they were alive, they'd pretty much abandoned her. Still, Darcy couldn't imagine watching a parent slip away.

Mason scooted his chair back and came to his feet. "I should be thanking you," he told her. "I'm sorry for your loss. Not that words can bring him back, but I am sorry. What was your dad's name?"

"Walt."

Mason laid a hand on her shoulder and returned the soft smile. Darcy couldn't tear her eyes away from her bestie. Not only did he have looks that should be illegal, he had a heart of gold. Maybe he was a billionaire with sponsors and several multi-million dollar contracts that had turned him into a household name, but there was still that small-town boy inside of him that had compassion for others.

"I'm glad I could spend that night with you guys," Mason told her. "I wish things had gone differently for both your dad and me."

"I remember watching after you got hit. I was so worried," she told Mason. "I was scared for your future, but you look like you're doing remarkably well."

Darcy caught the muscle in Mason's jaw clenching. Not many people, if any, would notice that, but she knew everything about him. And she knew he was worried about his future as well.

"I'll be just fine," he assured the girl. "I'm on the road to recovery, but I had to hang up my cleats."

The barista glanced from Mason to Darcy and took a step back. "I'm sorry I interrupted. I just wanted to bring you a fresh scone I made and some coffee on the house to say thanks."

"No thanks necessary," he told her. "I'm grateful to have such loyal fans."

When the girl started to turn, she stopped herself and let out a small chuckle. "You know, my little brother is a senior at the local high school, and they need a new baseball coach. If you were looking for something to do while you're here."

Mason made some sound that fell between a grunt and a laugh as he turned back to Darcy. Obviously, she knew of his celebrity status, but seeing him interact one-on-one with fans and locals really touched her heart in ways she couldn't even explain.

"There's a new idea for you," Darcy muttered around the rim of her cup. "Ever thought about coaching at the old school?"

Mason shook his head. "Not once."

The idea seemed almost laughable in a way, but as the thought settled into her mind, she wondered if a to-tally different direction wouldn't be the best thing for Mason at this point. Selfishly, she thought him staying and taking on the lead role was the best plan all the way around. The school would have someone more than qualified to take over, and she would have her bestie back where she needed him. Maybe they could explore the new feelings that had developed between them. How could she not love the idea?

Realistically, though, she knew the chances of any of that happening were slim to none.

Mason picked up his scone and took a bite, likely moving on from any thoughts of local coaching. Something about the almost-joke seemed to dig into Darcy's brain, and she couldn't dismiss the idea so quickly. But she'd hold that kernel of information for another time.

"While I appreciate you helping me with Tanner, maybe tone it down a notch."

Mason paused mid-bite and brought that dark gaze up to land on her. A shiver of arousal slid through her. How could he garner such an instant, potent response from her with just a look? She never had these issues before those damn kisses.

"Why?" he asked.

Darcy blinked. "Why? Because the whole town thinks we're dating."

"Let them." He shrugged and took another bite before reaching for his coffee mug. "Do you know how many articles have been written about me? Only about five percent held any truth."

"Maybe so, but I'm not used to people gossiping about me. And I have a charter empire to build, which won't happen if I'm not taken seriously. We've been over this. The guys at the hangar will never let me live this down." She took a sip of her drink and curled her fingers around her glass as she leaned forward. "I like my nice, quiet life of flying and doing my own thing."

"That sounds fun, but lonely."

Darcy tipped her head. "Really? Coming from the man who has lived as a recluse since his injury?"

"I have a reason," he countered. "You are bright and lively and all that's good. I'm not sure why you're still single, honestly. I thought for sure you'd lose our marriage bet."

Oh, yeah. They'd made that bet back in high school. Their longest running to date. Whoever married first lost and owed the other one a thousand bucks. When they'd been seventeen, that had seemed like so much money... and it was. But they'd chosen a ridiculous amount because they hadn't known what else to choose.

"I haven't found anyone that makes me feel like I'm in the cockpit."

Mason jerked. "Come again?"

Darcy relaxed back in her seat and shrugged. "You know that feeling when you're doing something you absolutely love? I haven't found a man who makes me feel that way. I want that zing of anticipation that I have sitting on the runway right before I'm about to take off. I want that thrill I have with the controls in my hands. So, at this point in my life, I'm married to a Cessna Citation."

"You're saying you won't marry until you get that thrill from a guy?"

Darcy nodded. "Pretty much. Likely I'll be single forever. Looks like you'll be losing that bet, because women throw themselves at you all the time."

"The women who come after me aren't looking for marriage. More like money and sex."

Something akin to sadness flashed in his eyes. Some

celebrities wouldn't mind that setup, but she knew Mason. He had a heart, and he cared. Oh, sure, he had needs and no doubt had scratched that proverbial itch over the years. The tabloids had always glommed onto any gorgeous woman at his side, but he didn't do serious relationships. Like her, he'd opted to marry his career. Only now, his career as he knew it was over.

Maybe he regretted his fast lifestyle. The man she'd always known had been such a giver. Maybe the women and celebrity status that came with his career hadn't been what he'd expected or even wanted. She honestly didn't know.

Darcy didn't like the thought of a woman using him for his bank account or his bedroom. More the bedroom, though, which made no sense. It wasn't as if she had any claims on him, and she certainly wasn't a virgin. But he was more, so much more, than a quick fling. There was a genuine man with a loving soul beneath that sexy exterior.

Still, after those kisses and spending more time with him over these past few days than she had over the past few years, an unexpected burst of jealousy pumped through her at the thought of anyone else warming his sheets.

"Well, that doesn't mean you aren't going to settle down," she countered, hating the thought of another woman coming into his life. "You might fix up that farm and find yourself loving it. Next thing you know, you'll be coaching high school baseball and taking a wife to start having babies with and making your own team."

The look that passed across his face now was nothing less than horror. His mouth dropped, his brows rose, and those deep chocolate eyes widened.

"That's quite the life plan you have laid out for me."

A laugh bubbled up before she could stop herself.

"Well, you don't have to look like I just gave you a death sentence," she fired back. "Relax, Mason. Nobody is dragging you down the aisle or forcing you to stay here. I know you were meant for bigger things than Willowvale Springs."

A sliver of her always wondered if he was bigger than her as well, but every time they got together, things just clicked back into place like before. Still, she couldn't help but feel a void each time he left or their time apart stretched longer and longer.

Mason opened his mouth to say something, but his cell on the table vibrated. Darcy glanced at his screen but couldn't make out the name. When she looked back at him, he had a torn expression, as if he wasn't sure if he should answer or not.

"You need to get that?" she asked.

His eyes darted from the phone to her, then back down.

"It's my former manager."

"Sounds important."

He simply nodded, then finally slid his finger over the screen and lifted the phone to take the call. Darcy wondered if she should move to give him privacy, but he did take the call in public, so...

Attempting not to eavesdrop, she focused back on her laptop and her drink. She wanted to plug a few more flights into her schedule and follow up on some emails with potential new clients. The holiday season always brought in more customers, and she wanted to make sure they moved into the long-term client category. Once people decided to fly private, they had a difficult time going back to commercial, which meant even more job security for her, putting her one step closer to her own plane and the next level in her career.

"A coach?"

Darcy glanced up to find Mason's eyes locked onto hers as he continued his conversation.

"I'm not sure about that," he replied. "When would you need an answer?"

Darcy couldn't look away now. Was he being called back to LA? He'd just gotten here, and they wanted him back? Or would this be for another team? She knew he missed the sport, but did he want to be on the other side of the dugout?

"I understand," he went on. "I'll think about it and let you know."

He disconnected the call and set his cell back on the table. Without a word, he turned his attention to his coffee and took another sip.

"Well? Are you filling me in?" she asked after the much-too-long pregnant pause.

"I have the opportunity to coach my old team," he stated, his tone way too calm.

"You didn't expect this?"

Mason shook his head and set his mug down. Despite the bustling café, silence settled between them as he stared down at the black coffee as if trying to find the answer there.

"What are the odds of two coaching opportunities in one day?" she joked, trying to make light of the earlier proposal. But Mason said nothing, and Darcy knew that that phone call had upended his entire life once again.

And she had no idea what that meant for the farm or their relationship while he was here in Willowvale.

Eight

"What the hell is that?"

Mason stood in the doorway of the farmhouse and took in the sight. He didn't know whether to be shocked or amused.

Darcy was wrestling a live Christmas tree into a bucket and seemed to be trying to level the darn thing. In the middle of the ugly living room, with worn carpeting and a broken burgundy recliner, Darcy was attempting to bring some holiday cheer into the mix.

"It's a BMW." She straightened to look at him, kept one hand on the tree to hold it steady, and adjusted her glasses with her free hand. "It's a tree. What do you think it is?"

He stepped farther into the house and closed the door behind him to shut out the cold.

"Clearly, but you know I'm going to be tearing up

the majority of this house for renovations. Why would you choose to bring a tree in now two months early? We might be tearing out this entire first floor."

"Because this place is depressing, and it's close enough to the holidays. If you tear out the floor, then we'll move the tree upstairs." She raked her gaze up and down his body and laughed. "What were you doing?"

"I took the four-wheeler out and was looking around the property, and then it got dark on me."

Mason went to the bench along the staircase leading to the second story and took a seat. He untied his boots and toed them off before unzipping his overalls and shedding those as well. Layers were key here in this part of the West. December weather was no joke, and his body still hadn't acclimated back to this place. Sure, he'd grown up here, but he'd been gone so long that he had to pretty much wrap his entire body twice from head to toe just to go out for more than a few minutes. There was cold, and then there was Wyoming cold.

"What did you think?" she asked.

Once he'd stripped down to his socks, jeans, and flannel, he crossed the room to help her level the tree.

"I think the main barn is definitely salvageable, which will be a nice draw for someone who needs all of this land and has livestock."

Mason crouched down and grabbed the trunk as he shifted the tree slightly to the right.

"Where did you get this at, anyway?" he asked.

"The side yard. There's a bunch along the property line."

Mason glanced up to where she still held on to the top

portion. He met her gaze and realized she never ceased to amaze him. She flew planes on the daily, she obviously chopped down trees and insisted on a traditional Christmas, and she could kiss unlike any woman he'd ever known in his entire life.

And she held the all-important title of his very best friend.

"Do you ever ask for help with anything?"

Darcy shrugged. "When I need help, I do."

Of course she didn't think she needed help cutting down a tree and hauling it back inside, then putting it up. She would have had it all leveled and decorated had he not come in to assist.

Mason focused back on the tree and shifted it once more before shimmying out from beneath it. He came to his feet and brushed the pine needles from his pants.

"You have lights?"

"I have everything in my car. I ran and grabbed some ornaments and everything after my last flight. I wasn't about to head to the attic to see what Hank had kept."

Darcy released the tree and took a step back. She looked at the thing from all angles before nodding her approval.

"There." She clasped her hands together and shot him a wide smile. "The place already looks better, and you haven't had to do one renovation."

He scoffed. "A fresh Christmas tree doesn't instantly make this farmhouse better."

"Well, it makes me feel better." She narrowed her eyes. "I bet you never even put up a tree in your stuffy old penthouse apartment."

"My penthouse isn't stuffy," he countered.

"The fact that you dodged my question tells me all I need to know." She took a step toward him and patted the side of his face. "I bet you don't even have one present bought yet."

That simple touch of her warm skin against his sent a burst of arousal through him. Mason reached up and gripped her hand in his, then gave her a gentle tug until she landed against his chest.

"I actually purchased one today," he volleyed back. "So you'd lose that bet."

She muttered a curse beneath her breath, obviously hating the reality of defeat. Mason grinned, because she had no idea that the gift was for her. He had to wait until the right moment to present it, and he couldn't wait to see the look on her face.

Darcy licked her lips, pulling every bit of his focus from his thoughts to this vibrant woman in his arms. Well, partially in his arms. Definitely within kissing distance.

Did she want to be kissed again? Had she replayed their kisses over and over like he had? Had she lain awake at night fantasizing about the next steps? Because every single part of him wanted to take those next steps with her, but at the same time, the risk could blow up in his face.

"You given any more thought to going back to your team to coach?" she murmured.

Mason suppressed a grin. "Is that what you want to discuss?"

"It's something I want to know," she admitted. "But right now, I'm confused."

"About?"

"You kissing me and the way you're looking at me, like you want to do it again."

He inched a fraction closer. "Because I do," he whispered.

"Is this crazy, though?"

That soft question held absolutely no conviction. She continued to look back at him as if nothing else existed. Had she ever looked at him that way before? Oh, she'd given him her friend look, her compassionate look, and the one where she thought he was being ridiculous. Of course, they also had their inside joke looks they'd pass each other in public. Their silent communication had always been one of their strongest bonds. He knew Darcy inside and out, but part of him still wanted more. He couldn't explain his reasoning, even to himself. All he knew was that he wanted her in every sense of the word.

But he wasn't staying in Willowvale, and she didn't want a relationship.

But maybe…

Just maybe…

That meant they were on the same page. If neither wanted a commitment, but the chemistry kept pulling them together, then perhaps they—

"What's that look?" she muttered. "You have a different one now. Almost like…"

"Like I want you?" Mason grazed his lips across hers and replied, "I do."

Darcy's swift intake of breath, coupled with her tight

grip on his hand, had his gut tightening with anticipation. He'd had no clue how she'd respond to his bold,
yet honest, statement. But her reaction gave him hope…

"What about after?" she asked.

That anticipation rose to the next level. If she had
questions, then her curiosity had been piqued, and she
had been having similar thoughts.

"What about it?" he volleyed back. "We're adults,
Darcy. We can do what we want and nobody has to
know."

He waited a beat, but when she didn't answer, he went
on. "People think we're dating anyway," he reminded
her. "One night won't hurt anything."

He hoped. Hell, they'd come this far over the friend
line. What was one more step?

"Will things get weird between us?" she asked.

Mason freed her hand so he could use both of his to
frame her face. He wanted her full attention because,
above all else, he wanted her to know she'd be safe with
him.

"Absolutely not," he insisted. "I won't let that happen."

"You can't guarantee everything won't change between us."

"I can't," he agreed. "But I can tell you that we've been
friends for far too long for anything to get between us.
Our bond is too strong to ever be destroyed."

She continued to stare back, desire mixed with worry
swirling through her wide eyes. If she wanted him even
an iota of how much he wanted her, he'd make damn
sure she was comfortable every step of the way.

"But if you don't want this, then we won't." Another

vital point he needed to make. "I'll never do anything to hurt you. You're in control here."

A slow smile spread across her face as her eyes lit up. "I never thought those words would come out of your mouth."

"I never thought my best friend would consider letting me take her to bed."

Even though her smile faded, that sparkle in her eye transformed into a fiery passion he'd never seen from her before.

"How did we get here so fast?" she asked, sliding her hands up his biceps and over his shoulders. "I never looked at you as more than a friend. Never really thought I was in the same category as the women you've always been seen with. But then you kissed me for pretend—"

"Nothing about that kiss was pretend," Mason interjected. "I've always wondered what kissing you would be like, and I took full advantage of the opportunity to find out."

Darcy jerked. "Always?"

Damn. He hadn't meant to let that nugget of information slip.

He didn't reply. What would he say that hadn't already been said?

With her face firmly between his hands, Mason held her gaze as he grazed his mouth over hers. He waited for any sign of hesitancy or that she didn't want to push forward. But the moment her lids fluttered closed and her lips parted, he took that as the green light he'd been waiting for.

Finally. He honestly didn't know how long he'd

wanted this to happen between them, but it was way too damn long. And now that he was back in town for a bit, he had to take a chance.

Darcy wrapped her arms around him, sending another surge of desire through his entire body. He lifted her off the floor and carried her over to the worn sectional in the corner. He wanted to take his time in unwrapping the most precious gift, but her hands were moving in a flurry of activity, so who was he to stop the progress?

He worked at his own clothes, all the while keeping his focus on her sweet body as she peeled back each and every layer until she lay completely bare before him. She leaned back against the sofa cushions and reached up for him.

"Don't just stand there and stare," she demanded with a soft laugh. "You can't turn me on like this and leave me hanging."

"Oh, I'm definitely not leaving you hanging," he replied. "But I'm taking a good, long look, because I've fantasized about this for years."

"Years?"

Mason nodded. No shame in letting her know the power she'd held over him for a while now. She should know how much he wanted her and how he appreciated her physically. He'd never seen such perfection.

Darcy kept her gaze on his, quirked a brow, and propped one foot up onto the sofa. She completely exposed herself as if daring him to go another second without touching her.

Damn, she was good at this.

But he hadn't thought things would escalate this quickly.

"I have zero protection with me," he informed her, cursing himself.

"I trust you," she replied. "And I'm on something and clean. So…"

Mason didn't want to keep talking when she clearly wanted to move on. He rested a knee on the sofa and gripped her hips, yanking her closer to him and garnering a shrill laugh from her.

He couldn't help but smile at the sexy, playful side of Darcy. He'd had no idea how she'd be in bed, but he already loved it.

"You're certain?" he asked, needing that one last bit of confirmation.

"Mason, if you don't do something fast, I'm going to take care of things myself."

His entire body heated all over again at that instant image of her doing just that. And now he had new fantasies to consider.

With a swift, expert move, he lifted her and turned until he sat on the sofa and she could straddle his hips. He wanted her to be in control here. All of this was new territory for them, and he didn't want to take any chances that she was uncomfortable.

But the way she squirmed against him only proved how achy she was, and he intended to fulfill her every need.

Mason flattened his palm against her back as he kept the other hand on the crook of her upper thigh. Wearing only her glasses, she stared down at him, offered the sexiest, sultriest smirk, and eased herself down to join their bodies.

His head dropped against the cushion as he let out a groan he couldn't suppress.

Damn. He hadn't expected this. She remained still for a minute, far too long for his liking. He jerked his hips and brought his attention back to her. Those expressive eyes were still zeroed right in on him as she began to move. Her hips shifted back and forth, slowly, as she rested her hands against his bare chest.

He could watch her move against him forever…but forever wasn't in their future. This was just one night, or maybe more, while he was in town. Temporary only, but he'd damn sure to enjoy every second he could.

Darcy bit down on her lip and tossed her head back, thrusting her breasts closer to him. He didn't miss a chance to take one in his hand and draw out another soft moan from her. When he covered her with his mouth, she cried out, her hips moving even faster now. He simply couldn't get enough. She continued to arch against him, resting her hands on his shoulders, digging those short nails into his skin.

His name came out on a whisper through her lips, and he pulled away from her breast to curl his hand behind her neck and bring her mouth to his. She pumped harder, pushing him even closer to his own release. He had to wait, had to hold back for her. This whole ordeal was going much too fast, but he already knew he'd be taking her to the bedroom after this. No way in hell was this going to be just one time. He was already craving more.

She cried out his name again. This time her nails bit into him as her body stilled. The passion that consumed her, leaving her vulnerable and exposed, was the most erotic sight he'd ever seen. Having her come totally undone around him was all it took for him to lose control himself.

Mason didn't even try to hold back another second. He wanted to share this moment with her. She threaded her fingers through his hair and brought her lips to his once again as they rocked against each other. Wave after wave of pleasure consumed him as he allowed himself to be completely enveloped by his best friend.

While he hadn't cared one bit about relinquishing control, he sure as hell had never expected such a feeling of euphoria to wash over him. He had never expected her to be so absolutely perfect in every single way.

As her body relaxed against his, she nestled her head on his shoulder, nuzzling his neck. Her warm breath slid over his heated skin, and he ran his hands up and down her back, not wanting this moment to end. Obviously she didn't either, because she said nothing. Just the ticking of the clock in the corner filled the otherwise silent space, leaving Mason alone with his thoughts and wondering how they could ever go back to being just friends.

Nine

"I agree with your vision, but I'd love to take it all a step further with the design."

Mason crossed his arms as he listened to Allie Price tick off all she would add to make this farmhouse a place that would bring in multiple offers and drive the price up. Not that he needed the money, but he also didn't want to invest a chunk of his own and not get a return on his investment.

Not only was Allie a mega real estate agent, but she also designed and assisted her family, who were the top contractors in the area. Having her here was invaluable to him and the next step in this whole process. Her insight could help him decide just how far he wanted to go on his own before selling.

He remembered her from school, and she still had

that same infectious smile and sweet voice. With her dark hair in a high curled ponytail and wearing a sweater with jeans and boots, she hadn't aged a bit.

"Splurging a bit more on the en suite is always a good idea," she went on. "A massive shower, a nice soaker tub, definitely double vanities, and an added makeup area will go a long way. Let's face it, the woman decides what house a couple is buying."

Mason laughed as he leaned against the current single vanity of the bathroom.

"I don't care who decides to buy it, so long as it gets sold," he told her. "I want to do right by Hank and Edith and make their home beautiful again. There should be life in the house and on the grounds."

Allie nodded. "I completely agree. Hank's properties were all divided up, and I'm anxious to see how they're handled. I know he wouldn't have entrusted his land to just anyone, so the fact that you have his original homestead tells me he believed you'd definitely do the right thing."

Mason sure as hell hoped so.

"Do you know anything about the other property owners?" he asked.

Allie slid her hands into the pockets of her jeans and nodded. "The horse farm is Kahlil's now. There was some drama over him getting all of that property, because Dray Walker assumed it would have been willed to her since she had been a farmhand there for years. But I guess it all worked out since they're engaged now."

Engaged. Mason couldn't even imagine using that

term for his own life, but if Kahlil and Dray were happy together, that's all that mattered.

"Darcy did let me know that. Is there anything about the dude ranch or resort?" he asked. "I discussed those with Darcy, but she wasn't aware of any owners coming forward."

"I'm sure the attorney for the estate has sent out everything, but tracking everyone down and getting them to come here is a whole process, apparently."

"I'm anxious to see who Hank chose," Mason murmured. "With Kahlil and me both working for him, I bet Hank chose other workers as well."

"You know how he was with his estates and businesses," Allie added. "That man only accepted perfection and demanded everything from his workers."

"As he should. He taught a lot of us how to work for what we wanted. There were days I hated the grueling tasks, but as an adult, I appreciate all he showed me."

Allie smiled. "Hank and Edith were definitely pillars in our community. Their absence has left a void, for sure."

Mason blew out a sigh. The Carsons were well respected in this town, and no doubt, everyone felt the loss in some form or another. Hank had always been one of those people you thought would live to a ripe old age. He and Edith loved Willowvale, but more than that, they had a deep connection and undeniable love for each other that wasn't common today. Oh, he'd heard people say they were in love, but for a relationship to stand the test of time? So rare and special.

Did that even exist anymore? He loved Darcy and

had since grade school. She was his very best everything. But a love that lasted forever and until death? How did that even work?

"How soon do you think you guys can start?" Mason asked, wanting to circle back to the renovations. "I understand your family is in high demand."

Allie laughed. "We have a reputation that precedes us, yes. But we can spare a worker or two to get a jump start on this."

"That would be great." Mason led the way out of the bathroom and headed toward the stairs to the first floor. "I want this to be done right, and I want to oversee the progress, but at the same time, I don't want to be in Willowvale any longer than necessary."

Allie nodded. "I understand. We'll take your schedule into account when drawing up the plans, timeline, and budget. I'll get started on everything when I get back to the office today."

"I'd appreciate that. I'll be here whenever you want to run everything by me."

"Give me a few days."

He gestured for her to go down ahead of him. Once they reached the foyer, Mason took Allie's coat off the hook by the front door and assisted her in putting it on.

"How's it feel to be back?" she asked, buttoning the coat and adjusting the collar.

"Cold."

Her laugh echoed in the open space, and he couldn't help but smile himself. Allie had always been a beautiful woman and didn't look that much different than when they were in school, which might make some

dismiss her as just another pretty face. But that innocent look belied the kick-ass businesswoman she had
become. Darcy had been right that Allie knew her stuff
and was the one to deal with for this special project.

"Did you miss this place at all?" she countered.

Mason shrugged and propped his hands on his hips.
"I missed the simplicity and the local bond everyone
seems to have. I've been in town a couple times, and
it's nice to see how everyone supports small businesses.
You don't get that so much in LA."

"I imagine not. I love it here, but I know Darcy has
been itching to move on." Allie shook her head. "I don't
know why. That girl screams *small town*, and everyone here just loves her. I always tell her she'd miss this
place if she left."

Darcy wanted out? First the new plane and wanting
to build her own company, and now this? How long had
she been building her dreams while he'd been off living
his? He'd never known her to keep things from him,
but maybe that's what happened when he closed her off
for a few months while he threw himself a pity party.

"I'll call you as soon as I have a solid plan in place,"
Allie said.

Mason directed his attention back to her as she pulled
open the front door. He thanked her and made sure she
reached her car okay, without falling in the mounds of
snow. Shoveling really didn't matter at this point. Did
it ever stop?

He closed the door and went toward the office. There
was still so much stuff to purge, and he'd have to call
someone in to take all of these donations. Clothes,

knickknacks, old furniture. He had no need for any of that stuff, not with the new items coming in. But there would be pieces of Hank and Edith he'd want to incorporate into all the fresh and new things. He wasn't sure what piece or pieces yet, but he'd find something and work with Allie and her designs to see what would both fit in with the modern aesthetic and pay homage to the original homeowners.

A twinge of a headache threatened him, but he ignored the intrusion of his thoughts and went about his search. He hated the damn headaches that had been happening since his accident. His memory was definitely getting better, as was everything else, but sometimes his head would start pounding to the point that he couldn't handle any light or sound. If the pain persisted, he had meds in the bedroom he'd been using. He hoped one day to be off of those for good, but he had a hunch it wouldn't be anytime soon.

Mason surveyed the built-in shelves stretching across one entire wall. He made his way over, glancing at the various spines on the books. Most were on farming, some were cookbooks, and some were old-school family photo albums. He'd just pulled the first album out when the front door opened and closed.

"Mason."

Darcy's voice echoed through the first floor, and something deep inside him warmed. He hadn't talked to her since last night when she'd left. As much as he'd wanted her to stay in bed with him, they'd agreed on a one-time thing. Having an adult sleepover had moved them to a whole other level of intimacy.

But he'd wanted her to stay in his arms. For those moments, he'd wanted to forget the world outside and any problem that they might face. He'd wanted to keep her close where he could have her again, but common sense had prevailed, and he'd walked her to her car before going back to bed alone. When he awoke this morning, her lingering perfume had surrounded him. He wasn't sure if that had been mocking or comforting. All he'd known was that he regretted not asking her to stay.

How could he have ever predicted this? A temporary fling was one thing, but he'd had no idea of the full impact Darcy would and could have on him...and maybe he still didn't fully understand.

"Back here," he called.

Her footsteps grew louder as she made her way down the hallway. Mason took the album to the rickety desk in the corner and flipped open the cover. His breath caught in his throat at the first image. In an old black-and-white photograph of the front of the property, out by the street. Hank and Edith stood where the driveway was now, with wide smiles, posing for the camera. A field of weeds behind them would ultimately turn into the Carson farm and homestead. Mason couldn't imagine Willowvale Springs without this place.

"Can I come in?"

Mason glanced over his shoulder as Darcy stood in the doorway. She was still wearing her coat and scarf and had her hands shoved into her pockets.

"Did you think you weren't welcome here?" he asked.

She shrugged and stepped into the room, stopping just on the other side of the braided area rug.

"I have no idea what to think after last night," she admitted. "I was too busy today to text you, so I feel like this awkward wedge has settled between us."

Ignoring the photo album, Mason turned to fully face her.

"Do I look like I feel awkward?" He spread his arms, gesturing for her to come closer. "Last night doesn't change the fact that you're my best friend."

With a soft smile, she closed the gap between them and sank into his embrace.

"I was afraid things would be weird," she muttered against his chest before glancing up and tapping a kiss on his cheek. "Thank you for what you did earlier."

Confused, Mason jerked back. "What did I do? I haven't even talked to you today."

"The jersey you dropped off to Malia at the coffee shop?" She tipped her head back as tears welled up in her eyes. "Very sweet, Mason. Very sweet."

He'd tried to be discreet as possible, but going into a public establishment as a celebrity wasn't exactly a stealth move. Still, despite having his entire world turned upside down last night with Darcy, he'd had the notion on his heart to give the jersey he'd brought with him. Why not? The woman deserved it, and he wanted something good to come from that horrible night.

"Do you often travel with your uniform?" she asked.

Mason shifted and eased a hip on the edge of the desk for a seat. "It was the jersey I wore in my last game. It's been with me since."

Darcy let out a soft gasp. "Mason."

No. He didn't want the pity. She hadn't given it yet, and he sure as hell didn't want her to start now.

"It's no big deal," he insisted. "It's not like I'm using it anyway, and she deserved something. Maybe in some weird way, she'll feel closer to her dad. I don't know. That's dumb, isn't it?"

"Not at all. It's just another endearing quality that the public never gets to see."

"Why should they?" he countered. "The world doesn't need to know everything about my life and doing something nice for someone shouldn't be publicized."

"I agree, but I do wish everyone could see the side of you that I know."

Mason only wanted the world to see a strong, capable athlete, but here he was, clawing his way back to some type of normalcy, all while living on a run-down farm in the middle of nowhere.

"Your friend Allie left a bit ago." Mason wanted to get the topic off him and onto something else. "She knows her stuff, that's for sure."

"Oh, I'm sorry I missed her. She's great, isn't she?"

"Amazing," he agreed. "She had some really great ideas that I hadn't thought of and ways to drive the selling price up even more. I hope we get into a bidding war, to be honest."

Darcy crossed her arms over her chest. "I never took you for money-hungry."

"You know me better than that." He pushed off the desk and turned back to the album. His eyes locked onto the image of the younger Carson couple. "I want to do right by Hank and Edith. I'll establish some scholarship fund or something with the money. I don't want it."

Money had never meant anything to him. He'd gained celebrity status simply because he had fallen in love with a sport and happened to be damn good at it. Now he wasn't sure what the hell he'd be good at. He hadn't thought of life beyond baseball. Oh, he'd known he couldn't play forever, but he didn't think his career would end this soon. And it wasn't just the actual game he would miss. It was the conditioning with the guys, the traveling, the late nights and cold beers, talking of nothing and everything. He would get some of this back if he accepted the coaching position. But would that be enough? And now that he'd been with Darcy in the truest sense of the word, could he go back to seeing her only once in a blue moon?

Darcy came to stand beside him at the desk. "So, what's this?"

"I just found this old album when you got here."

She leaned over, the simple gesture sending her signature floral perfume wafting around him and teasing his senses. He shut his eyes for a second, fighting the urge to spin her around and lay her out on this desk. How the hell was he supposed to live with those memories from last night and pretend his life hadn't changed? Not to mention act like he wasn't more than ready for a repeat performance?

"That's the cutest picture." Darcy ran her fingertip over the image of the young couple. "I've never seen them at this stage, and I've never seen a photo of the land before the farm existed. I never thought about a time when the Carsons didn't dominate Willowvale."

"They were certainly a driving force for getting the town up and running," Mason agreed. "Which is why having this farm restored and sold to someone worthy is so important."

Darcy shifted her gaze to his. "Worthy. See? Another quality that makes you so sweet."

He nearly cringed. He'd been fantasizing about clearing the desk and seeing how sturdy it was, and she sat there thinking of how sweet he was. Maybe they weren't on the same wavelength at all. How the hell could she compartmentalize her thoughts and feelings so easily?

"Don't call me sweet in public," he joked. "You'll ruin my badass reputation."

Darcy snickered as she turned and hopped up on the edge of the desk. "I promise not to let anyone know you're sweet, but I'd say you already announced that when you took your jersey into the coffee shop."

Photo album forgotten, he took a step back, trying to distance himself from how tempting she was right now. Hands on either side of her hips, legs dangling, her glasses perched on her nose, and her hair in a messy knot on her head. She was the only woman he knew who could be both adorable and sexy at the same time.

"You're giving me that look again," she murmured, her smile faltering.

He attempted to gain control of his thoughts, but he couldn't help how he looked at her.

"Should we talk about last night?" she asked.

Talk? No. Reenact? Hell yes.

"What do you want to talk about?" he countered, wanting her to take the lead here. He wanted her to know that she had all the control when it came to their intimacy. He'd meant it when he'd said he'd keep her safe, and that included her mental state.

"I really have no idea."

She kept that beautiful brown gaze locked on him, not shying away from the topic, which only made her more attractive. He didn't want to be drawn deeper into her world. He wanted a physical connection and friendship. That was all.

"Are you sorry it happened?" he asked, almost afraid of the answer.

Darcy jerked back. Then a burst of laughter escaped her. "Sorry? Did I do something last night to make you think I was upset?"

Mason's lips twitched. "You seemed to enjoy yourself pretty well."

"Exactly. I'm just not sure how to act or what to say. I mean, you're still my best friend, but now I just know even more of your skills."

Mason raked a hand over the back of his neck. "I'm not sure I want to discuss my *skills*, as you put it."

"You have to know you're amazing. I can't be the first to say that."

Now he did cringe. "I'm not discussing my bedmates with you."

"No, I really don't want to go there, either."

Mason cocked his head and propped his hands on his hips. "Jealous?"

Darcy simply shrugged, and something about her

being jealous squashed any idea that she regretted what they'd done. If she was even one percent jealous, then she wanted more, which would play right into his own plans. Because he wasn't sure he could keep denying himself now that he knew how perfectly matched he and Darcy were physically.

But it was more than that. He'd never had this type of connection with anyone else. Not even close. So where did that leave him? Where did that leave *them*?

Another twinge of pain sliced through his head. Mason reached up, attempting to rub it away. He shut his eyes and took in a deep breath. Of all the times for his head to be a nuisance…

"Mason."

Darcy's hand came to his bicep, and the concern in her voice irked him. He hated being vulnerable, but even more, he hated having an audience.

"I just need to get my meds," he assured her. "I'll be okay."

"Where are they? I'll go."

The pain started to intensify, and he realized he'd waited too long. Sometimes the window was wider, but apparently, that time he had needed to get on top of the pain had passed.

"I'll go," he told her. "I need to lie down."

The last thing he wanted was to fall down or get ill in front of Darcy. He was damn tired of being weak and out of control of his own body and mind.

"Let me help you."

Darcy took hold of his arm, but he shrugged her off. He squinted through one eye at the room so he could find the doorway. This episode had come on faster than the others, and going to the second-story bedroom might as well be walking to the other side of town.

"I can make it," he growled, but she took his arm again, completely ignoring him.

"Wanna bet?"

If he'd had the energy, he would have laughed and taken that bet.

"I know you think you're superhuman, but just humor me," she added.

He didn't say another word as he squinted to see his way.

"Which bedroom are you using?"

He gestured toward the steps, and she assisted him, pressing his body between her own and the wall. Just this once, he wouldn't argue. But when the pounding in his head ceased, he'd talk to her about being so pushy.

Once they reached the landing, he pointed down the hall toward the last room on the right. He'd taken the room with the best view of the back of the farm, overlooking the pond. He didn't plan on doing much renovating to this room, so he could hide away in there while the rest of the house was in chaos.

Darcy led him to the bed, and he sat on the edge, rubbing his forehead.

"Where are your meds?" she asked.

"The black bag on the vanity." He motioned toward the attached bath. "It's the only prescription bottle in there."

As the jackhammer behind his eyes persisted, Mason squeezed his eyes shut. Soft sounds echoed from the bathroom as Darcy shuffled his things around in his kit. Water turned on and off seconds before her feet shuffled back across the hardwood floor. Then there was silence when she hit the rug. Mason held out his hand for the medication, and she dropped one pill onto his palm. Then he took the small glass of water she offered and swallowed the pill, hoping it kicked in soon.

Darcy took the glass from him and set it on the nightstand as he lay back against the pillows.

"What else can I do?" she asked.

"Nothing. I just wait for the pill to work." After a few moments, he heard her pad out of the room and quietly close the door behind her.

He kept his eyes shut and tried to think of anything but the pounding...such as the intimate moment he and Darcy had shared. What he wouldn't give to erase this headache and see if that chemistry between them had been a one-time thing or if there was more. He knew passion like that couldn't just be turned off like a switch. The main question was, did she want to keep up what they'd started, or did she want to pretend it never happened?

Damn it, this headache had come on at the absolute worst possible time. He and Darcy had said one night, but he wanted more. He wanted to explore what they'd started, to see why they had an even stronger connection than he ever could have imagined.

At the same time, he didn't want to mess with her heart or shake their bond so hard that it crumbled and could never be repaired.

Doors opening and closing, and other random noises,

filtered up from the first floor. He had no idea what she was doing down there, but he hoped she didn't feel obligated to stay and babysit.

Maybe she'd go on home and he could wallow in his self-pity alone. Tomorrow he could try again to not look like a completely broken, vulnerable, pathetic shell of a man.

Ten

————

Darcy scrolled, then stilled. Her finger hovered over her laptop keys as she stared at the most magnificent gown she'd ever seen. Emerald green had always been her favorite color, but the holiday red of this dress just exuded class and style. A full skirt, in contrast with a fitted bodice and draped shoulder... Darcy could already see her hair up in a stylish twist, her face glowing with subtle makeup, because this dress was all the statement she needed to make.

But she still hadn't decided if she wanted to attend the gala. Originally, she'd agreed to go with Tanner. Well, she hadn't agreed to go, but he'd assumed they'd go together. Obviously, that wouldn't be happening now. She should go. She *wanted* to go. While she loved her jeans and flannels or hoodies, she was still a woman, and a chance to dress up, especially around the holidays, was hard to pass up.

What fun would there be in dressing up and going alone? Not only would that be boring, but she'd look pathetic. Good thing she hadn't ordered the dress yet. She'd been on the fence about what she wanted to purchase, but now that she didn't have a date, she'd just saved herself some money.

Her eyes drifted from the dress to the price, and she nearly choked. Who in their right mind would pay that for one dress to wear on one night? Maybe if she wore it every single day for the rest of her life, she could justify the expense.

"That's insane," she muttered.

"Online shopping?"

Darcy jerked around, knocking her laptop onto the cushion beside her on the sofa. Mason stood just behind her, and she had no clue how long he'd been there, because she'd gotten lost in her own thoughts.

"Daydreaming," she said, correcting him.

Darcy shifted, resting her arm on the back of the couch as she looked up at Mason's bare torso. Water droplets were clinging to his muscular form and glistening in his chest hair. She'd seen him without a shirt before, but now that they'd accelerated their relationship to a physical level, she had a whole new appreciation for his body.

"Feeling better?" she asked.

"Much. The rest and shower helped." He raked a hand down his chest, as if she needed help keeping her focus on that impressive muscle tone. "You didn't have to stay."

Darcy resisted the urge to roll her eyes. "No, I didn't, but I'm your friend and wanted to make sure you were okay. Besides, I had my laptop in the car, so I just brought it in to do some work, but I've been shopping."

"You're probably already done shopping for the holidays."

"Not yet," she countered. "I do have a few things done, though. There's still plenty of time."

Mason made his way around the couch and picked up her laptop. He stared at the screen as he took a seat next to her. She waited as he studied the gown she'd been ogling and readjusted herself back to a comfortable position. Darcy removed her glasses and propped them on top of her head as she stifled a yawn.

"You should have gone home to sleep." He glanced back at her but held on to her laptop. "It's late."

"I'm fine," she assured him. "I'll leave when I'm ready."

He shook his head and muttered something about her being stubborn as he redirected his attention back to her screen.

"You buying this?" he asked.

"Oh, mercy no. Do you see the price tag?"

"Do you like it?"

Darcy laughed. "What's not to love? It's elegant, fun, and screams *holidays*."

"Where on earth would you wear something like that?" he asked.

Darcy reached across to the old, scarred wooden table and grabbed her cell. She pulled up the invitation for the upcoming party to celebrate the Christmas season and benefit the town—the one she had no date for. Darcy turned the phone toward Mason for him to see.

He blinked, taking the device to read the text.

"Sounds fancy for Willowvale Springs," he muttered. "Black-tie affair to raise funds for the new parks and athletic complex. Surf and turf, orchestra…that all seems a bit over-the-top just to get money for an area for sports."

Darcy laughed. "Our schools haven't had new anything for any sports since we were there. Parents are ready to take their kids to other districts. You understand the importance, I'm sure."

Mason nodded and handed her cell back. "Of course I do. I just don't see the need to dress up for it. But, we'll go. Order your dress."

"You'll go?" The significance of this wasn't lost on Darcy. It was a huge step in Mason's recovery. Her heart swelled.

"Yeah, I'll go. Don't make me change my mind."

Darcy snorted. "As for the dress, you clearly didn't look at the price tag."

She tucked her phone under her leg and gestured toward her laptop. "I don't care what event I'm going to. I'm not spending that on one dress."

Mason shot her a glare. "When do you ever buy anything for yourself? Or splurge on something fun?"

"I got two cups of coffee this week from the café," she retorted, tipping her chin up in defiance.

Mason set her laptop on the table and shifted until he faced her completely. "Coffee is a necessity. So, what else do you have?"

Darcy tried to think of the last time she bought some-thing simply because she wanted it. Did that pack of underwear last month count?

"You can't think of anything, can you?" he asked.

She blew out a sigh. "Listen, I wasn't raised to just make frivolous purchases. My parents were much too frugal for that. Besides, I have everything I need."

"Do you have a dress for the gala?"

She pursed her lips, and he laughed, totally mocking her.

"Then you don't have everything you need," he tacked on with a wink.

Darcy groaned and dropped her head against the back of the cushion. "You should've been an attorney. You love to argue and be right."

"Too much reading for me." He scoffed. "And I can't help that I'm always right."

She rolled her head to the side and met his gaze. "Your ego is out of control."

"I'm quite in control lately." He smirked, stretching his arm along the back of the couch.

The simple gesture brought him closer, drawing her attention once again to that delicious bare torso and his woodsy cologne or body wash—or something entirely him—reminding her of the potency of his masculinity and sex appeal.

He might be in control, but everything inside of her had spiraled into chaos since that first kiss. And their steamy night together hadn't helped matters.

"I'm not ordering that dress." She circled back to the topic of the gala and tried to ignore the overpowering presence of her hottie bestie. "And who says we're going together anyway?"

"Come on, now. The whole town thinks we're dating. You plan on showing up alone? Tanner will swoop in on you and make his play for another chance."

"Even if I went alone, I'm not giving Tanner another chance."

"Then it's settled."

Darcy shook her head. "What's settled?"

"You're my date. Do you need to RSVP with your plus-one?"

"I thought you were hiding from people."

Mason shrugged, pulling her attention back to all the dark exposed skin.

"I'm not hiding," he said. "I've just been keeping my distance while I recover. But I'm all for a fundraiser, especially when it comes to young kids playing a sport. Keeps them out of trouble and gives a little structure to their lives."

That same feeling of warmth—and something even more intimate—spread through her. Beneath Mason's physical perfection lay a heart of gold. He was truly the entire package, and she teetered on the brink of falling hard into a territory she could never come back from.

"I never thought you'd be all about kids," she stated.

"Really? Just because I don't want to have them doesn't mean I don't want to see them succeed or want to encourage them into that transition to adulthood."

Yeah, she'd known he never wanted a family. That was actually something they agreed on. She enjoyed her career, and once she reached one goal, she set another.

One day, she'd love to marry and share her dreams with her spouse, but having kids wasn't on her radar.

Maybe that's why both she and Mason were still single. They loved their jobs and made no apologies about it. But they'd entered into this new phase together, and there was more to explore than she'd ever realized. She enjoyed their intimacy and wanted more; she wouldn't be sorry or ashamed for any of that.

"What should I wear?" he asked, wiggling his brows.

Darcy laughed. "Something more than what you have on now, that's for sure. Don't you have a shirt to put on?"

Mason's wicked grin widened. "I typically don't bundle up to be inside, and it's warm enough with the fire going. You having trouble keeping your hands to yourself?"

Actually, she was, which irritated the hell out of her. They'd had their one night. She shouldn't still want more…yet she did.

"My hands are perfectly fine right here," she informed him, clasping her fingers together in her lap.

The arm behind her stretched farther as he leaned in just a bit closer. "Is that right?"

His mocking question, coupled with the knowing smirk, only exacerbated all those tingles spiraling through her body. Yeah, even though he'd handed her the reins during their night together, he was in control, and they both knew it. Honestly, she didn't mind, simply for the fact that she loved how he made her feel, all feminine and desired. He knew her soul, knew her mind, and now he knew how to pleasure her.

Which is precisely what he did next, leaving Darcy with no more thoughts of what they would or wouldn't wear to the charity event.

Eleven

"This place is a dump."

Mason nodded in agreement as he huddled deeper inside his coat. Kahlil had come to the old homestead to check things out and visit.

Mason's old friend adjusted his glasses and glanced around the old barn with a look of absolute disgust on his face. What was once the thriving stomping ground for cattle, donkeys, and a couple of horses seemed so depressing now with no livestock to be seen. Broken and missing boards gave way for daylight to creep in, not to mention the blustery winter air.

"Are you planning on renovating the barn, too?" Kahlil asked, turning his attention back to Mason.

Mason's high school friend barely showed any age.

Something about small-town living was good for those he remembered.

Time and success had been good to him. Kahlil had definitely bulked up more, as shown by his broader shoulders, but those double dimples still made him look as young as the teen Mason remembered.

Mason pulled in a heavy breath, not fully confident in his answer. "I feel I'll have to since I'm completely updating the house. I need the entire property to be one cohesive unit when I put it up for sale, but that project will have to wait for spring. It's too damn cold and snowy."

He'd grumbled about the weather each day he'd been here. Growing up in Willowvale Springs, with its hot summers and frigid winters, had just been the norm. But playing baseball didn't lead to many snowy places, so his body had acclimated quite nicely to the warmer weather.

"I know some people who could turn this back into something even better than it was when Hank had it, if you're interested," Kahlil offered.

"I'd appreciate that," Mason replied. "I assume whoever buys this place will want to supply their own livestock, so I'm not getting involved in any of that. I just want to fix it up and get it out of my life."

Kahlil chuckled. "I wanted the horse farm out of my life, but ended up with not only that, but a fiancée. You never know what curveballs life will throw at you."

Mason cringed. He didn't want a farm or a fiancée, but he couldn't deny that Kahlil did appear to be extremely happy. Maybe love did exist and worked for some people. That had never been a box on his list of life goals he felt he needed to check off. Granted, his entire list had shifted, and he'd have to create some new boxes, but he wasn't quite sure what those would be quite yet. He had given some thought to the coaching offer from his old team, but thinking of any kind was becoming difficult now that Darcy was regularly in his bed—well, it had been two times, but he wasn't sure he could give it up.

He did know that his feelings of desperation and hopelessness had drastically faded since coming back to Willowvale Springs. There was nobody other than Darcy to thank for that. He owed her so much, but there would be no way to ever show her or repay her for all she'd done for his mental state.

For the first time in a long time, he saw a glimmer of hope for his future. Maybe he didn't know exactly what that looked like right this minute, but Darcy had managed to remove the dark cloud hovering over his potential paths.

Should he actually take the position on the coaching staff for his old team? He'd never thought of coaching before, but he had to admit, the idea of getting back into the dugout with guys who had become his family held a vast amount of appeal.

But what if he tried and hated it? What if that side of the dugout wasn't meant for him? What if he was meant to be on the field and not the bench? If he tried and quit, he'd be ridiculed, and the last thing he wanted was to have his name spread through the media circus once again, this time for being a failure or unable to perform his job.

"So, you have no plans of staying?" Kahlil asked.

Mason shook his head. "None. How are you still here, though? Don't you have some big tech company in Washington?"

"I still run it." Kahlil adjusted the knit cap down over his ears before shoving his hands back in his pockets. "There's some traveling back and forth, but to make this relationship work with Dray, I would have done anything. I let her slip away once, and there was no way in hell I was going to let that happen again. Second chances don't always happen."

No, they didn't. So what should he do about this second chance with his team?

Or a chance with Darcy?

Unnamed emotions clenched his heart with a viselike grip. Where the hell had that come from? Darcy was his best friend and now lover. A relationship wouldn't even be possible. She had big dreams, ones bigger than Willowvale could hold, and he... Well, he was a mess trying to sort out all these pieces of his life.

"I'm happy for you both," Mason stated. "It's good to see you after all these years."

"I feel like I still know you just from watching all your games." Kahlil chuckled. "Man, you were a beast on that mound."

As much as Mason hated the term "was" when referring to his career, he couldn't help but smile at the compliment. Knowing he had done his job so well kept that warm, comforting feeling alive deep inside him. No injury could steal that emotion.

"Hate that it ended the way it did," his friend went on. "But you sure as hell left a legacy and big shoes to fill."

"Thanks, man. That means a lot." Mason shivered against the cold air and started toward the entrance of the main house. "Let's head inside and grab some coffee or something. It's too damn cold in this town for me."

"Got used to the warm climate, I see," Kahlil stated, falling in step beside Mason. "Winters here can certainly be brutal. But you'll get used to it if you're here long enough."

Yeah, that was the thing. Mason didn't want to get used to this town again. He wanted more…he just wished like hell he knew what that looked like.

"What's the emergency?"

Mason stood in the doorway between Darcy's foyer and living room as his eyes scanned the area. She simply crossed her arms over her chest and ground her teeth as she nodded toward the gigantic open box on her oversized ottoman.

Mason's stepped further into the room and stared at the package. "Oh, good. It arrived on time."

Darcy stared back at Mason, still unsure how to feel. She couldn't decide whether to be furious, confused, elated, or flat-out irritated. So far she had a healthy dose of all those emotions.

"You can't do this," she exclaimed. "I told you I'd find something."

Mason jerked back slightly and unzipped his coat.

He took his time to place it neatly over the back of her sofa before coming even closer to the box.

"You wanted this dress, right?"

Darcy laughed. "I want a lot of things, Mason. I can't just go buy them."

"You didn't buy this," he corrected her. "I did."

"Fine. You can't just go around buying things."

"I haven't bought you anything in a long time, and I haven't even thought about a Christmas present." He shrugged as he reached for the dress in the clear plastic garment bag. "We'll call this Christmas if that makes you feel better, even though we're still two months away."

Darcy resisted the urge to scream.

"That doesn't make me feel better," she grumbled. "I'd never spend that much on you."

Mason's laughter filled the room as he slowly unzipped the bag.

"Don't do that," she scolded. "I am sending this back. If you really want to get me something for Christmas, go buy a candle or a nice scarf. Not a dress that costs more than my entire grocery budget for a year."

"We're not sending this back. Don't be ridiculous."

"Ridiculous?" She snorted. "The price of this thing is what is ridiculous."

Mason sighed as he dropped the bag back into the box. He moved around the ottoman and came to stand directly in front of her. He reached for her arms and gently pried them apart, all the while keeping his dark gaze locked onto hers.

"I want to gift this to you, so do not ruin this for me," he ordered. "I want my date to look as good as I do."

Darcy's lips twitched. She shouldn't find him ador-able and endearing, not when she needed to be strong and hold her ground. She couldn't take frivolous gifts like this, and certainly not since they'd been sleeping together.

"You're more concerned about how you look, is that it?" she asked.

"If that will make you keep this dress, then yes." He gripped her hands in his as he brought them up between their chests. "You're going to look stunning, and every man there will be jealous that you're with me."

"Is that your goal? To make people jealous?"

"Not at all," he countered. "Just stating the truth."

"Did you buy all of your other lovers lavish gifts?" Darcy muttered a curse. "Don't answer that. I shouldn't have asked, and it's none of my business."

"I've bought many gifts over the years for people in my life." He gave her hands a gentle squeeze. "But this dress was made for you, and I want you to have it. Pre-tend cost isn't a factor and just accept the gift."

The wind in her sails of anger vanished. He wanted to do this for her because he cared, not because he was showing off or tossing money around. He'd seen that she'd liked something and had gifted it to her; it was as simple and as sweet as that.

"Unless you're saying thank you," he added, "I don't need to hear anything else."

This was one argument she wasn't going to win, and she had to admit that a small part of her was ut-terly thrilled she could wear something so striking and showstopping to the gala. The fact that he'd thought to do this for her really touched her, and she couldn't help but wonder if they'd moved into yet another level of intimacy.

"How did you know what size to order?" she asked.

Mason released her hands but didn't move away. Instead he settled his hands around the dip in her waist.

"You think I don't know every part of your body at this point?" he asked. "I guarantee if you try this on, it will fit perfectly."

Shivers raced through her body. The more she was around him, the harder she found it to keep her thoughts off their nights together. She'd assumed crossing that line would feel weird or off somehow, but nothing about what they were doing seemed wrong. And as he'd said before, they were adults who wanted the same thing, and they weren't hurting anyone.

"Thank you."

A wide grin spread across his face. "See? I knew you'd come around."

"You're literally impossible," she stated, shaking her head. "Do you ever take no for an answer?"

"Not when I want something."

"And you wanted this red dress?"

He tugged her closer until their hips lined up perfectly. "I want *you* in the red dress."

Mason's lips grazed hers, just enough to have her entire body heating and a thrill of arousal spiraling through her.

"And then I want you out of it," he muttered against her mouth.

Darcy curled her fingers around his taut shoulders and smiled against his lips.

"I think you definitely bought this dress for you and not me."

His soft chuckle vibrated against her chest. "Oh, we'll both benefit."

He completely covered her mouth with his, and she had no choice but to hold on…to the man and the moment.

Alarm bells constantly went off in her head as of late, but she couldn't simply dismiss the way he made her feel. Had anyone made her feel such a range of emotions before? She had no clue if all of this excitement stemmed from the fact that they were already best friends and shared such a solid bond or if Mason meant more to her than she'd ever realized.

Was this a fling or a stepping stone to something neither of them had planned—something more permanent?

Mason jerked back with a curse and reached for his pocket. Darcy blinked, trying to take in what had just happened. She pressed her lips together as if she could hold in that tingling feeling of their heated kisses.

She watched as he stared down at his phone. The muscle in his jaw clenched, and a conflicted look crossed his face. She didn't have to look at the phone to know that the caller had to be his agent, his former manager, or his therapist. He had demons that still haunted him, and she hadn't taken the time to dive into his problems. She'd been too busy enjoying their time together and being utterly selfish.

"I'll give you some privacy," she told him. "You need to take that."

Whoever the caller happened to be, Mason needed to face them and whatever turmoil he had in his life. Running wouldn't make the issue go away.

"I can call them back," he insisted.

"Take the call."

Darcy didn't wait for him to give her an excuse. She stepped from the room and headed toward the kitchen, which was in the back of the house. She had a new cookie bar recipe she'd been wanting to try, so since her nerves were on edge, now would be the perfect time to keep her hands busy and her mind on something else.

Despite everything going on between them that left her confused and wanting more, Mason needed help, and he needed her to be a friend. She had to stay in that zone until she knew exactly what they were dealing with and what he needed to do next to keep his life on a healing path.

Twelve

"And do you think you want to return to your team in that position?"

Mason stared out the front window of Darcy's bungalow and gripped his cell. His therapist, Adam, had only asked the logical question that Mason had been rolling over in his own mind for days. Yet when someone else presented the idea, Mason's stomach twisted into a ball of nerves.

"I don't want to be seen as a failure if I do," he admitted. "So I'm not sure what the answer is. My old high school needs a coach, too."

"Now, there's an option," Adam stated. "And how do you feel about that?"

"That was a joke," Mason said. "I mean, they do need a coach, but that person can't be me."

"And why is that?"

Mason stared at the blanket of snow covering the front yard, noticing the tracks from the various wildlife that had trekked through. Wyoming had some gorgeous animals roaming around. Some were dangerous to get in close contact with, but this time of year was always something to behold, with the majesty of nature on full display. There was also a peacefulness here that he didn't get or feel back in LA. Willowvale Springs had always been serene and a haven of sorts when he'd been a teen. Now maybe that former connection was sealing the deep hole in his battered soul.

"Mason?"

He blinked, pulling himself from the view and turning back toward the living room. The box and the red dress still sat on the ottoman where they'd left them. He wasn't sorry he'd bought the gift and knew without a doubt how magnificent she'd look in it. And out of it.

"I'm here," he finally replied. "Just thinking."

"I want to know why you dismissed the school position so easily," Adam repeated.

Mason shrugged, even though nobody could see him. "The idea was said in passing, and nothing serious, so I didn't think it was a practical option."

"Do you think a position in a small town would be a downgrade?" Adam asked.

Mason didn't really know what he thought, because he hadn't let that notion take up space in his mind. He'd had too many other things occupying space...namely his best-friend-turned-lover. His life seemed easier now with her. He hadn't expected easy or relaxed, but

Darcy and this town managed to do both for him at this point in his life. There were reasons to want to stay, he couldn't deny that, but he had a life he'd built elsewhere, and walking away didn't seem right, either.

"I never said it would be a downgrade."

"But you thought it. Am I right?"

Mason sighed. "Not really. I dismissed the thought before it could even take shape. I sure as hell am not cut out to coach teenagers. That sounds like an utter nightmare."

Adam chuckled on the other end. "It's certainly a position for someone special who knows the game and wants to see the next generation come up."

The next generation. That made Mason feel so damn old.

"It might be something to just roll around in your mind," Adam went on. "At this stage in your life and your career, you should explore all options, even if you're only exploring them mentally. Don't dismiss anything until you have a valid reason to or a solid plan for moving forward. That's what will help you heal and get over this hurdle—to have something tangible to look forward to. Not only that, but something you want to do that you have control of."

Clanking and commotion filtered down the hall from the kitchen, and Mason couldn't help but smile. Yeah, there was certainly something for him to look forward to, but only in the short term. He needed something long-term to strive for; he just wished like hell he knew what.

"Our time is about up," Adam stated. "I'm going to

send you a few things I'd like you to work on during the week, and then we'll talk again next Tuesday."

Wonderful. Just what Mason loved…homework.

He disconnected the call and slid his cell into his pocket before making his way toward Darcy. He hadn't heard anything from her during his thirty-minute session—one he had thought about dodging until Darcy forced him to answer—but clearly, she was having some type of altercation with her dishes.

When he stepped through the wide, arched doorway leading from the hall into the kitchen, he stopped and attempted to smother his laughter.

"Problem?" he asked.

Darcy stood barefoot on her countertop, reaching inside the top shelf in her cabinet. Plastic bowls and measuring cups had been scattered about on the floor. She tossed a glance over her shoulder.

"Single-girl problems," she explained. "Nothing to see here."

"Do you always reach things that way?"

She stood on her tiptoes and slid her hand around the shelf until she stopped and pulled down a tray.

"Considering I live alone, yes."

"I would have helped you, had you waited."

In a move that seemed both graceful and impressive, Darcy hopped down from the counter with a serving tray in hand.

"I didn't need help." She flashed a wide smile and motioned for him to move. "I need to get to the oven."

That's when he realized that an amazing aroma had

filled the house. Something sweet, but he had no clue what. He'd also had no clue she could bake.

"What did you make?" he asked as he bent to pick up the items that had fallen from her cabinet during her search.

"Well, it's a first attempt at these cranberry bars I love at the coffee shop. I looked up a recipe and thought I'd give it a shot."

"They smell delicious."

She reached for the pot holder on the counter and pulled the pan from the oven before setting it on the stovetop. Mason returned all of the fallen dishes to the cabinet, while Darcy busied herself with cutting the bars and placing each one on a cooling rack.

"Do you want to talk about the call?" she asked without turning around.

Mason leaned against the center island and kept his focus on her delicate hands as she worked. "It was my therapist."

"That's good. Do you think you're making progress?"

Mason ran a hand over the back of his neck, hating how vulnerable he'd become over the past several months. He'd never been one to talk about feelings, and now he couldn't escape them. Everyone wanted him to discuss them, to get his thoughts out in the open and examine them from every single angle.

"I guess I am," he finally admitted. "I don't have the urge to hang up on him anymore."

Darcy tossed a smile over her shoulder. "You just want to dodge the calls altogether."

Mason shrugged. "Only because I was busy doing

other things. I honestly forgot about our session today, or I would have told you I'd be over later."

Her eyes held his for a moment before she went back to the bars. "While I'm glad I can be a distraction, your mental and physical health are much more important."

"I know. I just... I hate this."

Darcy set the knife down and wiped her hands on the decorative towel hanging on the oven handle. She turned and crossed her arms as she tipped her head.

"You're human. Your life has been turned upside down, so cut yourself some slack."

Mason snorted. "You sound like Adam."

"Your therapist?"

He nodded and attempted to gather his thoughts, because Darcy deserved more.

"He says I need something to look forward to," Mason went on. "Something that gives me a purpose and to make me feel like I'm in control of my life right now."

Darcy pursed her lips. "That sounds like an excellent idea. Is there anything that you can think of that would make you feel like you're getting your life back?"

"Not really. I mean, I'm going back and forth about the coaching position with my old team, but I'm not sure that's where I'm meant to be."

Darcy's arms fell to her sides as she took a step toward him. With her hair curled around her shoulders, the soft yellow sweater falling off one delicate shoulder, and her leggings, which had been paired with animal-print slippers, she looked too damn adorable. No one had ever charged him up the way she managed to.

Darcy rested her hip against the island as she flattened her palm next to his. Those wide, expressive eyes came up to meet his. At first he thought pity flashed through her stare, but no. All he saw looking back was concern and hope.

"Maybe you're meant to be right here," she suggested. "Maybe the timing of you receiving a letter from Hank's attorney was absolutely perfect and just what you needed. Maybe Hank knew that you were supposed to make your mark in Willowvale Springs and this is where you'll find your new purpose."

The fear of the unknown gripped Mason once again. Being in Willowvale certainly wasn't the long-term plan he'd been thinking of. There had to be something more in store for him than renovations and farming. Mason might have worked on a farm, but he was certainly no farmer. He couldn't just take this all on and really do right by Hank. Mason could guide the next owner and give them suggestions if they didn't already know how to start things off. This estate would be beautiful and functional once again—it just wouldn't be his.

"I'm not sure how long I want to be here," he admitted.

A smile flirted around the edge of her lips. "Am I not a draw to staying?"

"Oh, you're the only draw." He laughed. "The damn cold weather and crappy living conditions are enough to make me want to run away."

"But you won't."

"No," he agreed. "I'm here for now, but you are aware that I'll be going."

A veil of sadness swept over her face only a fraction of a second before she tipped her chin up and pulled in a deep breath. "We're both destined for better things," she stated. "But there's no reason we can't enjoy each other while we're both here, right?"

"Sure…but where *are* you going?"

"Yeah, that's where my plan falls apart." Darcy wrinkled her nose as she glanced away. "I've been doing some research, and I still want to stay in the West or the Northwest. Everything will depend on hangar space and taxes and leasing options. I have a lot to consider, but there are a couple of places I've looked into. There are so many remote locations where television shows and movies are filmed. I'd love to have an elite clientele. But definitely a bigger town than Willowvale."

Mason listened to her talk about her dreams. She clearly wanted the small-town feel, but the big-city life. He understood that, to a point. He'd wanted to hold on to his small town a little bit when he'd first left, but once he got out, he didn't miss anything back here. He'd missed Darcy, of course, but not his unsupportive family and not the farm. He'd cared for nothing but baseball…just like Darcy cared for flying.

"You belong here." The words were out of his mouth before the thought had fully formed, but he truly believed Darcy just fit in Willowvale Springs. "You're just…home."

Her brows drew inward. "What?"

"When I think of this place, I think of you. Like home, you know?" Mason muttered a curse under his breath and shook his head. "Never mind. That sounds ridiculous."

Her small hand covered his, and he couldn't help but glance to where they were joined. Her creamy skin against his dark skin. Her soft curves to his hard planes. They were so completely different, yet they blended so well in so many areas and on a variety of levels.

"That doesn't sound ridiculous, because when I think of home, you are the first person that pops into my head."

Her bold, soft statement struck a nerve deep inside, and he wasn't quite sure what to make of it. But one of her signature sweet smiles quickly put him at ease.

"I don't say that so you'll stay," she added. "I say that so you know how important you are in my life. That's all."

But that wasn't all. Their relationship, both past and present, couldn't be that simple. Mason had no clue how this would play out. He just hoped like hell nobody got hurt.

Thirteen

Mason stepped from the hardware store with a new crowbar, more than ready to tackle those scratched baseboards and get a jump start on the renovations. This way, not only could he speed up the process, but he could also get more of his frustrations out. His therapist said he needed to work on something he could control—well, this sure as hell fit the proverbial bill.

He glanced across the street to the coffee shop, but figured he should head home and work instead of indulging in more caffeine. He'd already had three cups before heading out this morning. Before he could glance back toward his car, something slammed into him.

"Oof."

No. *Someone.*

Mason gripped the crowbar in one hand and held out the other to steady the guy who'd hit him.

"Hey, buddy. You okay?" Mason asked.

The young man gripped his cell as his eyes focused on Mason.

"Oh my gosh." The teen gasped. "Mason Clark. I can't believe I ran into you like that. I'm so sorry."

Mason shook his head. "No worries. Might want to look up from your phone every now and then, though," he joked.

"Yeah, I'm just trying to get some conditioning scheduled, but my team doesn't take me seriously." He sighed as he slid his cell into his coat pocket. "I really am sorry. This is so embarrassing, to meet my idol and then—"

"Think nothing of it," Mason replied. "What team do you have?"

"Baseball, but it's not mine. I mean, I'm a player, but we don't have a coach right now. I'm just trying to keep the guys conditioning through the winter so we keep up our stamina and stay strong for when the season rolls around. But since I'm not the coach, I can only get about two of them to listen."

Mason could relate to what the frustrated teen was saying. Keeping in shape in the off-season was what made good athletes great.

"Sorry," the young boy stated. "I didn't mean to unload on you. I'll let you get going. It was really nice to meet you."

The boy started to turn, and Mason reached for his arm.

"What's your name?"

"Trevor Abrahms. Remember that name. You might hear it again one day."

Mason laughed, loving this kid's attitude. "What position you play?"

Trevor's lips twitched. "Pitcher, and I'm about to beat your high school record for most strikeouts."

Every part of Mason wished he'd be around in the spring to watch this kid. Not only did he have the mentality of a great player, he had the drive if he was frustrated with his team for not pulling their weight. This kid would definitely be going places, and Mason had no doubt he'd hear Trevor's name again.

"I hope you do," Mason stated honestly. "I'll be in town a while. Maybe I'll see you around."

"That would be awesome. I'm sorry I ran into you and vented."

Mason shrugged. "Think nothing of it, and if you need help getting those boys into the weight room, you come find me. I'm at Hank's old farmhouse."

Trevor's brows rose as his mouth dropped. "I couldn't bother you."

"It's no bother," Mason assured him. "I wouldn't have offered if I didn't mean it. Better yet, tell your crew that you're meeting for conditioning this Saturday at 8:00 a.m., and you have a surprise for everyone who shows up."

The words were out of his mouth before he could think better of it.

"What's the surprise?" Trevor asked.

"Me. I'll be leading the conditioning this week, but

don't tell anyone that. I want them to come because they want to be there, not because of me."

"Are you serious?" Trevor asked.

Mason couldn't believe it himself, but what was one day? Maybe this would light a fire under the team, and they would gather more often. Donating a couple hours of his time might actually be a good thing and give him a taste of what coaching for his old team might be like if he accepted their offer.

"My appearance has to be between us until then," Mason reiterated. "Got it?"

"If you are willing to donate even five minutes of your time to us, I'll keep any secret you want." Trevor laughed. "Do you know where the new school is? We have a weight room off the gym there in the back."

"I'll find it," Mason assured him. "See you then."

He turned away and headed toward his SUV as another blast of frigid wind encircled him. He hated this damn weather, but he'd done something that he could be proud of and was completely within his control. A couple of hours this weekend working with young athletes didn't sound miserable at all. In fact, part of him actually looked forward to the challenge.

Darcy opened the front door to the farmhouse and froze. The entire living room was in shambles, as if a tornado had whipped through. But in the midst of the chaos stood Mason, wearing jeans, boots, and a fitted tee, swiping a black bandana across his forehead.

"I take it you're getting a jump start on the progress here?"

Darcy stepped on inside, careful of where she moved, and closed the door behind her.

"I've been in touch with Allie, and there are some things I'm going to get done while they finish on another site. That way, we're a little ahead of schedule."

"And what schedule did you set?" she asked, hating that an end date loomed in the distance.

"I hope to be gone mid-December." He tapped the crowbar against the side of his thigh as he turned to survey the mess. "I know this will be far from done, but there will be good progress, and I can come and go. But I have to get back to my life in LA."

Even though she knew their time was limited, a piece of her heart broke knowing that he'd be leaving again.

"So you've decided to go coach?" she asked.

Mason shrugged. "Not yet, but that's where my penthouse is and my friends. I've made a life I'm not ready to just give up on yet."

A sliver of pride slid through her at the fact he had a bit more confidence than when he'd first arrived. He was taking action at the house and in his life instead of hiding away with that vulnerable, worried look.

The selfish side of her wanted him to fall in love with their hometown. She wanted him to stay with her so she didn't feel so lonely, but she'd never voice that to him or anyone else. He deserved to find a new life. He had to start over, and she wanted nothing but the absolute best for him—even if that meant him moving away from her again.

"I've gotten spoiled having you here," she admitted, offering a grin so she didn't come across as needy or desperate. "You better get that spare room ready for me, because I'm visiting all the time now that you won't be on the road so much."

"If I'm not coaching," he amended.

"Yeah, that." She swallowed and forced the unknowns of the future and any negative thoughts from her mind. "But I won't let you push me away anymore. Not for any reason."

Her voice had cracked on that last sentence. She hadn't meant to let her emotions get the best of her. The crowbar dropped to the floor with a metallic clang as Mason stepped over the pile of baseboards and crown moldings. His tee stretched across broad shoulders and showed damp areas around his pecs, proof of how hard he had worked.

"No, don't coddle me." She put her hands up and shook her head. "I wasn't looking for sympathy and didn't meant to say that."

"But you meant it," he countered, placing his hands on her shoulders. "I did let you down, and we haven't addressed that."

"Let me down?" Darcy repeated. "You think I'm upset about my feelings? I'm upset because you pushed me away after your injury, but that's only because I knew you were alone and scared, though you'd never admit it. I knew you wouldn't want people near, but that's when you needed them the most. I'm hurt because I couldn't help you, not because of anything to do with me. I hated the thought of you in pain, physical or emotional."

Mason's dark brows drew in as his eyes searched

her face. Confusion set in as silence surrounded them. The weight of his hands on her and the intensity of his stare had her reaching for him as well. She framed his face, the coarse stubble of his cropped beard tickling her palms.

"I wanted to help you," she murmured. "I needed to see that you were okay and to let you know that you had a support system. I know you have a manager and agent and all that, but you didn't have me. No matter what happens between us or the distance that keeps us apart, we're still a team. I just didn't want you to think anything else."

Mason covered her hands with his own as he leaned his forehead against hers. Darcy closed her eyes and held tight to the moment. Their bond had always been unbreakable, but since they had stepped into a more intimate relationship, Darcy couldn't deny the added level of chemistry. She had no idea what label or term to put on what they shared now, but she knew they were even deeper rooted than before.

"I never once thought you wouldn't be there for me," he said. "I didn't want anyone near me unless they could magically fix things to the way they were before."

A lump formed in Darcy's throat. The burn in her eyes and sting in her nose were extremely unwelcome, but she couldn't stop her emotions any more than she could stop herself from falling for her best friend.

Oh, no. No, no, no.

She wasn't falling for Mason…was she?

"Why the tears?" he asked, swiping the pad of his thumb across her cheek. "I'm practically good as new, other than a few brain hiccups. Could've been much worse."

Yeah, it could have. Maybe that one hit could have changed her entire world, and he'd be gone. Maybe he'd been spared for this moment in time…for her. Was this their chance to explore more? Just weeks ago, Mason had lived in that best-friend category, and now he… well, he'd become so much more. She wasn't ready for this to end or for him to leave.

"We could have missed this," she said.

She stared into his eyes and wondered where they were headed. Fear could consume her, but she wanted to live in the moment. Mason's injury had proved to her that they weren't promised another day together.

"But we didn't," he replied with a slight grin.

Mason slid her glasses off and put them on the counter. A thrill of anticipation pumped through her. Each time with him seemed like the first. Would that feeling of excitement ever wear off? She truly didn't think so.

Before she could think or even say anything, Mason bent down and lifted her up into his arms. Instinctively, Darcy looped her arms around his neck.

She laughed. "Are you trying to be romantic?" she asked.

Mason glanced around the room before taking a careful step over a pile of trim. He maneuvered his way toward the steps and carried her with ease.

"Trying?" he asked with a chuckle. "Clearly I'm failing if you have to ask."

Darcy closed her eyes and rested her head against

his shoulder. The salty, musky scent from his hard labor enveloped her. How could she not be attracted to a man who worked hard, trying to claw his way back to a normal life? He might not know his future yet, but he knew he wanted to do right here with this farm and honor the Carsons' legacy.

"I'm just surprised," she told him as they reached the top landing. "Nobody has ever tried to romance me."

Mason glanced down at her. "Then it's past time, and you've been with the wrong men."

Another burst of admiration slithered through her, adding to her attraction and desire. How had she not seen all of these sides to Mason before? How had she just seen him as a good time and a shoulder to cry on? Never once had she considered anything more with him…until recently.

"You're thinking too hard," he murmured. "Just you and me right now, D. Got it?"

Her heart swelled. Hadn't they always been the perfect team? Now they were even stronger, and maybe there could be more if she took the risk and told him that her feelings were growing well beyond a friendship level.

"For how long?"

She hadn't meant to let that question slip out, but she couldn't help herself and wasn't sorry the words were out in the open.

"I bet we'll figure it out."

Mason moved on into the bedroom and through to the adjoining bath. Carefully he set her down and turned on the shower before slowly undressing her. Darcy pushed aside the worry that would no doubt be there tomorrow and let the man and the moment consume her.

Fourteen

Mason couldn't believe the progress that had taken place in just a week. The crew had left for the day, and he'd purposely tried to stay out of their way. Over the past several days, he'd done a good bit of driving around town, seeing the old and the new since he'd last lived here.

But today he'd worked with the baseball conditioning crew, and he still didn't know what to feel about that. The guys had been amazed that Mason had taken the time to come in, and they had done every single thing he'd asked of them. No questions, no complaints. Damn. They had some drive, and he saw himself in each of them. There was nothing like the innocence of the game, and the hope that lived in the off-season that the upcoming one would be their best yet. He remembered those days…and he hadn't realized how much he missed them until now.

If his life were simple, he'd stay here in this town and start to build a life without all the press and lights and stress. But his life wasn't simple. In fact, his world seemed to be more complicated than ever, and he wasn't sure which way to turn.

Did he want his old life back? Did he want to go back to the city, to the team he'd called family for several years now? Is that the new chapter he wanted to start?

He pulled his cell from his pocket and shot Darcy a quick text.

Kitchen in shambles. Grabbing takeout and heading your way.

Mason started for the steps to grab a bag with some overnight things, but hesitated. They hadn't talked about sleepovers, and that seemed to be a whole other level of intimacy they'd yet to venture into. Would she think him too arrogant and cocky to just assume he could stay the night? Probably, but he would only stay if she agreed. With the house more demolished than it had been yesterday, he could stay put, but he could also be comfortable in a place without all the dust and real walls.

He started up the steps as his cell vibrated in his hand.

Not a good day. I'm having issues. Won't be home until late.

Confused, he started to type back to see what issues she was having, but if she wanted help, she would have asked. Mason went ahead and quickly packed a bag, called in a food order to The Getaway for those amazing wings and a few other things, and locked the place back up. If she was having a bad day, all the more reason to have dinner ready for her, and he could be there as her sounding board…or however else she wanted to release her tension.

The more time he spent with Darcy, the more he wanted to be with her. He wanted to wake up next to her tomorrow, but he didn't know what that meant for the long term. Staying still wasn't in his plans, but his only other option was to go back to his cold, sterile penthouse apartment. He'd never thought of it that way until Darcy had said something about it, but she'd been right. Of course, he wouldn't tell her any such thing. But staying in Willowvale Springs didn't feel right, either. He couldn't forget that he'd run fast and far the moment he'd had the opportunity to years ago.

But that had been to pursue a dream. And he'd done that. Now he needed to find a new goal. Obviously, his possibilities were endless, and he had the financial means to do anything. Maybe he should travel around the world, relax and unwind, take months to de-stress.

Instantly, images of Darcy traveling with him flooded his mind, which was absolutely ridiculous. She had her own goals and aspirations and was still chasing them. Besides, they weren't on some honeymoon or lover's retreat. They were friends who happened to be enjoying a brief physical relationship. That's all.

At least, that's what he told himself.

After he got the food, Mason headed toward her house. Part of him was damn proud he hadn't gotten lost since that first day. Maybe this cold mountain air was helping in his recovery…or maybe it was all this time with Darcy. Someone familiar, someone who made him feel whole again.

The moment he stepped into her cozy home, he took a minute to truly appreciate the life she'd built here. She'd done everything on her own. Like him, she hadn't had the support from her parents. She'd worked hard and pushed herself to where she wanted to be, and now she wanted to go even further.

What did that look like, though? Would she move somewhere and start her own fleet like she wanted? Fall in love with another pilot and build a dynasty with him?

A surge of jealousy threatened to choke him. Just the idea of his Darcy with another man really pissed him off, especially now that he'd had her. But she wasn't *his*; she belonged only to herself and had to make her own decisions.

And he wouldn't hold her back.

He needed to support her just like she'd done for him all these years.

Still, a niggling sense of loss settled in deep. At some point, this affair would end. Then where would they be?

Darcy's headlights slashed through the night as she pulled into her drive. She still didn't know whether to shed more tears or throw a tantrum. Very likely both, but she'd had to leave the hangar before anyone saw her having her well-deserved meltdown.

She spotted Mason's SUV parked up by her wrap-around porch. On a sigh, she pulled up beside him. As much as she adored him, she wasn't in the mood for company—or anything else tonight. She had no energy, physical or mental, to put into anything other than maybe drawing a bubble bath and attempting to calm her nerves.

She needed to regroup, look at her finances, and pray for a miracle. Christmas was coming. Maybe the magical holiday would bring along that miracle. It was all that would save her career at this point.

As she stepped from her car and pulled her coat tighter around her chest, she glanced at the porch to see Mason in the doorway. She stilled, and her breath caught in her throat. She wasn't used to anyone waiting on her, let alone a sexy silhouette backlit with a soft glow. Her stomach coiled in a series of knots as she realized she could get used to the idea of someone to come home to at the end of the day. She'd gotten so accustomed to being alone and dealing with her problems all on her own. She wondered what had made him want to grab dinner and come here. She'd told him not to, yet here he was.

Had he also had a bad day? Did she need to be there for him? Finding strength right now seemed utterly exhausting, but she'd do whatever Mason needed.

As she mounted the porch steps, she caught his gaze. His smile and relaxed stance eased some of her worries. He hadn't had a bad day. If anything, he'd had a damn good day. She hadn't seen such a genuinely relaxed look from him since he'd gotten to town.

The second she reached the top step, his smile faltered.

"What happened?" he asked.

Her throat clogged with another round of tears. She hated being vulnerable and helpless. Tears never solved anything, so she simply shook her head.

"You didn't have to come. I'm not good company."

He shifted to the side to allow her in. Once she stepped over the threshold, Mason slid her coat off her shoulders and hung it on the peg by the door.

"All the more reason you need someone," he countered, taking her by the shoulders to face him. "Now, do you want to talk about it or eat first? Or do you need to just go put your feet up in front of the fire?"

Darcy blinked and jerked slightly. "You started a fire?"

"It's damn cold here, in case you forgot." He chuckled. "I can't get warm."

"I'll be adding long underwear to your Christmas list."

"You told a joke and didn't even crack a smile." He pulled her into his arms, and she willingly fell against his chest. "Now tell me what I can do to fix this."

"Get me a new plane," she muttered against his chest.

He eased her back slightly and smoothed her hair from her face. "Say that again."

"A part on my plane broke," she amended. "Well, the plane I share with another pilot, but the part broke, and it's expensive. Even if we could afford it, the part cannot be here for nearly two months. I was doing my preflight check—Allie and I had plans to take the plane somewhere for dinner—and I a warning light on the control panel that our mechanic needs to check into.

Allie had to cancel anyway, but it's still pretty much a nightmare, considering I'd just booked new customers and was hoping their business would lead to something more. They're an elite family with many connections."

Mason's lips thinned as he pulled in a deep breath. "Is it too early to give you a Christmas present? Besides the dress for the gala?"

Oh right, the gala. How would she woo new clients there if she didn't have a plane? Darcy snorted. "Seriously? You assume giving me presents will brighten my day?"

She thought for a second before continuing. "I mean, I'm not going to turn it down. Did you bring it with you?"

He stepped back and laughed. "Not exactly. Want to make this more interesting and place a wager on it?"

Mentally, this day had drained her. She didn't know if she had the energy for a fun game…or fun according to him.

"What's the wager?" she asked, cautious yet intrigued.

Mason pulled his cell from his pocket and waved it. "You guess your gift in five tries and I'll show you."

"Seems easy enough," she replied. "And if I don't guess it?"

A flirty smirk danced over his lips. "I'm spending the night."

Darcy's heart clenched. They'd never even discussed adult sleepovers. They'd entered this fling without saying one word about "after," and she'd assumed the unspoken rule of leaving before morning always applied.

Was this something he wanted? Clearly it was, or he wouldn't have mentioned it.

"How long have you been wanting to ask me that?" she countered in lieu of an answer.

"Since the first time," he admitted with a shrug. "Unless you're not comfortable with that."

She'd never let a man stay in her bed. That was her private space, but the idea of waking up next to her best friend didn't frighten her or make her want to back away from what they'd started. Mason had always been her safe space in life, and she trusted him to continue to hold that vital position, no matter what the future held for them. She didn't want to dismiss the idea or pretend they hadn't come further than she had ever thought they would. They were on this path together and she had to see where they would go, because she certainly wasn't ready to end what they'd started.

"Deal." She crossed her arms and rolled some ideas through her mind. "So, I get five guesses. Can you give me any hints?"

"It's something you'll love, but you'll never guess."

"That's all I get?" she groaned.

He merely smiled as he waited for her to start guessing.

Darcy pursed her lips as possibilities hit her. She had no clue what direction Mason would go. Was he doing something sexy? Something on a friendship level? Somewhere in between?

"Lingerie."

"No, but I like that idea. You might get another gift."

Darcy rolled her eyes. "Of course you'd go buy something else. Let's see…"

"How about we head to the kitchen and eat those wings while you work on this?"

She followed him toward the back of the house as she continued to think of gift ideas.

"How about a massage at that little spa in town?" she asked, taking a seat at her island.

Mason moved to the other side of the counter and pulled the wings from the carton.

"Nope. Only three tries left."

"You bought me a hot tub for my house."

"Oh, damn. That's a good one. We'll definitely need one of those."

He worked on getting drinks and paper plates while she continued to guess.

"You bought me a new car?" She laughed.

"No. Do you need one?"

The way he shot her a serious look as he asked told her he would go buy her one right now if she wanted him to.

"No." She held her hands up. "You're not buying me a new car. That's a bit more than I'll be spending on you."

"Money doesn't matter to me." He shrugged as he set a plate in front of her and then came around to take the stool next to hers. "Might as well spend my money on someone I care about. I don't need anything."

"Well, you're not buying me a car." She scoffed. "I don't know, and I only have one guess left. Hmm… I give up. You bought me a plane."

She couldn't help but laugh at her own joke. Of

course he didn't buy her a plane. That would be even more ridiculous than the car and a hell of a lot more than the winter gear she planned on buying him.

But she noticed that he wasn't laughing one bit.

Wings forgotten, she jerked her attention toward him and caught his dark stare.

"Mason."

Her whispered word settled between them as he tapped his phone on the island between them and pulled up an image.

Darcy's breath caught in her throat as she took in the exact Cessna she'd been lusting over. The very one she'd shown him only a week ago.

"You didn't," she murmured, unable to tear her eyes away from the picture.

She literally stared at the very thing that would help her get to that next step in her goal of owning her own fleet with her own crew. But...she couldn't accept this.

Finally, she turned back to him, and he merely smiled.

"It was going to be delivered here closer to Christmas, but I'll make a call and have it here tomorrow," he explained. "We'll get your charters back on track."

Darcy couldn't believe what she was seeing, what she was *hearing*. She came to her feet and paced her kitchen, then walked into her open living room and back. She rubbed her head, trying to make sense of his gift.

"Are you okay?" he asked.

Darcy whirled around and threw her arms in the air. "No, Mason. I am not okay. Who the hell gifts someone an airplane?"

"I believe I just did."

"Well, take it back," she demanded. "That's no... This isn't..."

He sat there calm as you please, just staring back at her, making her feel even more foolish. She wasn't sure if she was angry over the insane amount of money he'd spent or the fact that he'd handed her the very thing she needed to succeed in life.

How the hell could she stop herself from falling in love with this man now?

Fifteen

Mason didn't know why she was so upset. Not only did this solve her immediate crisis, but also it would catapult her to the next stage of her career.

At least she'd stopped pacing. Now she tore into those wings on her plate like she was pissed off at the world... or, at least, him.

Considering he was hungry, he opted to eat instead of saying anything else. At this point, he didn't know what to say, and clearly, she was working some things out in her head. No doubt, she'd clue him in when she figured out all her thoughts.

The cell, still sitting between them, vibrated. Mason took a quick glance and saw Trevor's name on the screen.

Thanks for an awesome practice.

He reached for the phone but not before Darcy snatched it up.

"Practice?" She held the cell up, glancing at him. "What practice?" she asked.

"Just helped a few of the high school boys this morning. No big deal."

She jerked back slightly and clutched the device to her chest. "No big deal?" she repeated. "You are full of legit surprises today. How did you fall into helping the team? I didn't realize this was baseball season."

"Athletes are made in the off-season."

"Oh, I remember you busting your ass all winter in the weight room."

"That's all I did," he informed her. "It's just conditioning."

She handed his phone over and laughed. "I'm sure to high school boys, having a superstar pitcher in their presence was more than just conditioning. I bet they worked harder than ever."

He nodded. "They were hard workers. That's a good group of kids."

Her eyes held his, and he couldn't quite make out the look on her face.

"What?"

"You liked it."

Mason lifted a shoulder. "Of course I did. Helping kids want to do better in a sport I love, what's not to like?"

She tipped her head up in that adorable way she always did when she had a thought. Why did he have to be so drawn to her? Sex was easy. The act itself was physical and detached. Any other feeling delved deeper into the core of something more intimate and emotional. She had forced him to grow emotionally, encouraging him to keep going, even though there had been a time not long ago when he'd thought about giving up.

"Does this mean you're going to be their new coach?" she asked.

"No." He turned his attention back to his plate and dug into his wings. "I'm not the coach. Just giving them some tips while I'm here."

"So this was a one-time thing?"

He stilled.

"That's what I thought," she tacked on. "There's nothing wrong with considering that position. You have endless options, Mason."

Yeah, he was well aware. But over the past few weeks, he'd only been worried about the farm and Darcy. He wasn't quite ready to make that next commitment.

He pushed his plate back and came to his feet. Too many thoughts swirled around in his broken mind. He could drive himself crazy trying to keep up with all the directions his ideas were taking him.

Instead of talking, he busied himself with tidying up the island and throwing the trash away. Then, when he looked and nothing else could be done, he flattened his palms on the counter and dropped his head between his shoulders.

"You know, my whole life, everything was decided for me," he started, not necessarily wanting her to answer, just needing to get some of these thoughts out. "I loved baseball so much and got recognized early. I was ushered from high school to the Minors to the Majors. Every step I took was decided by a manager or my agent. Of course I wanted to play the sport, but I didn't make too many decisions on my own. And now...hell, I don't know what I'm doing."

He risked a glance across the island and found her wide eyes locked on him. She slid off her glasses and set them on the island, then rested her arms in front of her. She said nothing, but was just fully intent on listening to him. He didn't even know if he ultimately wanted advice, but he wanted someone else clued into his thoughts. There was nobody else he trusted more than Darcy.

"I don't have to work," he went on. "I'm set financially, but the game was never about the money. I was doing something I loved, and now I have to figure out what else I love or what I'm good at."

"And you think coaching isn't it?" she finally asked.

"Could be, but where? Here, for a high school? Coming back to my roots?" He let out a groan and pushed off the counter, raking a hand over the back of his neck. "Do I go back to my team? Or do I try to go somewhere new altogether?"

She'd been right in saying his options were endless. That was the part that irritated the hell out of him. He just didn't know what the best decision was for his future.

"Where do you see yourself this time next year?" she asked.

"Somewhere warmer."

Darcy chuckled as she slid from her stool. "Well, is

that in LA or do you intend on vacationing somewhere tropical?"

An instant image of Darcy stretched out in a red bikini beside some beach cabana hit him, and he figured that wasn't a bad goal to work toward. But a year from now? Would they still be doing this in a year? The term *fling* had never applied here, though he'd tried to tell himself that in the beginning. Darcy had always been more and would always *be* more.

"I don't hate it here," he finally confessed. "I'm just not a fan of being in pain when I'm outside."

Her brows drew in as she moved in closer. "Pain?"

"Yeah. That damn frigid air hurts."

Darcy froze just before she reached him and started laughing. Not just a normal ha-ha laugh, but doubled-over, holding-her-abs laughing. Mason propped his hands on his hips and waited while she got this out of her system at his expense. Once she composed herself, she still didn't wipe away her mocking grin.

"Finished yet?"

She curled her lips in and nodded. "I'm done. We've established you're a wimp. Now, what were you saying?"

In one swift move, he took a step toward her and hoisted her up and over his shoulder.

"Wimp, my ass," he muttered. "You'll regret those words."

Her laughter warmed something deep inside of him as he playfully smacked her rear end, which was positioned by his face. He made his way through the living room and on to the opposite side of the house, toward her bedroom.

"I'm kidding!" she yelled between bouts of laughter. "Put me down."

He stepped to the edge of her bed and dropped her with a soft bounce. She continued to laugh, and the wide smile that had spread across her face was a far cry from how defeated she'd looked when she'd first gotten home.

Home.

He couldn't—and *shouldn't*—think of her cozy bungalow as "home." He had a home, and just because he'd brought an overnight bag in the hopes of staying, it did not make this place his temporary residence while in town.

"I take back saying you were a wimp."

Darcy continued to stare up at him with those eyes that sparkled when she smiled. His heart clenched and that was something else that couldn't happen…heart-strings. Whether he decided to stay or go, or wherever he ended up, he and Darcy weren't a couple, so he had to keep any heart connection out of the picture.

"But I won't take the plane," she told him, her smile still in place but her voice stern. "That's just… That's the nicest, most insane thing anyone has ever done for me, but it's too much."

"Nothing is too much for you, D." He reached behind his neck and pulled off his shirt, flinging it to the side without a care. "You deserve to have every single thing you've ever wanted. And if I can help in any way, I will."

She sat up and leaned back on her hands as her eyes traveled over his bare torso. Damn, he loved when she looked at him like she couldn't get enough. He felt the exact same way. In every single aspect, he couldn't get enough of her. Not their easy banter, their emotional connection, and sure as hell not this physical relationship they'd uncovered.

"For now, I just want you," she murmured.

The soft glow of an accent lamp on her nightstand seemed to shine directly onto her and the center of the bed. Mason wasn't sure if the raw emotions that had built inside of him over the past several months had made him more vulnerable and aware of his feelings, but there was something about Darcy that he hadn't recognized in all their years of friendship. Or maybe there was something deep inside himself he hadn't recognized.

All thoughts vanished when she eased off the bed and stripped off every stitch of clothing she had on. Then she went to work on his clothes. She flattened her palms on his chest and shoved him down onto the bed with that naughty grin he'd truly come to appreciate in the bedroom.

"You've done enough for one day," she told him, coming down to straddle his lap. "And I need to decompress from mine. I assume you're on board for that?"

Mason gripped her hips and guided her to exactly where he wanted her. "I'm on board for everything with you."

She stilled, and he inwardly cringed. That hadn't come out the way he'd intended.

"Darcy—"

She joined their bodies, again cutting off any and every thought he might have. They could talk later.

Right now, he fully intended to enjoy this woman, this moment.

Her hands rested on his chest as she started to move, and he tightened his grip on her hips as he shifted beneath her. A low, sultry moan escaped her and seemed to echo around him. He loved knowing he could elicit such emotions from her, that he could touch her in the most basic yet primal way and have her ready to come undone.

He'd never had a lover like Darcy, and he wasn't sure he ever would again.

She leaned down, bracing her hands on either side of his face now as her hair came to curtain all around them. Mason framed her face and pulled her mouth to his. He wanted to be completely consumed by her in every way possible. He jerked his hips up and down beneath hers as she continued to work her own sweet body against him. He parted her mouth with his tongue, drawing another soft groan from her.

He slid one hand around to the back of her neck, he reached with the other to cup her backside, urging her on even faster. He simply couldn't get enough, and yet he still wanted more.

So he took it.

Mason maneuvered their bodies and flipped her over onto her back. She gasped and laughed, then stared up at him. With pink flushed cheeks and her chest heaving with deep breaths, she parted her legs as he settled between them. He hooked his arms behind her knees and lifted them slightly, wanting to give her the absolute best sensation as he rejoined their bodies.

And he wasn't disappointed. Darcy arched her back and cried out, reaching behind her to grip the top of the upholstered headboard. Mason knew she was close, and there was nothing he wanted more than to watch her come completely undone because of him. There was no one else for her. He wanted to ruin her for any other man in the future.

He jerked faster, forcing himself to contain his own release until she hit hers.

She panted his name, her knees clenched at his sides, and he went faster, harder.

Her cry enveloped him, and that was all he needed to let go and follow her. He gritted his teeth but kept his eyes locked onto her as she thrashed beneath him, letting the wave of the climax consume her.

That's all he wanted. To consume her.

As their bodies slowly came down from their high, he gathered her in his arms and lay next to her without a word. They hadn't discussed whether he'd stay or not, but he wasn't going anywhere…and he didn't know that he ever really wanted to.

Sixteen

A plane. A new-to-her shiny Cessna that she'd been eyeing for months.

And here she sat in the hangar at Willowvale Springs Airport. Obviously, bows weren't made large enough to wrap this beast.

Not only had Mason insisted on having the plane delivered within forty-eight hours, he'd also spent the night at her place the past two nights. He'd casually mentioned that the plumbing was being replaced in the farmhouse, but honestly, she wouldn't have kicked him out. She'd never had a man sleep over before, and she didn't mind having Mason there one single bit.

Actually, she wanted him to stay right there until he left town…if he in fact planned on leaving. As much as she wanted him to stay, that had to be his decision.

She couldn't make him love this place or love her or be there as she followed her dreams.

Now that she had her very own plane, she had more freedom for flights, customers, saving for her own business. But what if she had more? What if Mason did stay? What would that look like for them? She was human, so she couldn't help but fantasize about keeping him here or wherever she decided to be. They were attending the gala together tonight, so she could keep that fantasy going a bit longer.

"Girl, that is impressive."

Darcy spun away from her plane as Allie's familiar voice echoed through the hangar. Her beautiful friend strode through the space wearing knee-high boots, jeans, and a wrap coat that made her look as if she'd just stepped off a magazine photo shoot.

"You look nice," Darcy replied. "What are you doing here?"

"Oh, I just had lunch in town with a client. I was heading to get my hair done for the gala tonight and stopped by your office. The guys told me you were out here drooling over your new plane."

"I'm not exactly drooling—petting, maybe." Darcy slid her hands into the pouch of her hoodie sweatshirt. "Did you need me for anything?"

"I just wanted to apologize for canceling our girls' night out plans the other night. I know I sent you a text, but I feel awful."

Darcy offered a smile. "I understand business comes first. It's not like we won't reschedule."

"I know. I just value our friendship, and believe me,

I wanted you to whisk me away in your plane to some amazing restaurant for dinner."

"The plane wasn't working anyway. But now I have a new plane, and we can be fancier getting there," Darcy replied. "Think nothing of it."

When Allie had sent the text that a last-minute business meeting had come up with her family and a new client, Darcy hadn't been upset. As a self-employed woman herself, Darcy understood sometimes plans had to change.

"So, the guys in the office gossip like old ladies and were quick to tell me this plane was a gift." Allie shot Darcy a wink and a knowing grin. "Sounds like you two aren't just fake-dating to throw off Tanner."

Throwing off Tanner hadn't even crossed Darcy's mind in days, or maybe even a week or so. She'd forgotten how all of this had started, mainly because she'd fallen so hard, so fast, so *deep* with her best friend.

"You know Mason and I are just friends," she stated.

"Is that why his truck is always at your place?" Allie's smile widened. "Girl, I'm not judging. I'm happy for you. Mason is one fine-looking man, and your smile really says it all."

Darcy inwardly cringed. Her facial expressions had a mind of their own. While she wouldn't deny she was happier than she'd been in a long time, all of this was temporary. She didn't know when Mason would head back home—or even if that's where he would go—but she knew Willowvale was too small to contain someone so dynamic and iconic.

Allie took a step closer. "Now, you don't have to tell

me details, but is this serious, or are you guys just having fun?" she asked, her voice low. "Because buying someone a plane sure as hell seems serious."

Darcy tried to think of a logical response, but nothing came to her. How could she explain something she didn't even fully understand herself? If Mason had intentions of staying in town, maybe they could discuss being serious, but he had no idea where he would end up, and honestly, she wasn't quite sure where she would end up, either. Everything had changed with this damn plane—the dynamics of their relationship and her outlook on her career.

Should she keep going with her goal of leaving Willowvale and trying for a fleet in a larger city? That had always been her endgame, but lately she'd been so content. She knew that all her happiness could be linked back to Mason. He'd changed so much in her life in such a short time.

"Oh no," Allie said.

Darcy blinked, focusing back on Allie. "What?" Darcy asked.

"You've fallen for him," Allie murmured.

Darcy's breath caught in her throat for a fraction of a second, and she cursed the facial expressions she must have been making. She also cursed herself for falling so hard and fast when she'd vowed to herself to keep this fling casual.

"I have not," she fired back, absolutely lying through her teeth. "Mason and I have been best friends since kindergarten."

"So you already had a solid foundation." Allie's

smile widened, and then her eyes widened. "Oh my word, this is wonderful. You guys are going to be such a powerhouse couple."

Darcy held her hands up, palms out. "Hold up. We are not a couple. He's staying at my place because Hank's farmhouse is under construction, as you are well aware. And this plane is an exorbitantly priced early Christmas present. Won't he be disappointed when he opens long underwear from me?"

Darcy laughed at her own joke, but Allie continued flashing that knowing smile. There really was no sense in lying to her friend.

She let out an exasperated sigh. "I have no clue what's going on," she admitted. "I mean, yeah, I have deeper feelings for him, but do I tell him, or do I ignore them and hope they go away? I can't lose him as my friend, and I don't want to make things weird."

Allie reached for Darcy's hand and squeezed. "Oh, honey. You guys are so strong, and he deserves to know how you feel. You owe it to yourself, too. Who knows? Maybe he feels the same."

Darcy pointed over her shoulder. "I can't tell if that's the sweetest gesture of friendship ever or a blatant sign that he wants more."

Allie chuckled and released Darcy's hand. "I see how you can be confused. I assume Mason is your date for the night?"

"He is," she confirmed. "I'll talk to him after the gala. I'm not sure what to say, and I still don't know what I feel."

"I won't say a word, but I'm cheering you guys on.

I think you'd be amazing together if you can get on the same page. Maybe he'd want to stay here and take over the farm."

Darcy shook her head. "He's not a farmer. He just worked there for several summers. He's an athlete, and being here is killing him."

"He might change his mind once he sees what we can do to that place," Allie stated. "Plus, we're ahead of schedule, so once he starts seeing even more progress, maybe that will sway his decision."

"You think a fancy house will make him stay?" Darcy joked. "He's not like that."

"No, the house is just icing on the cake."

Darcy laughed. "Am I the cake?"

"You know it," Allie replied with a wink. "I hope you're wearing something tonight that will make his jaw drop."

Darcy thought back to the stunning red dress that went from online to her closet in a flash once Mason knew she wanted it.

"It's red, and he bought that, too."

Allie's snorted. "Girl, he's all but told you he loves you, so open up to him and go get your man."

Go get your man. Darcy slid those bold words deep inside so she could use them later. Maybe she should go after what she wanted. She'd never found anyone like Mason, and perhaps all this time and all these roads had led them back together for a reason.

Now she had to decide if she wanted to make the riskiest move of her entire life and confess her feelings or let this opportunity and a potential future of happiness pass her by.

* * *

Mason adjusted his black bow tie as he stared at his reflection in the floor-length mirror of Darcy's guest bedroom. She'd requested he get ready in here because she wanted to surprise him with her entire look. Personally, he wanted to help her into that dress now and out of it later, but he didn't mind waiting to build the anticipation.

His cell chimed from the chest of drawers in the corner. Mason gave himself one last look and figured his tux didn't matter with Darcy on his arm. She'd be a show-stopper in that red gown.

A series of buzzes from his phone interrupted his thoughts. He rounded the four-poster bed and grabbed it, eyeing a very familiar name on the screen.

"Hey, man," he answered. "What's up?"

"You have a second?" Dalton asked. "I have a proposition for you."

Intrigued, Mason gripped his cell. "I have a few minutes."

"Listen, I haven't talked to you about the coaching position here because I've been giving you time to think. But apparently you haven't made up your mind yet, and I wanted to tell you that I'm thinking of retiring as a player. I'd like to take on coaching this team with you."

Mason didn't know what to say, so he said nothing.

"We've been the dynamic duo for years now," Dalton went on. "The pitcher and catcher turned coaching staff would really draw the positive press our team needs—"

"—since the black cloud from my accident," Mason finished.

"That's not at all what I was going to say."

For the first time, the memory of that day and all he'd lost didn't haunt him nearly as much. He had no idea why, but maybe he'd mentally been set free in some manner. Maybe coming back here and distancing himself from the professional sports world and the high-society, high-stress lifestyle had helped him heal.

"Well, I wanted to tell you first that if you decide to coach, I want to be right there with you," Dalton went on. "I know you and I can take this team where it needs to be."

Mason listened to his best friend and teammate lay out the idea, and he honestly had no clue what to think. It sounded incredible. Him and Dalton back together? He had never thought that chance would come around again.

They would make the team amazing, there wasn't a doubt in Mason's mind.

"You've been silent the entire time I've been talking," Dalton stated. "You're either considering this notion of mine, or you're letting me ramble so you can tell me you've decided to stay in the middle of nowhere you came from."

Mason had always referred to Willowvale Springs as the "middle of nowhere," but something about hearing his hometown in a negative tone now agitated him. This place had shaped Mason into the man he was today.

Had Hank wanted Mason to return here? Had that been his plan all along? The man had obviously known of Mason's success and career. Yet Mason couldn't help but wonder if Hank had wanted the guys to stick around, and that's why he'd left them his properties. Granted, right now the only other person Mason knew of was Kahlil, so he was anxious to see who else might pop up.

"And if I don't come back?" Mason asked. He couldn't believe those words were coming out of his mouth.

"Is that what you're saying?"

Mason tipped his head back and closed his eyes, willing some type of miracle to occur. Some answer to hit him out of nowhere, because he still didn't know what to do.

All career moves aside, he hated the idea of leaving Darcy, but neither one had talked about anything long-term.

There really was nothing else holding him here. He knew without a doubt he could sell the farm and could do that from anywhere in the world. Being on the coaching staff with his best friend from the team sounded like a dream job. He had never thought Dalton would retire without being forced out.

"Why now?" Mason asked, turning around to look for his wallet.

"Why retire?" Dalton said. "Because the season won't be the same without you. Besides, we're getting too old for this job. My joints and back hurt all the damn time."

Mason laughed, mostly because that was a fact. The older he got, the more he had to get massaged and sit in the hot tub to loosen his muscles, and the longer it took to recover from games.

Still thriving in the sport but not taking all the physical hits seemed like a win-win…right?

Damn it. He just wished he knew he had all the answers.

"Tell me you'll at least think about this," Dalton added. "I can't do this without you, man."

The whole concept seemed like a dream career move.

"You think this will be approved?" Mason asked.

"Are you kidding me? They'll be damn lucky to have us."

Yeah, they would be lucky to have them. The idea had taken hold of Mason, and the more he rolled it over in his mind, the more he thought this sounded like just the opportunity he'd been waiting for.

"They would, wouldn't they?" Mason chuckled.

"You're thinking, aren't you?"

Mason shifted his cell to the other ear and gave himself one last glance in the mirror. "Absolutely. When do you need an answer?"

"Now?" Dalton snickered, then sighed. "Soon, though. Like, within the next few days. I know it's short notice, but you already had the offer on the table. I'm just adding myself into the mix. I'll need to decide on my next move pretty soon, and I want to know you're on board with me."

Every part of Mason wanted to say yes, but something held him back. He just couldn't jump at this chance.

"I'll let you know," Mason promised. "I'm heading out the door now, so I'll be in touch."

"Can't wait to be back in the dugout with you."

Dalton disconnected the call with those parting words, leaving Mason wanting to head back to LA to start this exciting new chapter…but for reasons he couldn't explain, he just couldn't commit.

Seventeen

"If I didn't tell you already, you look damn sexy."

Darcy stepped into the courthouse rotunda, which had been transformed into a winter wonderland with towering evergreens and twinkling lights that were suspended from the ceiling like stars. But Mason's whisper into her ear as they moved toward the throng of people had her smiling.

"At least ten times," she murmured.

"I'll likely say it ten more times before we're done here tonight," he informed her, placing a hand on the small of her back. "This dress might be one of my best investments. Too bad you won't be wearing it long. We're not staying more than an hour, right?"

Darcy scanned the crowds as she tried not to laugh… or get too heated here.

"We need to stay for a bit," she warned. "Smile and mingle. And feel free to leave a healthy donation. It's a good cause."

The whole purpose of tonight was to get more funds for a new athletic facility that could house all sports during the various seasons. Apparently, these things took quite a bit of money, but considering she'd spent her teen years learning the skies and various plane controls, she didn't know much about sports. Well, she had gone to Mason's games, but she didn't know what exactly went into making star players.

"What if I make a sizeable donation?" he suggested, guiding her toward the tables set up for silent auctions. "Then nobody will care if we are here or not."

Darcy glanced over her shoulder to meet his gaze. "You are going to have to control yourself."

"If you weren't so tempting, there wouldn't be a problem," he ground out.

"So this is my fault?" She reached up and patted his bearded cheek. "I will be worth the wait. Promise."

He let out a low growl as she turned back to check out the auction items. Her eyes scanned the table. By the time she got to the end, she froze at the massive display of signed memorabilia from Mason's team. Jerseys, game balls, rosters signed by all the players, a team photo, season passes.

She turned and quirked a brow. "You didn't tell me you had all of this donated."

He shrugged as if his donation was no big deal. To him it probably wasn't, but this package would bring in a good bit of money.

"I asked my former manager to send some things," Mason replied, sliding his hands into the pockets of his tux pants.

The man did sinful things to such a basic, traditional suit. There was no manner of dress—or undress—in which she didn't find Mason utterly irresistible.

"Mr. Clark."

Darcy and Mason both turned to a man Darcy didn't recognize.

"I'm sorry to interrupt," the guy started. "I'm Bart Calhoun. My son plays first base for the high school here, and he was at the conditioning the other morning with you. I can't tell you how much that meant to him and the other boys."

Darcy gathered her full skirt and took a step to the side. She didn't want to interfere in this exchange, because any praise, especially when it came to baseball, was important to Mason's recovery. He needed any positivity in his life to help him move forward...with whatever he decided.

As soon as they got back to her place tonight, she had every intention of telling him she'd fallen for him. The risk terrified her, but never knowing what could have come of her honesty scared her even more.

"I enjoyed being with them," Mason replied. "That's a great group of kids."

"You definitely lit a fire under them," Bart went on. "They'd been pretty down, thinking they wouldn't have a season because the school has still not hired a coach. But now they are optimistic someone will step up. They were just glad to have some guidance, not to mention spend a couple hours with a Major League player."

Darcy listened as the guy's discussion rolled into stats from Mason's team and how they'd move on, without Mason. She spotted Allie across the room and made her way over. The extremely selfish part of her wanted to flat-out tell Mason to try staying for a year. Just stay through the baseball season in the spring and see how it went. Maybe he'd love it. Maybe he'd love her.

But only he could decide what was best for him. Even if she thought that what was best was her and the future they could make together.

"Girl, you didn't tell me your dress was straight from the runway."

Darcy laughed at Allie's declaration. Her friend looked stunning, as always, in a body-hugging gold strapless gown.

"Did you look in a mirror?" Darcy asked. "You are smokin' hot."

"Just good undergarments," she joked. "I see Mason has drawn a crowd."

Darcy shifted to check the area she'd just vacated, and indeed, four men had walked over to talk to him. She studied his face, looking for any sign that he wanted out of the situation. But he laughed at something one of them said and seemed to be perfectly fine.

"I can't believe he let you out of the house with that on," Allie added.

"He's already asked if we can leave early." Darcy reached for a flute of champagne as a server strode by. "I'm going to need a quick drink to get up my courage."

"Honey, that dress and the way you look tonight is all you need. No man can deny anything when you look like that."

Maybe not, but she wasn't going to use sex or his attraction to get what she wanted. She could, no doubt. She could talk him into staying longer than he'd intended. But then what? Would that lead to resentment later, down the road? What would happen if she decided to move her charter business somewhere else? She didn't expect him to just follow along like a dog.

Maybe once he figured out what he wanted, they could figure out if there was a future for the two of them. She could see that life together so clearly in her mind. Mason coaching the high school team, them living on the old farm and maybe having some livestock, or even just chickens. The possibilities were endless, and she was ready to explore all of that with him.

Of course, that was assuming Mason accepted what she had to say to him tonight.

"I still think you have nothing to worry about," Allie added. "I think you and Mason are meant to be, but maybe I'm a hopeless romantic."

Darcy's heart swelled a little more. "I never thought I was, but maybe there's a bit of that inside me, too."

Part of her couldn't help but wonder if all of those ball dads huddled around Mason were just shy of begging him to stay for the team. No way did Darcy want to interrupt that, so she sipped her champagne and took a walk around the floor to mingle with Allie. Plus, with her new Cessna, she had some flights to book.

The truth was, the longer she waited to confront Mason, the more her nerves amped up. But she wouldn't back down.

Mason's gut tightened as he maneuvered through the streets back toward Darcy's house. Silence filled the small space of his SUV, and there was too much going through his mind for him to say a word. His eyes scanned the road as he turned onto another familiar lane.

The phone call from Dalton earlier had hyped him up, made him feel as if this nightmare could be over soon and he might get back to the life he'd known, just in a different manner. He'd already imagined him and Dalton spitting sunflower seeds in the dugout and high-fiving the guys as they came back in from a grand slam.

But the more he'd talked to the men at the gala, the more he'd seen the need right here in Willowvale. His heart was still with his team, the guys he'd been with for the past eight years. He didn't want to just walk away and leave them when he had an opportunity to return... and with Dalton at his side.

Mason pulled into the drive and killed the engine. Without a word, he stepped out and rounded the hood to assist Darcy. She'd gathered the full red skirt and moved toward the porch. Once they were inside, he took the wrap from her shoulders and draped it over the hook next to their coats.

Somehow, he'd slowly moved in over the past several days. Seeing their things hung side by side sent a shiver of fear through him. Were they moving too fast? They'd gone from amazing sex to practically living together, and while he could see himself here with her, what did the rest of his life look like? Giving up the career and lifestyle he'd worked so hard for? Was it going to be that easy to transition from high-stakes and fast-paced to low-key and laid-back?

"Okay, let's have it."

Darcy's words filtered through the foyer and pulled him from his own thoughts.

"Have what?" he asked.

She tipped her head and locked those striking eyes directly on him. She'd gone with contacts tonight and had done something sexy and sultry to her eyes. He'd never thought she needed makeup to be stunning, but whatever she'd done wasn't lost on him.

"You've been sulking since we left the gala," she told him. "Your mood changed while we were there. I'm sure others didn't notice, but I know you too well. Something happened."

Mason reached up to loosen his bow tie. He didn't quite know what to say because his thoughts were all over the place.

To make matters more confusing, Dalton had sent a picture of the two of them from years ago when they'd both been rookies. No words, just the image.

Mason moved through the foyer and into the living area. He needed to stay busy, to do something so he could sort through his thoughts. He headed to the fireplace and grabbed another log from the pile.

He didn't want to mess up here. Each word and action had to be thought through, because the last person he'd ever want to hurt was Darcy.

"I got a call before we left," he started, keeping his focus on the task and not Darcy's face. "My best teammate and catcher, Dalton, asked if I'd come back. You met him at some of my games."

"Yes, I remember him. I knew you had a coaching offer on the table," Darcy supplied from behind him. "Did something else happen?"

"He wants to retire and coach alongside me. He hasn't mentioned retiring to anyone else yet; he wants to see what my plans are before committing to that step."

"And you want to go back," she murmured, her voice closer this time.

He struck the match on the side of the box and tossed the flame onto the wood. He waited, making sure the fire took hold.

"Yeah, I do." He hadn't realized until just that minute how much he wanted the opportunity dangling right in front of him. "I'd be a fool to turn down a chance like this."

"Yes, you would," she agreed, her tone much softer. "This sounds like another dream job for you, and it's unheard-of to have two dreams fulfilled in the same lifetime."

That's where his mind had gone as well. To return from a head injury and be able to dive back into the same team, the same guys, and have an even bigger role, was something he'd never imagined.

Now he turned, and wished like hell he hadn't.

Darcy stood there in all of her beauty, with that full

gown and dipped front, her exposed shoulders just begging for his touch. But the unshed tears in her eyes clenched his heart.

The sweetest smile spread across her face. "I'm really happy for you," she told him, taking a step forward. "Are you leaving before the renovations are done?"

Mason swallowed the lump in his throat and nodded. "Most likely. I trust Allie and her family to keep me posted, and I was hoping I could talk you into being my eyes and ears."

Darcy nodded. "Of course. You can always count on me for anything."

Yeah, he knew that, which was why it was so damn difficult to tell her he was leaving again.

"We don't have the specifics worked out yet," he went on, forcing himself to focus on the positive decision he'd just made. "I'll need to let Dalton know for sure, but I'll likely be heading back in the next few days."

She jerked back slightly as her smile became strained. "That's really soon," she murmured. "I was hoping to have a little longer with you, but that's selfish of me. I'm glad you found your way back to what you love."

He couldn't look away. She mesmerized him with both her beauty and the sadness in her eyes. He wanted to comfort her and wrap his arms around her, but he wasn't sure if that was the right move here. The very last thing he ever wanted was to hurt her, but apparently his decision was doing just that.

"Darcy—"

She took a step back and tipped her chin up. "It's been a long day. I'm going to go change."

An invisible wall slid into place between them, cutting off anything he might want to tell her or ask. But he wanted to know her thoughts, wanted to know how he could make this transition better for her. Their relationship went so much deeper than friendship or even intimacy. She was his everything, but he couldn't be both the coach and the partner in two different states.

Just as she turned and started from the room, he called her name. She stilled, her shoulders hunched slightly, but didn't turn around.

"What are you thinking?" he asked, almost afraid of her answer.

She let out the softest sigh. "That this isn't how I thought the night would end."

Now she did glance over her shoulder as one lone tear slid down her cheek. He took a step toward her, but she shook her head.

"No. Stay there," she commanded in a low, heartbreaking tone. "I'm fine. This was the night I was going to tell you how I feel. I intended to lay out my plan for you, for our life together, to tell you that I've fallen in love with you and wanted to see if we could make this work here on Hank's farm."

Mason's knees went weak, but he forced himself to remain strong. If her tears didn't cripple him, her raw, honest words sure as hell did the job.

"But that's not meant to be, and I was naive to think someone as big and bold as you could be contained in a small town," she went on. "I decided earlier that I would be staying here. That with my new plane, I still have all the freedoms I wanted and can continue to save to bring on my own employees and build my company in Willowvale. Foolish, I know, but I also thought you'd fall in love with the idea of coaching the high school team. But you're too far advanced for that."

"That's not why I'm leaving," he muttered, but his words seemed stale and moot.

"You don't have to explain anything to me, Mason," she went on. "I love you no matter what you decide, and I'll always be your best friend. I guess, after all we'd shared, I was simply wishing for more. That's nobody's fault but mine."

She turned back around to head toward the steps.

"I'll get the guest room ready for you."

That sentence floated back to him like a smack in the face. But a few weeks ago, when they were still only in the friend zone, she would have made up that room for him and he wouldn't have thought twice.

Obviously, they were taking several steps back to that part of their relationship, and he'd just have to be content with being only her friend. After all, he was the one who made this decision.

Would he still have made that decision had he known her feelings? He couldn't even wrap his mind around the fact she loved him. She *loved* him. And she'd meant that as more than a friend.

While he'd been trying to figure out where to go with his career, she'd been planning her life with him, putting her dreams of moving away aside and coming up with a solution to be with him here.

And that made him a selfish prick to not even see that she had been putting him first all this time.

Mason turned back to the crackling fire, knowing he should go get some sleep, but he sank onto the sofa and watched the embers change from gold to red. He had to get out of town. The sooner he left, the sooner he'd see that he'd made the right decision in the long run.

Eighteen

Mason glanced around his new office at the stadium and already had mentally rearranged it. His awards would line the shelves behind the L-shaped desk, but everything needed to be moved around. Something about this room didn't feel right.

"You're here."

Mason turned just as Dalton stepped through the doorway. The wide grin on his face calmed Mason, but still…something seemed so off. Must be the new position.

"You look good in here, Coach," Dalton stated with a slap on Mason's shoulder. "Hopefully my office will be as nice as yours."

Dalton still hadn't been officially approved, considering he'd just given his bid for the open position, but he was the only candidate, and there was no way in hell the owner would choose anyone else.

"Ready to get back into the blue-and-white uniform?" his friend asked.

"Ready to start training again, that's for sure," Mason replied.

His mind flashed to the dank locker room at the school where fifteen boys had given him their undivided attention. Mason wondered how much money had been raised at the gala and how much more they needed to complete their new facility. Those boys deserved all the breaks they could get.

"You with me?" Dalton asked, waving a hand. "I lost you for a second."

Mason nodded. "I'm good. Just thinking."

Dalton's brows drew in as his hand fell back to his side. "You don't look near as happy as I thought you would coming back for this position."

Happy? Yeah, he was happy. But...

"I've only been in town two days, and this is my first time back to the stadium," Mason replied. "I'm adjusting to what this new role will look like."

Dalton took a step back and propped his hands on his hips. "Even your tone seems off. What's really going on?"

What was going on? Well, three nights ago he'd lain awake on Darcy's sofa only to get up and leave like some cheap lover...only he hadn't been her lover that night. Then he'd called to tell her he was leaving but ended up with her voice mail. He'd come straight to LA on very little sleep and crashed once he hit his penthouse. The place had seemed cold, empty...lonely. So this morning, he'd gotten up and come here to check out his new space, and everything seemed to be hitting him at once.

He would be the coach for his old team. He was back in the life he'd created and worked so damn hard for.

And he'd essentially lost Darcy.

She hadn't responded to his voice mail and she hadn't texted. He'd hurt her, unintentionally, but still, the damage had been done. Maybe she just needed space and time to recover from the whirlwind that had been their physical relationship.

Or maybe she wanted to move on and pretend that it had never happened.

"Dude. You all right?"

Mason rubbed the back of his neck and shook his head. "I don't know. I thought for sure coming here would feel right and I'd just know this is where I belong."

"And you don't feel that way?" Dalton asked.

Mason glanced around the mostly empty office. All he had to do was move his stuff in and get started, but something held him back from even thinking that far ahead.

"I'm not confident this is where I need to be, no," Mason finally stated.

He stared at the empty desk and tried to imagine himself there. He tried to imagine himself as more of an enforcer than a player. There was so much to this business aspect when stepping into a coaching position of this caliber.

"You miss your hometown already?" Dalton asked, but his stern face indicated he was dead serious, not mocking in any way.

Mason snorted. "Damn. I think I do. I hadn't been back in over a decade, and I spend a few weeks there and am already homesick."

Guilt niggled at his gut. Someone would be disappointed no matter what decision he made, so at this point, he had to do what his heart wanted and not worry about anything—or anyone—else.

"You need to work through some things?" Dalton asked. "Let's go get some lunch. My treat, and you can tell me what's really going on."

A sounding board was exactly what he needed right now. Maybe then he could clear his head and figure out what the hell to do with his life.

Darcy did her preflight inspection from the exterior. She had a new customer who had notified her via email late last night of his need for a last-minute flight from Willowvale Springs to Helena, Montana. She loved that area of the country, with the gorgeous snowy peaks she could see so clearly from the sky. She never took such beauty for granted from the high altitude.

But her heart wasn't in flying today. This would be her first trip since Mason left. How could she fly this plane without him in her life? Every time she looked at the thing she thought of him…not that she needed the reminder. Mason had ingrained himself so deeply into her life, there was no way she could ever forget the time they shared and all that they'd experienced together.

Nor could she be angry at the decision he'd made to leave. She was truly happy that he was getting another chance to do something he loved. She didn't know what she would have done in his position. Granted, he had never returned her declaration of love, so perhaps he wasn't in the same place as her. Maybe their time together had just been a fling for him. There wasn't a doubt in her mind that he cared for her, but it must not be enough to make him want to explore a relationship further or stick around and at least try.

"Is this where I check in for my flight?"

Darcy spun around. Striding through the hangar just as casual as you please was the man who had kept her awake the past few nights—more out of frustration or heartbreak, she wasn't sure.

"What are you doing here?" she asked, remaining still and clutching her checklist against her chest.

He continued to make his way across the open space, his dark eyes firmly locked onto hers. "Catching my flight to Helena."

Confused, Darcy adjusted her glasses. "I got an email from a new client last night. That wasn't you."

"That was Dalton." Mason's signature cocky grin spread across his face. "You know, my friend and teammate who wanted to coach with me?"

Darcy nodded, still confused about what was going on here.

"I don't get why he emailed me for you and why you're going to Helena," she replied. "Do you have a recruit you're going to look at or something?"

"Or something," he muttered as he came to stand within inches of her.

Had it just been a few days ago that he had walked out of her life? She'd replayed his voice mail over and over like some pathetic lovesick teen. She hadn't replied, because she really didn't know what to say. Part of her wished she could erase telling him how she truly felt, while the other part was damn proud of herself for putting everything on the line.

"Forgive me."

His words halted her thoughts.

"For what?" she asked.

Mason reached for her, curling his hands around her shoulders as he stepped into her. "Everything," he replied. "Not being more open to you, leaving with only a phone call, making you cry. There's an entire list, but I'm hoping you'll let me make it up to you in Helena."

Darcy's breath caught in her throat as nerves of anticipation curled through her.

"Come with you to Helena?" she asked with a laugh. "We're due to take off in thirty minutes, and I can't go somewhere with no clothes or anything. I needed a bit of a heads-up here."

"Not necessary," he replied with a smirk. "I have everything you need in my rental car."

"You do?" she asked. "And how did you get my stuff from my house without me knowing?"

"I didn't." He dropped his hands and rocked back on his heels. "I incorporated the help of Allie. She bought everything I said we'd need and whatever else she thought you'd want for a week's getaway."

"A week? I can't just leave for a week, and why would I go away with you anyway?"

While she had hope that he was back, she was also irritated that he just assumed she'd jump at a chance to go away with him.

"You should come away with me so I can spend that time telling you how sorry I am for being an ass and confusing you," he started. "You should come away so I can tell you every single day how much I love you and I can't live without you. So I can tell you how I left my team for good and I already accepted the high school coaching position."

"You did?" she gasped.

He nodded and went on. "With the stipulation that any salary for that position goes back into a scholarship fund to help the players go to college."

Tears pricked her eyes, and her heart swelled more than she'd ever thought possible.

"Yes," she cried. "I'll go."

He chuckled. "I'm not done telling you why."

Darcy dropped her preflight checklist onto the floor and wrapped her arms around his neck. "I don't care anymore. You're back, you're staying, and that's all I need to know."

"There is one more thing," he stated. "I'd really like to live on the farm once it's done. I believe that Hank led me back here for a reason, and I might as well try my hand at farming. It's not like I didn't work the place enough, but how do you feel about that?"

Darcy plastered kisses all over his face. "Let's talk about putting my house up for sale."

"There's no hurry." He lifted her off the ground and did quick spin before setting her back down. "Just to be clear, I do love you, Darcy. There's no one else in this world for me but you."

He slid the pads of his thumbs over her damp cheeks as she stared back at him. She didn't recall ever being as happy in her entire life as she was right now.

"I'm glad you came to your senses," she told him. "So, what are we doing in Helena?"

"I purchased a getaway home in the mountains, and we're about to go make good use of every single room and all of the privacy the place has to offer."

Darcy couldn't wait to get there and start what would be the rest of their lives together.

* * * * *

UNDER THE SAME ROOF & KEEPING A LITTLE SECRET

UNDER THE SAME ROOF
Texas Cattleman's Club: Diamonds and Dating Apps
by Niobia Bryant
Investigator Tremaine Knowles was hired to find stolen jewels—not seduce the prime suspect. But Alisha Winters is captivating...and hiding a secret that could change the case *and* the ongoing Winters-Del Rio family feud...

KEEPING A LITTLE SECRET
Texas Cattleman's Club: Diamonds and Dating Apps
by Cynthia St. Aubin
Nothing will derail Preston Del Rio's plan to take over his family's oil empire—except a tryst with Tiffany Winters, daughter of his father's bitter rival. And now there's a baby on the way...

RANCHER UNDER THE MISTLETOE & ONE NIGHT WITH A COWBOY

RANCHER UNDER THE MISTLETOE
Kingsland Ranch • by Joanne Rock
Outcast Clayton Reynolds is back in Montana for Christmas, and all he wants is local veterinarian Hope Alvarez. But she wants no part of the man who ghosted her three years ago, until a heated kiss tempts her to play with fire!

ONE NIGHT WITH A COWBOY
by Tanya Michaels
Workaholic Dr. Mia Zane decides the perfect cure for stress is one wild night with a sexy cowboy. Mia never expected that ranch hand Jace Malone would turn out to be a billionaire...or that she would be expecting his baby!

BREAKING THE BAD BOY'S RULES & THEIR WHITE-HOT CHRISTMAS

BREAKING THE BAD BOY'S RULES
Dynasties: Willowvale • by Reese Ryan
When former rock star drummer Vaughn Reed inherits a run-down ranch, he hires his best friend's sister to fix it up. But annoying little Allie Price is now all grown up—and too dang tempting...

THEIR WHITE-HOT CHRISTMAS
Dynasties: Willowvale • by Jules Bennett
Ruthless businessman Paxton Hart says he always chooses money over love. So life coach Kira Lee vows to show the town's resident Scrooge that Christmas miracles can happen—and their fiery kisses are just the first step!

You can find more information on upcoming Harlequin titles, free excerpts and more at Harlequin.com.

HD2in | CNM1023

HARLEQUIN
PLUS

Try the best multimedia subscription service for romance readers like you!

Read, Watch and Play.

Experience the easiest way to get the romance content you crave.

Start your **FREE TRIAL** at
www.harlequinplus.com/freetrial.